PRAIS... ...OR

JULIE KAGAWA

'Katniss Everdeen better watch out.'
—*Huffington Post* on *The Immortal Rules*

'Julie Kagawa is one killer storyteller.'
—MTV's *Hollywood Crush* blog

...e Kagawa's Iron Fey series is the next *Twilight*."
—*Teen.com*

...ans of Melissa Marr... will enjoy the ride.'
—*Kirkus Reviews* on *The Iron Queen*

'wholly satisfying'
—*Realms of Fantasy* on *The Iron Queen*

'a book that will keep its readers glued to the
pages until the very end.'
...lew York Journal of Books* on *The Iron Daughter*

'...The Iron King* surpasses the greater majority
of dark fantasies.'
—*teenreads.com*

Also by **Julie Kagawa**
from

The Iron Fey series
(in reading order)

Blood of Eden series

JULIE KAGAWA

THE LOST PRINCE

Published in Great Britain 2012
Mira Ink, an imprint of Harlequin (UK) Limited,
Eton House, 18-24 Paradise Road,
Richmond, Surrey, TW9 1SR

© Julie Kagawa 2012

ISBN 978 1 848 45154 4

47-0113

To Guro Ron, and all the 'badges of courage'
I received in class.

PART 1

CHAPTER ONE
NEW KID

My name is Ethan Chase.

And I doubt I'll live to see my eighteenth birthday.

That's not me being dramatic; it just is. I just wish I hadn't pulled so many people into this mess. They shouldn't have to suffer because of me. Especially…her. God, if I could take back anything in my life, I would never have shown her my world, the hidden world all around us. I *knew* better than to let her in. Once you see Them, they'll never leave you alone. They'll never let you go. Maybe if I'd been strong, she wouldn't be here with me as our seconds tick away, waiting to die.

It all started the day I transferred to a new school. Again.

The alarm clock went off at 6:00 a.m., but I had been awake for an hour, getting ready for another day in my weird, screwed-up life. I wish I was one of those guys who roll out of bed, throw on a shirt and are ready to go, but sadly, my life isn't that normal. For instance, today I'd filled the side pockets of my backpack with dried Saint-John's-wort and stuffed a canister of salt in with my pens and notebook. I'd also driven three nails into the heels of the new boots Mom had bought me for the semester. I wore an iron cross on a chain beneath my shirt, and just last summer I'd gotten my ears pierced with metal studs. Originally, I'd gotten a lip ring and an eyebrow bar, too, but Dad had thrown a roof-shaking fit when I came home like that, and the studs were the only things I'd been allowed to keep.

Sighing, I spared a quick glance at myself in the mirror, making sure I looked as unapproachable as possible. Sometimes, I catch Mom looking at me sadly, as if she wonders where her little boy went. I used to have curly brown hair like Dad, until I took a pair of scissors and hacked it into jagged, uneven spikes. I used to have bright blue eyes like Mom and, apparently, like my sister. But over the years, my eyes have become darker, changing to a smoky-blue-gray—from constant glaring, Dad jokes. I never used to sleep with a knife under my mattress, salt around my windows, and a horseshoe over my door. I never used to be "brooding" and "hostile" and "impossible." I used to smile more, and laugh. I rarely do any of that now.

I know Mom worries about me. Dad says it's normal teenage rebellion, that I'm going through a "phase," and that I'll grow out of it. Sorry, Dad. But my life is far from normal. And I'm dealing with it the only way I know how.

"Ethan?" Mom's voice drifted into the room from beyond the door, soft and hesitant. "It's past six. Are you up?"

"I'm up." I grabbed my backpack and swung it over my white shirt, which was inside out, the tag poking up from the collar. Another small quirk my parents have gotten used to. "I'll be right out."

Grabbing my keys, I left my room with that familiar sense of resignation and dread stealing over me. *Okay, then. Let's get this day over with.*

I have a weird family.

You'd never know it by looking at us. We seem perfectly normal; a nice American family living in a nice suburban neighborhood, with nice clean streets and nice neighbors on either side. Ten years ago we lived in the swamps, raising pigs. Ten years ago we were poor, backwater folk, and we were happy. That was before we moved into the city, before we joined civilization again. My dad didn't like it at first; he'd spent his whole life as a farmer. It was hard for him to adjust, but he did, eventually. Mom finally convinced him that we needed to be closer to people, that *I* needed to be closer to people, that the constant isolation was bad for me. That was what she told Dad, of course, but I knew the real reason. She was afraid. She was afraid of Them, that They would take me away again, that I would be kidnapped by faeries and taken into the Nevernever.

Yeah, I told you, my family is weird. And that's not even the worst of it.

Somewhere out there, I have a sister. A half sister I haven't seen in years, and not because she's busy or married or across the ocean in some other country.

No, it's because she's a queen. A faery queen, one of Them, and she can't ever come home.

Tell me *that's* not messed up.

Of course, I can't ever tell anyone. To normal humans, the fey world is hidden—glamoured and invisible. Most people wouldn't see a goblin if it sauntered up and bit them on the nose. There are very few mortals cursed with the Sight, who can see faeries lurking in dark corners and under beds. Who know that the creepy feeling of being watched isn't just their imagination, and that the noises in the cellar or the attic aren't really the house settling.

Lucky me. I happen to be one of them.

My parents worry, of course, Mom especially. People already think I'm weird, dangerous, maybe a little crazy. Seeing faeries everywhere will do that to you. Because if the fey *know* you can see them, they tend to make your life a living hell. Last year, I was kicked out of school for setting fire to the library. What could I tell them? I was innocent because I was trying to escape a redcap motley that followed me in from the street? And that wasn't the first time the fey had gotten me into trouble. I was the "bad kid," the one the teachers spoke about in hushed voices, the quiet, dangerous kid whom everyone expected would end up on the evening news for some awful, shocking crime. Sometimes, it was infuriating. I didn't really care what they thought of me, but it was hard on Mom, so I tried to be good, futile as it was.

This semester, I'd be going to a new school, a new location. A place I could "start clean," but it wouldn't matter. As long as I could see the fey, they would never leave me alone. All I could do was protect myself and my family, and hope I wouldn't end up hurting anyone else.

Mom was at the kitchen table when I came out, waiting for me. Dad wasn't around. He worked the graveyard shift at UPS and often slept till the middle of the afternoon. Usually, I'd see him only at dinner and on weekends. That's not to say he was happily oblivious when it came to my life; Mom might know me better, but Dad had no problem doling out punishments if he thought I was slacking, or if Mom complained. I'd gotten one D in science two years ago, and it was the last bad grade I'd ever received.

"Big day," Mom greeted me as I tossed the backpack on the counter and opened the fridge, reaching for the orange juice. "Are you sure you know the way to your new school?"

I nodded. "I've got it set to my phone's GPS. It's not that far. I'll be fine."

She hesitated. I knew she didn't want me driving there alone, even though I'd worked my butt off saving up for a car. The rusty, gray-green pickup sitting next to Dad's truck in the driveway represented an entire summer of work—flipping burgers, washing dishes, mopping up spilled drinks and food and vomit. It represented weekends spent working late, watching other kids my age hanging out, kissing girlfriends, tossing away money like it fell from the sky. I'd *earned* that truck, and I certainly wasn't going to take the freaking bus to school.

But because Mom was watching me with that sad, almost fearful look on her face, I sighed and muttered, "Do you want me to call you when I get there?"

"No, honey." Mom straightened, waving it off. "It's all right, you don't have to do that. Just…please be careful."

I heard the unspoken words in her voice. *Be careful of* Them. *Don't attract their attention. Don't let Them get you into trouble. Try to stay in school this time.*

"I will."

She hovered a moment longer, then placed a quick peck on my cheek and wandered into the living room, pretending to be busy. I drained my juice, poured another glass, and opened the fridge to put the container back.

As I closed the door, a magnet slipped loose and pinged to the floor, and the note it was holding fluttered to the ground. *Kali demonstration, Sat.*, it read. I picked it up, and I let myself feel a tiny bit nervous. I'd started taking kali, a Filipino martial art, several years ago, to better protect myself from the things I knew were out there. I was drawn to kali because not only did it teach how to defend yourself empty-handed, it also taught stick, knife and sword work. And in a world of dagger-toting goblins and sword-wielding gentry, I wanted to be ready for anything. This weekend, our class was putting on a demonstration at a martial arts tournament, and I was part of the show.

If I could stay out of trouble that long, anyway. With me, it was always harder than it looked.

★ ★ ★

Starting a new school in the middle of the fall semester sucks.

I should know. I've done all this before. The struggle to find your locker, the curious stares in the hallway, the walk of shame to your desk in your new classroom, twenty or so pairs of eyes following you down the aisle.

Maybe third time's the charm, I thought morosely, slumping into my seat, which, thankfully, was in the far corner. I felt the heat from two dozen stares on the top of my head and ignored them all. *Maybe this time I can make it through a semester without getting expelled. One more year—just give me one more year and then I'm free.* At least the teacher didn't stand me up at the front of the room and introduce me to everyone; that would've been awkward. For the life of me, I couldn't understand why they thought such humiliation was necessary. It was hard enough to fit in without having a spotlight turned on you the first day.

Not that I'd be doing any "fitting in."

I continued to feel curious glances directed at my corner, and I concentrated on not looking up, not making eye contact with anyone. I heard people whispering and hunched down even more, studying the cover of my English book.

Something landed on my desk: a half sheet of notebook paper, folded into a square. I didn't look up, not wanting to know who'd lobbed it at me. Slipping it beneath the desk, I opened it in my lap and looked down.

U the guy who burned down his school? it read in messy handwriting.

Sighing, I crumpled the note in my fist. So they'd already heard the rumors. Perfect. Apparently, I'd been in the local paper: a juvenile thug who was seen fleeing the scene of the crime. But because no one had actually *witnessed* me setting the library on fire, I was able to avoid being sent to jail. Barely.

I caught giggles and whispers somewhere to my right, and then another folded piece of paper hit my arm. Annoyed, I was going to trash the note without reading it this time, but curiosity got the better of me, and I peeked quickly.

Did u really knife that guy in Juvie?

"Mr. Chase."

Miss Singer was stalking down the aisle toward me, her severe expression making her face look pinched behind her glasses. Or maybe that was just the dark, tight bun pulling at her skin, causing her eyes to narrow. Her bracelets clinked as she extended her hand and waggled her fingers at me. Her tone was no-nonsense. "Let's have it, Mr. Chase."

I held up the note in two fingers, not looking at her. She snatched it from my hand. After a moment, she murmured, "See me after class."

Damn. Thirty minutes into a new semester and I was already in trouble. This didn't bode well for the rest of the year. I slumped farther, hunching my shoulders against all prying eyes, as Miss Singer returned to the front and continued the lesson.

I remained in my seat after class was dismissed, listening to the sounds of scraping chairs and shuffling bodies, bags being tossed over shoulders. Voices surged around me, students talking and laughing with each other, gelling into their own little groups. As they began to file out, I finally looked up, letting my gaze wander over the few still lingering. A blond boy with glasses stood at Miss Singer's desk, rambling on while she listened with calm amusement. From the eager, puppy-dog look in his eyes, it was clear he was either suffering from major infatuation or was gunning for teacher's pet.

A group of girls stood by the door, clustered like pigeons, cooing and giggling. I saw several of the guys staring at them as they left, hoping to catch their eye, only to be disappointed. I snorted softly. *Good luck with that.* At least three of the girls were blonde, slender and beautiful, and a couple wore extremely short skirts that gave a fantastic view of their long, tanned legs. This was obviously the school's pom squad, and guys like me—or anyone who wasn't a jock or rich—had no chance.

And then, one of the girls turned and looked right at me.

I glanced away, hoping that no one noticed. Cheerleaders, I'd discovered, usually dated large, overly protective football stars whose policy was punch first, ask questions later. I did not want to find myself pressed up against my locker or a bathroom stall on my first day, about to get my face smashed in, because I'd had the gall to look at the quarterback's girlfriend. I heard more whispers, imagined fingers pointed my way, and then a chorus of shocked squeaks and gasps reached my corner.

"She's really going to do it," someone hissed, and then footsteps padded across the room. One of the girls had broken away from the pack and was approaching me. Wonderful.

Go away, I thought, shifting farther toward the wall. *I have nothing you want or need. I'm not here so you can prove that you're not scared of the tough new kid, and I do not want to get in a fight with your meathead boyfriend. Leave me alone.*

"Hi."

Resigned, I turned and stared into the face of a girl.

She was shorter than the others, more perky and cute than graceful and beautiful. Her long, straight hair was inky-black, though she had dyed a few strands around her face a brilliant sapphire. She wore sneakers and dark jeans, tight enough to hug her slender legs, but not looking like she'd painted them on. Warm brown eyes peered down at me as she stood with her hands clasped behind her, shifting from foot to foot, as if it was impossible for her to stay still.

"Sorry about the note," she continued, as I shifted back to eye her warily. "I told Regan not to do it—Miss Singer has eyes like a hawk. We didn't mean to get you in trouble." She smiled, and it lit up the room. My heart sank; I didn't want it to light up the room. I didn't want to notice anything about this girl, especially the fact that she was extremely attractive. "I'm Kenzie. Well, *Mackenzie* is my full name, but everyone calls me Kenzie. *Don't* call me Mac or I'll slug you."

Behind her, the rest of the girls gaped and whispered to each other, shooting us furtive glances. I suddenly felt like some kind of exhibit at the zoo. Resentment simmered. I was just a curiosity to them; the dangerous new kid to be stared at and gossiped about.

"And…you are…?" Kenzie prompted.

I looked away. "Not interested."

"Okay. Wow." She sounded surprised, but not angry, not yet. "That's…not what I was expecting."

"Get used to it." Inwardly, I cringed at the sound of my own voice. I was being a dick; I was fully aware of that. I was also fully aware that I was murdering any hope for acceptance in this place. You didn't talk this way to a cute, popular cheerleader without becoming a social pariah. She would go back to her friends, and they would gossip, and more rumors would spread, and I'd be shunned for the rest of the year.

Good, I thought, trying to convince myself. *That's what I want. No one gets hurt this way. Everyone can just leave me alone.*

Except…the girl wasn't leaving. From the corner of my eye, I saw her lean back and cross her arms, still with that lopsided grin on her face. "No need to be nasty," she said, seeming unconcerned with my aggressiveness. "I'm not asking for a date, tough guy, just your name."

Why was she still talking to me? Wasn't I making myself clear? I didn't want to talk. I didn't want to answer her questions. The longer I spoke to anyone, the greater the chance that *They* would notice, and then the nightmare would begin again. "It's Ethan," I muttered, still staring at the wall. I forced the next words out. "Now piss off."

"Huh. Well, aren't we hostile." My words were not having the effect I wanted. Instead of driving her off, she seemed almost...excited. What the hell? I resisted the urge to glance at her, though I still felt that smile, directed at me. "I was just trying to be nice, seeing as it's your first day and all. Are you like this with everyone you meet?"

"Miss St. James." Our teacher's voice cut across the room. Kenzie turned, and I snuck a peek at her. "I need to speak with Mr. Chase," Miss Singer continued, smiling at Kenzie. "Go to your next class, please."

Kenzie nodded. "Sure, Miss Singer." Glancing back, she caught me looking at her and grinned before I could look away. "See ya around, tough guy."

I watched her bounce back to her friends, who surrounded her, giggling and whispering. Sneaking unsubtle glances back at me, they filed through the door into the hall, leaving me alone with the teacher.

"Come here, Mr. Chase, if you would. I don't want to shout at you over the classroom."

I pulled myself up and walked down the aisle to slouch into a front-row desk. Miss Singer's sharp black eyes watched me over her glasses before she launched into a lecture about her no-tolerance policy for horseplay, and how she understood my situation, and how I could make something of myself if I just focused. As if that was all there was to it.

Thanks, but you might as well save your breath. I've heard this all before. How difficult it must be, moving to a new school, starting over. How bad my life at home must be. Don't act like you know what I'm going through. You don't know me. You don't know anything about my life. No one does.

If I had any say in it, no one ever would.

I got through my next two classes the same way—by ignoring everyone around me. When lunchtime rolled around, I watched the students filing down the hall toward the cafeteria, then turned and went in the opposite direction.

My fellow classmates were starting to get to me. I wanted to be outside, away from the crowds and curious looks. I didn't want to be trapped at a table by myself, dreading that someone would come up and "talk." No one would do it to be friendly, I was fairly certain. By now, that girl and her friends had probably spread the story of our first meeting through the whole school, maybe embellishing a few things, like how I called her awful names but somehow came on to her at the same time. Regardless, I didn't want to deal with angry boyfriends and indignant questions. I wanted to be left alone.

I turned a corner into another hall, intent on finding an isolated part of the school where I could eat in peace, and stumbled across the very thing I was trying to avoid.

A boy stood with his back to the lockers, thin shoulders hunched, his expression sullen and trapped. Standing in front of him were two larger boys, broad-shouldered and thick-necked, leering down at the kid they had pinned against the wall. For a second, I thought the kid had whiskers. Then he looked at me, quietly pleading, and through a mop of straw-colored hair, I caught a flash of orange eyes and two furred ears poking up from his head.

I swore. Quietly, using a word Mom would tear my head off for. These two idiots had no idea what they were doing. They couldn't See what he really was, of course. The "human" they had cornered was one of Them, one of the fey, or at least part fey. The term *half-breed* shot through my mind, and I clenched my fist around my lunch bag. Why? Why couldn't I ever be free of them? Why did they dog me every step of my life?

"Don't lie to me, freak," one of the jocks was saying, shoving the boy's shoulder back into the lockers. He had short, ruddy hair and was a little smaller than his bull-necked companion but not by much. "Regan saw you hanging around my car yesterday. You think it's funny that I nearly ran off the road? Huh?" He shoved him again, making a hollow clang against the lockers. "That snake didn't crawl in there by itself."

"I didn't do it!" the half-breed protested, flinching from the blow. I caught the flash of pointed canines when he opened his mouth, but of course, the two jocks couldn't see that. "Brian, I swear, that wasn't me."

"Yeah? So, you calling Regan a liar, then?" the smaller one asked, then turned to his friend. "I think the freak just called Regan a liar, did you hear that, Tony?" Tony scowled and cracked his knuckles, and Brian turned back to the half-breed. "That wasn't very smart of you, loser. Why don't we pay a visit to the bathroom? You can get reacquainted with Mr. Toilet."

Oh, great. I did not need this. I should turn around and walk away. *He's part faery*, my rational mind thought. *Get mixed up in this, and you'll attract Their attention for sure.*

The half-breed cringed, looking miserable but resigned. Like he was used to this kind of treatment.

I sighed. And proceeded to do something stupid.

"Well, I'm so glad this place has the same gorilla-faced morons as my old school," I said, not moving from where I stood. They whirled on me, eyes widening, and I smirked. "What's the matter, Daddy cut off your allowance this month, so you have to beat it out of the losers and freaks? Does practice not give you enough manhandling time?"

"Who the hell are you?" The smaller jock, Brian, took a menacing step forward, getting in my face. I gazed back at him, still smirking. "This your boyfriend, then?" He raised his voice. "You got a death wish, fag?"

Now, of course, we were beginning to attract attention. Students who had been averting their eyes and pretending not to see the trio against the locker began to hover, as if sensing violence on the air. Murmurs of "Fight" rippled through the crowd, gaining speed, until it felt as if the entire school was watching this little drama play out in the middle of the hall. The boy they'd been picking on, the half-breed, gave me a fearful, apologetic look and scurried off, vanishing into the crowd. *You're welcome,* I thought, resisting the urge to roll my eyes. Well, I had stepped into this pile of crap—I might as well go all out.

"New kid," grunted Brian's companion, stepping away from the lockers, looming behind the other. "The one from Southside."

"Oh, yeah." Brian glanced at his friend, then back at me. His lip curled in disdain. "You're that kid who shanked his cellmate in juvie," he continued, raising his voice for the benefit of the crowd. "After setting fire to the school and pulling a knife on a teacher."

I raised an eyebrow. *Really? That's a new one.*

Scandalized gasps and murmurs went through the student body, gaining speed like wildfire. This would be all over school tomorrow. I wondered how many more crimes I could add to my already lengthy imaginary list.

"You think you're tough, fag?" Bolstered by the mob, Brian stepped closer, crowding me, an evil smile on his face. "So you're an arsonist and a criminal, big deal. You think I'm scared of you?"

At least one more.

I straightened, going toe-to-toe with my opponent. "Arsonist, huh?" I said, matching his sneer with my own. "And here I thought you were as stupid as you look. Did you learn that big word in English today?"

His face contorted, and he swung at me. We were extremely close, so it was a nasty right hook, coming straight at my jaw. I ducked beneath it and shoved his arm as the fist went by, pushing him into the wall. Howls and cheers rose around us as Brian spun furiously and swung at me a second time. I twisted away, keeping my fists close to my cheeks, boxer style, to defend myself.

"Enough!"

Teachers descended from nowhere, pulling us apart. Brian swore and fought to get to me, trying to shove past the teacher, but I let myself be pulled off to the side. The one who grabbed me kept a tight hold of my collar, as if I might break free and throw a punch at him.

"Principal's office, Kingston," ordered the teacher, steering Brian down the hall. "Get moving." He glared back at me. "You, too, new kid. And you better pray you don't have a knife hidden somewhere on you, or you'll be suspended before you can blink."

As they dragged me off to the principal's office, I saw the half-faery watching me from the crowd. His orange eyes, solemn and grim, never left mine, until I was pulled around a corner and lost from view.

CHAPTER TWO
HALF-BREED

I slumped in the chair in the principal's office, arms crossed, waiting for the man across the desk to notice us. The gold sign on the mahogany surface read *Richard S. Hill, Principal*, though the sign's owner hadn't given us more than a glance when we were brought in. He sat with his eyes glued to the computer screen, a small, balding man with a beaky nose and razor-thin eyebrows, lowered into a frown. His mouth pursed as he scanned the screen, making us wait.

After a minute or two, the jock in the chair next to mine blew out an impatient sigh.

"So, uh, do you need me anymore?" he asked, leaning forward as if preparing to stand. "I can go now, right?"

"Kingston," the principal said, finally glancing up. He blinked at Brian, then frowned again. "You have a big game this weekend, don't you? Yes, you can go. Just don't get into any more trouble. I don't want to hear about fights in the hallways, understand?"

"Sure, Mr. Hill." Brian stood, gave me a triumphant sneer, and swaggered out of the office.

Oh, that's fair. Jock-boy was the one who threw the first punch, but we don't want to jeopardize the team's chance of winning the game, do we? I waited for the principal to notice me, but he had gone back to reading whatever was on the computer. Leaning back, I crossed my legs and gazed longingly out the door. The ticking of the clock filled the small room, and students stopped to stare at me through the window on the door before moving on.

"You've quite the file, Mr. Chase," Hill finally said without looking up.

I suppressed a wince.

"Fighting, truancy, hidden weapons, arson." He pushed back his chair, and those hard black eyes finally settled on me. "Is there anything you'd like to add? Like assaulting the school's star quarterback on your very first day? Mr. Kingston's father is part of the school board, in case you did not realize."

"I didn't start that fight," I muttered. "He was the one who swung at me."

"Oh? You were just minding your own business, then?" The principal's sallow lips curled in a faint smile. "He swung at you out of nowhere?"

I met his gaze. "He and his football buddy were about to stick some kid's head down a toilet. I stepped in before they could. Jock-boy didn't appreciate me ruining his fun, so he tried smashing my face in." I shrugged. "Sorry if I like my face as it is."

"Your attitude does you no credit, Mr. Chase," Hill said, frowning at me. "And you should have gotten a teacher to take care of it. You're on very thin ice as it is." He folded pale, spiderlike hands on his desk and leaned forward. "Since it is your first day here, I'll let you go with a warning this time. But I will be watching you, Mr. Chase. Step out of line again, and I won't be so lenient. Do you understand?"

I shrugged. "Whatever."

His eyes glinted. "Do you think you're special, Mr. Chase?" A note of contempt had entered his voice now. "Do you think you're the only 'troubled youth' to sit in this office? I've seen your kind before, and they all go the same way—straight to prison, or the streets, or dead in the gutter somewhere. If that's the path you want, then, by all means, keep going down this road. Drop out. Get a dead-end job somewhere. But don't waste this school's time trying to educate you. And don't drag those who are going somewhere down with you." He jerked his head at the door. "Now get out of my office. And don't let me see you here again."

Fuming, I pulled myself upright and slid out the door.

The hallways were empty; everyone was back in their class-rooms, well into postlunch stupor, counting down the min-utes to the final bell. For a moment, I considered going home, leaving this sorry excuse of a new school and a clean start, and just accepting the fact that I would never fit in and be normal. No one would ever give me the chance.

But I couldn't go home, because Mom would be there. She wouldn't say anything, but she would look at me with that sad, guilty, disappointed expression, because she wanted so badly for me to succeed, to be normal. She was hoping that *this* time, things would work out. If I went home early, no matter the reason, Mom would tell me I could try again tomorrow, and then she would probably lock herself in her room and cry a little.

I couldn't face that. It would be worse than the lecture Dad would give me if he found out I skipped class. Plus, he'd been very fond of groundings lately, and I didn't want to risk another one.

It's just a couple more hours, I told myself and reluctantly started back to class, which would be the middle of trig by now, joy of joys. Why did every curriculum decide to teach math right after lunch when everyone was half-asleep? *You can survive a couple more hours. What else can happen, anyway?*

I should've known better.

As I turned a corner, I got that cold, prickly sensation on the back of my neck, the one that always told me I was being watched. Normally, I would've ignored it, but right then, I was angry and less focused than usual. I turned, glancing behind me.

The half-breed stood at the end of the hall next to the bathroom entrance, watching me in the frame. His eyes glowed orange, and the tips of his furry ears twitched in my direction.

Something hovered beside him, something small and humanoid, with buzzing dragonfly wings and dark green skin. It blinked huge black eyes at me, bared its teeth in a razor grin, then zipped into the air, flying up toward the ceiling tiles.

Before I could stop myself, my gaze followed it. The piskie blinked, startled, and I realized my slip-up.

Furious, I wrenched my stare down, but it was too late. *Dammit. Stupid, stupid mistake, Ethan.* The half-breed's eyes widened as he stared from me to the piskie, mouth gaping open. He knew. He knew I could see Them.

And now, They were aware, as well.

I managed to avoid the half-breed by going to class. When the last bell rang, I snatched up my backpack and hurried out the door, keeping my head down and hoping for a quick escape.

Unfortunately, he trailed me to the parking lot.

"Hey," he said, falling into step beside me as we crossed the lot. I ignored him and continued on, keeping my gaze straight ahead. He trotted doggedly to keep up. "Listen, I wanted to thank you. For what you did back there. Thanks for stepping in, I owe you." He paused, as if expecting me to say something. When I didn't, he added, "I'm Todd, by the way."

"Whatever," I muttered, not looking directly at him. He

frowned as if taken aback by the reaction, and I kept my expression blank and unfriendly. *Just because I rescued you from the jock and his goon doesn't mean we're buds now. I saw your little friend. You're playing with fire, and I want nothing to do with it. Go away.* Todd hesitated, then followed me in silence for a few steps, but he didn't leave.

"Uh, so," he continued, lowering his voice as we approached the end of the lot. I had parked my truck as far as I could from the Mustangs and Camaros of my fellow students, wanting it to avoid notice, as well. "When did you become able to see Them?"

My gut twisted. At least he didn't say *faeries* or *the fey,* because voicing their name out loud was a surefire way to attract their attention. Whether that was deliberate or ignorant on his part, I wasn't sure. "I don't know what you're talking about," I said coolly.

"Yes, you do!" He stepped in front of me, brow furrowed, and I had to stop. "You know what I am," he insisted, all subtlety gone. There was a hint of desperation in his eyes as he leaned forward, pleading. "I saw you, and Thistle caught you looking, too. You can see Them, and you can see what I really look like. So don't play dumb, okay? I know. We both do."

All right, this kid was pissing me off. Worse, the more I talked to him, the more attention I would draw from Them. His little "friends" were probably watching us right now, and that scared me. Whatever this half-breed wanted from me, it needed to end.

I sneered at him, my voice ugly. "Wow, you *are* a freak. No wonder Kingston picks on you. Did you not take your happy pills this morning?" Anger and betrayal flashed in Todd's orange eyes, making me feel like an ass, but I kept my voice mocking. "Yeah, I'd love to stay and chat with you and your imaginary friends, but I have real-world things to do. Why don't you go see if you can find a unicorn or something?"

His face darkened even more. I shoved past him and continued on, hoping he wouldn't follow. This time, he did not. But I hadn't gone three steps when his next words stopped me in my tracks.

"Thistle knows about your sister."

I froze, every muscle in my body coiling tight as my stomach turned inside out.

"Yeah, I thought you might be interested in that." Todd's voice held a note of quiet triumph. "She's seen her, in the Nevernever. Meghan Chase, the Iron Queen—"

I spun and grabbed the front of his shirt, jerking him forward off his feet. "Who else knows?" I hissed as Todd cringed, flattening his ears. "Who else has heard of me? Who knows I'm here?"

"I don't know!" Todd held up his hands, and short claws flashed in the sunlight. "Thistle is hard to understand sometimes, ya know? All she said was that she knew who you were—the brother of the Iron Queen."

"If you tell anyone…" I balled my fist, resisting the urge to shake him. "If you tell any of Them, I swear—"

"I won't!" Todd cried, and I realized then how I must have looked, teeth bared, eyes wild and crazy. Taking a deep breath, I forced myself to calm down. Todd relaxed, shaking his head. "Jeez, take it easy, man. So They know who you are—it's not the end of the world."

I sneered and shoved him backward. "You must be very sheltered, then."

"I was adopted," Todd shot back, catching himself. "How easy do you think it's been, pretending to be human when my own parents don't know what I am? No one here gets me, no one has any idea what I can do. They keep stepping on me, and I keep pushing back."

"So you *did* put a snake in Kingston's car." I shook my head in disgust. "I should've let him stick your head down a toilet this afternoon."

Todd sniffed and straightened the front of his shirt. "Kingston's a dick," he said, as if that justified everything. "He thinks he owns the school and has the teachers and the principal in his pocket. He believes he's untouchable." He smirked, orange eyes glittering. "Sometimes I like to remind him that he's not."

I sighed. *Well, it serves you right, Ethan. This is what happens when you get involved with Them. Even the half-fey can't keep themselves from pranking humans every chance they get.*

"The Invisible Folk are the only ones who understand me," Todd went on, as if trying to convince me. "They know what I'm going through. They're only too happy to help." His smirk grew wider, more threatening. "In fact, Thistle and her friends are making that jock's life very unpleasant right now."

A chill slid up my back. "What did you promise them?"

He blinked. "What?"

"They never do anything for free." I took a step forward, and he shrank back. "What did you promise them? What did they take?"

"What does it matter?" The half-breed shrugged. "The jerk had it coming. Besides, how much harm can two piskies and a boggart do?"

I closed my eyes. *Oh, man, you have no idea what you've gotten yourself into.* "Listen," I said, opening my eyes, "whatever bargains you've made, whatever contracts you've agreed to, stop. You can't trust them. They'll use you, because it's their nature. It's what they do." Todd raised a disbelieving eyebrow, and I scrubbed my scalp at his ignorance. How had he survived this long and not learned anything? "*Never* make a contract with Them. That's the first and most important rule. It doesn't ever go how you imagine, and once you've agreed to something, you're stuck. You can't ever get out of it, no matter what they ask for in return."

Todd still looked unconvinced. "Who made you the expert on all things faery?" he challenged, and I winced as he finally said the word. "You're human—you don't understand what it's like. So I made a few deals, promised a few things. What's that to you?"

"Nothing." I stepped back. "Just don't drag me into whatever mess you're creating. I want nothing to do with Them, or you, got it? I'd be happy if I never saw them again." And without waiting for an answer, I turned, opened my car door, and slammed it shut behind me. Gunning the engine, I squealed out of the parking lot, ignoring the half-breed's desolate figure as he grew smaller and smaller in my rearview mirror.

"How was school?" Mom asked as I banged through the screen door and tossed my backpack on the table.

"Fine," I mumbled, making a beeline for the fridge. She stepped out of the way with a sigh, knowing it was useless to talk to me when I was starving. I found the leftover pizza from last night and shoved two slices in the microwave while chewing on a cold third. Thirty seconds later, I was about to take my plate up to my room when Mom stepped in front of me.

"I got a call from the principal's office this afternoon."

My shoulders sank. "Yeah?"

Mom gestured firmly to the table, and I slumped into one of the chairs, my appetite gone. She sat down across from me, her eyes hooded and troubled. "Anything you want to tell me?"

I rubbed my eyes. No use trying to hide it, she probably already knew—or at least she knew what Hill told her. "I got into a fight."

"Oh, Ethan." The disappointment in her voice stabbed me like tiny needles. "On your first day?"

It wasn't my fault, I wanted to say. But I'd used that excuse so many times before, it seemed empty. Any excuse seemed empty now. I just shrugged and slouched farther in my seat, not meeting her eyes.

"Was it…was it Them?"

That shocked me. Mom almost never spoke of the fey, for probably the same reasons as me; she thought it might attract their attention. She would rather close her eyes and pretend they didn't exist, that they weren't still out there, watching us. It was one of the reasons I never talked openly to her about my problems. It just made her too frightened.

I hesitated, wondering if I should tell her about the half-breed and his invisible friends, lurking in the halls. But if Mom found out about them, she might pull me out of school. And as much as I hated going to class, I did not want to go through the whole "starting over" thing one more time.

"No," I said, fiddling with the edge of my plate. "Just these two dicks that needed a lesson in manners."

Mom gave one of her frustrated, disapproving groans. "Ethan," she said in a sharper voice. "It's not your place. We've gone over this."

"I know."

"If you keep this up, you'll be kicked out again. And I don't know where we can send you after that. I don't know…" Mom took a shaky breath, and covered her eyes with her hand.

Now I felt like a complete ass. "I'm sorry," I offered in a quiet voice. "I'll…try harder."

She nodded without looking up. "I won't tell your father, not this time," she murmured in a weary voice. "Don't eat too much pizza or you'll spoil your appetite for dinner."

Standing, I hooked my backpack over one shoulder and

took it and the plate into my room, kicking the door shut behind me.

Slumping to my desk, I ate my pizza while halfheartedly jiggling my laptop to life. The episode with Kingston, not to mention the talk with the half-breed, had made me edgy. I went to YouTube and watched videos of students practicing kali, trying to pick out the weaknesses in their attacks, poking holes in their defenses. Then, to keep myself occupied, I grabbed my rattan sticks from the wall and practiced a few patterns in the middle of my room, smacking imaginary targets with Brian Kingston's face, being careful not to hit the walls or ceiling. I'd put a couple of holes in the drywall already, by accident of course, before Dad made the rule that all practice must be done outside or in the dojo. But I was much better now, and what he didn't know wouldn't hurt him.

As I was finishing a pattern, I caught a flash of movement from the corner of my eye and turned. Something black and spindly, like a giant spider with huge ears, crouched on the windowsill outside, watching me. Its eyes glowed electric green in the coming darkness.

I growled a curse and started forward, but when the creature realized I'd spotted it, it let out an alarmed buzz and blinked out of sight. Yanking up the window, I peered into the darkness, searching for the slippery little nuisance, but it was gone.

"Damn gremlins," I muttered. Stepping back, I glared around my room, making sure everything was in place. I checked my lights, my clock, my computer; they all still worked, much to my relief. The last time a gremlin had been in my room, it had shorted out my laptop, and I'd had to spend my own money to get it fixed.

Gremlins were a special type of faery. They were Iron fey, which meant all my precautions and protections from the faery world didn't work on them. Iron didn't faze them, salt barriers didn't keep them out, and horseshoes over doors and windows did nothing. They were so used to the human world, so integrated with metal and science and technology, that the old charms and protection rituals were too outdated to affect them at all. I rarely had problems with Iron fey, but they were everywhere. I guessed even the Iron Queen couldn't keep track of them all.

The Iron Queen. A knot formed in my stomach. Shutting the window, I put my sticks away and dropped into the computer chair. For several minutes, I stared at the very top drawer of my desk, knowing what was inside. Wondering if I should torment myself further by taking it out.

Meghan. Do you even think of us anymore? I'd seen my half sister only a few times since she'd disappeared from our world nearly twelve years ago. She never stayed long; just a few hours to make sure everyone was okay, and then she was gone again. Before we moved, I could at least count on her to show up for my birthday and holidays. As I got older, those visits grew fewer and fewer. Eventually, she'd disappeared altogether.

Leaning forward, I yanked open the drawer. My long-lost older sister was another taboo subject in this household. If I so much as spoke her name, Mom would become depressed for a week. Officially, my sister was dead. Meghan wasn't part of this world anymore; she was one of Them, and we had to pretend she didn't exist.

But that half-breed knew about her. That could be trouble. As if I needed any more, as if being the delinquent, broody, don't-let-your-daughter-date-this-hooligan wasn't enough, now someone knew about my connection to the world of Faery.

Setting my jaw, I slammed the drawer shut and left the room, my thoughts swirling in a chaotic, sullen mess. I was human, and Meghan was gone. No matter what some half-breed faery said, I didn't belong to that world. I was going to stay on this side of the Veil and not worry about what was happening in Faery.

No matter how much it tried to drag me in.

CHAPTER THREE
FAERIES IN THE GYM BAG

Day two.

Of purgatory.

My "fight" with the school quarterback and my discussion in the principal's office hadn't gone unnoticed, of course. Fellow students stared at me in the halls, whispering to their friends, muttering in low undertones. They shied away from me as if I had the plague. Teachers gave me the evil eye, as if worried that I might punch someone in the head or pull a knife, maybe. I didn't care. Maybe Principal Hill had told them what had gone on in his office; maybe he'd told them I was a lost cause, because as long as I kept my head down, they ignored me.

Except for Miss Singer, who actually called on me several times during class, making sure I was still paying attention. I answered her questions about *Don Quixote* in monotones, hoping that would be enough to keep her off my back. She seemed pleasantly surprised that I'd read the homework assignment the night before, despite being somewhat distracted by the thoughts of gremlins lurking around my computer. Apparently satisfied that I could listen and stare out the window at the same time, Miss Singer finally left me alone, and I went back to brooding in peace.

At least Kingston and his flunky were absent today, though I did notice Todd in one of my classes, looking smug. He kept glancing at the quarterback's empty desk, smirking to himself and nodding. It made me nervous, but I swore not to get involved. If the half-breed wanted to screw around with the notoriously fickle Fair Ones, I wasn't going to be there when he got burned.

When the last bell rang, I gathered my backpack and rushed out, hoping to evade a repeat of the day before. I saw Todd as I went out the door, watching me as if he wanted to talk, but I quickly lost myself in the crowded hallway.

At my locker, I stuffed my books and homework into my pack, slammed the door—and came face-to-face with Kenzie St. James.

"Hey, tough guy."

Oh, no. What did she want? Probably to tear me a new one about the fight; if she was on the pom squad, Kingston was likely her boyfriend. Depending on which rumor you'd heard, I had either sucker-punched the quarterback or I'd threatened him in the hallway and had gotten my ass kicked before the teachers pulled us apart. Neither story was flattering, and I'd been wondering when someone would give me crap about it. I just hadn't expected it to be her.

I turned to leave, but she smoothly moved around to block my path. "Just a second!" she insisted, planting herself in front of me. "I want to talk to you."

I glared at her, a cold, hostile stare that had given redcaps pause and made a pair of spriggans back down once. Kenzie didn't move, her determined stance never wavering. I slumped in defeat. "What?" I growled. "Come to warn me to leave your boyfriend alone if I know what's good for me?"

She frowned. "Boyfriend?"

"The quarterback."

"Oh." She snorted, wrinkling her nose. It was kind of cute. "Brian's not my boyfriend."

"No?" That was surprising. I'd been so sure she was going to rip into me about the fight, maybe threaten to make me sorry if I hurt her precious football star. Why else would this girl want to talk to me?

Kenzie took advantage of my surprise and stepped closer. I swallowed and resisted the urge to step back. Kenzie was shorter than me by several inches, but that fact seemed completely lost on her. "Don't worry, tough guy. I don't have a boyfriend waiting to slug you in the bathrooms." Her eyes sparkled. "If it comes to that, I'll slug you myself."

I didn't doubt she'd try. "What do you want?" I asked again, more and more perplexed by this strange, cheerful girl.

"I'm the editor for the school paper," she announced, as if it was the most natural thing in the world. "And I was hoping you would do me a favor. Every semester, I interview the new students who started late, you know, so people can get to know them better. I'd love to do an interview with you, if you're up for it."

For the second time in thirty seconds, I was thrown. "You're an editor?"

"Well, more of a reporter, really. But since everyone else hates the technical stuff, I do the editing, too."

"For the paper?"

"That is generally what reporters report for, yes."

"But...I thought..." I gave myself a mental shake, collecting my scattered thoughts. "I saw you with the pom squad," I said, and it was almost an accusation. Kenzie's slender eyebrows rose.

"And, what? You thought I was a cheerleader?" She shrugged. "Not my thing, but thank you for thinking so. Heights and I don't really get along very well, and I can barely walk across the gym floor without falling down and bruising myself. Plus, I'd have to dye my hair blond, and that would just fry the ends."

I didn't know if she was serious or joking, but I couldn't stay. "Look, I have to be somewhere soon," I told her, which wasn't a lie; I had class tonight with my kali instructor, Guro Javier, and if I was late I'd have to do fifty pushups and a hundred suicide dashes—if he was feeling generous. Guro was serious about punctuality. "Can we talk later?"

"Will you give me that interview?"

"Okay, yes, fine!" I raised a hand in frustration. "If it will get you off my back, fine."

She beamed. "When?"

"I don't care."

That didn't faze her. Nothing did, it seemed. I'd never met someone who could be so relentlessly cheerful in the face of such blatant jack-assery. "Well, do you have a phone number?" she continued, sounding suspiciously amused. "Or, I could give you mine, if you want. Of course, that means you'd actually have to call me...." She gave me a dubious look, then shook her head. "Hmm, never mind, just give me yours. Something tells me I could tattoo my number on your forehead and you wouldn't remember to call."

"Whatever."

As I scribbled the digits on a scrap of paper, I couldn't help but think how weird it was, giving my phone number to a cute girl. I'd never done this before and likely never would again. If Kingston knew, if he even saw me talking to her, girlfriend or not, he'd probably try to give me a concussion.

Kenzie stepped beside me and stood on tiptoe to peer over my shoulder. Soft, feathery strands of her hair brushed my arm, making my skin prickle and my heart pound. I caught a hint of apple or mint or some kind of sweet fragrance, and for a second forgot what I was writing.

"Um." She leaned even closer, one slender finger pointing to the messy black scrawl on the paper. "Is this a six or a zero?"

"It's a six," I rasped, and stepped away, putting some distance between us. Damn, my heart was still pounding. What the hell was that about?

I handed over the paper. "Can I go now?"

She tucked it into the pocket of her jeans with another grin, though for just a moment she looked disappointed. "Don't let me stop you, tough guy. I'll call you later tonight, okay?"

Without answering, I stepped around her, and this time, she let me.

Kali was brutal. With the tournament less than a week off, Guro Javier was fanatical about making sure we would give nothing less than our best.

"Keep those sticks moving, Ethan," Guro called, watching me and my sparring partner circle each other, a rattan in each hand. I nodded and twirled my sticks, keeping the pattern going while looking for holes in my opponent's guard. We wore light padded armor and a helmet so that the sticks wouldn't leave ugly, throbbing welts over bare skin and we could really smack our opponent without seriously injuring him. That's not to say I didn't come home with nice purple bruises every so often—"badges of courage," as Guro called them.

My sparring partner lunged. I angled to the side, blocking his strike with one stick while landing three quick blows on his helmet with the other.

"Good!" Guro called, bringing the round to a close. "Ethan, watch your sticks. Don't let them just sit there, keep them moving, keep them flowing, always. Chris, angle out next time—don't just back up and let him hit you."

"Yes, Guro," we both said, and bowed to each other, ending the match. Backing to the corner, I wrenched off my helmet and let the cool air hit my face. Call me violent and aggressive, but I loved this. The flashing sticks, the racing adrenaline, the solid crack of your weapon hitting a vital spot on someone's armor…there was no bigger rush in the world. While I was here, I was just another student, learning under Guro Javier. Kali was the only place where I could forget my life and school and the constant, judging stares, and just be myself.

Not to mention, beating on someone with sticks was an awesome way to relieve pent-up aggression.

"Good class, everyone," Guro called, motioning us to the front of the room. We bowed to our instructor, touching one stick to our heart and the other to our forehead, as he continued. "Remember, the tournament is this Saturday. Those of you participating in the demonstrations, I would like you there early so you can practice and go over the forms and patterns. Also, Ethan—" he looked at me "—I need to talk to you before you leave. Class dismissed, everyone." He clapped his hands, and the rest of the group began to disperse, talking excitedly about the tournament and other kali-related things. I stripped off my armor, set it carefully on the mats and waited.

Guro gestured, and I followed him to the corner, gathering up punch mitts and the extra rattan sticks scattered near the wall. After stacking them neatly on the corner shelves, I turned to find Guro watching me with a solemn expression.

Guro Javier wasn't a big guy; in fact, I had an inch or two on him in my bare feet, and I wasn't very tall. I was pretty fit, not huge like a linebacker, but I did work out; Guro was all sinew and lean muscle, and the most graceful person I'd ever seen in my life. Even practicing or warming up, he looked like a dancer, twirling his weapons with a speed I had yet to master and feared I never would. And he could strike like a cobra; one minute he'd be standing in front of you demonstrating a technique, the next, you'd be on the ground, blinking and wondering how you got there. Guro's age was hard to tell; he had strands of silver through his short black hair, and laugh lines around his eyes and mouth. He pushed me hard, harder than the others, drilling me with patterns, insisting I get a technique close to perfect before I moved on. It wasn't that he played favorites, but I think he realized that I wanted this more, needed this more, than the other students. This wasn't just a hobby for me. These were skills that might someday save my life.

"How is your new school?" Guro asked in a matter-of-fact way. I started to shrug but caught myself. I tried very hard not to fall back into old, sullen habits with my instructor. I owed him more than a shrug and a one-syllable answer.

"It's fine, Guro."

"Getting along with your teachers?"

"Trying to."

"Hmm." Guro idly picked up a rattan and spun it through the air, though his eyes remained distant. He often did that stick twirling when thinking, demonstrating a technique, or even talking to us. It was habit, I guessed; I didn't think he even realized he was doing it.

"I've spoken to your mother," Guro continued calmly, and my stomach twisted. "I've asked her to keep me updated on your progress at school. She's worried about you, and I can't say I like what I've heard." The whirling stick paused for a moment, and he looked directly at me. "I do not teach kali for violence, Ethan. If I hear you've been in any more fights, or that your grades are slipping, I'll know you need to concentrate more on school than kali practice. You'll be out of the demonstration, is that clear?"

I sucked in a breath. *Great. Thanks a lot, Mom.* "Yes, Guro."

He nodded. "You're a good student, Ethan. I want you to succeed in other places, too, yes? Kali isn't everything."

"I know, Guro."

The stick started its twirling pattern again, and Guro nodded in dismissal. "Then I'll see you on Saturday. Remember, thirty minutes early, at least!"

I bowed and retreated to the locker room.

My phone blinked when I pulled it out, indicating a new message, though I didn't recognize the number. Puzzled, I checked voice mail and was greeted by a familiar, overly cheerful voice.

"Hey, tough-guy, don't forget you owe me an interview. Call me tonight, you know, when you're done robbing banks and stealing cars. Talk to you later!"

I groaned. I'd forgotten about her. Stuffing the phone into my bag, I slung it over my shoulder and was about to leave when the lights flickered and went out.

Oh, nice. Probably Redding, trying to scare me again. Rolling my eyes, I waited, listening for footsteps and snickering laughter. Chris Redding, my sparring partner, fancied himself a practical joker and liked to target people who kicked his ass in practice. Usually, that meant me.

I held my breath, remaining motionless and alert. As the silence stretched on, annoyance turned to unease. The light switch was next to the door—I could see it through a gap in the aisles, and there was no one standing there. I was in the locker room alone.

Carefully, I eased my bag off my shoulder, unzipped it and drew out a rattan stick, just in case. Edging forward, stick held out in front of me, I peered around the locker row. I was not in the mood for this. If Redding was going jump out and yell *"rah,"* he was going to get a stick upside the head, and I'd apologize later.

There was a soft buzz, somewhere overhead. I looked up just as something tiny half fell, half fluttered from the ceiling, right at my face. I leaped back, and it flopped to the floor, twitching like a dazed bird.

I edged close, ready to smack it if it lunged up at me again. The thing stirred weakly where it lay on the cement, looking like a giant wasp or a winged spider. From what I could tell, it was green and long-limbed with two transparent wings crumpled over its back. I stepped forward and nudged it with the end of the stick. It batted feebly at the rattan with a long, thin arm.

A piskie? What's it doing here? As fey went, piskies were usually pretty harmless, though they could play nasty tricks if insulted or bored. And, tiny or no, they were still fey. I was tempted to flick this one under the bench like a dead spider and continue on to my truck, when it raised its face from the floor and stared up at me with huge, terrified eyes.

It was Thistle, Todd's friend. At least, I thought it was the same faery; all piskies looked pretty much the same to me. But I thought I recognized the sharp pointed face, the puff of yellow dandelion hair. Its mouth moved, gaping wide, and its wings buzzed faintly, but it seemed too weak to get up.

Frowning, I crouched down to see it better, still keeping my rattan out in case it was just faking. "How did you get in here?" I muttered, prodding it gently with the stick. It swatted at the end but didn't move from the floor. "Were you following me?"

It gave a garbled buzz and collapsed, apparently exhausted, and I hesitated, not knowing what to do. Clearly, it was in trouble, but helping the fey went against all the rules I'd taught myself over the years. Don't draw attention to yourself. Don't interact with the Fair Folk. Never make a contract, and never accept their help. The smart thing to do would be to walk away and not look back.

Still, if I helped this once, the piskie would be in my debt, and I could think of several things I could demand in exchange. I could demand that she leave me alone. Or leave Todd alone. Or abandon whatever scheme the half-breed was having her do.

Or, better yet, I could demand that she tell no one about my sister and my connection to her.

This is stupid, I told myself, still watching the piskie crawl weakly around my rattan, trying to pull herself up the length of the stick. *You know faeries will twist any bargain to their favor, even if they owe you something. This is going to end badly.*

Oh, well. When had I ever been known for doing the smart thing?

With a sigh, I bent down and grabbed the piskie by the wings, lifting her up in front of me. She dangled limply, half-delirious, though from what I had no idea. Was it me, or did the faery seem almost…transparent? Not just her wings; she flickered in and out of focus like a blurry camera shot.

And then, I saw something beyond the piskie's limp form, lurking in the darkness at the end of the locker room. Something pale and ghostlike, long hair drifting around its head like mist.

"Ethan?"

Guro's voice echoed through the locker room, and the thing vanished. Quickly, I unzipped my bag and stuffed the piskie inside as my instructor appeared in the doorway. His eyes narrowed when he saw me.

"Everything all right?" he asked as I shouldered the bag and stepped forward. And, was it my imagination, or did he glance at the corner where the creepy ghost-thing was? "I thought I heard something. Chris isn't hiding in a corner ready to jump out, is he?"

"No, Guro. It's fine."

I waited for him to move out of the doorway so I wouldn't have to shoulder past him with my bag. My heart pounded, and the hair on the back of my neck stood up. Something was still in the room with me; I could feel it watching us, its cold eyes on my back.

Guro's eyes flicked to the corner again, narrowing. "Ethan," he said in a low voice, "my grandfather was a *Mang-Huhula*— you know what that means, yes?"

I nodded, trying not to seem impatient. The *Mang-Huhula* was the spiritual leader of the tribe, a faith-healer or fortune teller of sorts. Guro himself was a *tuhon,* someone who passed down his culture and practices, who kept the traditions alive. He'd told us this before; I wasn't sure why he was remind-ing me now.

"My grandfather was a wise man," Guro went on, hold-ing my gaze. "He told me not to put your trust in only your eyes. That to truly see, sometimes you had to put your faith in the invisible things. You had to believe what no one else was willing to. Do you understand what I'm saying?"

I heard a soft slither behind me, like wet cloth over cement, and my skin crawled. It took all my willpower not to draw my rattan and swing around. "I think so, Guro."

Guro paused a moment, then stepped back, looking faintly disappointed. Obviously, I'd just missed something, or he could tell I was really distracted. But all he said was, "If you need help, Ethan, all you have to do is ask. If you're in trou-ble, you can come to me. For anything, no matter how small or crazy it might seem. Remember that."

The thing, whatever it was, slithered closer. I nodded, trying not to fidget. "I will, Guro."

"Go on, then." Guro stepped aside, nodding. "Go home. I'll see you at the tournament."

I fled the room, forcing myself not to look back. And I didn't stop until I reached my truck.

My phone rang as soon as I was home.

After closing my bedroom door, I dropped my gym bag on the bed, listening to the buzz of wings from somewhere inside. It seemed the piskie was still alive, though it probably wasn't thrilled at being zipped into a bag with used gym shorts and sweaty T-shirts. Smirking at the thought, I checked the trilling phone. Same unfamiliar number. I sighed and held it to my ear.

"God, you're persistent," I told the girl and heard a chuckle on the other end.

"It's a reporter skill," she replied. "If every newscaster got scared off by the threat of violence or kidnapping or death, there wouldn't be any news at all. They have to brave a lot to get their stories. Consider yourself practice for the real world."

"I'm so honored," I deadpanned. She laughed.

"So, anyway, are you free tomorrow? Say, after school? We can meet in the library and you can give me that interview."

"Why?" I scowled at the phone, ignoring the angry buzzing coming from my gym bag. "Just ask me your questions now and be done with it."

"Oh, no, I never do interviews over the phone if I can help it." The buzzing grew louder, and my bag started to shake. I gave it a thump, and it squeaked in outrage.

"Phone interviews are too impersonal," Kenzie went on, oblivious to my ridiculous fight with the gym bag. "I want to look at the person I'm interviewing, really see their reactions, get a glimpse into their thoughts and feelings. I can't do that over the phone. So, tomorrow in the library, okay? After the last class. Will you be there?"

A session alone with Kenzie. My heart beat faster at the thought, and I coldly stomped it down. Yes, Kenzie was cute, smart, popular and extremely attractive. You'd have to be blind not to see it. She was also obscenely rich, or her family was, anyway. The few rumors I'd heard said her father owned three mansions and a private jet, and Kenzie only went to public school because she wanted to. Even if I was anywhere near normal, Mackenzie St. James was way out of my league.

And it was better that way. I couldn't allow myself to get comfortable with this girl, to let my guard down for an instant. The second I let people get close to me, the fey would make them targets. I would not let that happen ever again.

My bag actually jumped about two inches off the bed, landing with a thump on the mattress. I winced and dragged it back before it could leap to the floor. "Sure," I said distractedly, not really thinking about it. "Whatever. I'll be there."

"Awesome!" I could sense Kenzie's smile. "Thanks, tough guy. See you tomorrow."

I hung up.

Outside, lightning flickered through the window, showing a storm was on its way. Grabbing my rattan stick, I braced myself and unzipped the gym bag in one quick motion, releasing a wave of stink and a furious, buzzing piskie into my room.

Not surprisingly, the faery made a beeline for the window but veered away when it noticed the line of salt poured along the sill. It darted toward the door, but an iron horseshoe hung over the frame and a coil of metal wire had been wound over the doorknob. It hummed around the ceiling like a frantic wasp, then finally drifted down to the headboard, alighting on a bedpost. Crossing its arms, it gave me an annoyed, expectant look.

I smiled nastily. "Feeling better, are we? You're not getting out of here until I say so, so sit down and relax." The piskie's wings vibrated, and I kept my rattan out, ready to swat if it decided to dive-bomb me. "I saved your life back there," I reminded the faery. "So I think you owe me something. That's generally how these things work. You owe me a life debt, and I'm calling it in right now."

It bristled but crossed its legs and sat down on the post, looking sulky. I relaxed my guard, but only a little. "Sucks being on that end of a bargain, doesn't it?" I smirked, enjoying my position, and leaned back against the desk.

The piskie glared, then lifted one arm in an impatient gesture that clearly said, *Well? Get on with it, then*. Still keeping it in my sights, I crossed my room and locked the door, more to keep curious parents out than annoyed faeries in. Life debt or no, I could only imagine the trouble the piskie would cause if she managed to escape to the rest of the house.

"Thistle, right?" I asked, returning to the desk. The piskie's head bobbed once in affirmation. I wondered if I should ask about Meghan but decided against it. Piskies, I'd discovered, were notoriously difficult to understand and had the attention span of a gnat. Long, drawn-out conversations with them were virtually impossible, as they tended to forget the question as soon as it was answered.

"You know Todd, then?"

The piskie buzzed and nodded.

"What did you do for him recently?"

The result was a garbled, high-pitched mess of words and sentences, spoken so quickly it made my head spin. It was like listening to a chipmunk on speed. "All right, enough!" I said, holding up my hands. "I wasn't thinking." *Yes or no answers,*

Ethan, remember? The piskie gave me a confused frown, but I ignored it and continued. "So, were you following me today?"

Another nod.

"Why—"

The piskie gave a terrified squeal and buzzed frantically about the room, nearly smacking into me as it careened around the walls. I ducked, covering my head, as it zipped across the room, babbling in its shrill, squeaking voice. "Okay, okay! Calm down! Sorry I asked." It finally hovered in a corner, shaking its head, eyes bulging out of its skull. I eyed it warily.

Huh. That was…interesting. "What was that about?" I demanded. The piskie buzzed and hugged itself, wings trembling. "Something was after you tonight, wasn't it? That thing in the locker room—it was chasing you. Piss off an Iron faery, then?" The fey of the Iron Queen's court were the only creatures I could think of that could provoke such a reaction. I didn't know what it was like in the Nevernever, but here, the old-world faeries and the Iron fey still didn't get along very well. Generally, the two groups avoided each other, pretending the other didn't exist. But faeries were fickle and destructive and violent, and fights still broke out between them, usually ending fatally.

But the piskie shook its head, squeaking and waving its thin arms. I frowned. "It wasn't an Iron fey," I guessed, and it shook its head again, vigorously. "What was it?"

"Ethan?" There was a knock, and Dad's voice came through the door. "Are you in there? Who are you talking to?"

I winced. Unlike Mom, Dad had no problem invading my personal space. If it were up to him, I wouldn't even have a door. "On the phone, Dad!" I called back.

"Oh. Well, dinner is ready. Tell your friend you'll call back, okay?"

I grunted and heard his footsteps retreat down the hall.

The piskie still hovered in the corner, watching me with big black eyes. It was terrified, and even though it was fey and had probably played a million nasty pranks on unsuspecting humans, I suddenly felt like a bully.

I sighed. "You know what?" I told it, moving to the window. "Forget it. This was stupid of me. I'm not getting involved with any of you, life debt or no." Sweeping away the salt, I unlocked the window and pushed it open, letting in a blast of cool, rain-scented air. "Get out of here," I told the piskie, who blinked in astonishment. "You want to repay me? Whatever you're doing for that half-breed, stop it. I don't want you hanging around him, or me, ever again. Now beat it."

I jerked my head toward the window, and the piskie didn't hesitate. It zipped past my head, seeming to go right through the screen, and vanished into the night.

CHAPTER FOUR

AN UNEXPECTED VISITOR

Storms always made me moody. More so than usual, anyway.

Don't know why; maybe they reminded me of my child-hood, back in the swamps. We'd gotten a lot of rain on our small farm, and somehow the drumming of water on the tin roof always put me to sleep. Or maybe because, when I was very small, I would creep out of bed and into my sister's room, and she would hold me as the thunder boomed and tell me stories until I fell asleep.

I didn't want to remember those days. They just reminded me that she wasn't here now, and she never would be again.

I loaded the last plate into the dishwasher and kicked it shut, wincing as a crash of thunder outside made the lights flicker. Hopefully, the power would stay on this time. Call me para-noid, but stumbling around in the dark with nothing but a candle made me positive that the fey were lurking in shadowy corners and darkened bathrooms, waiting to pounce.

I finished clearing the table, walked into the living room and flopped down on the couch. Dad had already gone to work, and Mom was upstairs, so the house was fairly still as I flipped on the television, turning up the volume to drown out the storm.

The doorbell rang.

I ignored it. It wasn't for me, that was for certain. I didn't have friends; no one ever came to my house to hang out with the weird, unfriendly freak. Most likely it was our neighbor, Mrs. Tully, who was friends with Mom and liked to glare at me through the slits in her venetian blinds. As if she was afraid I would throw eggs at her house or kick her yappy little dog. She liked to give Mom advice about what to do with me, claiming she knew a couple of good military schools that would straighten me right out. Most likely, she was huddled on our doorstep with an umbrella and a bag of extra candles, using the storm as an excuse to come in and gossip, probably about me. I snorted under my breath. Mom was too nice to tell her to take a hike, but I had no such convictions. She could just stay out there as far as I was concerned.

The doorbell rang again, and it sounded louder this time, more insistent.

"Ethan!" Mom called from somewhere upstairs, her voice sharp. "Will you get that, please? Don't leave whoever it is standing there in the rain!"

Sighing, I dragged myself upright and went to the door, expecting to see a plump old woman glaring disapprovingly as I yanked it open. It wasn't Mrs. Tully, however.

It was Todd.

At first, I didn't recognize him. He had on a huge camouflage jacket that was two sizes too big, and the hood had fallen over his eyes. When he raised a hand and shoved it back, the porch light caught his pupils and made them glitter orange. His hair and furry ears were drenched, and he looked even smaller than normal, huddled in that enormous coat. A bike lay on its side in the grass behind him, wheels spinning in the rain.

"Oh, good, this is the right house." Todd grinned at me, canines flashing in the dim light. A violet-skinned piskie peeked out of his hood, blinking huge black eyes, and I recoiled.

"Hey, Ethan!" the half-breed said cheerfully, peering past me into the house. "Nasty weather, isn't it? Uh, can I come in?"

I instantly shut the door in his face, leaving no more than a few inches open to glare at him through the crack. "What are you doing here?" I hissed. He flattened his ears at my tone, looking scared now.

"I need to talk to you," he whispered, glancing back over his shoulder. "It's important, and you're the only one who might be able to help. Please, you gotta let me in."

"No way." I kept a firm foot on the edge of the door, refusing to budge an inch as he pushed forward. "If you're in trouble with Them, that's your problem for getting involved. I told you before—I want nothing to do with it." I glared at the piskie who crouched beneath Todd's hood, watching it carefully. "Get lost. Go home."

"I can't!" Todd leaned in frantically, eyes wide. "I can't go home because *They're* waiting for me."

"Who?"

"I don't know! These weird, creepy, ghostly *things*. They've been hanging around my house since yesterday, watching me, and they keep getting closer."

A chill spread through my stomach. I gazed past him into the rainy streets, searching for glimmers of movement, shadows of things not there. "What did you do?" I growled, glaring at the half-phouka, who cringed.

"I don't know!" Todd made a desperate, helpless gesture, and his piskie friend squeaked. "I've never seen these type of fey before. But they keep following me, watching me. I think they're after us," he continued, gesturing to the fey on his shoulder. "Violet and Beetle are both terrified, and I can't find Thistle anywhere."

"So, you came *here,* to pull my family into this? Are you crazy?"

"Ethan?" Mom appeared behind me, peering over my shoulder. "Who are you talking to?"

"No one!" But it was too late; she'd already seen him.

Glancing past me, Todd gave a sheepish smile and a wave. "Um, hey, Ethan's Mom," he greeted, suddenly charming and polite. "I'm Todd. Ethan and I were supposed to trade notes this evening, but I sorta got caught in the rain on the way here. It's nothing—I'm used to biking across town. In the rain. And the cold." He sniffled and glanced mournfully at his bike, lying in the mud behind him. "Sorry for disturbing you," he said, glancing up with the most pathetic puppy dog eyes I'd ever seen. "It's late. I guess I'll head on home now...."

"What? In this weather? No, Todd, you'll catch your death." Mom shooed me out of the doorway and gestured to the half-phouka on the steps. "Come inside and dry off, at least. Do your parents know where you are?"

"Thank you." Todd grinned as he scurried over the threshold. I clenched my fists to stop myself from shoving him back into the rain. "And yeah, it's okay. I told my Mom I was visiting a friend's house."

"Well, if the rain doesn't let up, you're more than welcome to stay the night," Mom said, sealing my fate. "Ethan has a spare sleeping bag you can borrow, and he can take you both to school tomorrow in his truck." She fixed me with a steely glare that promised horrible repercussions if I wasn't nice. "You don't mind, do you?"

I sighed. "Whatever." Glancing at Todd, who looked way too pleased, I turned away and gestured for him to follow. "Come on, then. I'll get that sleeping bag set up."

He trailed me to my room, gazing around eagerly as he stepped through the frame. That changed when I slammed the door, making him jump, and turned to glare at him.

"All right," I growled, stalking forward, backing him up

to the wall. "Start talking. What's so damned important that you had to come here and drag my family into whatever mess you created?"

"Ethan, wait." Todd held up clawed hands. "You were right, okay? I shouldn't have been screwing around with the fey, but it's too late to go back and undo…whatever I did."

"What *did* you do?"

"I told you, I don't know!" The half-breed bared his canines in frustration. "Little things, nothing I haven't done before. Teensy contracts with Thistle and Violet and Beetle to help with some of my tricks, but that's all. But I think something bigger took notice of us, and now I think I'm in real trouble."

"What do you want *me* to do about it?"

"I just…" Todd stopped, frowning. "Wait a minute," he muttered, and pushed his hood back. It flopped emptily. "Violet? Where'd she go?" he said, stripping out of the coat and shaking it. "She was here a few minutes ago."

I smirked at him. "Your piskie friend? Yeah, sorry, she couldn't get past the ward on the front door. No faery can get over the threshold without my permission, and I wasn't about to set that thing free in my house. It doesn't work on half-breeds, sadly."

He looked up, eyes wide. "She's still outside?"

A tap came on the window, where a new line of salt had been poured across the sill. The dripping wet piskie stared through the glass at us, her small features pinched into a scowl. I grinned at her smugly.

"I knew it," Todd whispered, and dropped his wet jacket onto a chair. "I knew you were the right person to come to."

I eyed him. "What are you talking about?"

"Just…" He glanced at the piskie again. She pressed her face to the glass, and he swallowed. "Dude, can I…uh….let her in? I'm scared those things are still out there."

"If I refuse, are you going to keep bothering me until I say yes?"

"More or less, yeah."

Annoyed, I brushed away the salt and cracked open the window, letting the piskie through with a buzz of wings and damp air. Two faeries in my room in the same night; this was turning into a nightmare. "Don't touch anything." I glowered at her as she settled on Todd's shoulder with a huff. "I have an antique iron birdcage you can sit in if anything goes missing."

The piskie made irritated buzzing sounds, pointing at me and waving her arms, and Todd shook his head. "I know, I know! But he's the Iron Queen's brother. He's the only one I could think of."

My heart gave a violent lurch at the mention of the Iron Queen, and I narrowed my eyes. "What was that?"

"You have to help us," Todd exclaimed, oblivious to my sudden anger. "These things are after me, and they don't look friendly. You're the brother of the Iron Queen, and you know how to keep the fey out. Give me something to keep them away from me. The common wards are helping, but I don't think they're strong enough. I need something more powerful." He leaned forward, ears pricked, eyes eager. "You know how to keep Them away, right? You must, you've been doing it all your life. Show me how."

"Forget it." I glared at him, and his ears wilted. "What happens if I give you all my secrets? You would just use it to further your stupid tricks. I'm not revealing everything just to have it bite me in the ass later." His ears drooped even more, and I crossed my arms. "Besides, what about your little friends? The wards I know are for *all* fey, not just a select few. What happens to them?"

"We can get around that," Todd said quickly. "We'll make it work, somehow. Ethan, please. I'm desperate, here. What do you want from me?" He leaned forward. "Give me a hint. A tip. A note scribbled on a fortune cookie, I'll try anything. Talk to me this one time, and I swear I'll leave you alone after this."

I raised an eyebrow. "And your friends?"

"I'll make sure they leave you alone, as well."

I sighed. This was probably monumentally stupid, but I knew what it was like to feel trapped, not having anyone I could turn to. "All right," I said reluctantly. "I'll help. But I want your word that you'll stop all bargains and contracts after today. If I do this, no more 'help' from the Good Neighbors, got it?"

The piskie buzzed sadly, but Todd nodded without hesitation. "Deal! I mean…yeah. I swear."

"No more contracts or bargains?"

"No more contracts or bargains." He sighed and made an impatient gesture with a claw. "Now, can we please get on with it?"

I had major doubts that he could keep that promise—half fey weren't bound by their promises the way full fey were— but what else could I do? He needed my help, and if something *was* after him, I couldn't stand back and do nothing. Rubbing my eyes, I went to my desk, opened the bottom drawer and pulled out an old leather journal from under a stack of papers. After hesitating a moment, I walked forward and tossed it onto my bed.

Todd blinked. "What is that?"

"All my research on the Good Neighbors," I said, pulling a half-empty notepad off my bookshelf. "And if you mention it to anyone, I *will* kick your ass. Here." I tossed him the pad, and he caught it awkwardly. "Take notes. I'll tell you what you need to know—it'll be up to you to go through with it."

We stayed there for the rest of the evening, him sitting on

my bed scribbling furiously, me leaning against my desk reading wards, charms and recipes from the journal. I went over the common wards, like salt, iron and wearing your clothes inside out. We went over things that could attract the fey into a house: babies, shiny things, large amounts of sugar or honey. We briefly discussed the most powerful ward in the book, a circle of toadstools that would grow around the house and render everything inside invisible to the fey. But that spell was extremely complicated, required rare and impossible ingredients, and could be safely performed only by a druid or a witch on the night of the waning moon. Since I didn't know any local witches, nor did I have any powdered unicorn horn lying around, we weren't going to be performing that spell anytime in the near future. Besides, I told a disappointed Todd, you could put a wrought-iron fence around your house with less effort than the toadstool ring, and it would do nearly the same job in keeping out the fey.

"So," Todd ventured after a couple of hours of this. I sensed he was getting bored, and marveled that the half-phouka had lasted this long. "Enough talk about the fey already. Word around school is that you were a total douche to Mackenzie St. James."

I looked up from the journal, where I was making small corrections to a charm using ragwort and mistletoe. "Yeah? So what?"

"Dude, you'd better be careful with that girl." Todd put down his pen and gazed at me with serious orange eyes. The piskie buzzed from the top of my bookshelf to land on his shoulder. "Last year, some guy kept following her around, trying to ask her out. Wouldn't leave her alone even when she turned him down." He shook his shaggy head. "The whole football team took him out behind the bleachers to have 'a talk' about Kenzie. Poor bastard wouldn't even look at her after that."

"I have no interest in Kenzie St. James," I said flatly.

"Good to hear," Todd replied. "'Cause Kenzie is off-limits. And not just to people like you and me. Everyone at school knows it. You don't bother her, you don't start rumors about her, you don't hang around, you don't make yourself *unwanted*, or the Goon Squad will come and leave an impression of your face in the wall."

"Seems a little drastic," I muttered, intrigued despite myself. "What, did she have a nasty breakup with one of the jocks, and now he doesn't want anyone to have her?"

"No." Todd shook his head. "Kenzie doesn't have a boyfriend. She's *never* had a boyfriend. Not once. Why is that, you wonder? She's gorgeous, smart, and everyone says her dad is loaded. But she's never gone out with anyone. Why?"

"Because people don't want their heads bashed in by testosterone-ridden gorillas?" I guessed, rolling my eyes.

But Todd shook his head. "No, I don't think that's it," he said, frowning at my snort of disbelief. "I mean, think about it, dude—if Kenzie wanted a boyfriend, do you think anyone, even Chief Tool Kingston himself, would be able to stop her?"

No, I thought, *he wouldn't*. No one would. I had the distinct feeling that if Kenzie wanted something, she would get it, no matter how difficult or impossible it was. She had wheedled an interview out of *me*—that was saying something. The girl just didn't take no for an answer.

"Kinda makes you wonder," Todd mused. "Pretty girl like that, with no boyfriend and no interest in any guy? Do you think she could be—"

"I don't care," I interrupted, pushing thoughts of Mackenzie St. James to the back of my mind. I couldn't think about her. Because even if Kenzie was pretty and kind and had treated

me like a decent human being, even though I was a total ass
to her, I could not afford to bring someone else into my dangerous, screwed-up world. I was spending the evening teach-
ing anti-faery charms to a piskie and a half-phouka; that was
a pretty good indication of how messed up my life was.

A crash of thunder outside rattled the ceiling and made the
lights flicker just as there was a knock on the door and Mom
poked her head in. I quickly flipped the journal shut, and Todd
snatched the notebook from where it lay on the bed, hiding
the contents as she gazed down at us.

"How are you boys doing?" Mom asked, smiling at Todd,
who beamed back at her. I kept a close eye on his piskie, making sure it didn't dart through the crack into the rest of the
house. "Everything all right?"

"We're fine, Mom," I said quickly, wishing she would close
the door. She frowned at me, then turned to my unwanted
guest.

"Todd, it looks like it's going to storm all night. My husband is at work, so he can't drive you home, and I am not
sending you out in this weather. It looks like you'll have to
stay here tonight." He looked relieved, and I suppressed a
groan. "Make sure you call your parents to let them know
where you are, okay?"

"I will, Mrs. Chase."

"Did Ethan set you up with a sleeping bag yet?"

"Not yet." Todd grinned at me. "But he was just about to,
right, Ethan?"

I glared daggers at him. "Sure."

"Good. I'll see you boys tomorrow morning, then. And
Ethan?"

"Yeah?"

She gave me a brief look that said *be nice or your father will hear about this.* "It's still a school night. Lights out before too long, okay?"

"Fine."

The door clicked shut, and Todd turned to me, wide-eyed. "Wow, and I thought my parents were strict. I haven't heard 'lights out' since I was ten. Do you have a curfew, as well?" I gave him a hooded stare, daring him to go on, and he squirmed. "Um, so where's the bathroom, again?"

I rose, dug a sleeping bag from my closet, and tossed it and an extra pillow on the floor. "Bathroom's down the hall to the right," I muttered, returning to my desk. "Just be quiet—my dad gets home late and might freak out if he doesn't know about you. And the piskie stays here. It doesn't leave this room, got it?"

"Sure, man." Todd closed the notebook, rolled it up, and stuffed it in a back pocket. "I'll try some of these when I get home, see if any of them work. Hey, Ethan, thanks for doing this. I owe you."

"Whatever." I turned my back on him and opened my laptop. "You don't owe me anything," I muttered as he started to leave the room. "In fact, you can thank me by never mentioning this to anyone, ever."

Todd paused in the hallway. He seemed about to say something, but when I didn't look up, turned and left silently, the door clicking shut behind him.

I sighed and plugged my headphones into my computer, pulling them over my head. Despite Mom's insistence that I go to bed soon, sleep wasn't likely. Not with a piskie and a half-phouka sharing my room tonight; I'd wake up with my head glued to the baseboard, or find my computer taped to the ceiling, or something like that. I shot a glare at the piskie sitting on my bookshelf, legs dangling over the side, and she glared back, baring sharp little teeth in my direction.

Definitely no sleep for Ethan tonight. At least I had coffee and live-streaming to keep me company.

"Oh, cool, you like *Firefly?*" Todd came back into the room, peering over my shoulder at the computer screen. Grabbing a stool, he plunked himself down next to me, oblivious to my wary look. "Man, doesn't it suck that it was canceled? I seriously thought about sending Thistle with a few of her friends to jinx FOX until they put it on again." He tapped the side of his head, indicating my headphones. "Dude, turn it up. This is my favorite episode. They should've just stuck with the television series and not bothered with that awful movie."

I pulled the headphones down. "What are you talking about? *Serenity* was awesome. They needed it to tie up all the loose ends, like what happened with River and Simon."

"Yeah, after killing everyone that was important," Todd sneered, rolling his eyes. "Bad enough that they offed the preacher dude. Once Wash died I was done."

"That was brilliant," I argued. "Made you sit up and think, hey, if *Wash* died, no one was safe."

"Whatever, man. You probably cheered when Anya died on *Buffy,* too."

I smirked but caught myself. What was happening here? I didn't need this. I didn't need someone to laugh and joke and argue the finer points of Whedon films with me. *Friends* did that sort of thing. Todd was not my friend. More important, I wasn't anyone's friend. I was someone who should be avoided at all costs. Even someone like Todd was at risk if I didn't keep my distance. Not to mention the pain he could bring down on me.

"Fine." Pulling off the headphones, I set them on the desk in front of the half-breed, not taking my hand away. "Knock yourself out. Just remember…" Todd reached for the headphones, and I pulled them back. "After tonight, we're done.

You don't talk to me, you don't look for me, and you *definitely* don't show up at my front door. When we get to school, you'll go your way and I'll go mine. Don't ever come here again, got it?"

"Yeah." Todd's voice, though sullen, was resigned. "I got it."

I pushed myself to my feet, and he frowned, pulling the headphones over his furry ears. "Where are you going?"

"To make some coffee." I shot a glance at the piskie, now on my windowsill, staring out at the rain, and resigned myself to the inevitable. "Want some?"

"Ugh, usually that would be a 'no,'" Todd muttered, pulling a face. Following my gaze to the window, his ears flattened. "But, yeah, go ahead and make me a cup. Extra strong… black…whatever." He shivered as he watched the storm raging beyond the glass. "I don't think either of us will be getting much sleep tonight."

CHAPTER FIVE
THE GHOST FEY

"Uh-oh," Todd muttered from the passenger seat of my truck. "Looks like Kingston is back."

I gave the red Camaro a weary look as we cruised past it in the parking lot, not bothering to think about what Todd might be implying. Hell, I was tired. Staying up all night as Todd watched reruns of *Angel* and *Firefly,* listening to the half-breed's running commentary and drinking endless cups of coffee to keep myself awake, wasn't high on my list of favorite things to do. At least one of us had gotten a few hours' sleep. Todd had finally curled up on the sleeping bag and started to snore, but the piskie and I had given each other evil glares until dawn.

Today was going to suck, big-time.

Todd opened the door and hopped out of the truck almost before I turned off the engine. "So, uh, I guess I'll see you around," he said, edging away from me. "Thanks again for last night. I'll start setting these up as soon as I get home."

Whatever, I wanted to say, but just yawned at him instead. Todd hesitated, as if he was debating whether or not to tell me something. He grimaced.

"Also, you might want to avoid Kingston today, man. I mean, like the plague. Just a friendly warning."

I gave him a wary look. Not that I had any intention of talking to Kingston, ever, but... "Why?"

He shuffled his feet. "Oh, just...because. See ya, Ethan." And he took off, bounding over the parking lot, his huge coat flapping behind him. I stared after him, then shook my head.

Why do I get the feeling I've just been had?

Yep, the half-breed had definitely been hiding something, because Kingston was out for blood. I wouldn't have noticed, except he made a point of glaring at me all through class, following me down the hallway, cracking his knuckles and mouthing "you're dead, freak," at me over the aisles. I didn't know what his problem was. He couldn't still be pissed about that fight in the hallway, if you could even call it a fight. Maybe he was mad because he hadn't gotten to knock my teeth out. I ignored his unsubtle threats and made a point of not looking at him, vowing that the next time I ran into Todd, we were going to have a talk.

Other than glaring at me, Kingston left me alone in the halls to and from class. But I expected him to try something during lunch, so I found a hidden corner in the library where I could eat in peace. Not that I was afraid of the football star and his gorillas, but I wanted to go to that damn demonstration, and they weren't going to ruin it by getting me expelled.

The library was dim and smelled of dust and old pages. A No Food or Drink sign was plastered to the front desk, but I stuffed my sandwich under my jacket, slipped my soda can into my pocket, and retreated to the back. The head librarian stared as I walked past her desk, her hawk eyes glinting behind her glasses, but she didn't stop me.

Opening my soda, making sure it didn't hiss, I sank down on the floor between aisles M–N and O–P with a relieved sigh. Leaning against the wall, I gazed through the cracks in the books, watching students moving down the mazelike corridors. A girl came down my aisle once, book in hand, and came to an abrupt halt, blinking. I glared stonily, and she retreated without a word.

Well, my life had certainly reached a new low. Hiding out in the library so the star quarterback wouldn't try to stick my head through a wall or put his fist between my teeth. Return the favor, and I'd be expelled. Morosely, I finished the last of my sandwich and checked my watch. Still thirty-five minutes to class. Restless, I plucked a book off the shelf next to me and skimmed through it: *The History of Cheeses and Cheesemaking.* How fascinating.

As I put it back, my thoughts drifted to Kenzie. I was supposed to meet her here after school for that stupid interview. I wondered what she would ask, what she wanted to know. Why had she even singled me out, after I'd made it perfectly clear that I wanted nothing to do with her?

I snorted. Maybe that was the reason. She liked a challenge. Or maybe she was intrigued by someone who wasn't tripping over himself to talk to her. If you believed what Todd said, Mackenzie St. James probably had everything handed to her on a silver platter.

Stop thinking about her, Ethan. It doesn't matter why; after today you'll go back to ignoring her, same as everyone else.

There was a buzz somewhere overhead, the soft flutter of wings, and all my senses went rigidly alert.

Casually, I picked up the book again and pretended to flip through it while listening for the faery atop the shelves. If the piskie tried anything, it would be squashed like a big spider under *The History of Cheeses and Cheesemaking.*

The piskie squeaked in its excited, high-pitched voice, wings buzzing. I was tempted to glance up to see whether it was the piskie I'd saved in the locker room or Todd's little purple friend. If either were back to torture me after I just saved their miserable lives and stuck my neck out for the half-breed, I was going to be really annoyed.

"There you are!"

A body appeared at the end of the aisle, orange eyes glowing in the dim light. I suppressed a groan as the half-breed ducked into the corridor, panting. His ears were pressed flat to his skull, and his canines were bared as he flung himself down next to me.

"I've been looking everywhere for you," he whispered, peering through the books, eyes wild. "Look, you've got to help me. They're still after us!"

"Help you?" I glared at him, and he shrank back. "I've already helped you far more than I should have. You swore you would leave me alone after this. What happened to that?" Todd started to reply, and I held up my hand. "No, forget that question. Let me ask another one. Why does Kingston want to bash my head in today?"

He fiddled with the end of his sleeve. "Dude…you have to understand…this was before I knew you. Before I realized something was after me. If I'd known I'd be asking for your help…you can't get mad at me, okay?"

I waited, letting the silence stretch. Todd grimaced.

"Okay, so I…uh… might've asked Thistle to pay him back for what he did, but to make sure he didn't connect it to me. She put something in his shorts that…er…made him swell up and itch like crazy. That's why he wasn't here yesterday. But, the catch is, he knows someone did it to him."

"And he thinks it was me." Groaning, I leaned my head back and thumped it against the wall. So that's why the quarterback was on the warpath. I raised my head and glared at him. "Give me one good reason I shouldn't kick your ass right now."

"Dude, They are *here!*" Todd leaned forward again, apparently too panicked to take my threat seriously. "I've seen them, peering in through the windows, staring right at me! I can't go home while they're out there! They're just waiting for me to step outside."

"What do you want me to do about it?" I asked.

"Make them go away! Tell them to leave me alone." He grabbed my sleeve. "You're the brother of the Iron Queen! You have to do *something.*"

"No, I don't. And keep your voice down!" I stood and glared down at them both. "This is your mess. I told you before, I want nothing to do with Them, and your friends have caused me nothing but trouble since the day I got here. I stepped in front of Kingston for you, I let a piskie and a half-phouka into my room last night, and look where it got me. That's what I get for sticking my neck out."

Todd wilted, looking stunned and betrayed, but I was too angry to care. "I told you before," I growled, backing out of the aisle, "we're done. Stay away from me, you hear? I don't want you or your friends around me, my house, my family, my car, anything. I've helped you as much as I can. Now leave. Me. *Alone.*"

Without waiting for an answer, I whirled and stalked away, scanning the room for invisible things that might be lurking in the corners, ready to pounce. If the fey were hanging around the school like Todd said, I would have to up the ante on some of my protection wards, both for my truck and my person. Also, if Kingston was ready to put my head through a bathroom stall, I should probably head back to class and lay low until he and the gorilla squad cooled off a bit.

As I neared the librarian's desk, however, a faint, muffled sob came from one of the aisles behind me, and I stopped.

Dammit. Closing my eyes, I hesitated, torn between anger

and guilt. I knew what it was like, being hunted by the fey. I knew the fear, the desperation, when dealing with the Fair Folk who meant you harm. When you realized that it was just you against Them and no one could help you. When you realized *They* knew it, too.

Spinning on a heel, I walked back to the far aisle, cursing myself for getting involved one more time. I found Todd sitting where I had left him, huddled in the aisle looking miserable, the piskie crouched on his shoulder. They both glanced up when I approached, and Todd blinked, furry ears pricking hopefully.

"I'll drive you home," I said, watching his face light up with relief. "Last favor, all right? You have what you need to keep Them away from you—just follow the instructions I gave you and you'll be fine. Don't thank me," I said as he opened his mouth. "Just meet me here after class. I have this interview with the school reporter I have to do first, but it shouldn't take long. We'll leave when I'm done."

"School reporter?" Todd's smile shifted to an obnoxious leer in the space of a blink. "You mean St. James. So, she's got you wrapped around her little finger, too, huh? That didn't take long."

"You wanna walk home?"

"Sorry." The smirk vanished as quickly as it had come. "I'll be here. In fact, I think Violet and I are just going to stay right here until classes are over. You go do your interview thing. We'll be close, probably hiding under a table or something."

I made a mental note to check under the table before I did any interviews that afternoon, and left without another word. This time I did not look back.

Damn the fey. Why couldn't they leave me alone? Or Todd, for that matter? Why did they make life miserable for anyone caught up in their twisted sights? Human, half-breed, young, old, it didn't matter. I was no safer today than I had been thirteen years ago, just more paranoid and hostile. Was it always going to be like this, constantly looking over my shoulder, being alone so no one else got hurt? Was I ever going to be free of Them?

As I stepped through the library doors, my thoughts still on the conversation with the half-breed, something grabbed my shoulder and slammed me into the wall. My head struck the cement with a painful crack, expelling the air from my lungs. Stars danced across my vision for a second, and I blinked them away.

Kingston glared down at me, one fist in the collar of my shirt, pinning me to the wall. Two of his goons stood at his shoulders, flanking him like growling attack dogs.

"Hey there, asshole," Kingston's hot breath whipped at my face as he leaned close, reeking of smoke and spearmint. "I think we need to have a little talk."

The demonstration, Ethan. Keep it together. "What do you want?" I snarled, forcing myself not to move, not to shoot my arm up his neck, wrench his head down and drive my knee into his ugly mouth. Or grab the hand on my collar, spin around, and slam his thick face into the wall. So many options, but I kept myself still, not meeting his eyes. "I haven't done anything to you."

"Shut up!" His grip tightened, pressing me harder against the cement. "I know it was you. Don't ask me how, but I know. But we'll get to that in a minute." He brought his face close to mine, lips curling into a grim smile. "I hear you've been talking to Mackenzie."

You've got to be kidding me. All this time I've been saying "go away," and this still happens? "So what?" I challenged stupidly, making Kingston narrow his eyes. "What are you going to do, pee on her locker to let everyone know she's off-limits?"

Kingston didn't smile. His free fist clenched, and I kept a close eye on it in case it came streaking at my face. "She's off-limits to *you*," he said, dead serious now. "And unless you want me to make it so that all your food comes through a straw, you'll remember that. You don't talk to her, you don't hang around her, you don't even look at her. Just forget you ever heard her name, you got that?"

I would love to, I thought sourly. *If the girl would leave* me *alone.* But at the same time, something in me bristled at the thought of never talking to Kenzie again. Maybe I didn't respond well to threats, maybe Todd's unknown faeries had me itching for a fight, but I straightened, looked Brian Kingston right in the eye and said, "Piss. Off."

He tensed, and his two friends swelled up behind him like angry bulls. "Okay, freak," Kingston said, and that evil smirk came creeping back. "If that's how you want it. Fine. I still owe you for making me miss practice yesterday. And now, I'm gonna make you beg." The pressure on my shoulder tightened, pushing me toward the floor. "On your knees, freak. That's how you like it, right?"

"Hey!"

A clear, high voice rang through the hall, a second before I would've exploded, demonstration or no. Mackenzie St. James came stalking toward us, a stack of books under one arm, her small form tight with fury.

"Let him go, Brian," she demanded, marching up to the startled quarterback, a bristling kitten facing down a Rottweiler. "What the hell is your problem? Leave him alone!"

"Oh, hey, Mackenzie." Brian grinned at her, looking almost sheepish. *Taking your eyes off your opponent,* I thought. *Stupid move.* "What a coincidence. We were just talking about you to our mutual friend, here." He shoved me against the wall again, and I fought down a knee-jerk reaction to snap his elbow. "He's promised to be a lot nicer to you in the future, isn't that right, freak?"

"Brian!"

"Okay, okay." Kingston raised his hands and stepped away, and his cronies did the same. "Take it easy, Mac, we were just fooling around." He turned a sneer on me, and I glared back, daring him to step forward, to grab me again. "You got lucky, freak," he said, backing away. "Remember what I told you. You won't always have a little girl around to protect you." His friends snickered, and he winked at Kenzie, who rolled her eyes. "We'll see you around, real soon."

"Jerk," Kenzie muttered as they sauntered off down the hall, laughing and high-fiving each other. "I don't know what Regan sees in him." She shook her head and turned to me. "You okay?"

Embarrassed, fuming, I scowled at her. "I could've handled it," I snapped, wishing I could put my fist through a wall or someone's face. "You didn't have to interfere."

"I know, tough guy." She gave me a half smile, and I wasn't sure if she was being serious. "But Regan is fond of the big meathead, and I didn't want you to beat him up *too* badly."

I glared in the direction the jocks had gone, clenching my fists as I struggled to control my raging emotions, the urge to stalk down the hall and plant Kingston's face into the floor. *Why me?* I wanted to snap at her. *Why won't you leave me alone? And why do you have the entire football team ready to tear someone in half for looking at you funny?*

"Anyway," Kenzie continued, "we're still on for that interview, right? You're planning on showing up, I hope. I'm dying to know what goes on in that broody head of yours."

"I don't brood."

She snorted. "Tough guy, if brooding was a sport, you'd

have gold medals with scowling faces lining the walls of your room."

"Whatever."

Kenzie laughed. Sweeping past me, she pushed open the library door, pausing in the frame. "See you in a couple hours, Ethan."

I shrugged.

"I'm holding you to it, tough guy. Promise me you won't run off or conveniently forget."

"Yes." I blew out a breath as she grinned, and the door swung shut. "I'll be there."

I didn't go.

Not that I didn't try. Despite the incident in the hall—or maybe because of it—I wasn't about to let anyone tell me who I could or could not hang out with. Like I said, I don't respond well to threats, and if I was being honest with myself, I was more than a little curious about Mackenzie St. James. So after the last bell, I gathered my stuff, made sure the hall was clear of Kingston and his thugs, and headed toward the library.

About halfway there, I realized I was being followed.

The halls were nearly empty as I went by the cafeteria. The few bodies I passed were going the other way, to the parking lot and the vehicles that would take them home. But as I made my way through the quiet hallways, I got that strange prickle on the back of my neck that told me I wasn't alone.

Casually, I stopped at a water fountain, bending down to get a quick drink. But I slid my gaze off to the side, scanning the hall.

There was a shimmer of white at the edge of my vision, as something glided around a corner and stopped in the shadows, watching.

My gut tightened, but I forced myself to straighten and walk down the hall as if nothing was wrong. I could feel the presence at my back following me, and my heart began to thud in my chest. It was the same creature, the one that I'd seen in the locker room that night, when the piskie found me. What was it? One of the fey, I was certain, but I'd never seen this kind before, all pale and transparent, almost ghostlike. A bean sidhe, perhaps? But bean sidhes usually announced their presence with hair-raising shrieks and wails; they didn't silently trail someone down a dark corridor, being careful to stay just out of sight. And I certainly wasn't about to die.

I hoped.

What does it want with me? I paused at the library door, grasping the handle but not pulling it open. Through the small rectangular window, I saw the front desk, the librarian's gray head bent over the computer. Kenzie would be in there, somewhere, waiting for me. And Todd. I'd promised I would meet them both, and I hated breaking my word.

A memory flashed: one of myself, fleeing the redcaps, taking refuge in the library. Pulling a knife as I hunkered between the aisles, waiting for them. The sadistic faeries setting fire to the wall of books to flush me into the open. I escaped, but my rush to get out was taken as me fleeing the scene of the crime, leading to my expulsion from school.

I drew in a quiet breath, pausing in the door frame, anger and fear spreading through my stomach. No, I couldn't do this. If I went in, if They saw me talking to Kenzie, they could use her to get to me. I didn't know what They wanted, but I wasn't going to draw another person into my dangerous, messed-up life. Not again.

Releasing the handle, I stepped away and continued down the hall. I felt the thing follow me, and as I turned the corner, I thought I heard the library door creak open. I didn't look back.

I walked out to the parking lot, but I didn't stop there. Getting in my truck and driving home might lose my tail, but it wouldn't give me any answers as to why it was following me. Instead, I passed the rows of cars, stepped over the curb, and continued on to the football field. Thankfully, it was empty today. No practice, no screaming coaches, no armored jocks slamming into each other. If Kingston and his friends saw me sauntering casually across their turf in a very blatant show of *Screw you, Kingston, what are you gonna do about it?* they would try to bury me here. I wondered if anyone else could see me, and if they did, would they tell the quarterback I was figuratively pissing on his territory? I smirked at the thought, vaguely tempted to stop and make it literal, as well. But I had more important things to deal with, and a pissing contest with Kingston wasn't one of them.

Behind the bleachers, I stopped. A fence separated the field from a line of trees on the other side, so it was cool and shady here. I wished I had my knife. Something sharp, metal and lethal between me and whatever was coming my way. But I'd been caught with a knife before, and it had gotten me in a *lot* of trouble, so I'd left it at home.

Putting my back to the fence, I waited.

Something stepped around the bleachers, or rather, *shimmered* around the bleachers, barely visible in the sun. And even though it was a bright fall afternoon, with enough sunlight to melt away the chill, I suddenly felt cold. Sluggish. Like my thoughts and emotions were slowly being drained, leaving behind an empty shell.

Shivering, I gazed stonily at the thing hovering a few feet away. It was unlike any faery I'd seen before. Not a nymph, a sidhe, a boggart, a dryad, *anything* I recognized. Not to say I was an expert on the different types of faeries, but I'd seen more than most people, and this one was just…weird.

It was shorter than me by nearly a foot and so thin it didn't seem possible that its legs could hold it up. In fact, its legs ended in needle-sharp tips, so it looked as if it was walking on toothpicks instead of feet. Its face was hatchet thin, and its fingers were those same thin points, as if it could poke its nail right through your skull. The skeletons of what used to be wings protruded from its bony shoulders, broken and shattered, and it hovered a few inches off the ground, as if the earth itself didn't want to touch it.

For a few seconds, we just stared at each other.

"All right," I said in an even voice, as the creepy fey floated there, still watching me. "You followed me out here—you obviously wanted to see me. What the hell do you want?"

Its eyes, huge and multifaceted like an insect's, blinked slowly. I saw myself reflected a hundred times in its gaze. Its razor slit of a mouth opened, and it breathed:

"I bring a warning, Ethan Chase."

I resisted the urge to cringe. There was something very… wrong…about this creature. It didn't belong here, in the real world. The faeries I had seen, even the Iron fey, were still a part of reality, sliding back and forth between this realm and the Nevernever. *This* thing…it was as if its body was out of sync with the rest of world, the way it flickered and blurred, as if it wasn't quite there. Wasn't quite solid.

The faery raised one long, bony finger and pointed at me.

"Do not interfere," it whispered. "Do not become involved in what will soon happen around you. This is not your fight. We seek no trouble with the Iron Court. But if you meddle in our affairs, human, you put those you care about at risk."

"Your affairs? What *are* you?" My voice came out raspier than I wanted it to. "I'm guessing you're not from the Seelie or Unseelie Courts."

The faery's slitted mouth might've twitched into a smile.

"We are nothing. We are forgotten. No one remembers our names, that we ever existed. You should do the same, human."

"Uh-huh. So, you make a point of making certain I know you're there, of tracking me down and threatening my family, to tell me I should forget about you."

The faery drew back a step, gliding over the ground. "A warning," it said again and tossed something at my feet, something small and gray. "This is what will happen to those who interfere," it whispered. "Our return has just begun."

I crouched, still keeping a wary eye on the faery, and spared a glance at what lay on the ground.

A piskie. The same one I'd seen earlier that day with Todd, I was sure of it. But its skin was a dull, faded gray, as if all the color had been sucked out of it. Gently, I reached down and picked it up, cradling it in my palm. It rolled over and blinked, huge eyes empty and staring. It was still alive, but even as I watched, the faery's tiny body rippled and then…blew away. Like mist in the breeze. Leaving behind nothing at all.

My insides felt cold. I'd seen faeries die—they turned into leaves, branches, flowers, insects, dirt, and sometimes they did just vanish. But never like this. "What did you do to it?" I demanded, surging back to my feet.

The thing didn't answer. It shimmered again, going transparent, as if it, too, were in danger of blowing away on the wind. Raising its hands, it gazed at its fingers, watching as they flickered like a bad television channel.

"Not enough," it whispered, shaking its head. "Never enough. Still, it is something. That you can see me, talk to me. It is a start. Perhaps the half-blood will be stronger."

It drifted back. "We will be watching you, Ethan Chase," it warned, and suddenly turned, as if glimpsing something off to the side. "You do not want even more people hurt because of you."

More people? *Oh, no,* I thought, as it dawned on me what the faery was implying. The dead Thistle, the "half-blood" it mentioned. *Todd.* "Hey!" I snapped, striding forward. "Hold it right there. What are you?"

The faery smiled, rippled in the sunlight and drifted away, over the fence and out of sight. I would've given chase, but the sound of movement behind the bleachers caught my attention, and I turned.

Kenzie stood beside the benches, a notepad in one hand, staring at me. From the look on her face, she'd heard every word.

CHAPTER SIX
VANISHED

I ignored Kenzie and strode quickly across the football field, not looking back.

"Hey!" Kenzie cried, scrambling after me.

My mind was spinning. *Todd was right,* it whispered. *Something was after him. Damn, what* was *that thing? I've never seen anything like it before.*

My chest felt tight. It was happening again. It didn't matter what that thing was, the damned faeries were out to ruin my life and hurt everyone around me. I had to find Todd, warn him. I just hoped that he was okay; the half-breed might be annoying and ignorant, but he shouldn't have to suffer because of me.

"Ethan! Just a second! Will you please hold up?" Kenzie put on a burst of speed as we reached the edge of the field, blocking my path. "Will you tell me what's going on? I heard voices, but I didn't see anyone else. Was someone threatening you?" Her eyes narrowed. "You're not into anything illegal, are you?"

"Kenzie, get out of here," I snapped. The creepy faery could still be watching us. Or creeping closer to Todd. I had to get away from her, now. "Just leave me alone, okay? I'm not doing the damn interview. I don't give a crap about what you or this school or anyone else thinks of me. Put *that* in your article."

Her eyes flashed. "The parking lot is the other way, tough guy. Where are you going?"

"Nowhere."

"Then you won't mind if I come along."

"You're not coming."

"Why not?"

I swore. She didn't move, and my sense of urgency flared. "I don't have time for this," I growled, and brushed past her, sprinting down the hall toward the library. The girl followed, of course, but I wasn't thinking about her anymore. If that faery freak got close to Todd, if it did something to him like it had the piskie, it would be my fault. Again.

The librarian gave me the evil eye as I burst through the library doors, followed closely by the girl. "Slow down, you two," she barked as we passed the desk. Kenzie murmured an apology, but I ignored her, striding toward the back, searching for the half-breed in the aisles. Empty, empty, a couple making out in the history section, empty. My unease grew. Where *was* he?

"What are we looking for?" Kenzie whispered at my back.

I turned, ready to tell her to get lost, futile as it might be, when something under the window caught my eye.

Todd's jacket. Lying in a crumpled heap beneath the sill. I stared at it, trying to find an explanation as to why he would leave it behind. Maybe he just forgot it. Maybe someone stole it as a prank and ditched it here. A cold breeze whispered through the window, ruffling my clothes and hair. It was the only open window in the room.

Kenzie followed my gaze, frowned, then walked forward and picked up the jacket. As she did, something white fell out of the pocket and fluttered to the floor. A note, written on a torn half sheet of paper. I lunged forward to grab it, but Kenzie had already snatched it up.

"Hey," I said sharply, holding out a hand. "Give me that."

She dodged, holding the paper out of reach. Defiance danced in her eyes. "I don't see your name on it."

"It was for me," I insisted, stalking forward. She leaped away, putting a long table between us, and my temper flared. "Dammit, I'm not playing this game," I growled, keeping my voice down so the librarian wouldn't come stalking toward us. "Hand it over, now."

Kenzie narrowed her eyes. "Why so secretive, tough guy?" she asked, deftly maneuvering around the table, keeping the same distance between us. "Are these the coordinates for a drug deal or something?"

"What?" I grabbed for her, but she slid out of reach. "Of course not. I'm not into that crap."

"A letter from a secret admirer, then?"

"No," I snapped, and stopped edging around the table. This was ridiculous. Were we back in the third grade? I eyed her across the table, judging the distance between us. "It's not a love letter," I said, silently fuming. "It's not even from a girl."

"Are you sure?"

"Yes."

"Then you won't mind if I read it," she said and flipped open the note.

As soon as her attention left me, I leaped over the table and slid across the surface, grabbing her arm as I landed on the other side. She yelped in surprise and tried to jerk back, unsuccessfully. Her wrist was slender and delicate, and fit easily into my grasp.

For a second, we glared at each other. I could see my scowling, angry reflection in her eyes. Kenzie stared back, a slight smirk on her lips, as if this newest predicament amused her.

"What now, tough guy?" She raised a slender eyebrow. And, for some reason, my heart beat faster under that look.

Deliberately, I reached up and snatched the paper from her fingers. Releasing her, I turned my back on the girl, scanning the note. It was short, messy and confirmed my worst suspicions.

They're here! Gotta run. If you find this, tell my folks not to worry. Sorry, man. Didn't mean to drag you into this. —Todd.

I crumpled the note and shoved it into my jeans pocket. What did he expect me to do now? Go to his parents, tell them a bunch of creepy invisible faeries were out to get their son? I'd get thrown into the loony bin for sure.

I felt Kenzie's eyes on my back and wondered how much of the note she'd seen. Had she read anything in that split second it had taken me to get across the table?

"It sounds like your friend is in trouble," Kenzie murmured. Well, that answered *that* question. All of it, apparently.

"He's not my friend," I replied, not turning around. "And you shouldn't get involved. This is none of your business."

"The hell it's not," she shot back. "If someone is in trouble, we have to do something. Who's after him? Why doesn't he just go to the police?"

"The police can't help." I finally turned to face her. "Not with this. Besides, what would you tell them? We don't even know what's going on. All we have is a note."

"Well, shouldn't we at least see if he made it home okay?"

I sighed, rubbing my scalp. "I don't know where he lives," I said, feeling slightly guilty that I knew so little. "I don't have his phone number. I don't even know his last name."

But Kenzie sighed. "Boys," she muttered, and pulled out her phone. "His last name is Wyndham, I think. Todd Wyndham. He has a couple of classes with me." She fiddled with her phone without looking up. "Just a second. I'll Google it."

I tried to stay calm while she looked it up, though I couldn't stop scanning the room for hidden enemies. What were these transparent, ghostlike fey, and why had I not seen them before? What did they want with Todd? I remembered the piskie's limp body, an empty, lifeless husk before it disappeared, and shivered. Whatever they were, they were dangerous, and I needed to find the half-breed before they did the same to him. I owed him that, for not being there like I promised.

"Got it," Kenzie announced. "Or, at least, I have his house number." Glancing up from her phone, she looked at me and raised an eyebrow. "So, do you want to call them or should I?"

I dug out my phone. "I'll do it," I said, dreading the task but knowing I had to finish what I started.

She recited a string of numbers, and I punched them into my phone. Putting it to my ear, I listened to it ring once, twice, and on the third, someone picked up.

"Wyndham residence," said a woman's voice. I swallowed.

"Um, yeah. I'm a…friend of Todd's," I said haltingly. "Is he home?"

"No, he isn't back from school yet," continued the voice on the other end. "Do you want me to give him a message?"

"Uh, no. I was…um…hoping to catch him later today so we could…hang." I winced at how lame I sounded, and Kenzie giggled. I frowned at her. "Do you know his cell phone number?" I added as an afterthought.

"Yes, I have his number." Now the woman sounded suspicious. "Why do you want to know? Who is this?" she continued sharply, and I winced. "Are you one of those boys he keeps talking about? You think I don't notice when he comes home with bruises and black eyes? Do you think it's funny, picking on someone smaller then you? What's your name?"

I was tempted to hang up, but that would make me look even more suspicious, and it would get me no closer to Todd.

I wondered if he'd even told her that he spent the night at my house. "My name is Ethan Chase," I said in what I hoped was a calm, reasonable voice. "I'm just…a friend. Todd stayed at my place last night, during the storm."

"Oh." I couldn't tell if Todd's mother was appeased or not, but after a moment, she sighed. "Then, I'm sorry. Todd doesn't have many friends, none that have called the house, anyway. I didn't mean to snap at you, Ethan."

"It's fine," I mumbled, embarrassed. *I'm used to it.*

"One moment," she continued, and her voice grew fainter as she put the phone down. "I have his number on the fridge. Just a second."

A minute later, I thanked Todd's mom and hung up, relieved to have that over with. "Well?" asked Kenzie, watching expectantly. "Did you get it?"

"Yeah."

She waited a moment longer, then bounced impatiently. "Are you going to call him, then?"

"I'm getting to it." Truthfully, I didn't want to. What if he was perfectly fine, and that note was just a prank, revenge for some imagined slight? What if he was halfway home, laughing at how he pulled a fast one on the stupid human? Todd was half-phouka, a faery notorious for their mischievous nature and love of chaos. This could be a great, elaborate joke, and if I called him, he would have the last laugh.

Deep down, though, I knew those were just excuses. I hadn't imagined that creepy faery, or the dead piskie. Todd wasn't pretending to be terrified. Something was happening, something bad, and he was right in the middle of it.

And I didn't want to be drawn in.

Too late now, I suppose. Pressing in Todd's number, I put the phone to my ear and held my breath.

One ring.

Two rings.

Thr—

The phone abruptly cut off, going dead without sending me to voice mail. A second later, the dial tone droned in my ear.

"What happened?" Kenzie asked as I lowered my hand. "Is Todd all right?"

"No," I muttered, looking down at the phone, and the end call button at the bottom of the screen. "He's not."

I went home after that, having convinced Kenzie that there was nothing we could do for Todd right then. She was stubborn, refusing to believe me, wanting to call the police. I told her not to jump to conclusions as we didn't exactly know what was going on. Todd could've turned off his phone. He could be on his way home and was just running late. We didn't have enough evidence to start calling the authorities. Eventually, she caved, but I had the feeling she wouldn't let it go for long. I just hoped she wouldn't do anything that would attract Their attention. Hanging around me was bad enough.

Back home, I went straight to my room, locking the door behind me. Sitting at my desk, I opened the first drawer, reached all the way to the back, and pulled out the long, thin envelope inside.

Leaning back in the chair, I stared at it for a long while. The paper was wrinkled and brittle now, yellow with age, and smelled of old newspapers. It had one word written across the front: Ethan. My name, in my sister's handwriting.

Flipping it over, I opened the top and pulled out the letter within. I'd read it a dozen times before and knew it word for word, but I scanned the note one more time, a bitter lump settling in my throat.

Ethan,

I've started this letter a hundred times, wishing I knew the right words to say, but I guess I'll just come out and say it. You probably won't see me again. I wish I could be there for you and Mom, even Luke, but I have other responsibilities now, a whole kingdom that needs me. You're growing up so fast—each time I see you, you're taller, stronger. I forget, sometimes, that time moves differently in Faery. And it breaks my heart every time I come home and see that I've missed so much of your life. Please know that you're always in my thoughts, but it's best that we live our own lives now. I have enemies here, and the last thing I want is for you and Mom to get hurt because of me.

So, this is goodbye. I'll be watching you from time to time, and I'll do everything in my power to make sure you and Mom and Luke can live comfortably. But please, Ethan, for the love of all that's holy, do not try to find me. My world is far too dangerous; you of all people should know that. Stay away from Them, and try to have a normal life.

If there is an emergency, and you absolutely must see me, I've included a token that will take you into the Nevernever, to someone who can help. To use it, squeeze one drop of your blood onto the surface and toss it into a pool of still water. But it can only be used once, and after that, the favor is done. So use it wisely.

I love you, little brother. Take care of Mom for me.
—Meghan

I closed the letter, put it on the desk, and turned the envelope upside down. A small silver coin rolled into my open palm, and I closed my fingers around it, thinking.

Did I want to bring my sister into this? Meghan Chase, the freaking Queen of the Iron Fey? How many years had it been since I'd seen her last? Did she even remember us anymore? Did she care?

My throat felt tight. Pushing myself up, I tossed the coin on the desk and swept the letter back in the drawer, slamming it shut. No, I wasn't going to go crying to Meghan, not for this or anything. Meghan had left us; she was no longer part of this family. As far as I was concerned, she was Faery through and through. And I'd been through enough faery torment to last several lifetimes. I could handle this myself.

Even if it meant I had to do something stupid, something I'd sworn I would never do.

I was going to have to contact the fey.

CHAPTER SEVEN
THE EMPTY PARK

At 11:35 p.m., my alarm went off. I slapped it silent and rolled out of bed, already dressed, snatching my backpack from the floor. Creeping silently down the hall, I checked to see if Mom's light was off; sometimes she stayed up late, waiting for Dad to get home. But tonight, the crack under her door was dark, and I continued my quiet trek out the front door to the driveway.

I couldn't take my truck. Dad would be home later, and he'd know I was gone if he saw my truck was missing. Sneaking out in the middle of the night was highly frowned upon and tended to result in groundings, lectures and technology banishment. So I dug my old bike out of the garage, checked to see that the tires were still inflated and walked it down to the sidewalk.

Overhead, a thin crescent moon grinned down at me behind ragged wisps of cloud, and a cold autumn breeze sliced right through my jacket, making me shiver. That nagging, cynical part of me hesitated, reluctant to take part in this insanity. *Why are you getting involved?* it whispered. *What's the half-breed to you, anyway? Are you willing to deal directly with the fey because of him?*

But it wasn't just Todd now. Something strange was happening in Faery, and I had a feeling it was going to get worse. I needed to know what was going on and how I could defend myself from transparent ghost-fey that sucked the life right out of their victims. I didn't want to be left in the dark, not with those things out there.

Besides, Mr. Creepy Faery had threatened not only me but my family. And *that* pissed me off. I was sick of running and hiding. Closing my eyes, hoping They would leave me alone wasn't working. I doubted it ever had.

Hopping on my bike, I started pedaling toward the one place I'd always avoided until now. A place where, I hoped, I would get some answers.

If the damn fey wanted me as an enemy, bring it on. I'd be their worst nightmare.

Even in gigantic, crowded cities, where steel buildings, cars and concrete dominate everything, you can always find the fey in a park.

It doesn't have to be a big park. Just a patch of natural earth, with a few trees and bushes scattered about, maybe a little pond, and that's all they need. I'm told Central Park in New York City has hundreds, maybe thousands of faeries living there, and several trods to the Nevernever, all within its well-groomed perimeter. The tiny park three and a half miles from my house had about a dozen fey of the common variety—piskies, goblins, tree sprites—and no trods that I knew of.

I parked my bike against an old tree near the entrance and gazed around. It wasn't much of a park, really. There was a picnic bench with a set of peeling monkey bars and an old slide, and a dusty fire pit that hadn't been used in years. At least, not by humans. But the trees here were old, ancient things—huge oaks and weeping willows—and if you stared very hard be-

tween the branches, you sometimes caught flickers of movement not belonging to birds or squirrels.

Leaving the bike, I walked to the edge of the fire pit and
looked down. The ashes were cold and gray, days or weeks
old, but I had seen two goblins at this pit several weeks ago,
roasting some sort of meat over the fire. And there were several piskies and wood sprites living in the oaks, as well. The
local fey might not know anything about their creepy, transparent cousins, but it couldn't hurt to ask.

Crouching, I picked up a flat rock, dusted it off, and set
it in the center of the fire pit. Digging through my pack, I
pulled out a bottle of honey, stood and drizzled the golden
syrup onto the stones. Honey was like ambrosia to the fey;
they couldn't resist the stuff.

Capping the bottle, I tossed it into my pack and waited.

Several minutes passed, which was a surprise to me. I knew
the fey frequented this area. I was expecting at least a couple
of goblins or piskies to appear. But the night was still, the
shadows empty—until there was a soft rustle behind me, the
hiss of something moving over the grass.

"You will not find them that way, Ethan Chase."

I turned, calmly. *Rule number two: show no fear when dealing
with the Fair Folk.* I could have drawn my rattan sticks, and in
all honesty I really wanted to, but that might have been taken
as a sign of nervousness or unease.

A tall, slight figure stood beneath the weeping willow,
watching me through the lacy curtain. As I waited, a slender hand parted the drooping branches and the faery stepped
into the open.

It was a dryad, and the weeping willow was probably her
tree, for she had the same long green hair and rough, bark-
like skin. She was impossibly tall and slender, and swayed
slightly on her feet, like a branch in the wind. She observed

me with large black eyes, her long hair draped over her body, and slowly shook her head.

"They will not come," she whispered sadly, glancing at the swirl of honey at my feet. "They have not been here for many nights. At first, it was only one or two that went missing. But now—" she gestured to the empty park "—now there is no one left. Everyone is gone. I am the last."

I frowned. "What do you mean, you're the last? Where are all the others?" I gazed around the park, scanning the darkness and shadows, seeing nothing. "What the hell is going on?"

She drifted closer, swaying gently. I was tempted to step back but held my ground.

The dryad tilted her head to one side, lacy hair catching the moonlight as it fell. A large white moth flew out of the curtain and fluttered away into the shadows. "You have questions," the dryad said, blinking slowly. "I can tell you what you wish to know, but you must do something for me in return."

"Oh, no." I did step away then, crossing my arms and glaring at her. "No way. No bargains, no contracts. Find someone else to do your dirty work."

"Please, Ethan Chase." The dryad held out an impossibly slender hand, mottled and rough like the trunk of the tree. "As a favor, then. You must go to the Iron Queen for us. Inform her of our fate. Be our voice. She will listen to you."

"Go find Meghan?" I thought of the coin lying abandoned on my desk and shook my head. "You expect me to go into the Nevernever," I said, and my stomach turned just thinking about it. Memories crowded forward, dark and terrifying, and I shoved them back. "Go into Faery. With Mab and Titania and the rest of the crazies." I curled my mouth into a sneer. "Forget it. That's the *last* place I'll ever set foot in."

"You must." The dryad wrung her hands, pleading. "The courts do not know what is happening, nor would they care.

The welfare of a few half-breeds and exiles does not concern them. But you…you are the half brother of the Iron Queen— she will listen to you. If you do not…" The dryad trembled, like a leaf in a storm. "Then I'm afraid we will all be lost."

"Look." I stabbed a hand through my hair. "I'm just trying to find out what happened to a friend. Todd Wyndham. He's a half-breed, and I think he's in trouble." The dryad's pleading expression didn't change, and I sighed. "I can't promise to help you," I muttered. "I have problems of my own to worry about. But…" I hesitated, hardly believing I was saying this. "But if you can give me any information about my friend, then I'll…try to get a message to my sister. I'm still not promising anything!" I added quickly as the dryad jerked up. "But if I see the Iron Queen anytime in the near future, I'll tell her. That's the best I can offer."

The dryad nodded. "It will have to do," she whispered, shrinking in on herself. She closed her eyes as a breeze hissed through the park, rippling her hair and making the leaves around us sigh. "More of us have disappeared," she sighed. "More vanish with every breath. And they are coming closer."

"Who *are* they?"

"I do not know." The faery opened her eyes, looking terrified. "I do not know, nor do any of my fellows. Not even the *wind* knows their names. Or if it does, it refuses to tell me."

"Where can I find Todd?"

"Your friend? The half-breed?" The dryad took a step away, looking distracted. "I do not know," she admitted, and I narrowed my gaze. "I cannot tell you now, but I will put his name into the wind and see what it can turn up." She looked at me, her hair falling into her eyes, hiding half her face. "Return tomorrow night, Ethan Chase. I will have answers for you, then."

Tomorrow night. Tomorrow was the demonstration, the

event I'd been training for all month. I couldn't miss that, even for Todd. Guro would kill me.

I sighed. Tomorrow was going to be a long day. "All right," I said, stepping toward my bike. "I'll be here, probably some time after midnight. And then you can tell me what the hell is going on."

The dryad didn't say anything, watching me leave with unblinking black eyes. As I yanked my bike off the ground and started down the road, hoping I would beat Dad home, I couldn't shake the creeping suspicion that I wouldn't see her again.

CHAPTER EIGHT
THE DEMONSTRATION

The next day was Saturday, but instead of sleeping in like a normal person, I was up early and in the backyard, swinging my rattan through the air, smacking them against the tire dummy I'd set up in the corner. I didn't need the practice, but beating on something was a good way to focus, to forget the strangeness of the night before, though I still couldn't shake the eerie feeling whenever I remembered the dryad's last warning.

More of us have disappeared. More vanish with every breath. And they are coming closer.

"Ethan!"

Dad's voice cut through the rhythmic smacking of wood against rubber, and I turned to find him staring blearily at me from the patio. He wore a rumpled gray bathrobe, his face was grizzled and unshaven, and he did not look pleased.

"Sorry, Dad." I lowered the sticks, panting. "Did I wake you up?"

He shook his head, then stepped aside as two police officers came into the yard. My heart and stomach gave a violent lurch, and I tried to think of any crimes I might've committed without realizing it, or anything the fey might've pinned on me.

"Ethan?" one of them asked, as Dad watched grimly and

Mom appeared in the door frame, her hands over her mouth. "Are you Ethan Chase?"

"Yeah." I kept my arms at my sides, my sticks perfectly still, though my heart was going a mile a minute. The sudden thought of being arrested, being handcuffed in my own back-yard in front of my horrified parents, nearly made me sick. I swallowed hard to keep my voice steady. "What do you want?"

"Do you know a boy named Todd Wyndham?"

I relaxed, suddenly aware of where this was going. My heart still pounded, but I kept my tone light, flippant, and I shrugged. "Yeah, he's in a few of my classes at school."

"You called his home yesterday afternoon, correct?" the policeman continued, and when I nodded, he added, "And he spent the night at your house the day before?"

"Yeah." I feigned confusion, looking back and forth between them. "Why? What's going on?"

The policemen exchanged a glance. "He's missing," one of them said, and I raised my eyebrows in fake surprise. "His mother reported that he didn't come home last night, and that she had received a call from Ethan Chase, a boy from his school, on the afternoon before his disappearance." His gaze flickered to the sticks in my hand, then back up to me, eyes narrowing slightly. "You wouldn't know anything about his whereabouts, would you, Ethan?"

I forced myself to be calm, shaking my head. "No, I haven't seen him since yesterday. Sorry."

It was pretty clear he didn't believe me, for his mouth thinned, and he spoke slowly, deliberately. "You have no clue as to what he was doing yesterday, no idea of where he could have gone?" When I hesitated, his voice became friendlier, encouraging. "Any information would be useful to us, Ethan."

"I told you," I said, firmer this time. "I don't know any-thing."

He gave an annoyed little huff, as if I was being deliberately evasive—which I was, but not for the reasons he thought. "Ethan, you realize we're only trying to help, don't you? You aren't protecting anyone if you hide information from us."

"I think that's enough." Dad suddenly came into the yard, bathrobe and all, glaring at the policemen. "Officers, your concern is appreciated, but I believe my son has told you all he knows." I blinked at Dad in shock as he came to stand beside me, smiling but firm. "If we find anything out, we'll be sure to call you."

"Sir, you don't seem to realize—"

"I realize just fine, officers," Dad said, his polite smile never wavering. "But Ethan has already given you his answer. Thank you for stopping by."

They looked irritated, but Dad wasn't a small man and had this stance that could be compared to a friendly but stubborn bull; you weren't going to get him to move once he'd made up his mind. After a lengthy pause—as if hoping I would fess up at the last second, perhaps—the officers gave curt nods and turned away. Muttering polite "ma'ams" to Mom, they swept by her, and she followed them, I assumed to the front door.

Dad waited a few seconds after the back door clicked shut before turning to me. "Todd Wyndham is the boy who came over the other night. Anything you'd like to tell me, son?"

I shook my head, not looking at him. "No," I muttered, feeling bad for lying, especially after he'd just gotten rid of the policemen for me. "I swear I don't know anything."

"Hmm." Dad gave me an unreadable look, then shuffled back into the house. But Mom appeared in the doorway again, watching me. I saw the fear on her face, the disappointment. She knew I was lying.

She hesitated a moment longer, as if waiting for me to confess, to tell her something different. But what could I say?

That the kid who'd spent the night with us was part faery, and this creepy new breed of fey were after him for some reason? I couldn't drag her into this; she would flip out for sure, thinking I was next. There was nothing either of them could do to help. So, I averted my gaze, and after a long, achingly uncomfortable pause, she slipped inside, slamming the door behind her.

I winced. Great, now they were both pissed at me. Sighing, I switched my rattan sticks to one hand and went in myself. I wished I could smack the tire dummy a while longer, but keeping a low profile seemed like a good idea now. The last thing I wanted was a grilling session where they would both ask questions I couldn't answer.

Mom and Dad were talking in the kitchen—probably about me—so I slipped into my room and gently closed the door.

My phone sat on the corner of my desk. For a second, I thought about calling Kenzie. I wondered what she was doing now, if the police had shown up on her doorstep, asking about a missing classmate. I wondered if she was worried about him…or me.

What? Why would she worry about you, you psychopath? You've been nothing but a jackass to her, and besides, you don't care, remember?

Angry now, I stalked to my bed and flopped down on it, flinging an arm over my face. I had to stop thinking of her, but my brain wasn't being cooperative this morning. Instead of focusing on the demonstration and the missing half-breed and the creepy Fey out to get us both, my thoughts kept going back to Kenzie St. James. The idea of calling her, just to see if she was all right, grew more and more tempting, until I jumped up and stalked to the living room, flipping on the television to drown out my traitorous thoughts.

★ ★ ★

The day passed in a blur of old action movies and commercials. I didn't move from the couch, afraid that if I went into my room, I'd see my unblinking phone and know Kenzie hadn't called me. Or worse, that she *had,* and I'd be tempted to call her back. I lounged on the sofa, the remains of empty chip bags, dirty plates and empty soda cans surrounding me, until late afternoon when Mom made an exasperated comment about rotting brains and bumps on logs or something, and ordered me to do something else.

Flipping off the television, I sat up, thinking. I still had a couple of hours till the demonstration. Wandering back to my room, I again noticed the phone on the corner of the desk. Nothing. No missed calls, texts, anything. I didn't know whether to be relieved or disappointed.

As I reached for it, though, it rang. Without checking the number, I snatched it up and put it to my ear.

"Hello?"

"Ethan?" The voice on the other end wasn't Kenzie, as I'd hoped, though it was vaguely familiar. "Is this Ethan Chase?"

"Yeah?"

"This...this is Mrs. Wyndham, Todd's mother."

My heart skipped a beat. I swallowed hard and gripped the phone tightly, as the voice on the other end continued.

"I know the police have already spoken to you," she said in a halting, broken voice, "but I...I wanted to ask you myself. You say you're Todd's friend...do you know what could have happened to him? Please, I'm desperate. I just want my son home."

Her voice broke at the end, and I closed my eyes. "Mrs. Wyndham, I'm sorry about Todd," I said, feeling like an ass. Worse than an ass, like a complete and utter failure, because I'd let another person down, because I couldn't protect them from the fey. "But I really don't know where he is. The last time we spoke was yesterday at school, before I talked to you, I swear." She gave a little sob, making my gut clench. "I'm really sorry," I said again, knowing how useless that sounded. "I wish I could give you better news."

She took a shaky breath. "All right, thank you, Ethan. I'm sorry to have bothered you." She sniffed and seemed about to say goodbye, but hesitated. "If…if you see him," she went on, "or if you find any information at all…will you let me know? Please?"

"Yeah," I whispered. "If I see him, I'll make sure he gets home, I promise."

After she hung up, I paced my room, not knowing what to do. I tried surfing online, watching YouTube, checking out various weapon stores, just to keep myself distracted, but it didn't help. I couldn't stop thinking of Todd, and Kenzie, caught in the twisted games of the fey. And it was partly my fault. Todd had been playing a dangerous game, and Kenzie was too stubborn to know when to back off, but the common denominator was me.

Now, one of them was gone and another family was torn apart. Just like last time.

Picking up my phone, I stuck it in my jeans pocket and snatched my keys from the desk. Grabbing my gym bag from the floor, I started to leave. Might as well head to the demonstration now; it was better than standing around here, driving myself crazy.

The silver coin on the desk glinted, and I paused. Sliding it into my palm, I stared at it, wondering where Meghan was, what she was doing. Did she ever think of me? Would she be disgusted, if she knew how I'd turned out?

"Ethan!" Mom's voice echoed from the kitchen. "Your

karate thing is tonight, isn't it? Do you want anything to eat before you go?"

I stuffed the coin in my pocket with the keys and left the room. "Kali, Mom, not karate," I told her, walking into the kitchen. "And no, I'll grab something on the way. Don't wait up for me."

"Curfew is still at eleven, Ethan."

Irritation flared. "Yeah, I know," I muttered. "It's been that way for five years. Why would it change now? It's not like I'm old enough to make my own decisions." Before she could say anything, I stalked past her and headed outside. "And, yes, I'll call if I'm going to be late," I threw back over my shoulder.

I could feel Mom's half angry, half worried gaze on my back as I slammed out the front door, making sure to bang it as I left. Stupid of me. If I had known what was going to happen at the demonstration that night, I would've said something much different.

The building was already full of people when I arrived. Tournaments had been going on for most of the afternoon, and shouts, *ki-yas,* and the shuffle of bare feet on mats echoed through the room as I ducked inside. Kids in their white gis tied with different colored belts threw punches and kicks within taped-off arenas; from the looks of it, it was the kempo students' turn on the mats.

I spotted Guro Javier and made my way over, weaving through students and onlookers, gritting my teeth as someone—a large kid with a purple belt—elbowed me in the ribs. I glared at him, and he smirked, as if daring me to try something. As if I'd start a fight with the brat in front of two hundred parents and about a dozen masters of various arts. Ignoring the kid's self-satisfied grin, I continued along the wall and stood next to my guro in the corner. He was watching the tournament with detached interest and gave a faint smile as I came up.

"You're very early, Ethan."

I shrugged helplessly. "Couldn't stay away."

"Are you ready?" Guro turned to me. "Our demonstration is after the kempo students are finished. Oh, and Sean sprained his ankle last night, so you're going to be doing the live weapon demo."

I felt a small, nervous thrill. "Really?"

"Do you need to practice?"

"No, I'll be fine." I thought back to the few times I'd handled Guro's real swords, which were short, single-edged blades similar to a machete. They were a little shorter then my rattan, razor sharp and about as deadly as they looked. They'd been in Guro's family for generations, and I was a bit in awe that I'd be wielding them tonight.

Guro nodded. "Go, get ready," he said, eyeing my holey jeans and T-shirt. "Warm up a bit if you want. We should start in about an hour."

I retreated to the locker room, changed into loose black pants and a white shirt, and carefully removed my wallet, keys and phone, ditching them in the side pocket of my gym bag. As I pulled my phone out, something bright tumbled to the floor, striking the ground with a ping.

The silver token. I'd forgotten about it. I stared at the thing, wondering if I should stuff it in my bag or just leave it on the floor. Still, it was my last connection to my sister, and even though Meghan didn't care about me, I didn't want to lose it just yet. I picked it up and slipped it into my pocket.

I stretched a bit, practiced several patterns empty-handed, making sure I knew what I was doing, then headed out to watch the tournament. The other kali students were starting to arrive, walking by me with brief nods and waves before flocking around Guro, but I didn't feel like socializing. Instead, I found an isolated corner behind the rows of chairs and leaned against it with my arms crossed, studying the matches.

"Ethan?"

The familiar voice caught me off guard. I jerked my head up as Kenzie slipped through the crowd and walked my way, a notebook in one hand and a camera around her neck. A tiny thrill shot through me, but I quickly squashed it.

"Hey," she greeted, giving me a friendly but puzzled smile. "I didn't expect to see you around. What are you doing here?"

"What are *you* doing here?" I countered, as though it wasn't obvious.

"Oh, you know." She held up her camera. "School paper stuff. A couple of the boys in our class take lessons here, and I'm covering the tournament. What about you?" Her eyes lit up. "Are you in the tournament? Will I actually get to see you fight?"

"I'm not fighting."

"But you do take something here, right? Kempo? Jujitsu?"

"Kali."

"What's that?"

I sighed. "A Filipino fighting style using sticks and knives. You'll see in a few minutes."

"Oh." Kenzie pondered this, then took a step forward, gazing up at me with thoughtful brown eyes. I swallowed the sudden dryness in my throat and leaned away, feeling the wall press against my back, preventing escape. "Well, you're just full of surprises, aren't you, Ethan Chase?" she mused with a small grin, cocking her head at me. "I wonder what other secrets are hiding in that broody head of yours."

I forced myself not to move, to keep my voice light and uncaring. "Is that why you keep hanging around me? You're curious?" I smirked and shook my head. "You're going to be disappointed. My life isn't that exciting."

I received a dubious look, and she took another step forward, peering into my eyes as if she could see the truth in them. My stomach squirmed as she leaned in. "Uh-huh. So, you keep your distance from everyone, take secret martial arts classes, and were expelled from your last school because the library mysteriously caught fire with you in it, and you're telling me your life isn't that exciting?"

I shifted uneasily. The girl was perceptive, I'd give her that. Unfortunately, she was now treading a little too close to the "exciting" part of my life, which meant I was either going to have to lie, pretend ignorance or pull the asshole card to drive her off. And right now, I didn't have it in me to be a jerk.

Meeting her gaze, I shrugged and offered a faint smile. "Well, I can't tell you all my secrets, can I? That would ruin my image."

She huffed, tossing her bangs. "Oh, fine. Be mysterious and broody. You still owe me an interview, you know." A wicked look crossed her face then, and she held up her notebook. "In fact, since you're not doing anything right now, care to answer a few questions?"

"Ethan!"

Strangely relieved and disappointed at the same time, I glanced up to see Guro waving me over. The rest of my classmates had gathered and were milling around nervously. It seemed the kempo matches were wrapping up.

Nice timing, Guro, I thought, and I didn't know if I was being serious or sarcastic. Pushing away from the wall, I turned to Kenzie with a helpless shrug. "I gotta go," I told her. "Sorry."

"Fine," she called after me. "But I'm going to get that interview, tough guy! I'll see you after your thing."

Guro raised an eyebrow as I came up but didn't ask who

the girl was or what I'd been doing. He never poked into our personal lives, for which I was thankful. "We're almost up," he said, and handed me a pair of short blades, their metal edges gleaming under the fluorescent lights. They weren't Guro's swords; these were different—a little longer, perhaps, the blades not quite as curved. I held them lightly, checking their weight and balance, and gave them a practice spin. Strangely enough, I felt they had been made especially for me.

I looked questioningly at Guro, and he nodded approvingly.

"I sharpened them this morning, so be careful," was all he said, and I backed away, taking my place along the wall.

The mats finally cleared, and a voice crackled over the intercom, introducing Guro Javier and his class of kali students. There was a smattering of applause, and we all went onto the mats to bow while Guro spoke about the origin of kali, what it meant, and how it was used. I could sense the bored impatience of the other students along the wall; they didn't want to see a demonstration, they wanted to get on with the tournament. I held my head high and kept my gaze straight ahead. I wasn't doing this for them.

There was a brief gleam of light along one side of the room: a camera flash. I suppressed a groan, knowing exactly who was taking pictures of me. Wonderful. If my photo ended up in the school paper, if people suddenly knew I studied a martial art, I could see myself being hounded relentlessly; people lining up to take a shot at the "karate kid." I cursed the nosy reporter under my breath, wondering if I could separate her from the camera long enough to delete the images.

The demonstration started with a couple of the beginner students doing a pattern known as Heaven Six, and the clacks of their rattan sticks echoed noisily throughout the room. I saw Kenzie take a few pictures as they circled the mats. Then the more advanced students demonstrated a few disarms, takedowns, and free-style sparring. Guro circled with them, explaining what they were doing, how we practiced, and how it could be applied to real life.

Then it was my turn.

"Of course," Guro said as I stepped onto the mats, holding the swords at my sides, "the rattan—the kali sticks—are proxies for real blades. We practice with sticks, but everything we do can be transferred to blades, knives or empty hands. As Ethan will demonstrate. This is an advanced technique," he cautioned, as I stepped across him, standing a few yards away. "Do not try this at home."

I bowed to him and the audience. He raised a rattan stick, twirled it once, and suddenly tossed it at me. I responded instantly, whipping the blades through the air, cutting it into three parts. The audience gasped, sitting straighter in their chairs, and I smiled.

Yes, these are real swords.

Guro nodded and stepped away. I half closed my eyes and brought my swords into position, one held vertically over one shoulder, the other tucked against my ribs. Balanced on the balls of my feet, I let my mind drift, forgetting the audience and the onlookers and my fellow students watching along the wall. I breathed out slowly and let my mind go blank.

Music began, drumming a rhythm over the loudspeakers, and I started to move.

I started slowly at first, both weapons whirling around me, sliding from one motion to the next. *Don't think about what you're doing, just move, flow.* I danced around the floor, throwing a few flips and kicks into the pattern because I could, keeping time with the music. As the drums picked up, pounding out a frantic rhythm, I moved faster, faster, whipping the blades around my body, until I could feel the wind from their passing, hear the vicious hum as they sliced through the air around me.

Someone whooped out in the audience, but I barely heard them. The people watching didn't matter; nothing mattered except the blades in my hands and the flowing motion of the dance. The swords flashed silver in the dim light, fluid and flexible, almost liquid. There was no block or strike, dodge or parry—the dance was all of these things, and none, all at once. I pushed myself harder than I ever had before, until I couldn't tell where the swords ended and my arms began, until I was just a weapon in the center of the floor, and no one could touch me.

With a final flourish, I spun around, ending the demonstration on one knee, the blades back in their ready position. For a heartbeat after I finished, there was absolute silence. Then, like a dam breaking, a roar of applause swept over me, laced with whistles and scraping chairs as people surged to their feet. I rose and bowed to the audience, then to my master, who gave me a proud nod. He understood. This wasn't just a demonstration for me; it was something I'd worked for, trained for, and finally pulled off—without getting into trouble or hurting anyone in the process. I had actually done something right for a change.

I looked up and met Kenzie's eyes on the other side of the mats. She was grinning and clapping frantically, her notebook lying on the floor beside her, and I smiled back.

"That was awesome," she said, weaving around the edge of the mat when I stepped off the floor, breathing hard. "I had no idea you could do…that. Congratulations, you're a certified badass."

I felt a warm glow of…something, deep inside. "Thanks," I muttered, carefully sliding the blades back into their sheaths before laying them gently atop Guro's bag. It was hard to give them up; I wanted to keep holding them, feeling their perfect weight as they danced through the air. I'd seen Guro practice with his own blades, and he looked so natural with them, as if they were extensions of his arms. I wondered if I'd looked the same out there on the mat, the shining edges coming so close to my body but never touching it. I wondered if Guro would ever let me train with them again.

Our instructor had called the last student to demonstrate knife techniques with him, and he had the audience's full attention now. Meanwhile, I caught several appreciative gazes directed at Kenzie from my fellow kali students, and felt myself bristle.

"Come on," I told her, stepping away from the others before Chris could jump in and introduce himself. "I need a soda. Want one?"

She nodded eagerly. Together, we slipped through the crowds, out the doors, and into the hallway, leaving the noise and commotion behind.

I fed two dollars into the vending machine at the end of the hall, choosing a Pepsi for myself, then a Mountain Dew at Kenzie's request. She smiled her thanks as I tossed it to her, and we leaned against the corridor wall, basking in the silence.

"So," Kenzie ventured after several heartbeats. She gave me a sideways look. "Care to answer a few questions now?"

I knocked the back of my head against the wall. "Sure," I muttered, closing my eyes. The girl wouldn't let me be until we got this thing over with. "Let's have at it. Though I promise, you're going to be disappointed by how dull my life really is."

"I somehow doubt that." Kenzie's voice had changed. It was uncertain, now, almost nervous. I frowned, listening to the flipping of notebook paper, then a quiet breath, as if she was steeling herself for something. "First question, then. How long have you been taking kali?"

"Since I was twelve," I said without moving. "That's…

what…nearly five years now." Jeez, had it really been that long? I remembered my first class as a shy, quiet kid, holding the rattan stick like it was a poisonous snake, and Guro's piercing eyes, appraising me.

"Okay. Cool. Second question." Kenzie hesitated, then said in a calm, clear voice, "What, exactly, is your take on faeries?"

My eyes flew open, and I jerked my head up, banging it against the wall again. My half-empty soda can dropped from my fingers and clanked to the floor, fizzing everywhere. Kenzie blinked and stepped back as I gaped at her, hardly believing what I'd just heard. *"What?"* I choked out, before I thought better of it, before the defensive walls came slamming down.

"You heard me." Kenzie regarded me intently, watching my reaction. "Faeries. What do you know about them? What's your interest in the fey?"

My mind spun. Faeries. Fey. She knew. How she knew, I had no idea. But she couldn't continue this line of questioning. This had to end, now. Todd was already in trouble because of Them. He might really be gone. The last thing I wanted was for Mackenzie St. James to vanish off the face of the earth because of me. And if I had to be nasty and cruel, so be it. It was better than the alternative.

Drawing myself up, I sneered at her, my voice suddenly ugly, hateful. "Wow, whatever you smoked last night, it must've been good." I curled my lip in a smirk. "Are you even listening to yourself? What kind of screwed-up question is that?"

Kenzie's eyes hardened. Flipping several pages, she held the notebook out to me, where the words *glamour, Unseelie* and *Seelie Courts* were underlined in red. I remembered her standing behind the bleachers when I faced that creepy transparent faery. My stomach went cold.

"I'm a reporter," Kenzie said, as I tried wrapping my brain around this. "I heard you talking to someone the day Todd disappeared. It wasn't hard to find the information." She flipped the notebook shut and stared me down, defiant. "Changelings, Fair Folk, All-Hallow's Eve, Summer and Winter courts, the Good Neighbors. I learned a lot. And when I called Todd's house this afternoon, he still wasn't there." She pushed her hair back and gave me a worried look. "What's going on, Ethan? Are you and Todd in some sort of pagan cult? You don't actually *believe* in faeries, do you?"

I forced myself to stay calm. At least Kenzie was reacting like a normal person should, with disbelief and concern. Of course she didn't believe in faeries. Maybe I could scare her away from me for good. "Yes," I smirked, crossing my arms. "That's exactly right. I'm in a cult, and we sacrifice goats under the full moon and drink the blood of virgins and babies every month." She wrinkled her nose, and I took a threatening step forward. "It's a lot of fun, especially when we bring out the crack and Ouija boards. Wanna join?"

"Very funny, tough guy." I'd forgotten Kenzie didn't scare easily. She glared back, stubborn and unmovable as a wall. "What's really going on? Are you in some kind of trouble?"

"What if I am?" I challenged. "What are you going to do about it? You think you can save me? You think you can publish one of your little stories and everything will be fine? Wake up, Miss Nosy Reporter. The world's not like that."

"Quit being a jerkoff, Ethan," Kenzie snapped, narrowing her eyes. "You're not really like this, and you're not as bad as you think you are. I'm only trying to help."

"No one can help me." Suddenly, I was tired. I was tired of fighting, tired of forcing myself to be someone I wasn't. I didn't want to hurt her, but if she continued down this path, she would only rush headlong into a world that would do its best to tear her apart. And I couldn't let that happen. Not again.

"Look." I sighed, slumping against the wall. "I can't explain it. Just…leave me alone, okay? Please. You have no idea what you're getting into."

"Ethan—"

"Stop asking questions," I whispered, drawing away. Her eyes followed me, confused and sad, and I hardened my voice. "Stop asking questions, and stay the hell away from me. Or you're only going to get hurt."

"Advice you should have followed yourself, Ethan Chase," a voice hissed out of the darkness.

CHAPTER NINE
TOKEN TO THE NEVERNEVER

They were here.

The creepy, transparent fey, floating a few inches off the tile floors, drifting toward us down the hall. Only now there were a whole lot of them, filling the corridor, their bony fingers and shattered wings making soft clicking sounds as they eased closer.

"We told you," one whispered, regarding me with shiny black eyes, "we told you to forget, to not ask questions, to not interfere. You were warned, and you chose to ignore us. Now, you and your friend will disappear. No one will endanger our lady's return, not even the mortal kin of the Iron Queen."

"Ethan?" Kenzie gave me a worried look, but I couldn't tear my eyes away from the ghostly faeries, creeping toward us. She glanced back down the hall, then turned to stare at me again. "What are you looking at? You're starting to freak me out."

Backing away, I grabbed Kenzie's wrist, ignoring her startled yelp, and fled back into the main room.

"Hey!" She tried to yank free as I bashed through the doors, nearly knocking down three students in white gis. "Ow! What the hell are you doing? Let go!"

We were starting to attract attention, despite the noise of battle and sparring, and several parents turned to give me the evil eye. I pulled Kenzie into the corner where I'd left my bag and released her, watching the door we'd just come through. She glared at me, rubbing her wrist. "Next time, a little warning would be nice." When I didn't answer, she frowned and dropped her wrist. "Are you okay? You look like you're about to hurl. What's going on?"

The creepy fey drifted through the door frame, rising over the crowd like skeletal wraiths, black eyes scanning the floor. No one saw them, of course. They flickered, fading from sight for just a second before, as one, their faceted black eyes locked onto me.

I whispered a curse. "Kenzie," I muttered, as the fey started to float toward us. "We have to get out of here. Will you trust me, just this once, without asking any questions?" She opened her mouth to protest, and I whirled on her frantically. "Please!"

Her jaw snapped shut. Whether it was from the look on my face or something else, she nodded. "Lead the way."

Shouldering my bag, I fled along the wall with Kenzie right behind me, weaving through students and watching parents, until we reached the back of the dojo. The fire door stood slightly ajar, propped open to let in the cool autumn air, and I lunged toward it.

Just as I hit the metal bar, pushing it open, something struck my arm, sending a flaring pain up my shoulder. I stifled a yell and staggered down the steps, dragging Kenzie with me, seeing the hatchet-face of the faery glaring at me from behind the door.

"Ethan," Kenzie gasped as I pulled her across the back lot. It had rained again, and the pavement smelled like wet asphalt. Puddles glimmered under the streetlamps, pooling in cracks and potholes, and we splashed our way through the black, oily water.

"Ethan!" Kenzie called again. She sounded frantic, but all

my thoughts were on getting to my truck around front. "Oh, my God! Wait a second. Look at your arm!"

I looked back, and my skin crawled. Where the faery had hit me, the entire sleeve of my shirt was soaked with red. I pushed back the sleeve, revealing three long, vivid slashes across my triceps. Blood was starting to trickle down my arm.

"What the hell?" Kenzie gasped, as the pain suddenly hit like a hot knife peeling back my skin. I gritted my teeth and clamped a hand over the wound. "Something tore the crap out of your arm. You need to go to the hospital. Here." She reached for me, putting a gentle hand on my uninjured shoulder. "Give me your bag."

"No," I rasped, backing away. They were coming down the stairs now, pointed stick legs skipping over the puddles. One of them stared at me and raised a thin, bloody claw to his mouth slit, licking the blood with a pale, wormlike tongue.

The sound of movement rippled behind us, and I turned to see more of them floating around the corner of the building, spreading out and trapping us between them.

My stomach felt tight. Is this what had happened to Todd, surrounded on all sides by creepy transparent fey, torn apart with long needle fingers?

I shivered, trying to be calm. My rattan sticks were in my bag, feeble weapons against so many, but I had to do something.

For just a moment, I caught a reflection of myself in the puddle at my feet, grim-faced and hollow-eyed. There was a dark smear on my cheek, my own blood, from where I'd rubbed my face after touching the wound....

Wait. Blood. Standing water.

The fey drifted closer. I stuck my hand into my pocket, and my bloody fingers closed around the silver coin. Pulling it out, I faced Kenzie, who was giving me that worried, be-wildered stare, still insisting we go to a doctor.

"Kenzie," I said, taking her hand as the clicking around us grew very loud in my ears, "do you believe in faeries?"

"What?" She blinked at me, looking confused and almost angry that I'd brought up something so ridiculous. "Do I... no! Of course not, that's crazy."

I closed my eyes. "Then, I'm sorry," I whispered. "I didn't want to do this. But try not to freak out when we get there."

"Get...where?"

The circle of fey hissed and flowed toward us, claws reaching out, mouths gaping. Praying this would work, I squeezed Kenzie's hand in a death grip and flung the token into the puddle at my feet.

A flash of blinding white, a ripple of energy with no sound. I felt my stomach pulled inside out, the ground spinning under my feet, and held my breath. The mad hisses and clicking of the transparent fey cut out, and suddenly I was falling.

I hit the ground on my stomach, biting my lip as the gym bag landed on my shoulder and sent a flare of pain up my arm. Beside me, I heard Kenzie's breathless yelp as she thumped to the dirt and lay there, gasping.

"What...what in the hell?" she panted, and I heard her struggle to get up. "What just happened? Where are we?"

"Well, well," answered a cool, amused voice from some-where above us. "And here you are again. Ethan Chase, your family does have a knack for getting into trouble."

PART II

CHAPTER TEN

CAVE OF THE CAIT SITH

I jerked upright, pushing off the bag. The motion sent a blaze of agony across my back and shoulder. Clenching my jaw, I struggled to my feet and searched for the source of the elusive voice. We were in some sort of a cave with a sandy bottom and a small pool near the back. Along the walls, enormous spotted toadstools glowed with eerie luminance. Tiny glowing balls, like blue and green fireflies, drifted over the pool, throwing rippling splashes of light over the cavern, but I couldn't see anyone besides Kenzie and myself.

"Who's there?" Kenzie demanded, in a far more steady voice than I'd expect. "Where are you? Show yourself."

"As usual, you mortals have not the slightest ability to see what is right in front of your faces," continued the voice in a bored tone, and I thought I heard a yawn. "Very well, humans. Up here, if you would."

There was a shimmer of movement along the far wall. I followed it up to a rocky shelf about fifteen feet off the ground. For a moment, the shelf appeared empty. Then, two glowing yellow eyes blinked into existence, and a second later a large gray cat sat there with its tail curled around itself, peering down on us haughtily.

"There." It sighed, sounding exceptionally weary, as if it had held this entire conversation before. "See me now?"

A memory flickered to life—the image of a metal tower, crumbling all around us, and a furry gray cat leading us to safety. A name hovered at the edge of my mind, eluding me for the moment, but the image of the golden-eyed cat was clear. Of course, it hadn't changed a bit.

Kenzie took two staggering steps backward, staring at the feline as if in a daze. "O-kay," she breathed, shaking her head slightly. "A cat. A cat that talks. I'm going crazy." She glanced at me. "Or you slipped something into my drink at the tournament. One or the other."

"How predictable." The cat sighed again and stuck its hind leg into the air to lick its toes. "I believe there is nothing wrong with your eyes or ears, human. My previous statement still stands."

I glared at it. "Lay off, cat," I said. "She's never seen one of you before, let alone been *here*." My arm throbbed, and I sank onto a nearby rock. "Dammit, I don't why *I'm* here. Why am I here? I was hoping I'd never see this place again."

"Please," the cat said in that annoyingly superior voice, eyeing me over its leg. "Why are you even surprised, human? Your last name is Chase, after all. I was expecting your arrival any day now." It sniffed and glanced at Kenzie, who was still staring at it openmouthed. "Minus the girl, of course. But I am sure we can work around that. First things first, however." The golden eyes shifted to me. "You are dripping blood everywhere, human. Perhaps you should try to put a stop to that. We would not want to attract anything nasty, would we?"

I exhaled, hard. Well, here I was, in the Nevernever. Nothing to be done now but try to get out as quickly as I could. Pulling my bag toward me, I tugged it open and rifled through it one-handed, biting my lip as pain continued to claw at my shoulder. Blood still oozed sluggishly down my arm, and the left side of my shirt was spattered with red.

"Here." Kenzie suddenly knelt across from me, stopping

my hand. "Don't hurt yourself. Let me do it." Taking off her camera, she started going through the bag. "You have gauze in here somewhere, right?"

"I can get it," I said quickly, not wanting her to see my old clothes and smelly belongings. I reached forward, but she gave me such a fierce glare that I sat back with a grimace, leaving her to it. Setting her jaw, she rummaged around, pushing aside rattan sticks and old T-shirts, pulling out a rag and the roll of gauze I kept for sports-related injuries. Her lips were pressed in a thin line, her eyes hard and determined, as if she was going to take care of this little problem before she faced anything else. For a second, I felt a weird flicker of pride. She was taking things remarkably well.

"Take off your shirt."

I blinked, feeling my face heat. "Uh. What?"

"Shirt, tough guy." She gestured to my blood-spattered T-shirt. "I don't think you're going to want it after this, anyway. Off."

Her words were almost too flippant, like someone forcing a smile after a horrible tragedy. I hesitated, more out of concern than embarrassment—though there was that, too. "You sure you're okay with this?"

"Oh, do as she says, human." The cat thumped its tail. "Otherwise we will be here all night."

Gingerly, I eased off my shirt and tossed the bloodied rag aside. Kenzie soaked the cloth in the pool, wrung it out, and crouched behind me in the sand. For a moment, she hesitated, and I tensed, suddenly feeling highly exposed—half-naked and bleeding in front of a strange girl and a talking cat. Then her fingers brushed my skin, cool and soft, and my stomach turned into a pretzel.

"God, Ethan." She laid one palm gently against my shoulder, leaning in to examine the tears down my arm. I closed my eyes, forcing myself to relax. "These are nasty. What the hell was after you, demon cougars?"

I sucked in a ragged breath. "You wouldn't believe me if I told you."

"Oh, I'm willing to believe just about anything right now." She pressed the cloth to the jagged claw marks, and I set my jaw. We were both silent as she dabbed blood off my shoulder and wrapped the gauze around my arm. I could sense Kenzie was still a little dazed from the whole situation. But her fingers were gentle and sure, and I shivered each time they touched my skin, leaving goose bumps behind.

"There," she said, dusting off her knees as she stood. "That should do it. Those first aid sessions in Ms. Peters's class didn't go to waste, at least."

"Thanks," I muttered. She gave me a shaky smile.

"No problem." She watched as I reached into my bag and pulled out another T-shirt, shrugging into it with a grimace. "Now, before I start screaming, will someone—you or the talking cat or a freaking flying goat, I don't care—please tell me what the hell is going on?"

"Why are mortals so boring?" the cat asked, landing on the sandy floor without a sound. Padding toward us, it leaped atop a flat rock and observed us both critically, waving its tail, before its gaze settled on the girl. "Very well, I will be the voice of reason and sanity once again. Listen closely, human, for I will explain this only once." It sat down with a sniff, curling its tail around its feet. "You are in the Nevernever, the home of the fey. Or, as you mortals insist upon calling them, faeries. Yes, faeries are real," it added in its bored tone, as Kenzie took a breath to speak. "No, mortals cannot normally see them in the real world. Please save all unnecessary questions until I am finished.

"You are here," it continued, giving me a sideways look, "because Ethan Chase apparently cannot stay out of trouble

with the fey and has used a token to bring you both into the
Nevernever. More important, into my home—one of them,
anyway. Which begs the question…" The cat blinked and
looked at me now, narrowing its eyes. "Why *are* you here,
human? The token was to be used only in the most dire circumstances. By your wounds, I would guess something was
chasing you, but why drag the girl into this, as well?"

"I didn't have a choice," I said, avoiding Kenzie's eyes. "They
were after her, too."

"They?" asked Kenzie.

I scrubbed my good hand over my face. "There's something
out there," I told the cat. "Something different, some type
of fey I've never seen before. They're killing off exiles and
half-breeds, and they've taken a friend of mine, a half-phouka
named Todd Wyndham. When I tried to find out more…"

"They came to silence you," the cat finished solemnly.

"Yeah. Right in the open. In front of a couple hundred
people." I felt Kenzie's gaze on me and ignored her. "So," I
asked the cat, "do you know what's going on?"

The cat twitched an ear. "Perhaps," it mused, managing
to look bored and thoughtful all at once. "There have been
strange rumors circling the wyldwood. They have me curious." It yawned and casually licked a foot. "I believe it is time
to pay a visit to the Iron Queen."

I stood up. "No," I said a little too forcefully, though the
cat didn't even look up from its paw. "I can't go to Meghan. I
have to get home! I have to find Todd and see if my family is
all right. They're gonna freak out if I don't come back soon." I
remembered what Meghan said about time in the Nevernever,
and groaned. "God, they're probably freaking out right now."

"The Iron Queen needs to be informed that you are here,"
the cat said, calmly rubbing the paw over his whiskers. "That
was the favor—should you ever use that token, I would bring

you to her. Besides, I believe she will be most interested in what is happening in the mortal world, and this new type of fey. I think one of the courts needs to know about this, do you not agree?"

"Can't you at least take Kenzie home?"

"That was not the bargain, human." The cat finally looked at me, unblinking. "And, were I you, I would think long and hard about sending her back alone. If these creatures are still out there, they could be waiting for you both to return."

A chill ran down my back. I glanced at Kenzie and found her looking completely lost as she stared from me to the cat and back again. "I have no idea what's going on here," she said matter-of-factly, though her eyes were a bit glazed. "I just hope that when I wake up, I'm not in a padded room with a nice man in a white suit feeding me pills."

I sighed, feeling my life unravel even more. *I'm sorry, Kenzie*, I thought, as she hugged herself and stared straight ahead. *I didn't want to drag you into this, and this is the very last place I want to be. But the cat's right; I can't send you back alone, not with those things out there. They already got Todd; I won't let them have you, too.*

"All right," I snapped, glaring at the feline. "Let's go see Meghan and get this over with. But I'm not staying. I have to get home. I have a friend who's in trouble, and I have to find him. Not even Meghan can help me with that."

The cat sneezed several times, curling his whiskers in mirth. I didn't see what was so funny. "This should be most amusing," it said, hopping down from the rock. "I suggest you remain here for the night," it continued as he padded away over the sand. "Nothing will harm you in this place, and I am in no mood to lead wounded humans around the wyldwood in the dark. We will start out for the Iron Realm in the morning."

"How long will it take to get there?" I asked, but there was no answer. Frowning, I glanced around the cave. The cat was gone.

Oh, yeah, I thought, remembering something then, from long ago. *Grimalkin. He does that.*

Kenzie still seemed unnaturally quiet as I sat down and started fishing in my bag, taking stock of what I had. Rattan sticks, extra clothes, bottled water, a smashed box of energy bars, a container of aspirin and a couple of small, secret items I kept handy for pests of the invisible variety. I wondered if my little charms would work in the Nevernever, the fey's home territory. I would find out soon enough.

I shook four painkillers into my palm and tossed them back, swallowing them with a grimace, then sliding the bottle into my pocket. My shoulder still ached, but against all odds, it seemed to be nothing more than a flesh wound. I just hoped the strange, creepy fey didn't have venomous claws.

"Here," I muttered, pulling out a slightly crushed energy bar, offering it to the girl sitting across from me. She blinked and stared at it blankly. "We should probably eat something. You don't want to take anything anyone offers you here. No food, drinks, gifts, anything, got it? Oh, and never agree to do someone a favor, or make any kind of deal or say 'thank you.'" She continued to watch me without expression, and I frowned. "Hey, are you listening to me? This is important."

Great, she's gone into shock. What am I supposed to do now? I stared at her, wishing I had never pulled her into this, wishing we could both just go home. I was worried for my parents; what would they say when they found out yet another child of theirs had disappeared from the face of the earth? *I'm not Meghan,* I promised, not knowing if it was to Mom, to Kenzie or myself. *I'll get us home, I swear I will.*

The girl still wasn't responding, and waggling the energy bar at her was getting me nowhere. I sighed. "Kenzie," I said, firmer this time, leaning forward over the bag. "Mackenzie. Hey!"

She jumped when I got right up in her face and grabbed her arm, jerking back with a startled look. I let her go, and she blinked rapidly, as if coming out of a trance.

"You all right?" I asked, sitting back, watching her cautiously. She stared at me for an uncomfortable moment, then took a deep breath.

"Yeah," she finally whispered, making me sag in relief. "Yeah, I'm good. I'm fine. I think." She gazed around the cave, as if making sure it was still there. "The Nevernever," she murmured, almost to herself. "I'm in the Nevernever. I'm in freaking Faeryland."

I watched her carefully, wondering what I would do if she started to scream. But then, sitting there on the log in the middle of the Nevernever, Kenzie did something completely unexpected.

She smiled.

It wasn't big or obvious. Just a faint, secret grin, a flicker of excitement crossing her face, as if this was something she'd been waiting for her whole life, only she hadn't known it. It raised the hairs on the back of my neck. Normal human beings did not react well to being dropped into an imaginary place with creatures that existed only in fairy tales. I was expecting fear, anger, rationalization. Kenzie's eyes nearly glowed with anticipation.

It made me very nervous.

"So," she said brightly, turning back to me, "tell me about this place."

I gave her a wary look. "You do realize we're in the *Nevernever,* home of *the fey.* Faeries? Wee folk? Leprechauns and pixies and Tinkerbell?" I held out the food bar again, watching her reaction. "Isn't this your cue to start explaining how faeries don't exist?"

"Well, I'm a reporter," Kenzie said, accepting the food package and fiddling with a corner. "I have to face facts. And it occurs to me that one of two things is happening right now. One, you slipped something into my drink at the dojo, and I'm having a really whacked-out dream. And if that's the case, I'll wake up soon and you'll go to jail and we'll never see each other again."

I winced.

"Or two…" She took a deep breath and gazed around the cavern. "This…is really happening. It's kind of silly to tell the talking cat he doesn't exist when he's sitting right there arguing with you."

I kept quiet, chewing on granola. You couldn't fault her reasoning, though she was still far more pragmatic and logical than I'd expected. Still, something about her reaction didn't feel right. Maybe it was her complete lack of fear and skepticism, as if she desperately wanted to believe that this was really happening. As if she didn't care at all about leaving what was real and sane and normal behind.

"Anyway," Kenzie went on, looking back at me, "you've been here before, right? From the way that cat was talking to you, it was like you knew each other."

I shrugged. "Yeah," I said, staring at the ground between my knees. Memories—the bad memories I tried so hard to forget—crowded in. Fangs and claws, poking at me. Glowing eyes and shrieking, high-pitched laughter. Lying in utter darkness, the stench of rust and iron clogging my nose, waiting for my sister to come. "But it was a long time ago," I muttered, shoving those thoughts away, locking them in the farthest corner of my mind. "I barely remember it."

"How long have you been able to see…um…faeries?"

I flicked a glance at her. She sat with her knees drawn to her chest, leaning against a rock, watching me gravely. The fluorescent toadstools on the walls gave off a black light effect, making the blue in her hair glow neon bright. I caught myself staring and looked down at the floor again.

"All my life." I hunched a little more. "I can't remember a time when I couldn't see them, when I didn't know they were there."

"Can your parents—?"

"No." It came out a bit sharper than I'd intended. "No one in my family can see them. Just me."

Except my sister, of course. But I didn't want to talk about her.

"Hmm." Kenzie rested her chin on her knees. "Well, this explains a lot about you. The secrecy, the paranoia, the weirdness at the tournament." My face heated, but Kenzie didn't seem to notice. "So how many…faeries…are out there in the real world?"

"Sure you want to know?" I challenged, smiling bitterly. "You might end up like me, mean and paranoid, staring at corners and out windows for things that aren't there. There's a reason no one ever talks about the fey, and not just because it draws their attention. Because normal people, the ones who can't see Them, will label you *weird* or *crazy* or *freak,* and will either treat you like you have the plague or will want to throw you in a cell."

"I never thought of you like that," Kenzie said softly.

Anger burned suddenly. At myself, for dragging her into this. At Kenzie, for being too damn stubborn to leave me alone, for refusing to stay away and not hate me like any normal, sane person would. And at myself, again, for allowing her to get this close, for wanting to be near someone. I had let down my guard the tiniest bit, and now look where we were.

"Well, maybe you should have," I said, standing and glaring down at her. "Because now you're stuck here with me. And I really don't know if we're going to make it out of here alive."

"Where are you going?" Kenzie asked as I stalked away toward the mouth of the cave. Ignoring her, hoping she wouldn't come after me, I walked to the entrance, just a foot or so from the edge of the cave, so I could see Faery for myself.

Peering into the darkness, I shivered. The wyldwood stretched away before me, tangled and ominous in the shadows. I couldn't see the sky through the canopy of leaves and branches, but I could see glimmers of movement far, far above, lights or creatures floating through the trees.

"Going somewhere?" came a voice above my head. Grimalkin sat in a tangle of roots that curled lazily from the ceiling. His huge eyes seemed to hover in the darkness.

"No," I muttered, giving him a cautious look. Grimalkin had helped my sister in the past, but I didn't know him well, and he was still fey. Faeries never did anything for free; his agreeing to guide us through the wyldwood into the Iron Realm was just part of a deal.

"Good. I would hate to have you eaten before we even started," he purred, raking his claws across the wood. "You appear to have the same recklessness as your sister, always rushing into things without thinking them through."

"Don't compare me to Meghan," I said, narrowing my eyes. "I'm not like her."

"Indeed. She, at least, had a pleasant personality."

"I'm not here to make friends." The cat was bugging the hell out of me, but I refused to let it show. "This isn't a reunion. I just want to get to the Iron Realm, talk to Meghan and go home." *Todd is still out there, counting on me.*

The cat stretched lazily on the branch. "Desire what you will, human," he said with a knowing, half-lidded stare. "With your family, I have found that it is never as easy as that."

CHAPTER ELEVEN
INTO THE WYLDWOOD

I didn't think I'd sleep, but I must've dozed off, because the next thing I knew, I was waking up on the sandy floor of the cave, and my shoulder was killing me. Pulling out the aspirin, I popped another three pills, crunched them down with a grimace and looked around for Kenzie and Grimalkin.

Unsurprisingly, the cat was nowhere to be seen, but a faint gray light was seeping in from the cave mouth, and the glowing fungi along the walls had dimmed, looking like ordinary toadstools now. I wondered how much time had passed, if a year had already flown by in the mortal world and my parents had given up all hope of ever seeing me again.

Grimacing, I struggled upright, cursing myself for falling asleep. Anything could've happened while I'd been out: something could've snuck up on me, stolen my bag, convinced Kenzie to follow it down a dark tunnel. Where was she, anyway? She didn't know about Faery, how dangerous it could be. She was far too trusting, and anything in this world could grab her, chew her up and spit her out again.

I spun, searching frantically, until I saw her sitting cross-legged near the entrance.

Talking to Grimalkin.

Oh, great. I hurried over, hoping she hadn't promised the cat anything she would regret, or we would regret, later. "Kenzie," I said as I swept up. "What are you doing? What are you two talking about?"

She glanced up at me, smiling, and Grimalkin yawned widely as he bent to lick his paws. "Oh, you're up," she said. "Grimalkin was just telling me a little about the Nevernever. It's fascinating. Did you know there's a whole huge city on the ocean floor that stretches for miles? Or that the River of Dreams supposedly runs to the End of the World before falling off the edge?"

"I don't want to know," I said. "I don't want to be here any longer than we have to, so don't think we're staying for the tour. I just want to go to the Iron Realm, talk to Meghan, and go home. How's that part coming along, cat?"

Grimalkin sniffed. "Your friend is far better company than you," he stated, and scrubbed the paw over his head. "And if you are so eager to get to the Iron Realm, we will leave whenever you are ready. However—" he peeked up at me, twitching his tail "—be absolutely sure you have everything you need, human. We will not be coming back to this place should you leave something behind."

I walked back to my gym bag, wondering what to leave. I couldn't take the whole bag, that was obvious. It was bulky and heavy, and I wasn't going to tote it across the Nevernever if I didn't have to. Besides, my arm still hurt like hell, so I wouldn't be carrying anything much larger than a stick.

I pulled out my rattan, the gauze, two bottles of water, and the last three power bars, then rifled around the side pocket for one more thing. Kenzie wandered over and knelt on the other side, watching curiously.

"What are you looking for?"

"This," I muttered, and pulled out a large, slightly rusted key, something I'd found half buried in the swamp when I was a kid. It was ancient, bulky and made of pure iron. I'd kept it as a lucky charm and a faery deterrent ever since.

"Here," I said, holding it out to her. It dangled from an old string, spinning lazily between us. I'd meant to get a chain for it but kept putting it off. "Keep this close," I told her as she stared at it curiously. "Iron is the best protection you can have against the creatures that live here. It's poison to them—they can't even touch it without being burned. It won't keep them away completely, but they might think twice about biting your head off if they smell that around your neck."

She wrinkled her nose, whether from the thought of having to wear a rusty old key or having her head bitten off, I didn't know. "What about you?" she asked.

I reached into my shirt and pulled out the iron cross on the chain. "Already have one. Here." I jiggled the key at her. "Take it."

She reached out, and my fingers brushed hers as they closed around the amulet, sending a rush of warmth up my arm. I jerked and nearly dropped the key, but she didn't pull back, her touch lingering on mine, watching me over our clasped hands.

"I'm sorry, Ethan."

I blinked and quickly pulled my hand back, frowning in confusion. My heart was pounding again, but I ignored it. "Why?"

"For not believing you at the tournament." She looped the heavy key around her neck, where it clinked softly against the camera. "I thought you might be into something dangerous and illegal, and had gotten Todd into trouble because of it. And that the faery thing was a cover for something else. I never thought they could be real." Her solemn gaze met mine over the gym bag. "They were at the tournament, weren't they?" she asked. "The faeries that grabbed Todd. That's what was chasing us, and you were trying to get us out." Her gaze flicked to my bandaged arm, and her brow furrowed. "I'm sorry for that, too."

I started to reply, but Kenzie rose and briskly dusted herself off, as if not wanting an answer. "Come on," she said in an overly cheerful voice. "We should get going. Grim is giving us the evil eye."

She started to walk away but paused very briefly, her fingers touching my shoulder as she passed. "Also…thanks for saving my life."

I sat there a moment, listening to Kenzie's footsteps pad quietly over the sand. What just happened here? Kenzie had nothing to apologize for. It wasn't her fault we were here, stuck in the Nevernever for who knew how long, that a bunch of ghostly, homicidal faeries were after us. Her life had been fairly normal before I came along. If anything, she should hate me for dragging her into this mess. I certainly hated myself.

My shoulder still prickled where she'd touched it.

An extremely loud yawn came from the mouth of the cave. "Are we going to start this expedition sometime in the next century?" Grimalkin called, golden eyes blinking in annoyance. "For someone who is in such a hurry to leave, you certainly are taking your time."

I rose, snatched my rattan sticks and water from the floor, and walked toward the cave entrance, leaving the bag behind. It, along with my dirty clothes and equipment, would have to stay in Faery. Hopefully it wouldn't stink up Grimalkin's home *too* badly.

"Finally." The cat sighed as I came up. He stood, tail waving, and sauntered to the mouth of the cave, looking out at the wyldwood beyond. "Ready, humans?"

"Hey, Grimalkin." Kenzie suddenly brought up her camera. "Smile."

The cat snorted. "That silly toy will not work here, mortal," he said as Kenzie pressed the button and discovered just that. Nothing happened. Frowning, she pulled back to look at it, and Grimalkin sniffed.

"Human technology has no place in the Nevernever," he stated. "Why do you think there are no pictures of dragons and goblins floating about the mortal world? The fey do not photograph well. We do not photograph at all. Magic and technology cannot exist together, except perhaps in the Iron Realm. And even there, your purely human technology will not work as you expect. The Iron Realm, for all its advancement, is still a part of the Nevernever."

"Well, shoot." Kenzie sighed and let the camera drop. "I was hoping to write a book called *My Trip to Faeryland*." Now how am I going to convince myself that I'm not completely loony?"

Grimalkin sneezed with laughter and turned away. "I would not worry about that, mortal. No one ever leaves the Nevernever completely sane."

The cave entrance vanished as soon as we stepped through, changing to a solid wall of stone when we looked back. Kenzie jumped, then reached out to prod the rock, a look of amazement and disbelief crossing her face.

"Better get used to things like that," I told her as she turned forward again, looking a bit stunned. "Nothing ever makes sense around here."

"I'm starting to see that," she murmured as we made our way down the rocky slope after Grimalkin. The cat trotted briskly ahead, neither slowing down nor glancing back to see if we were still there, and we had to scramble to keep up. I wondered if Meghan had had this same problem when she first came to the Nevernever.

Meghan. Flutters of both nerves and excitement hit my stomach, and I firmly shoved them down. I was going to see

my sister, the queen of the Iron Fey. Would she remember
me? Would she be angry that I'd come here, after she'd told
me not to look for her? Maybe she didn't want to see me at
all. Maybe she was glad to be rid of her human ties.

That thought sent a chill through me. Would she even be
the same Meghan I remembered? I had so many memories
of her, and she was always the same: the steady older sister
who looked out for me. When we got to the Iron Realm,
would I find the Iron Queen was insane and cruel like Mab,
or fickle and jealous like Titania? I hadn't met the fey queens,
of course, but the stories I'd heard about them told me everything I needed to know. Which was to stay far, far away
from them both.

"How old were you when you first came here?"

Kenzie voiced the question just as Grimalkin vanished into
the dark gray undergrowth. Alarmed, I stared hard between
the trees until I spotted him again and hurried to catch up. Except he did the same damn thing a minute later, and I growled
a curse, scanning the bushes. Catching sight of a bushy tail, I
hurried forward, Kenzie trailing doggedly beside me. I kept
silent, hoping Kenzie would forget the question. No such luck.

"Ethan? Did you hear me? How old were you the last time
you came to this place?"

"I don't want to talk about it," I said curtly, dodging a bush
with vivid blue thorns. Kenzie stepped deftly around it, keeping pace with me.

"Why?"

"Because." I searched for the cat, ignoring her gaze, and
tried to hold on to my temper. "It's none of your business."

"News flash, Ethan—I'm stuck in Faeryland, same as you.
I think that makes it my business—"

"I was four!" I snapped, turning to glare at her. Kenzie
blinked. "The fey took me from my home when I was four

and used me as *bait* so my sister would come rescue me. They stuck me in a cage and poked at me until I screamed, and when she finally did come, they took her away and turned her into one of Them. I have to pretend I don't have a sister, that I don't see anything weird or strange or unnatural, that my parents aren't terrified to let me do anything because they're scared the fey will steal me again! So, excuse me for not wanting to talk about myself or my screwed-up life. It's kind of a sore subject, okay?"

"Oh, Ethan." Kenzie's gaze was horrified and sympathetic, which was not what I was expecting. "I'm so sorry."

"Forget it." Embarrassed, I turned away, waving it off. "It's just…I've never told anyone before, not even my parents. And being back here—" I gestured to the trees around us "—it's making me remember everything I hated about this place, about Them. I swore I'd never come back. But, here I am and…" Exhaling, I kicked a rock into the undergrowth, making it rattle noisily. "And I managed to pull you in, as well."

Just like Samantha.

"Humans." Grimalkin appeared overhead, in the branches of a tree. "You are making too much noise, and this is not a safe place to do so. Unless you wish to attract the attention of every hungry creature in the area, I suggest attempting to continue on in silence." He sniffed and regarded us without hope. "Give it your best shot at least, hmm?"

We walked for the rest of the afternoon. At least, I thought we did. It was hard to tell time in the endless gray twilight of the wyldwood. My watch had, of course, stopped, and our phones were dead, so we trailed Grimalkin as best we could for several hours as the eerie, dangerous land of the fey loomed all around us. Shadows moved among the trees, keeping just out of sight. Branches creaked, and footsteps shuffled through the leaves, though I never saw anything. Sometimes I thought I heard voices on the wind, singing or whispering my name.

The colors of the wyldwood were weird and unnatural; everything was gray and murky, but then we'd pass a single tree that was a vivid, poisonous green, or a bush with huge purple berries hanging from the branches. Except for a few curious piskies and one hopeful will-o'-the-wisp, I didn't see any faeries, which made me relieved and nervous at the same time. It was like knowing a grizzly was stalking you through the woods, only you couldn't see it. I knew They were out there. I didn't know if I was happy that they were staying out of sight, or if I'd rather they try something now and get it over with.

"Careful through here," Grimalkin cautioned. We picked our way through a patch of thick black briars with thorns as long as my hand, shiny and evil-looking. "Do not take your eyes from the path. Pay attention to what is happening at your feet."

Bones hung in the branches and littered the ground at the base of the bushes, some tiny, some not. Kenzie shuddered whenever we passed one, clutching the key around her neck, but she followed the cat through the branches without a word.

Until a vine snaked around her ankle.

She pitched forward with a yelp, right toward a patch of nasty looking thorns. I caught her before she could impale herself on the spikes. She gasped and clung to my shirt while the offending vine slithered back into the undergrowth.

"You okay?" I asked. I could feel her shaking against me, her heart thudding against my ribs. It felt…good…to hold her like this. Her small body fit perfectly against mine.

With a start, I realized what I was doing and released her quickly, drawing back. Kenzie blinked, still trying to process what had happened, then glared down at the briar patch.

"It…the branch…it *tried* to trip me, didn't it?" she said, sounding incredulous and indignant all at once. "Jeez, not even the plant life is friendly. What did I ever do to it?"

We stepped out of the briar patch, and I looked around for Grimalkin. He had vanished once more, and I stared hard into the trees, searching for him. "Here's a hint," I told Kenzie, narrowing my eyes as I peered into the undergrowth and shadows. "And it might save your life. Just assume that everything here—plant, animal, insect, toadstool, whatever—is out to get you."

"Well, that's not very friendly of them. They don't even know me."

"If you're not going to take this seriously—"

"Ethan, I was just nearly impaled by a bloodthirsty killer bush! I think I'm taking this fairly well, considering."

I glanced back at her. "Whatever. Just remember, nothing in the Nevernever is friendly to humans. Even if the fey appear friendly, they all have ulterior motives. Not even the cat is doing this for free. And if they can't get what they want, they'll take something anyway or try to kill you. You can't trust the fey, ever. They'll pretend to be your friend and stab you in the back when it's most convenient, not because they're mean, or spiteful or hateful, but because it's their nature. It's just how they are."

"You must hate them a great deal," Kenzie said softly.

I shrugged, abruptly self-conscious. "You haven't seen what I have. It's not without cause, trust me." Speaking of which, Grimalkin still hadn't appeared. "Where's that stupid cat?" I muttered, starting to get nervous and a little mad. "If he's gone off and left us—"

A branch rustled somewhere in the woods behind us. We both froze, and Kenzie looked over warily.

"That sounded a little too big for a cat…"

Another branch snapped, closer this time. Something was coming. Something big and fast.

"Humans!" Grimalkin's voice echoed from nowhere, though the urgency in it was plain. "Run! Now!"

Kenzie jumped. I tensed, gripping my weapons. Before we could even think about moving, the bushes parted and a huge reptilian creature spilled out of the brambles into the open.

At first, I thought it was a giant snake, as the scaly green body was close to twenty feet long. But its head was more dragon than serpent, and two short, clawed forearms stuck out of its sides, just behind its shoulder blades. It raised its head, a pale, forked tongue flicking the air, before it reared up with a hiss, baring a mouthful of needlelike teeth.

Kenzie gasped, and I yanked her into the trees as the monster lunged, barely missing us. The snap of its jaws echoed horribly in my ears. We ran, weaving around trees, tearing through bramble and undergrowth, hearing the crashing of twigs and branches at our heels as it followed.

I dodged behind a thick trunk, pulling Kenzie behind me, and raised my sticks as the monster's head slithered around, forked tongue tasting the air. When it turned, I brought the rattan down across its snout as hard as I could, striking the rubbery nose three times before the thing hissed and pulled back with blinding speed. As it drew away, I spotted a place where we could make our stand and yanked Kenzie toward it.

"What is that thing?" Kenzie cried as I pulled her into a cluster of trees, their trunks grown close together to form a protective cage around us. No sooner had I squeezed through than the monster's head appeared between a crack, snapping narrow jaws at me. I whacked it across the head with my sticks, and it pulled back with a screech. I saw its scaly body through the circle of trees, coiling around us like a snake with a mouse, and fought to remain calm.

"Kenzie," I panted, trying to track the thing's head through the branches. My arms shook, and I focused on staying loose, holding my sticks in front of me. "Stay in the center as much as you can. Don't go near the edge of the trees."

The thing lunged again, snaking through the trunks, snapping at me. Thankfully, its body was just a bit too wide to maneuver at top speed, and I was able to dodge, cracking it in the skull as I did. Hissing, it pulled back, trying from a different, higher angle. I ducked, stabbing it in the throat, wishing I had a knife or a blade instead of wooden sticks. It gave an angry gurgle and backed out, eyeing me evilly through the trunks.

"Ethan!" Kenzie yelled, as the monster darted close again, "behind you!"

Before I could turn, a heavy coil snaked around my waist, slamming me back into a tree trunk, pinning me there. I struggled, cursing myself for focusing solely on the monster's head instead of the whole creature. My right arm was pinned to my side; I raised my left as the head snaked through the trees and came at me again. Timing it carefully, I stabbed up with the tip, jamming it into a slitted yellow eye.

Screeching, the monster drew back. With a hiss, it tightened its coils around my chest, cutting off my air. I gasped for breath, punching the end of my rattan into the monster's body, trying to struggle free. It only squeezed harder, making my ribs creak painfully. My lungs burned, and my vision began to go dark, a tunnel of hazy light that started to shrink. The creature's head drifted closer; its tongue flicked out to brush my forehead, but I didn't have the strength to raise my weapon.

And then, Kenzie stepped up and brought her iron key slashing down across the monster's hurt eye.

Instantly, the coils loosened as the monster reared up, screaming this time. Gasping, I dropped to my knees as it writhed and thrashed, scraping the side of its face against the trunk, snapping branches and smashing into the trees. A flailing coil struck Kenzie, knocking her back several feet. I heard her gasp as she hit the ground, and tried to push myself upright, but the ground was still spinning and I sagged to my knees again.

Cursing, I struggled to get up, to put myself between Kenzie and the snake in case it turned on her. But the iron key to the face seemed to have killed its appetite for humans. With a final wail, the monster slithered off. I watched it vanish into the undergrowth, then sagged in relief.

"Are you all right?" Kenzie dropped beside me, placing a slender hand on my arm. I could feel it shaking. I nodded, still trying to suck air into my burning lungs, feeling as if they'd been crushed with a vise.

"I'm fine," I rasped, pulling myself to my feet. Kenzie rose, dusting herself off, and I stared at her in growing astonishment. That thing had had me on the ropes, seconds away from being swallowed like a big mouse. If she hadn't been there, I'd be dead right about now.

"Kenzie, I…" I hesitated, grateful, embarrassed and angry all at once. "Thanks."

"Oh, no problem," Kenzie replied with a shaky grin, though her voice trembled. "Always happy to help with any giant snake monster issues that pop up."

I felt a weird pull somewhere in my stomach, and the sudden crazy urge to draw her close, to make sure we were both still alive. Uncomfortable, I retreated a step. "Sorry about your camera," I muttered.

"Huh? Oh." She held up the device, now very broken from the fall, and gave a dramatic sigh. "Well, it wasn't working anyway. Besides…" She reached out and gently squeezed my arm. "I owed you one."

My mouth was dry again. "I'll replace it. Once we get back to the real world—"

"Don't worry about it, tough guy." Kenzie waved it off. "It's just a camera. And I think surviving an attack by a giant snake monster was more important."

"Lindwurm," came a voice above our heads, and Grimalkin appeared in the branches, peering down at us. "That," he stated imperiously, "was a lindwurm, and a rather young one at that. An adult would have given you considerably more trouble." He flicked his tail and dropped to the ground, wrinkling his nose as he gazed at us. "There might be others around, as well, so I suggest we keep moving."

I glared at the cat as we maneuvered through the trees again, wincing as my bruised ribs twinged. "You couldn't have warned us any earlier?"

"I tried," Grimalkin replied with a sniff. "But you were too busy discussing hostile vegetation and how faeries are completely untrustworthy. I practically had to yell to get your attention." He glanced over his shoulder with a distinct I-told-you-so expression. "Next time, when I suggest you move silently through a dangerous part of the Nevernever, perhaps you will listen to me."

"Huh," Kenzie muttered, walking along beside me. "You know, if all cats are like him, I'm kinda glad they don't talk."

"That you know of, human," Grimalkin returned mysteriously, and continued deeper into the wyldwood.

CHAPTER TWELVE
THE BORDER

"The Iron Realm is not far, now."

I glanced up from where I sat on a fallen log, hot, sweaty and still sore from the recent battle. Kenzie slumped beside me, leaning against my shoulder, making it hard to concentrate on what the cat was saying. I didn't mind the contact—she was exhausted and probably just as sore—but I wasn't used to having anyone this close, touching me, and it was… distracting. I don't know how long we'd been walking, but it felt like the hours were stretching out just for spite. The wyldwood never changed; it was still as dark, murky and endless as it had been when we started. I didn't even know if we were walking in circles. Since fighting the lindwurm thing, I'd seen a wood sprite, several more piskies and a single goblin who might've given us trouble if he'd been with his pack. The short, warty fey had grinned evilly as it tried to block our path, but I'd drawn my weapons and Kenzie had stepped up beside me, glaring, and the goblin had suddenly decided it had other places to be. A will-o'-the-wisp had trailed us for several miles, trying to capture our attention so it could get us lost, but I'd told Kenzie to ignore the floating ball of light, and it eventually had given up.

I broke the last energy bar in half and handed the bigger part to Kenzie, who sat up and took it with a murmur of thanks. "How far?" I asked Grimalkin, biting into my half. The cat began grooming his tail, ignoring me. I resisted the urge to throw a rock at him.

I glanced at Kenzie. She sat hunched forward, her forearms resting on her knees, chewing methodically. There were circles under her eyes and a streak of mud across her cheek, but she hadn't complained once through the entire march. In fact, she had been very quiet ever since the fight with the lindwurm.

She saw me looking and managed a tired smile, bumping her shoulder against mine. "So, we're almost there, huh?" she said, brushing a strand of hair from her face. "I hope it's less…woodsy than this place. Do you know much about it?"

"Unfortunately," I muttered. Machina's tower, the gremlins, the iron knights, the stark, blasted wasteland. I remembered it all as if it was yesterday. "It's not as woodsy, but the Iron Realm isn't pleasant, either. It's where the Iron fey live."

"See, that's where I'm confused," Kenzie said, shifting to face me. "Everything I researched said faeries are allergic to iron." She held up the iron key. "That's why this thing worked so well, right?"

"Yes," I said. "And they are. At least, the normal faeries are. But the Iron fey are different. The fey—the entire Nevernever, actually—comes from us, from our dreams and imagination, as cheesy as that sounds. The traditional faeries are the ones you read about in the old myths—Shakespeare and the Grimm Brothers, for example. But, during the past hundred years or so, we've been…er…dreaming of other things. So, the Iron fey are a little more modern."

"Modern?"

"You'll see when we get there."

"Huh," Kenzie said, considering. "And you said the place is ruled by a queen?"

"Yeah," I said, quickly standing up. "The Iron Queen."

"Any idea what *she's* like?" Kenzie stood, too, unaware of my burning face. "I've read about Queen Mab and Titania, of course, but I've never heard of the Iron Queen."

"I dunno," I lied and walked over to Grimalkin, who was watching with amused golden eyes, the hint of a smile on his whiskered face. I shot a warning glare at the feline, hoping he would remain silent. "Come on, cat. The sooner we get there, the sooner we can leave."

We started off again, pushing through the trees, following the seemingly tireless cait sith as he glided through the undergrowth. Kenzie walked next to me, her eyes weary and dull, barely looking up from the ground. A tiny faery with a mushroom cap peeked at us from a nearby branch, but she didn't even glance at it a second time. Either the overwhelming weirdness of the Nevernever had driven her to a kind of numb acceptance or she was too tired to give a crap.

The tangled woods started to thin as the gray twilight was finally fading, giving way to night. Fireflies or faery lights began appearing through the trees, blinking yellow, blue and green.

Grimalkin stopped at the base of a tall black tree and turned to face us. I frowned as he swatted at a blue light, which zipped off into the woods with a buzz.

"Why are we stopping? Shouldn't we get out of the wyld-wood before night falls and the really nasty things start coming out?"

"You do not know where you are, do you?" Grimalkin purred. I gave him an irritated look, and he yawned. "Of course not. This," he stated, waving his tail languidly, "is the border of the Iron Realm. You are at the very edge of the Iron Queen's territory."

"What, right here?" I looked around but couldn't see anything unusual. Just black woods and a few blinking lights. "How can you tell? There's nothing here."

"One moment," the cat mused, a smug grin in his voice. "It should not be long."

I sighed. "We don't really have time for…"

I trailed off, as the tree behind Grimalkin flickered, then blazed with light. Kenzie gasped as neon lights erupted along the branches, like Christmas bulbs or those fiberglass trees in department stores. There were no wires or extension cords; the bulbs were growing right out of the branches. As the tree lit up, a swarm of multicolored fireflies spiraled up from the leaves and scattered to all parts of the forest, drifting around us like stray fireworks.

I blinked, dazzled by the display. Around us, the trees glimmered silver; trunks, leaves, branches and twigs shining as if they were made of polished metal. They reflected the drifting lights and turned the woods into a swirling galaxy of stars.

"Ethan," Kenzie breathed, staring transfixed at her arm. A tiny green bug perched on her wrist, blinking erratically. Its fragile body glittered in its own light, metallic and shiny, before it buzzed delicate transparent wings and zipped away into the woods. Kenzie held up her hand, and several more tiny lights hovered around her, landing on her fingers and making them glow.

For a second, I couldn't look away. My heartbeat picked up, and my mouth was suddenly dry, watching the girl in the center of the winking cloud, smiling as the tiny lights landed in her hair or perched on her arm.

She was beautiful.

"Okay," I muttered, tearing my gaze away before she noticed I was staring, "I can admit it—that's pretty cool."

Grimalkin sniffed. "So pleased you approve," he said. I frowned at him through the swirling lights, waving away several bugs drifting around my face. It occurred to me that we were on our own, now. Like the rest of the normal fey, Grimalkin couldn't set foot in the Iron Realm. Meghan's kingdom was still deadly to the rest of the Nevernever—only the Iron fey could live there without poisoning themselves. Grimalkin was showing us the border because he planned to leave us here.

"How far to the Iron Queen from here?" I asked.

The cat flicked a bug off his tail. "Still a few days by foot. Do not worry, though. Beyond this rise is a place that will take you to Mag Tuiredh, the site of the Iron Court, much faster than humans can walk."

"I suppose this is where you leave," I said.

"Do not be ridiculous, human." The cat yawned and stood up. "Of course I am coming with you. Besides your being highly amusing, the favor dictates that I see you all the way to Mag Tuiredh and dump you at the Iron Queen's feet. After that, you become her problem, but I will see you there, first."

"You can't go into the Iron Realm. It'll kill you."

Grimalkin gave me a bored look, turned and stalked off. Past the border and into the Iron Realm.

I hurried after him, Kenzie on my heels. "Wait," I said, catching up to him, frowning. "I *know* the Iron Realm is deadly to normal fey. How are you doing this?"

Grimalkin paused, looking over his shoulder with glowing, half-lidded eyes. His tail waved lazily. "There are things about this world that you do not realize, human," he purred. "Events that took place years ago, when the Iron Queen rose to power, still shape this world today. You do not know as much as you think you do. Besides…" He blinked, raising his head imperiously. "I am a cat."

And that was the end of it.

The fireflies continued to light up the forest as we walked on, blinking through leaves and branches, glinting off the trunks. Trees with flickering light bulbs illuminated the path to wherever Grimalkin was taking us. Kenzie kept staring at them, the amazement and disbelief back on her face.

"This…is impossible," she murmured once, brushing her fingers over a glittering trunk. Small glowing bulbs sprouted overhead like clusters of Christmas lights. Streetlamps grew right out of the dirt, lighting the path. "How…how can this be real?"

"This is the Iron Realm," I told her. "It's still Faery, just a different flavor of crazy."

Before she could answer, the trees fell away, and we found ourselves at the top of a rise, staring down at the lights of a small village on the edge of a massive lake. It looked sort of like a gypsy town or a carnival, all lit up with torches and strings of colored lights. Thatched huts stood on posts rising out of the water, and wooden bridges crisscrossed the spaces between. Creatures of all shapes and sizes roamed the walkways above the water.

At the edge of the town, a railroad arched away over the lake, vanishing to a point somewhere on the horizon.

"What is this place?" I muttered, as Kenzie pressed close to my back, peering over my shoulder. Grimalkin sat down and curled his tail over his feet.

"This is a border town, one of many along the edge of the Iron Realm. I forget its exact name, if it even has one. Many Iron fey gather here, for one reason." He raised a hind leg and scratched an ear. "Do you see the railroad, human?"

"What about it?"

"That will take you straight to Mag Tuiredh, the site of the Iron Court and the seat of the Iron Queen's power. It costs nothing to board, and anyone may use it. The railroad was one of the first improvements the queen made when she took the throne. She wished for everyone to have a safe way to travel to Mag Tuiredh from anywhere in the Iron Realm."

"We're going down there?" Kenzie asked, her eyes big as she stared at the creatures roaming about the bridges. Grimalkin sniffed.

"Do you see another way to get to the railroad, human?"

"But...what about the faeries?"

"I doubt they will bother you," the cat replied, unconcerned. "They see many travelers through this part of town. Do not speak to anyone, get on the train, and you will be fine." He raised a hind leg to scratch his ear. "That is where I will meet you, when you finally decide to show up."

"You're not coming?"

Grimalkin curled his whiskers in distaste. "Outside of Mag Tuiredh, I try to avoid contact with the denizens of the Iron Realm," he said in a lofty voice. "It circumvents tiresome, unnecessary questions. Besides, I cannot hold your hands the entire way to the Iron Queen." He sniffed and stood up, waving his tail. "The train will arrive soon. Do try not to miss it, humans."

Without another word, he disappeared.

Kenzie sighed, muttering something about impossible felines. And I realized, suddenly, that she looked very pale and tired in the moonlight. There were shadows under her eyes, and her cheeks looked hollow, wasted. Her normal boundless energy seemed to have deserted her as she rubbed her arm and gazed down the slope, shivering in the cold breeze.

"So," she said, turning to me. Even her smile looked weary as she stood at the edge of the rise, the wind ruffling her hair. "Head into the creepy faery town, talk to the creepy faery conductor and board the creepy faery train, because a talking cat told us to."

"Are you all right?" I asked. "You don't look so good."

"Just tired. Come on, let's go already." She backed up a step, avoiding my eyes, but as she turned, I saw something in the moonlight that made my stomach clench.

"Kenzie, wait!" Striding forward, I caught her arm as gently as I could. She tried squirming from my grip, but I pulled back her sleeve to reveal a massive purple stripe, stretching from her shoulder almost to her elbow. A dark, sullen blotch marring her otherwise flawless skin.

I sucked in a horrified breath. "When did you get this?" I demanded, angry that she hadn't told me, and that I hadn't noticed it until now. "What happened?"

"It's fine, Ethan." She yanked her arm back and tugged her sleeve down. "It's nothing. I got it when we were fighting the lindwurm thing."

"Why didn't you say anything?"

"Because it's not a big deal!" Kenzie shrugged. "Ethan, trust me, I'm all right. I bruise easily, that's all." But she didn't look at me when she said it. "I get them all the time, now can we please go? Like Grim said, we don't want to miss the train."

"Kenzie…" But she was already gone, dropping down the rise without looking back, striding merrily toward the lights and the railroad and the town of Iron fey. I blew out a frustrated breath and hurried to catch up.

After picking our way down the slope, we entered the town. Kenzie gazed around in wonder, her weariness forgotten, while I gripped my rattan and tensed every time something came near.

Iron fey surrounded us, weird, crazy and nightmarish. Creatures made entirely of twisted wire. A well-dressed figure in a top hat, holding the leash of a ticking clockwork hound. An old woman with the body of a giant spider scuttled past, her metallic, needlelike legs clicking over the wood. Kenzie let out a squeak and squeezed my hand, nearly crushing my fingers, until the spider-thing had disappeared.

We were getting stared at. Despite what Grimalkin said, the Iron fey *were* taking notice of us, and why not? It wasn't every day two humans strolled through their town, looking decidedly mortal and un-fey. Strangely enough, no one tried to stop us as we maneuvered the swaying bridges and walkways, passing shacks and odd-looking stores, feeling glowing fey eyes on my back.

Until we reached a large, circular deck where several walkways converged. I could see the railroad at the edge of town, stretching out over the lake. But as we headed toward it, a hunched figure dressed in rags suddenly reached out and grabbed Kenzie's wrist as she passed, making her yelp.

I spun, whipping my rattan down, striking the arm that held her, and the faery let go with a raspy cry. Shaking its fingers, it crept forward again, and I shoved Kenzie behind me, meeting the faery with my sticks raised.

"Humans," it hissed, and several rusty screws dropped out of its rags as it circled. "Humans have something for me, yes? A pocket watch? A lovely phone?" It raised its head, revealing a face put together with bits and pieces of machinery. One eye was a glowing bulb, the other the head of a copper screw. A mouth made of wires smiled at us as the thing eased forward. "Stay," it urged, as Kenzie recoiled in shock. "Stay and share."

"Back off," I warned, but a crowd was forming now, fey that had simply been watching before easing forward. They surrounded us on the platform, not lunging or attacking, but preventing us from going any farther. I kept an eye on both them and the machine-scrap faery; if they wanted a fight, I'd be happy to oblige.

"Stay," urged the faery in rags, still circling us, smiling. "Stay and talk. We help each other, yes?"

A piercing whistle rent the air, drawing the attention of several fey. Moments later, an enormous train appeared over the lake, trailing billowing clouds of smoke as it chugged closer. Bulky and massive, leaking smoke and steam everywhere, it pulled into the station with a roar and a screech of rusty gears before shuddering to a halt.

Several faeries began making their way toward the huge, smoking engine, as a copper-skinned faery in a conductor's uniform stepped out front, waving them forward. The crowd thinned a bit, but not enough.

"Dammit, I don't want to have to fight our way out," I growled, keeping an eye on the fey surrounding us. "But we need to get to that train now." The faery in rags eased closer, as if he feared we would turn and run. "This one isn't going to let us go," I said, feeling my muscles tense, and gripped my weapons. "Kenzie, stay back. This could get ugly."

"Wait." Kenzie grabbed my sleeve, a second before I would've lunged forward and cracked the fey in the skull. Pulling me to the side, she stepped forward and stripped off her camera. "Here," she told the ragged fey, holding it out. "You want a trade, right? Is this good enough?"

The Iron faery blinked, then reached out and snatched the camera, wire lips stretched into a grin. "Ooooh," it cooed, clutching it to its chest. "Pretty. So generous, little human." It shook the camera experimentally and frowned. "Broken?"

"Um…yeah," Kenzie admitted, and I tensed, ready to step in with force if the thing took offense. "Sorry."

The faery grinned again. "Good trade!" it rasped, tucking the camera into its robes. "Good trade. We approve. Luck on your travels, little humans."

With a hissing cackle, it hobbled down a walkway and vanished into the town.

The crowd began to disperse, and I slowly relaxed. Kenzie

pushed her hair back with a shaking hand and sighed in relief. "Well, there go the pictures for this week's sports article," she said wryly. "But, if you think about it, that camera has more than paid for itself today. I'm just sad no one will get to see your mad kali skills."

I lowered my sticks. That was twice now that Kenzie's quick thinking had gotten us out of trouble. Another few seconds, and I would've been in a fight. With a faery. In the middle of a faery town.

Not one of my smarter moments.

"How did you know what it wanted?" I asked as we headed toward the station again. Kenzie gave me an exasperated look.

"Really, Ethan, you're supposed to know this stuff. Faeries like gifts, all the Google articles say so. And since we don't have any jars of honey or small children, I figured the camera was the best bet." She chuckled and rolled her eyes at me. "This doesn't have to be a fight all the way to the Iron Queen, tough guy. Next time, let's try talking to the faeries before the sticks come out."

I would've said something, except...I was kind of speechless.

We boarded the train without trouble, receiving only a brief glare from the conductor, and made our way to a deserted car near the back. Hard wooden pews sat under the windows, but there were a few private boxes as well, and after a few minutes of searching, we managed to find an empty one. Sliding in behind Kenzie, I quickly shut the doors, locked them and lowered the blind over the window.

Kenzie sank down on one of the benches, leaning against the glass. I followed her gaze, seeing the glittering metal of the tracks stretch out over the dark waters until they were lost from view.

"How long do you think it'll be before we're there?" Kenzie asked, still gazing out the window. "What is this place called again?"

"Mag Tuiredh," I replied, sitting beside her. "And I don't know. Hopefully not long."

"Hopefully," Kenzie agreed, and murmured in a softer voice, "I wonder what my dad is doing right now?"

With a huff, the train began to move, chugging noisily at first, then smoothing out as it picked up speed. The lights of the village fell away until nothing could be seen outside the window but the flat, silvery expanse of the lake and the stars glittering overhead.

"I hope Grimalkin made it on," Kenzie said, her voice slurred and exhausted. She shifted against the window, crossing her arms. "You think he's here like he said he would be?"

"Who knows?" I watched her try to get comfortable for a few seconds, then scooted over, closing the distance between us. "Here," I offered, pulling her back against my shoulder. With everything she'd done for us, the least I could do was let her sleep. She leaned into me with a grateful sigh, soft strands of hair brushing my arm.

"I wouldn't worry about the cat," I went on, shifting to give her a more comfortable position. "If he made it, he made it. If not, there's nothing we can do about it."

She didn't say anything for a while, closing her eyes, and I pretended to watch the shadows outside the window, hyper-aware of her head on my shoulder, her slim hand on my knee.

"Mool onyurleg, m'surry," Kenzie mumbled, sounding half-asleep.

"What?"

"I said, if I drool on your leg, I'm sorry," she repeated. I chuckled at that, making her crack an eye open.

"Oh, wow, the broody one can laugh after all," she murmured, one corner of her mouth curling up. "Maybe we should alert the media."

Smirking, I looked down, ready to give a smart-ass reply.

And suddenly, my breath caught at how close our faces were, her lips just a few inches from mine. If I ducked my head just slightly, I would kiss her. Her hair was brushing my skin, the feathery strands tickling my neck, and the fingers on my leg were very warm. Kenzie didn't move, continuing to watch me with a faint smile. I wondered if she knew what she was doing, or if she was waiting to see what I would do.

I swallowed and carefully tilted my head back, removing the temptation. "Go to sleep." I told her. She sniffed.

"Bossy." But her eyes closed, and a few minutes later, a soft snore escaped her parted lips. I crossed my arms, leaned back, and prepared for a long, uncomfortable ride to Mag Tuiredh.

When I opened my eyes, it was light, and the sky through the window was mottled with sun and clouds. Groggily, I scanned the rest of the car, wondering if any faeries had crept up on us while I was asleep, but it seemed we were still alone.

My neck ached, and part of my leg was numb. I had drifted off with my chin on my chest, arms still crossed. I started to stretch but froze. Kenzie had somehow curled up on the tiny bench and was sleeping with her head on my leg.

For a few seconds, I watched her, the rise and fall of her slim body, the sun falling over her face. Seeing her like that filled me with a fierce protectiveness, an almost painful desire to keep her safe. She mumbled something and shifted closer, and I reached down, brushing the hair from her cheek.

Realizing what I was doing, I pulled my hand back, clenching my fists. Dammit, what was happening to me? I could not be falling for this girl. It was dangerous for the both of us. When we did go back to the mortal world, Kenzie would return to her old life and her old friends and her family, and I would do the same. She did not need someone like me hanging around, someone who attracted chaos and misery, who couldn't stay out of trouble no matter how hard he tried.

I'd already ruined one girl's life. I would not do that again. Even if I had to make her hate me, I would not do to Kenzie what I'd done to Sam.

"Hey," I said, jostling her shoulder. "Wake up."

She groaned, hunching her shoulders against my prodding. "Two more minutes, Mom."

It was mean, but I scooted away from her, letting her head thump to the bench. "Ow!" she yelped, sitting up and rubbing her skull. "What the hell, Ethan?"

I nodded out the window, ignoring the immediate stab of remorse. "We're almost there."

Kenzie still frowned at me, but when she looked out the glass, her eyes went wide.

Mag Tuiredh. The Iron Court. I'd never been there, never seen it. I'd only learned of the city from stories, rumors I'd heard over years of existing among the fey. Meghan herself had never told me where she lived and ruled from, though I'd asked her countless times before she disappeared. She didn't want me to know, to imagine it, to get ideas in my head that might lead me there, looking for her.

I had imagined it, of course. But as an ugly monstrosity, the images tainted by the memory of a stark black tower in the center of a blasted wasteland. The city at the end of the railroad tracks was anything but.

It was old, even from this distance, I could see that. Stone walls and mossy roofs, vines coiled around everything. Trees pushing up through rock, roots draped and curled around stone. Some of the buildings were huge—massively huge.

Not sprawling so much as they looked as if they were built by a race of giants.

But the city *gleamed,* too. Sunlight glinted off metal spires, lights glimmered in the haze and steam, glass windows caught the faint rays and reflected them back into the sky. It reminded me of a city under construction, with sleek metal towers rising up among the ancient moss- and vine-covered buildings. And above it all, gleaming spires stabbing into the clouds, the silhouette of a huge castle stood proud and imposing over Mag Tuiredh, like a glittering mountain.

The home of the Iron Queen.

The train came to a wheezing, clanking, chugging halt at the station. Gazing out the window, I narrowed my eyes. There were a lot more Iron fey here than at the tiny border town on the lake, a lot of guards and faeries in armor. Knights with the symbol of a great iron tree on their breastplates stood at attention or roamed the streets in pairs, keeping an eye on the populace.

"Well?" came a familiar voice from behind us, and we jerked around. Grimalkin sat on the bench across from us, watching us lazily. "Are you just going to sit there until the train starts moving again?"

"Where do we go from here?" Kenzie asked, peeking out the window again. "I guess we can't hail a taxi, right?"

Grimalkin sighed.

"This way," he said, walking along the edge of the bench before dropping to the ground. "I will take you to the Iron Queen's palace."

The palace, I thought, as we followed Grimalkin down the aisle toward the doors up front. I knew the huge castle must be hers. It was just hard to imagine Meghan living in a palace now. *Must be nice. Better than a rundown farmhouse or little home in the suburbs, anyway.*

Following Grimalkin, we stepped through the doors and walked down the steps into the hazy streets of Mag Tuiredh.

Aside from the crowds of fey, it was difficult to believe we were still in the Nevernever. Mag Tuiredh reminded me a little of Victorian England—the steampunk version. The streets were cobblestone and lined with flickering lanterns in hues of blue and green. Carriages stood at the edge of the sidewalks, pulled by strange, mechanical horses of bright metal and copper gears. Buildings crowded the narrow streets, some stony and vine-ridden and Gothic, others decidedly more modern. Pipes crisscrossed the sky overhead, leaking steam that trickled to the ground in lacy curtains. And, of course, there were the Iron fey, looking as if they'd stepped straight out of an alchemist's nightmare.

They stared at us as if *we* were the nightmares, the monsters, watching and whispering as we trailed Grimalkin through the cobblestone paths. The cat was nearly invisible in the haze and falling steam, as difficult to glimpse as a shadow in the wyldwood. I kept a tight grip on my weapons, glaring back at any fey who gave me a funny look. We were even more conspicuous here than we'd been at the border village. I hoped we could get to Meghan before anyone stepped up to challenge the two humans strolling through the middle of the faery capital.

Yeah, that wasn't going to happen.

As we passed beneath a stone archway, clanking footsteps rang out and a squad of faery knights stepped up to block our path. Weapons drawn, they surrounded us, a ring of bristling steel, their faces cold and hard beneath their helmets. I pulled Kenzie close, trying to keep her behind me, swinging my own weapons into a ready stance. Grimalkin, I noticed, had disappeared, and I cursed him under my breath. Fey gathered behind the knights, watching and murmuring, as the tension swelled and unspoken violence hung thick on the air.

"Humans." A knight stepped forward, pointing at me with his sword. He had a sharp face, pointed ears, and was covered head to toe in plate mail. His expression beneath the open helmet was decidedly unfriendly. "How did you get into Mag Tuiredh? Why are you here?"

"I'm here to see the Iron Queen," I returned, not lowering my weapons, though I had no idea what I could do against so many armored knights. I didn't think beating on them with a pair of wooden sticks would penetrate that thick steel. Not to mention, they had very sharp swords and lances, all pointed in our direction. "I don't want any trouble. I just want to talk to Meghan. If you tell her I'm here—"

An angry murmur went through the ranks of fey. "You cannot just walk into the palace and demand an audience with the queen, mortal," the knight said, swelling indignantly. "Who are you, to demand such things, to speak as if you know her?" He leveled his sword at my throat before I could reply. "Surrender now, intruders. We will take you to the First Lieutenant. He will decide your fate."

"Hold!" ordered a voice, and the knights straightened immediately. The ranks parted, and a faery came through, glaring at them. Instead of armor, he wore a uniform of black and gray, the silhouette of the same iron tree on his shoulder. His spiky black hair bristled like porcupine quills, and neon strands of lightning flickered and snapped between them.

As he came into the circle, he nodded to me in a genuine show of respect, before turning on the knight. Violet eyes glimmered as he stared him down. "What is the meaning of this?"

"First Lieutenant!" The knight jerked to attention as the

rest of the knights did the same. "Sir! We have apprehended these two mortal intruders. They were on their way to the palace, saying they wished an audience with the Iron Queen. We thought it best if we brought them to you. The boy claims to know her—"

"Of course he does!" the faery snapped, scowling, and the knight paled. "I know who he is, though it is apparent that you do not."

"Sir?"

"Stand down," said the First Lieutenant, and raised his voice, addressing all the faeries watching this little spectacle. "All of you, stand down! Bow to your prince!"

Uh. What?

CHAPTER THIRTEEN

THE IRON PRINCE

"Prince?"

I could feel Kenzie's disbelieving stare as all the fey surrounding us, knights, civilians and guards alike, lowered their heads and bent at the waist or sank to their knees. Including the First Lieutenant, who put a fist over his heart as he bowed. I wanted to tell them all to stop, to not bother, but it was too late.

Oh, great. I can already hear the questions this *is going to bring on.*

"Prince Ethan," the lieutenant said, straightening again. The knights sheathed their weapons, and a glare from a few of the armored fey quickly dispersed the crowd. "This is a surprise. Please excuse my guards. We were not expecting you. Are you here to see your sister?"

"Sister?" Kenzie echoed behind me, her voice climbing several octaves. I resisted the urge to groan.

"It's…Glitch, right?" I asked, dragging the name up from memory. Glitch was something of a legend even in the real world, the rebel Iron faery who'd joined with Meghan in defeating the false king. I'd seen him once or twice in the past, hanging around the house like a worried bodyguard when Meghan came to visit. I didn't mind his presence that much; it was another figure I hated, another faery who sometimes waited in the shadows for his queen to return, who never came into the house. He was a legend, too, even more so than Glitch, as one of the three who had taken down the false king and stopped the war. He was also the only normal fey (besides Grimalkin, apparently) who could survive in the Iron Realm. The rumors of how he'd accomplished such an impossible task were long and varied, but the reason behind it was always the same. Because he'd fallen in love with the Iron Queen and would do anything to be with her.

Including take her away from her family, I thought as the old, familiar anger spread through my chest. *Including making sure she never leaves Faery. It's because of you that she stayed, and it's because of you that she's gone. If you hadn't shown up that night to take her back, she would still be in the real world.*

But Glitch was still waiting for an answer and probably wouldn't appreciate my feelings concerning his boss. "Yeah, I came to see Meghan," I said, shrugging. "Sorry, we couldn't call ahead of time. She probably doesn't know I'm here."

Glitch nodded. "I will inform her majesty right away. If you and your…friend—" the faery lieutenant glanced at Kenzie "—would come with me, I will take you to the Iron Queen."

He gestured for us to follow, and we trailed him down the cobblestone paths as crowds of iron fey parted for us, bowing as we passed. The knights fell into rank behind us, their clanking echoing through the streets. I tried to ignore them and the way my stomach squirmed with every step that brought us closer to the palace and the Iron Queen.

"If you don't mind my asking, sire," Glitch continued, glancing back. His purple eyes regarded us with curious appraisal. "How did you cross over from the mortal world?"

"My doing," purred another familiar voice, and Grimalkin appeared, walking along the edge of a stone wall. Glitch looked up and sighed.

"Hello again, cat," he said, not sounding entirely pleased.

"Why am I not surprised to see you involved? What have you been scheming lately?"

The cat very deliberately ignored that question, pretending to be occupied with the tiny glittering moths that flitted around the streetlamps. Glitch shook his head, making the lightning in his hair flicker, then stopped at a corner and raised an arm.

A horse and carriage pulled up, both looking decidedly mechanical, the horse's body made of shifting copper gears and bright metal. The driver, green-skinned beneath his black-and-white coat, tipped his top hat at us. The clockwork dog sitting beside him thumped a wiry tail.

Grimalkin observed the carriage from atop the stone wall and wrinkled his nose.

"I believe I will find my own way to the palace," he stated, blinking in a bored manner as he looked down at me. "Human, please attempt to stay out of trouble for the last leg of the journey. Mag Tuiredh is not *that* big a place to become lost in. Do not make me have to come find you again."

Glitch's spines bristled. "I will make sure the prince gets to the palace, cait sith," he snapped, sounding indignant. "Any kin of the Iron Queen in Mag Tuiredh becomes my top priority. He will be perfectly safe here, I assure you."

"Oh, well, if you say so, Lieutenant, then it must be true." With a sniff, the cat disappeared, dropping off the wall and vanishing midleap.

Sighing, Glitch pulled open the door and nodded for us to get in. I climbed aboard, and Kenzie followed as the First Lieutenant helped her up the steps, then closed the door behind us.

"I will ride ahead and meet you at the palace," he told us through the window, and stepped back to the curb. "The queen will be informed of your arrival right away. Welcome to Mag Tuiredh, Prince Ethan."

He bowed once more, and the carriage started to move, taking his figure from sight. I stared out the window, watching the city of Mag Tuiredh scroll by, feeling Kenzie's gaze piercing my back. I knew it wouldn't be long before she started asking questions, and I was right.

"Prince?" she said softly, and I closed my eyes. "You're the prince of this place? You never told me that."

I sighed, turning to meet her bewildered, accusing gaze. "I didn't think it was important."

"Not *important?*" Kenzie's eyes bugged, and she threw up her hands. "Ethan, you're a freaking prince of Faeryland, and you didn't think that was important?"

"I'm not a real prince," I insisted. "It's not like you think. I'm not part faery, I'm just...related to the queen." Kenzie stared at me, waiting, and I stabbed my fingers through my hair. "The Iron Queen..." I sighed again and finally came out with it. "She's my half sister, Meghan."

Her mouth dropped open. "And you couldn't have mentioned that earlier?"

"No, I didn't want to talk about it!" I turned away to stare out the window again. Mag Tuiredh looked both bright and dark in the hazy light, a glittering realm of shadows and steam, stone and metal. "I haven't seen Meghan in years," I said in a quieter voice. "I don't know what she's like anymore. She told me to stay away from her, that she was cutting my whole family out of her life. Comes with being a faery queen, I guess." I heard the bitterness in my voice and struggled to control it. "I didn't want you to associate me with...Them," I told Kenzie. "Not like that."

Kenzie was quiet for a moment. Then, "So...when you were kidnapped, and your sister went into the Nevernever to rescue you..."

"Long story short, she became the Iron Queen, yeah."

"And…you blame them for taking her away. That's why you hate them."

My throat felt suspiciously tight. I swallowed hard to open it. "No," I growled, clenching my fist against the window-sill. "I blame her."

The Iron Queen's palace soared over the rest of the build-ings in the city, a huge pointed structure of glass, stone and steel. Banners emblazoned with the great iron tree flapped in the wind, and the path to the front gate was lined with enor-mous oaks, forming a tunnel of branches, leaves and lights. It was the strangest castle I'd ever seen, not really ancient or completely modern but caught somewhere between the two. It had mossy stone turrets, crawling with vines, but also tow-ers of shining glass and steel, catching the sunlight as they stabbed toward the sky. A pair of Iron knights bowed their heads as the carriage rolled through the gate into the court-yard, so apparently we were expected.

Past the gates, the road circled a massive green lawn strewn with metal trees, their leaves and branches glittering like tinsel as the light caught them. The stone walls of the castle rose up on either side, patrolled by more Iron knights. A small pond sat in the center of the courtyard, making me wonder what kind of fish swam beneath those waters. Iron goldfish, per-haps? Metallic turtles? I smirked at the thought.

Movement under one of the trees caught my attention. Two figures circled each other beneath the branches of a silver pine, a pair of swords held in front of them. One was easily rec-ognizable as an Iron knight, his armor and huge broadsword gleaming as he bore down on his opponent.

The other combatant was smaller, slighter and not wear-ing any armor as he danced around the much larger knight. He looked about my age, with bright silver hair tied back in a ponytail and an elegant curved blade in his hand.

And he knew how to move. Long years of watching Guro Javier made me appreciate a skilled fighter when I saw one. This kid reminded me of him: flowing, agile, deadly accurate. The knight lunged at him, stabbing at his head. He stepped aside, disarmed the knight faster than thought and pointed the blade at his throat.

Damn. He might even be faster than me.

As the carriage clopped past the fighters, the boy raised a hand to his opponent and turned to watch us.

The eyes under his silver brows were far too bright, a piercing ice-blue that made my skin crawl. He was fey, and *gentry,* that much was certain. I didn't need to see the tips of his pointed ears to know that. He watched me with a faint, puzzled smile, until the carriage took us around a bend in the road and he was lost from view.

We came to the steps of the palace and lurched to a halt. A tiny creature with a wrinkled face, carrying an enormous pile of junk on his hunched shoulders, stood waiting with a squad of knights as the carriage clanked and groaned and finally stilled.

"Prince Ethan," it squeaked as we climbed down from the carriage. It had an odd accent, as if English wasn't its first language. "Welcome to Mag Tuiredh. My name is Fix, and I will be your escort to the throne room. Please, come with me. The Iron Queen is expecting you."

My stomach churned, but I swallowed my nervousness and followed the creature across the road, up the steps and through the massive iron doors to the palace.

Things sort of went to hell from there.

Meghan's castle was pretty impressive, even I had to admit. I was expecting it to be old and slightly run-down on the inside, but the interior was bright and cheerful and very modern. Though it did have a few strange features that reminded you that this was still Faery, no matter what. The hallway of trees, for one, with glowing bulbs lighting the way through metal branches. And the computer mice that scurried over the floors on tiny red feet, chased by gremlins and clockwork hounds. One wall was covered in enormous brass and copper gears that, from what I could tell, served no purpose except to fill the air with deafening creaks, ticks and groans.

Kenzie stayed close to me as we followed the Iron faery through the hallways, but she couldn't stop staring at our surroundings, her eyes wide with amazement. I refused to be as captivated, glaring at the Iron fey passing us in the halls, trying to keep track of directions in this huge place. Fix finally led us down a long, brightly lit corridor, where Glitch bowed to me as we passed him in the hall. A pair of massive arching doors stood at the end of the corridor, flanked on all sides by armored knights.

"This is the queen's throne room," Fix explained as we stopped at the doors. "She and the Prince Consort are expecting you. Are you ready?"

My palms felt clammy, my stomach turning cartwheels. I nodded, and Fix pushed both doors open at once.

A huge, cathedral-like room greeted us as we stepped through the frame. Decorative pillars, twisted with vines and coils of tiny lights, soared up to a vaulted glass ceiling that showed off sun and sky. Our footsteps echoed in the empty chamber as we followed the guide down the strip of red carpet. The room was obviously used for large gatherings, but except for me, Kenzie and Fix, the floor appeared empty.

A large metal throne stood on a dais at the end of the room, and I noticed Grimalkin sitting on a corner step, calmly washing a paw. Rolling my eyes, I looked up at the throne itself.

And…there she was. Not sitting on the throne, but standing beside it, her fingers resting lightly on the arm.

My sister, Meghan Chase. The Iron Queen.

She looked exactly as I remembered. Even though it had been years since I'd seen her last, and back then she had been taller than me, she still had the same long, pale hair, the same blue eyes. She even wore jeans and a white shirt, much like she had when she'd lived at home. Nothing had changed. This Meghan could be the same girl who'd rescued me from Machina's tower, thirteen years ago.

My throat ached, and a flood of confusing emotions made my stomach feel tight. I didn't know what I would say to my sister now that I was finally here. *Why did you leave us? Why don't I ever see you anymore?* Useless questions. I already knew the answer, much as I hated it.

"Ethan." Her voice, so familiar, flowed across the room and drew me forward as if I was a little kid once more. Meghan smiled down at me, and any fears I had that she had changed, that she was some distant faery queen, were gone in an instant. Stepping from the dais, she walked up and, without hesitation, pulled me into a tight hug.

The dam broke. I hugged her back tightly, ignoring everyone else in the room, not caring what they thought. This was Meghan, the same Meghan who had looked out for me, who'd gone into the Nevernever to bring me home. And despite my anger, despite all those dark moments when I thought I hated her, she was still my sister.

Come home, I wanted to tell her, knowing it was useless. *Mom and Dad miss you. It's not the same since you left. And I'm tired of pretending you're dead, that I don't have a sister. Why did you always choose them instead of me?*

I couldn't say any of those things, of course. I'd tried, when I was younger, to get her to stay, or to at least visit more often. It had never worked; no matter how much I begged, pleaded or cried, she would always vanish back into the Nevernever,

leaving us behind. I knew she would never abandon her kingdom, not even for family. Not even for me.

Meghan drew back, smiling, holding me at arm's length.
I noticed with a strange thrill that I was taller than her now.
A weird sensation—the last time I'd seen my sister, she'd had
several inches on me. It really had been a long time.

"Ethan," she said again, with such undeniable affection I
instantly felt guilty for thinking the worst of her. "It's good to
see you." One hand rose, brushing hair from my eyes. "God,
you've gotten so tall."

I held her gaze. "And you haven't changed a bit."

Guilt flickered across her face, just for a moment. "Oh,"
she whispered, "you'd be surprised."

I didn't know what she meant by that, but my stomach
twisted. Meghan was immortal now, I reminded myself. She
looked the same, but who knew what she had done in the
time she had been the Iron Queen.

"Regardless," Meghan went on, her expression shifting to
puzzled concern. "Why are you here, Ethan? Grim told me
you were in the Iron Realm, that you had used his token. Is
something wrong at home?" Her fingers tightened on my
arms. "Are Mom and Luke okay?"

I nodded. "They're fine," I said, freeing myself and stepping back. "At least, they were fine when I left."

"How long ago was that?"

"About two days? Faery time?" I shrugged, nodding to the
gray lump of fur on the dais. "Ask him. The cat had us tromping all over the wyldwood. I don't know how long it's been
in the real world."

"They're probably worried sick." Meghan sighed, giving
me a stern look, then seemed to notice Kenzie hovering behind me. She blinked, and her brow furrowed. "And you

brought someone with you." She beckoned Kenzie forward. "Who is this?"

"Kenzie," I replied as the girl stepped around me and dropped into a clumsy curtsy. "Mackenzie St. James. She's one of my classmates."

"I see." I caught the displeasure in her voice, not directed at Kenzie, but that I would bring someone into the Never-never, perhaps. "And did she know anything about us before you dropped her into this world?"

"Oh, sure," I said flatly. "I talk about seeing invisible faeries every day, to whoever will listen. That always goes over so well."

Meghan ignored the jab. "Are you all right?" she asked Kenzie, her voice gentle. "I know it's a lot to take in. I was about your age when I first came here, and it was…interesting, to say the least." She gave her a sympathetic smile. "How are you holding up?"

"I'm okay, your…uh…your majesty," Kenzie said, and jerked her thumb in my direction. "Ethan sort of gave me the crash course in everything Faery. I'm still waiting to see if I wake up or not."

"We'll get you home soon," Meghan promised, and turned back to me. "I assume this visit wasn't just to say 'hi,' Ethan," she said in a firmer voice. "That token was only supposed to be used in emergencies. What's going on?"

"Wish I knew." I crossed my arms defensively. "I didn't want to come here. I would've been perfectly happy never seeing this place again." I paused to see if my words affected her. Except for a slight tightening of her eyes, her expression remained the same. "But there's a bunch of creepy fey hanging around the real world that I've never seen before, and they really didn't give me a choice."

"What do you mean, they didn't give you a choice?"

"I mean they kidnapped a friend of mine, a half-phouka, right from school, in broad daylight. And when I tried to find him, they came after us. Me and Kenzie both."

Meghan's eyes narrowed, and the air around her went still, like the sky before a storm. I could suddenly *feel* the power flickering around the Iron Queen, like unseen strands of lightning, making the hairs on my neck stand up. I shivered and took a step back, resisting the urge to rub my arms.

In that instant, I knew exactly how she had changed.

But the flare of energy died down, and Meghan's voice remained calm as she continued. "So, you came here," she went on, glancing from me to Kenzie and back again. "To escape them."

I nodded shakily.

The Iron Queen regarded me intently, thinking. "And you said they were a type of faery you've never seen before," she questioned, and I nodded again. "A new species, like the Iron fey?"

"No. Not like the Iron fey. These things are…different. It's hard to explain." I thought back to that night at the dojo, the ghostly, transparent faeries, the way they'd flickered in and out, as if they couldn't quite hold on to reality. "I don't know *what* they are, but I think they might be kidnapping exiles and half-breeds." I remembered the dead piskie, and my stomach churned. Todd might already be gone. "A dryad told me all the local fey are disappearing. Something is happening, but I don't know what they want. I don't even know what they are."

"And you're sure of this?"

"These things tried to kill me a couple days ago. Yeah, I'm sure."

"All right," Meghan said, turning from me. "If you say you've seen them, I believe you. I'll call a meeting with Summer and Winter, tell them there could be a new group of fey on the rise. If these faeries are killing off exiles and half-breeds, it could just be a matter of time before they start eyeing the Nevernever." She paced back to her throne, deep in thought. "Mab and Oberon will be skeptical, of course," she said in a half weary, half exasperated voice. "They're going to want proof before they act on anything."

"What about Todd?" I asked.

She turned back with an apologetic look. "I'll put out feelers in the mortal realm," she offered, "see if the gremlins or hacker elves can turn anything up. But my first responsibility is to my own kingdom, Ethan. And you."

I didn't like where this was going. It didn't sound as if she would try terribly hard to find Todd, and why would she? She was a queen who'd just been informed her entire kingdom could be threatened soon. The life of a single half-breed wasn't a high priority.

Meghan glanced at Kenzie, who looked confused but still trying to follow along as best she could. "I'll have someone take you home," she said kindly. "I'm sorry you had to go through all this. You should also be aware that time in the Nevernever flows differently than time in the mortal realm, which means you've probably been missing for several days now."

"Right," said Kenzie, a little breathlessly. "So, I'll have to make up a really good story for when I get home. I don't think 'stuck in Faeryland' is going to go over well."

"Better than the alternative," I told her. "At least you can lie and they'll believe you. After this, my parents aren't going to let me out of the house until I'm thirty."

Meghan gave me a sad smile. "I'll send someone over to explain what's happened," she said, and my nervousness increased. "But Ethan, I can't let you go home just yet. Until we figure out what's going on, I have to ask you to stay here, in Mag Tuiredh."

CHAPTER FOURTEEN
KEIRRAN

"Screw that!"

I glared at Meghan, feeling the walls of the Iron Court close in. She watched me sadly, though her stance and the determined look on her face didn't change.

"No way," I said. "Forget it. You can't keep me here. I have to get home! I have to find Todd. And to see if Mom and Dad are all right. You said it yourself—they're probably going crazy by now."

"I'll send someone to explain what's going on," Meghan said again, her voice and expression unyielding. "I'll go myself, if I must. But I can't send you home yet, Ethan. Not when something out there is trying to kill you."

"I'm fine!" I protested, somehow feeling like a toddler again, arguing to stay up one more hour. "Dammit, I'm not four anymore, Meghan. I can take care of myself."

Meghan's gaze hardened. Striding up to me, she reached out and pulled up my sleeve, revealing the filthy, bloody bandages wrapped around my arm. I jerked back, scowling, but it was too late.

"You're not as invincible as you think, little brother," Meghan said firmly. "And I won't put Mom and Luke through that again. They've been through enough. I can at least tell them that you're safe and that you'll be home soon. Please understand, I don't want to do this to you, Ethan. But you can't leave just yet."

"Try to stop me," I snarled, and whirled around intending to stalk out of the throne room. A stupid move, but my anger—at myself, at the fey, the Nevernever, everything— had emerged full force, and I wasn't thinking rationally. "I'll find my own way home."

I didn't make it out of the room.

A figure melted out of the shadows in the corner, stepping in front of the door, a sharp silhouette against the light. He moved like darkness itself, silent and smooth, dressed all in black, his eyes glittering silver as he blocked my exit. I hadn't noticed him until now, but as soon as he appeared, my gut contracted with hatred and the blood roared in my ears. A memory flickered to life: a scene of moonlight and shadows, and sitting on the couch with Mom and Meghan as the door slowly creaked open, spilling his shadow across the floor. Of this faery, stepping into the room, his eyes only for my sister. He'd said that it was time; he'd spoken of bargains and promises, and Meghan hadn't resisted. She'd followed him out the door and into the night, and from then on, nothing was the same.

I took a deep breath, trying to calm my shaking hands. How many nights in kali had I imagined fighting this very demon, taking my rattan and smashing in his inhumanly pretty face, or stabbing him repeatedly with my knife? Wild fantasies— I stood no chance against someone like him, even I realized that. And I knew Meghan…cared for him. Loved him, even. But this was the fey responsible for the state of our sad, broken family. If he'd never come to our house that night, Meghan would still be home.

she was still the Iron Queen, still fey, and I was a human intruder in her world.

Meghan nodded. "I won't force you," she said, annoying me that Kenzie had a choice and I didn't get one. "Stay if you wish—it might be safer for you here, anyway. Though I'm not sure when this issue will be resolved. You may be with us for some time."

"That's all right." Kenzie glanced at me and smiled bravely. "It's been several days in the real world, right? I might as well stay. I probably can't dig myself any deeper."

Ash moved, gliding into the room to stand by Meghan's side. I noticed he watched her carefully, as if she were the only person in the room, the only presence that mattered. I could be a gnat on the wall for all he cared. "I'll tell Glitch to send a message to the other courts," he said. "With Elysium approaching, we'll need to call this gathering soon."

Meghan nodded. "Grimalkin," she called, and the cat sauntered up, blinking lazily. "Will you please show Ethan and Kenzie to the guest quarters? The rooms in the north wing over the garden should be empty. Ethan..." Her clear blue eyes fixed on me, though they seemed tired and weary now. "For now, just stay. Please. We'll talk later, I promise."

I shrugged, not knowing what to say, and when the silence stretched between us, the queen nodded in dismissal. We followed Grimalkin out of the throne room and into the hall, where the motionless Iron knights lined the corridor. I glanced back at my sister as the doors started to close and saw her standing in the center of the room, one hand covering her face. Ash reached out, silently drawing her into him, and then the doors banged shut, hiding them from view.

You really are a jackass, aren't you? Guilt and anger stabbed at every part of me. *You haven't seen Meghan in years, and when you finally get to talk to her, what do you do? Call her names and try to make her feel guilty. Yeah, that's great, Ethan. Pushing people away is the only thing you know how to do, isn't it? Wonder what Kenzie thinks of you now?*

I stole a glance at her as we made our way down the halls of the Iron Court. Gremlins scuttled over the walls, laughing and making the lights flicker, and Iron knights stood like metal statues every dozen or so feet. I could feel their eyes on us as we passed, as well as the curious stares of the gremlins and every other Iron faery in the castle. If I wanted to get out of here unseen, it was going to be challenging to impossible.

Kenzie saw me looking at her and smiled. "Your sister seems nice," she offered as Grimalkin turned a corner without slowing down or looking back. "Not what I was expecting. I didn't think she would be our age."

I shrugged, grateful for the shift of focus, the chance to talk about something other than what had happened in the throne room. "She's not. Well, technically that's not right. I guess she is, but…" I struggled to explain. "When I saw her last, several years ago, she looked exactly the same. She doesn't age. None of them do. If I live to be a hundred years old, she still won't look a day over sixteen."

"Oh." Kenzie blinked. A strange look crossed her face, that same look I had seen back in Grimalkin's cave; thoughtful and excited, when she should have been disbelieving and terrified. "So, what about us? If we stay in the Nevernever, do we stop aging, too?"

I narrowed my eyes, not liking this sudden interest or the thought of staying here. But Grimalkin, sitting at a pair of doors facing each other across the wide hall, raised his head and yawned.

"Not to the extent that you are immortal," he explained, eying us lazily. "Humans in the Nevernever do age, but at a much slower rate. Sometimes countless years will pass before they notice any signs of decay. Sometimes they remain infants for centuries, and then one day they simply wake up old and withered. It is different for everyone." He yawned again and licked a paw. "But, no, human. Mortals cannot live forever. Nothing lives forever, not even the immortal Fey."

"And don't forget time is screwy here," I added, frowning at the contradiction but deciding to ignore it. "You might spend a year in Faery and go home to find twenty years have passed, or a hundred years. We don't want to stay here any longer than we have to."

"Relax, Ethan. I wasn't suggesting we buy a vacation home in the wyldwood." Kenzie's voice was light, but her gaze was suddenly far away. "I was just…wondering."

Grimalkin sniffed. "Well. Now, I am bored."

He stood, arched his tail over his back as he stretched, and trotted off down the hall. Even before he turned the corner, he vanished from sight.

I eyed the guards stationed very close to the "guest suites," and resentment simmered. "Guess these are our rooms, then," I said, crossing the hall and nudging a door open. It swung back to reveal a large room with a bed against one wall, a fireplace on the other and two giant glass doors leading to a balcony outside. "Fancy," I muttered, letting the door creak shut. "Nicest jail cell I've ever been in."

Kenzie didn't answer. She still stood in the same spot, gazing down the corridor where Grimalkin had vanished, her expression remote. I walked back, but she didn't look at me.

"Hey." I reached out and touched her elbow, and she started. "You all right?"

She took a breath and nodded. "Yeah," she said, a little too brightly. "I'm fine, just tired." She sighed heavily, rubbing her eyes. "I think I'm gonna crash for a bit. Wake me up when they announce dinner or something, okay?"

"Sure."

As I watched her walk toward her room, amazement and guilt clawed at me, fighting an equal battle within. Kenzie was still here. *Why* was she still here? She could've gone home, back to her family and friends and a normal life. Back to the real world. Instead, she'd chosen to stay in this crazy, upside-down nightmare where nothing made sense. I only hoped she would live to regret it.

"Ethan," Kenzie said as I turned away. I looked back, and she smiled from across the hall. "If you need to talk," she said softly, "about anything…I'm here. I'm willing to listen."

My heart gave a weird little lurch. No one had ever told me that, not with any real knowledge of what they were getting into. *Oh, Kenzie. I wish I could. I wish I could…tell you everything, but I won't do that to you. The less you know about Them—and me—the better.*

"To my whining?" I snorted, forcing a half grin. "Very generous of you, but I think I'll be fine. Besides, this is just another way of wheedling an interview out of me, right?"

"Darn, I've become predictable." Kenzie rolled her eyes and pushed her door open. "Well, if you change your mind, the offer still stands. Just knock first, okay?"

I nodded, and her door swung shut, leaving me alone in the hall.

For a moment, I thought about exploring the palace, seeing what my sister's home looked like, maybe checking for possible escape routes. But I had the feeling Meghan was keeping a close eye on me. She was probably expecting me to try something. I caught the impassive gaze of an Iron knight, watching me from the end of the hall, heard the gremlins snickering at me from the ceiling, and resentment boiled. She had no right to keep me here, especially after she was the one who'd left. She had no say in my life.

But they were watching me, a whole realm of Iron fey, making sure I wouldn't do anything against their queen's wishes. I didn't want a pack of gremlins trailing me through the palace, ready to scamper off to warn Meghan. And truthfully, I was exhausted. If I *was* going to pull something off, I needed to be awake and alert to do it.

Ignoring the buzz and snickers of the gremlins, I pushed my door open again. Thankfully, they didn't follow.

The room seemed even larger from inside, the high windows and arched balcony doors filling the air with sunlight. I spared a quick glance outside, confirming that the garden was several stories down and crawling with fey, before flopping back on the bed. My rattan dropped to the carpet, and I left them there, still within easy reach. Lacing my hands behind my head, I stared blankly at the ceiling.

Wonder what Mom and Dad are doing right now? I thought, watching the lines in the plaster blur together, forming strange creatures and leering faces. *They'll probably stick an ankle bracelet on me after this. I wonder if they've called the police yet, or if Mom suspects that I'm here.* I remembered my last words to Mom, snapped out in frustration and anger, and closed my eyes. *Dammit, I have to get back to the real world. Meghan isn't going to look hard for Todd. I'm the only one who has a chance of finding him.*

But there'd be no getting out today. Beyond this room, Meghan's Iron fey would be watching my every move. And I didn't know any trods from the Iron Court back to the real world.

My eyes grew heavy, and the faces in the ceiling blurred and floated off the plaster. I closed my eyes, feeling relatively safe for the first time since coming to the Nevernever, and let myself drift off.

★ ★ ★

A faint tapping sound had me bolting upright.

The room was dark. Silvery light filtered in from the windows, throwing long shadows over the floor. Beyond the glass, the sky was twilight-blue, dotted with stars that sparkled like diamonds. I gazed around blearily, noting that someone had left a tray of food on the table on the opposite wall. The moonlight gleamed off the metallic plate covers.

Swinging myself off the bed, I rubbed my eyes, wondering what had woken me. Maybe it was just a lingering nightmare, or I'd just imagined I'd heard the tap of something against the window....

Looking through the glass, my skin prickled, and I snatched a rattan from the side of the bed. Something crouched on the balcony railing, silhouetted against the sky, peering through the glass with the moonlight blazing down on him. It glimmered off his silver hair and threw his shadow across the balcony and into the room. I saw the gleam of a too-bright eye, the flash of perfectly white teeth as he grinned at me.

It was the faery from the courtyard, the gentry who had been practicing with the knight this afternoon. He was dressed in loose clothing of blue and white, with a leather strap across his chest, the hilt of a sword poking up behind one shoulder. Intense, ice-blue eyes glowed in the darkness as he peered through the glass and waved.

Gripping my weapon, I walked to the balcony doors and yanked them open, letting in the breeze and the sharp scent of metal. The faery still crouched on the railing, perfectly balanced, his elbows resting on his knees and a faint smile on his face. The wind tossed his loose hair, revealing the tips of the pointed ears knifing away from his head. I raised my stick and gave him a hard smile.

"Let me guess," I said, sliding through the door onto the

balcony. "You heard about the human in the castle, so you decided to come by and have a little fun? Maybe give him nightmares or put centipedes in his pillowcase?

The faery grinned. "That wasn't very friendly of me," he said in a surprisingly soft, clear voice. "And here I thought I was dropping by to introduce myself." He stood, easily balancing on the rails, still smiling. "But if you're so sold on me putting centipedes in your bed, I'm sure I can find a few."

"Don't bother," I growled at him, narrowing my eyes. "What do you want?"

"You're Ethan Chase, right? The queen's brother?"

"Who's asking?"

The faery shook his head. "They said you were hostile. I see they weren't exaggerating." He hopped off the railing, landing soundlessly on the veranda. "My name is Keirran," he continued in a solemn voice. "And I was hoping we could talk."

"I have nothing to say to you." Alarm flickered. If this faery had come by to propose a deal, I was beyond not interested. "Let me save you some time," I continued, staring him down. "If the next sentence out of your mouth includes the words *deal*, *bargain*, *contract*, *favor* or anything of the sort, you can leave right now. I don't make deals with your kind."

"Not even if I'm offering a way out of the Iron Realm? Back to the mortal world?"

My heart jumped to my throat. *Back to the mortal world. If I can go home…if I can get Kenzie home, and find Todd… I'd accomplished what I'd come here to do; I'd alerted Meghan to the threat of these new fey, and I doubted she was going to bring me into her inner circle anytime soon, not with her being so adamant about keeping me "safe." I had to get home. If this faery knew a way…*

Shaking my head, I took a step back. *No.* The fey always offered what you wanted the most, tied up in a pretty, sparkling package, and it always came at a high, high price. Too high a price. "No," I said out loud, firmly banishing any temptation to hear him out. "Forget it. Like I said, I don't make deals with you people. Not for anything. I have nothing to offer you, so go away."

"You misunderstand me." The faery smiled, holding up a hand. "I'm not here to bargain, or make a deal or a trade, or anything like that. I simply know a way out of the Iron Realm. And I'm offering to lead you there, free of charge. No obligation whatsoever."

I didn't trust him. Everything I knew was telling me this was some sort of trap, or riddle or faery word game. "Why would you do that?" I asked cautiously.

He shrugged, looking distinctly fey, and leaped onto the railing again. "Truthfully? Mostly because I'm *bored,* and this seems as good a reason to get out of here as any. Besides—" he grinned, and his eyes sparkled with mischief "—you're looking for a half-breed, right? And you said the exiles and half-breeds are disappearing from the mortal realm." I narrowed my eyes, and he made a placating gesture. "Gremlins talk. I listened. You want to find your friend? I know someone who might be able to help."

"Who?"

"Sorry." Keirran crossed his arms, still smiling. "I can't tell you until you've agreed you're coming along. You might go to the queen otherwise, and that would ruin it." He hopped onto one of the posts, inhumanly graceful, and beamed down at me. "Not to brag, but I'm sort of an expert at getting into and out of places unseen. But if we're going to leave, it should be soon. So, what's your answer? Are you coming, or not?"

This still seemed like a bad idea. I didn't trust him, and despite what he said, no faery did anything for free. Still, who knew how long it would take Meghan to figure out what was going on, how long before she would let me go? I might not get another chance.

"All right," I muttered, glaring up at him. "I'll trust you for now. But I'm not leaving Kenzie behind. She's coming with us, no matter what you say."

"I'd already planned for it." Keirran grinned more widely and crouched down on the pole. "Go on and get her, then," he said, looking perfectly comfortable, balanced on the top. "I'll wait for you here."

I drew back, grabbed my other stick from under the bed, and walked to the door, feeling his piercing eyes on me the whole way.

I half expected to find my door locked, despite Meghan's assurances that I was a guest in the palace. But it opened easily, and I slipped into the obscenely bright hallway, lit by glowing lanterns and metallic chandeliers. The guards were still there, pretending not to notice me as I crossed the hall to Kenzie's room.

Her door was closed, but as I lifted my knuckles to tap on it, I paused. Beyond the wood, I could hear faint noises coming from inside. Soft, sniffling, gasping noises. Worried, I reached down and quietly turned the handle. Her door was also unlocked, and it swung slowly inward.

Kenzie sat on the bed with her back to me, head bowed, her delicate shoulders heaving as she sobbed into the pillow held to her chest. Her curtains had been drawn, except for one, and a thin strand of moonlight eased through the crack and fell over her, outlining the small, shaking body.

"Kenzie." Quickly, I shut the door and crossed the room, coming to stand beside her. "Are you all right?" I asked, feeling completely stupid and awkward. Of course she wasn't all right; she was crying her eyes out into her pillow. I fully expected her to tell me to leave, or make some snarky comment that I totally deserved. But she wiped her eyes and took a deep breath, trying to compose herself.

"Yeah," she whispered, hastily rubbing a palm over her cheeks. "Sorry. I'm fine. Just…feeling a little overwhelmed, I guess. I think it's finally caught up to me."

I noticed her keys then, glinting on the mattress, and a small photograph encased in a plastic keychain. Looking to her for permission, I picked it up, making the keys jingle softly, and examined the picture. Kenzie and a small, dark-haired girl of maybe ten smiled up at me, faces close together. Kenzie's arm was raised slightly as if she was holding a camera up in front of them.

"My sister," she explained as I glanced back at her. "Alex. Or Alexandria. I'm not the only one in my family with a long, complicated name." She smiled, but I could see her trying to be brave, to not burst into tears again. "Actually, she's my stepsister. My mom died three years ago, and a year after that Dad remarried. I…I always wanted a sibling…." Her eyes glimmered in the darkness, and her voice caught. "We were supposed to go to the lake house this weekend. But…I don't know what's happening to them now. I don't know if they think I'm dead, or kidnapped or if Alex is waiting up for me to come home——" She buried her face in her pillow again, muffling her sobs, and I couldn't watch any longer.

Putting down the keys, I sat beside her and pulled her into my arms. She leaned against me and I held her quietly as she cried herself out. Dammit, here I was again, thinking only of myself. Why had it come to this before I realized Kenzie had a family, too? That she was just as worried for them as I was for mine?

"You never said anything," I murmured as her trembling subsided, trying not to make it sound like an accusation. "You didn't tell me you had a sister."

A shaky little laugh. "You didn't seem particularly open to listening, tough guy," she whispered back. "Besides, what could we do about it? You were already trying to get us out as fast as you could. Me whining about my home life wasn't going to speed anything up."

"Why didn't you go back this afternoon?" I pulled back to look at her. "Meghan offered to take you home. You could've gone back to your family."

"I know." Kenzie sniffed, wiping her eyes. "And I wanted to. But…we came here together, and I wouldn't have gotten this far…without you." She dropped her head, speaking quietly, almost a whisper. "I'm fully aware that you've saved my life on more than one occasion. With all the weirdness and faery cats and bloodthirsty snake monsters and everything else, I would've been dead if I had to do this by myself. It wouldn't be right, going back alone. And besides, I still have a lot to see here." She looked up at me then, her eyes wide and luminous in the shadows of the room. Her cheeks were tinged with color, though she still spoke clearly. "So, either we get out of here together, or not at all. I'm not leaving without you."

We stared at each other. Time seemed to slow around us, the moonlight freezing everything into a cold, silent portrait. Kenzie's face still glimmered with tears, but she didn't move. Heart pounding, I gently brushed a bright blue strand from her eyes, and she slid a cool hand up to my neck, soft fingers tracing my hairline. I shivered, unsure if I liked this strange, alien sensation twisting the pit of my stomach, but I didn't want it to stop, either.

What are you doing, Ethan? a voice whispered in my head, but I ignored it. Kenzie was watching me with those huge, trusting brown eyes, solemn and serious now, waiting. My heart contracted painfully. I didn't deserve that trust; I knew I should pull away, walk out, before this went too far.

A loud tap on the window made us both jump apart. Rising, I glared out the one open window, where a silver-headed face peered in curiously.

Kenzie yelped, leaping up, and I grabbed her arm. "It's all right!" I told her, as she looked at me in shock. "I know him. He's…here to help."

"Help?" Kenzie repeated, glaring at the fey boy, who waved at her through the glass. "Looks more like spying to me. What does he want?"

"I'll tell you in a second."

I opened the balcony doors, and Keirran ducked into the room. "So," the faery said, smiling as he came in, "Here we all are. I thought something might've happened to you, but if I'd known what was going on, I wouldn't have interrupted." His gaze slid to Kenzie, and his smile widened. "And you must be Kenzie," he said, walking over and taking her hand. But instead of shaking it, he brought her fingers to his lips, and she blushed. I stiffened, tempted to stride over and yank him away, but he dropped her hand before I could move. "My name's Keirran," he said in that soft, confident voice, and I noticed Kenzie gazing up at him with a slightly dazed look on her face. "Has Ethan told you the plan yet?"

Kenzie blinked, then glanced at me, confused. "What plan?"

I stepped between them, and the faery retreated with a faintly amused look. "We're leaving," I told her in a low voice. "Now. We don't have time for Meghan to decide to send us home—we have to find Todd now. Keirran says he knows a way out of the Nevernever. He's taking us back to the mortal world."

"Really?" Kenzie shot the fey boy a look, but it was more of curiosity than distrust. "Are you sure?"

The faery bowed. "I swear on my pointed ears," he said, before straightening with a grin. "But, like you said, we should leave now. While most of the castle is asleep." He gestured out the window. "The trod isn't far. We'll just have to get to it without anyone seeing us. Come on."

I snatched my weapons, gave Kenzie a reassuring nod, and together we followed the faery out the balcony doors onto the veranda. The night air was cool, and the silver moon seemed enormous, hovering so close I could practically see craters and ridges lining the surface. Below us, the garden was quiet, though the moonlight still glinted off the armor of several knights stationed throughout the perimeter.

Kenzie peered over the ledge, then drew back quickly. "There are so many guards," she whispered, looking back at Keirran. "How are we going to make it through without anyone seeing us?"

"We're not going that way," Keirran replied, hopping lightly onto the railing. He gazed up at the roof of the palace, at the great spires and towers lancing toward the sky. Putting two fingers to his lips, he blew out a soft whistle.

A knotted rope flew down from one of the towers, uncoiling in midair, dropping toward us with a faint hiss. Keirran glanced back at me and grinned.

"Hope you're not afraid of heights."

Even with a rope, it was difficult to scale the walls of the Iron Queen's palace. This high up, most of them were sheer metal or glass, making it hard to get a foothold. Keirran, unsurprisingly, moved like a squirrel or a spider, scrambling from ledge to ledge with the obnoxious natural grace of his kind. I had a hard time keeping up, and Kenzie struggled badly, though she never made a sound of complaint. We rested when we could, perched on narrow shelves that gave a stunning view of the city at night. Mag Tuiredh sparkled below us, a glittering carpet of lights and polished edges that reflected the moon. Even I had to admit, Meghan's kingdom was strangely beautiful under the stars.

"Come on," Keirran said encouragingly from a ledge above us. "We're almost there."

Heaving myself up the last wall, I turned and reached over the edge, pulling Kenzie up behind me. Her arms trembled as she took my hand and dragged herself onward, but as she reached the top, her legs gave out and she collapsed.

I caught her as she sagged against me, backing away from the edge. She shivered in my arms, her heart beating way too fast, her skin pale and cold. Wrapping my arms around her, I turned so that my body was between her and the slicing wind, feeling her delicate frame pressed against mine. Her fingers tangled in my shirt, and I wondered if she could feel the pounding beneath her palm.

"Sorry," Kenzie whispered, pulling away, standing on her own. She still kept a slender hand on my chest to steady herself, a tiny spot of warmth in the cold. "I guess a career in rock climbing isn't in my future."

"You don't have to do this," I told her gently, and she gave me a warning look. "You can stay here, and Meghan will send you back home—"

"Don't make me push you off this roof, tough guy."

Shaking my head, I followed her across a narrow rooftop flanked by a pair of towers, the wind whipping at our hair and clothes. Keirran stood a few feet away, talking to what looked like three huge copper and brass insects. Their "wings" looked like the sails on a hang glider, and their long dragonfly bodies were carried on six shiny jointed legs that gleamed in the cold light. As we stared, the creatures' heads turned in our direction, their eyes huge and multifaceted. They buzzed softly.

"These," Keirran said, smiling as he turned back to us,

"are gliders. They're the quickest and easiest way to get out of Mag Tuiredh without being seen. You just have to know how to avoid the air patrols, and luckily, I'm an expert." He scratched one glider on the head as if it was a favorite dog, and the thing cooed in response.

Standing beside me, Kenzie shuddered. "We're flying out of here on giant bugs?" she asked, eyeing the gliders as if they might swarm her any second.

"Be nice," Keirran warned. "They get their feelings hurt easily."

"Master!"

A different sort of buzz went through the air then, and a second later, something small, dark and fast zipped by us, leaping at Keirran with a shrill cry. Keirran winced but didn't move, and the tiny creature landed on his chest, a spindly, bat-eared monster with eyes that flashed electric green. Kenzie jumped and pressed closer to me, whispering: "What is *that*?"

"That's a gremlin," I answered, and she stared at me. "Yeah, it's exactly what you think it is. You know those sudden, un-explainable glitches when something just breaks, or when your computer decides to crash? Say hello to what causes it."

"Not all of them," Keirran said mildly, as the tiny fey scrab-bled to his shoulders, buzzing madly. "Give some credit to the bugs and the worms, too." He held up a hand. "Razor, calm down. Say hi to our new friends."

The gremlin, now perched on Keirran's arm, turned to stare at us with blazing green eyes and started crackling like a bad radio station.

"They can't understand you, Razor," Keirran said mildly. "English."

"Oh," said the gremlin. "Right." It grinned widely, baring a mouthful of sharp teeth that glowed neon-blue. "Hiiiiiiii."

"He knows French and Gaelic, too," Keirran said, as Razor

cackled and bounced on his shoulder. "It's surprisingly simple to teach a gremlin. People just underestimate what they're capable of."

Before we could say anything about this bizarre situation, Keirran plucked the gremlin off his shoulder and tossed it on the glider, where it scrambled to the front and peered out eagerly. "Shall we get going?" he asked, and the glider's wings fluttered in response. "Gliders are easy to control," he continued with absolute confidence, while I gave him a look that implied the exact opposite. "Steer them by pulling on their front legs and shifting your weight from side to side. They'll basically do the rest. Just watch me and do what I do."

He stepped to the edge of the roof and spread his arms. Instantly, the glider picked its way across the roof and crawled up his back, curling its legs around his chest and stomach. He glanced back at us and winked.

"Your turn."

A cry of alarm echoed from somewhere below, making me jump. I peered down and saw a packrat on the balcony of Kenzie's room, looking around wildly.

"Uh-oh," Keirran muttered, sounding remarkably calm. "You've been discovered. If we're going to do this, we need to do it now, before Glitch and the entire air squad is up here looking for us. Hurry!"

Without waiting for an answer, he dove off the building. Kenzie gasped, watching him plunge toward the ground, a streak of silver and gold. Then the glider's wings caught the breeze, and it swooped into the air again, circling the tower. I heard the gremlin's howl of glee, and Keirran waved to us as he soared by.

I glanced at Kenzie. "Can you do this? It's probably just going to get more dangerous from here on out."

Her eyes flashed, and she shook her head. "I already told

you," she said, her voice firm. "We go home together, or not at all. What, you think I'm scared of a couple giant bugs?"

I shrugged. She did look pale and a bit creeped out, but I wasn't going to comment on it. Kenzie frowned and stalked forward, her lips pressed into that tight line again. I watched her walk to the edge of the roof, hesitate just a moment, and spread her arms as Keirran had done. She shook a little as the glider crawled up her back, but she didn't shy away, which was remarkable considering she had a monstrous insect perching on her shoulders. Peering off the roof, she took a deep breath and closed her eyes.

"Just like Splash Mountain at Disneyland," I heard her whisper. Then she launched herself into empty space. She plummeted rapidly, and a shriek tore free, nearly ripped away by the wind, but then the current caught her glider and she rose into the air after Keirran.

My turn. I stepped forward, toward the last glider, but a shout from below made me pause.

"Prince Ethan!" Glitch's head appeared as the First Lieutenant hauled himself up the rope and onto the roof. His hair sparked green and purple lightning as he held out his hand. "Your highness, no!" he cried, as I quickly raised my arms. The glider inched over and crawled up my back, achingly slow. "You can't leave. The queen ordered you to stay. Did Keirran talk you into this? Where is he?"

Glitch knows Keirran, does he? "I'm not staying, Glitch," I called, backing up as the First Lieutenant eased forward. The glider gave an annoyed buzz, hastily wrapping its legs around my middle as I overbalanced it. "Tell Meghan I'm sorry, but I have to go. I can't stay here any longer."

"Ethan!"

I turned and threw myself off the roof, clutching the glider's legs as it plunged toward the ground. For a second, I thought we would smash headfirst into the garden below, but then the glider swooped upward, climbing in a lazy arc, the wind whipping at my face.

Keirran dropped beside me, wearing his careless grin, as Glitch's shouts faded away behind us. "Not bad, for your first time," he said, nodding as Kenzie swooped down to join us. Razor cackled and bounced on his shoulder, huge ears flapping in the wind. "We need to hurry, though," the faery said, glancing behind us. "Glitch will go straight to the queen, and she is *not* going to be happy. With either of us. And if Ash decides to pursue…" For the first time, a worried look crossed his face. He shook it off. "The trod isn't far, but we'll have to cross into the wyldwood to get to it. Follow me."

The gliders were surprisingly fast, and from this height, the Iron Realm stretched out before us, beautiful and bizarre. Far below, the railroad cut through the grassy plateau, snaking between huge iron monoliths that speared up toward the sky and around bubbling pools of lava, churning red and gold in the darkness. We passed mountains of junk, metal parts glinting under the stars, and flew over a swamp where strands of lightning flickered and crawled over oily pools of water, mesmerizing and deadly.

Finally, we soared over a familiar canopy, where the trees grew so close together they looked like a lumpy carpet. Keirran's glider dropped down so that it was nearly brushing the tops of the branches.

"This way," I heard him call, and he dropped from sight, vanishing into the leaves. Hoping Kenzie and I wouldn't fly headfirst into the branches, I followed, passing through the canopy into an open clearing. Darkness closed on us instantly as the light of the moon and stars disappeared and the gloom of the wyldwood rose up to replace it.

I could just make out the bright gleam of Keirran's hair

through the shadows, and spiraled down, dodging branches, until my feet lightly touched the forest floor. As soon as I landed, the glider uncurled its legs and pulled itself up to an overhanging limb, clinging there like a huge dragonfly.

"Well," Keirran said, as Kenzie landed and her glider did the same, hanging next to mine. "Here we are."

An ancient ruin rose up before us, so covered in vines, moss and fungi it was nearly impossible to see the stones beneath. Huge gnarled trees grew from the walls and collapsed ceiling, thick roots snaking around the stones.

"The trod to the mortal realm is inside," Keirran explained, as Kenzie pressed close to me, staring at the ruins in amazement. I was tempted to reach down and take her hand, but I was glad I hadn't when Keirran abruptly drew his sword with a soft rasping sound. I glared at him and drew my weapons as well, putting myself between her and the faery. He glanced over his shoulder with a faintly apologetic look.

"Forgot to tell you," he said, gesturing to the ruin, "this place is normally unoccupied, but it is right in the middle of goblin territory. So, we might run into a few locals who won't be happy to see us. Nothing you can't handle, right?"

"You couldn't have told us earlier?" I growled as we started toward the ruins. Keirran shrugged, his curved steel blade cutting a bright path through the darkness. Razor chattered on his shoulder, only his eyes and neon grin visible in the gloom.

"It's just a few goblins. Nothing to—whoops."

He ducked, and a spear flew overhead, striking a nearby tree. Kenzie yelped, and Razor blipped out of sight like an image on a television screen as a chorus of raucous voices erupted from the ruins ahead. Glowing eyes appeared in the stones and among the roots. Pointed teeth, claws and spear tips flashed in the shadows, as about a dozen short, evil fey poured from the ruins and shook their weapons at us.

"A *few* goblins, huh?" I glared at Keirran and backed away. He grinned weakly and shrugged.

The goblins started forward, cackling and jabbing the air with their spears. I quickly turned to Kenzie and pressed one of my sticks into her hands.

"Take this," I told her. "I'll try to keep them off us, but if any gets too close, smack it as hard as you can. Aim for the eyes, the nose, whatever you can reach. Just don't let them hurt you, okay?"

She nodded, her face pale but determined. "Tennis lessons, don't fail me now." I started to turn, but she caught my wrist, holding it tightly as she gazed up at me. "You be careful, too, Ethan. We're going home together, okay? Just remember that."

I squeezed her hand and turned back to the approaching horde. Keirran was waiting for them calmly, sword in hand.

I joined him, and he gave me a curious look from the corner of his eye. "Interesting," he mused, smiling even as the horde prepared to attack. "I've never seen anyone fight goblins with half a broom handle."

I resisted the impulse to crack him in the head. "Just worry about yourself," I told him, twirling my weapon in a slow arc. "And I'll do the same."

A bigger, uglier goblin suddenly leaped onto a rock and leered at us. "Humans," he rasped with a flash of yellow teeth. "I thought I smelled something strange. You sure picked the wrong spot to stumble into. Trying to get home, are we?" He snickered, running a tongue along his jagged fangs. "We'll save you the trouble."

"We don't have to do this," Keirran said mildly, seemingly unconcerned about the approaching horde. "Surely there are other travelers you can accost."

The goblins edged closer, and I eased into a ready stance, feeling an almost savage glee as they surrounded us. No rules now; no teachers, principals or instructors to stop me. I felt the old anger rise up, the hatred for all of Faery bubbling to the surface, and grinned viciously. There was nothing to hold me back now; I didn't have to worry about hurting anyone. I could take my anger out on the goblins' ugly, warty skulls, and there would be no consequences.

"And miss out on three tasty humans, wandering through my territory?" The goblin chief snorted, shaking his head. "I don't think so. We eat well tonight, boys! Dibs on the liver!"

Cheering, the goblins surged forward.

One charged me with its spear raised, and I swung my rattan, felt my weapon connect beneath the goblin's jaw. It flew back with a shriek, and I instantly slashed down again, cracking another's lumpy green skull. A third goblin scuttled in from the other side, stabbing its spear up toward my face. I dodged, snaked my free arm around the spear, and yanked it out of the faery's grasp. It had a split second to gape in surprise before I bashed the side of its head with its own weapon and hurled it away.

Beside me, Keirran was moving, too, spinning and twirling like a dancer, his sword flashing in deadly circles. Though I couldn't see exactly what he was doing, he was inhumanly fast. Goblin body parts flew through the air, horrific and disgusting, before turning into mud, snails or other unpleasant things.

Three more goblins came at me, one of them the big goblin who'd spoken before, the chief. I shuffled away, blocking their attacks, whipping my rattan from one spear to the next. The frantic clacking of wood echoed in my ears as I waited for an opening, a chance to strike. The goblin's size was actually a handicap for me; they were so short, it was hard to hit them. A spear tip got through my defenses and tore through my sleeve, making me grit my teeth as I twisted away. Too close.

Suddenly, Kenzie was behind them, bringing her stick

smashing down on a goblin's head. It met with a satisfying crack, and the goblin dropped like a stone. Kenzie gave a triumphant yell, but then the chief whirled with a snarl of rage, swinging his spear at her legs. It struck her knee, and she crumpled to the dirt with a gasp.

The chief lunged forward, raising his spear, but before either of us could do anything, a tiny black form landed on his head from nowhere. Razor buzzed like a furious wasp, hissing and snarling as the goblin flailed.

"Bad goblin!" the gremlin howled, clinging like a leech. "Not hurt pretty girl! Bad!" He sank his teeth into the goblin's ear, and the chief roared. Reaching up, the goblin managed to grab the tiny Iron fey, tear him off, and hurl him into the brush.

With a snarl, I kicked a goblin into a stone wall, snatched Kenzie's rattan from the ground, and attacked the chief. I didn't see the other fey. I didn't see Keirran. I forgot everything Guro taught me about fighting multiple opponents. All I knew was that this thing had hurt Kenzie, had tried to kill her, and it was going to pay.

The goblin scuttled backward under my assault, frantically waving his spear, but I knocked it from his claws and landed a solid blow between his ears. As he staggered back, dazed, I pressed my advantage, feeling the crack of flesh and bone under my sticks. My rattan hissed through the air, striking arms, teeth, face, neck. The goblin fell, cringing, in the dirt, and I raised my weapons to finish it off.

"Ethan!"

Keirran's voice brought me up short. Panting, I stopped beating on the goblin and looked up to see that the rest of the tribe had run off with the fall of their chief. Keirran had already sheathed his weapon and was watching me with a half amused, half concerned expression. Kenzie still sat where she had fallen, clutching her leg.

"It's over," Keirran said, nodding to the empty forest around us. "They're gone."

I glanced at my sticks, and saw that my weapons, as well as my hands, were spattered with black goblin blood. With a shiver, I looked back at the chief, saw him curled around himself in the dirt, moaning through bloody lips, his teeth shattered and broken. My gut heaved, and I staggered away.

What am I doing?

The chief groaned and crawled away, and I let him go, watching the faery haul itself into the bushes. Through the horror and disgust of what I'd just done, I still felt a nasty glow of vindication. Maybe next time, they would think twice about assaulting three "tasty" humans.

Keirran watched it go as well, then walked over to Kenzie, holding out a hand. "Are you all right?" he asked, drawing her to her feet, holding her steady. I clenched my fists, wanting to stalk over there and shove him away from her. Kenzie grimaced, her face tightening with pain, but she nodded.

"Yeah." Her cheeks were pale as she gingerly put weight on her injured leg, wincing. "I don't think anything's broken. Though my knee might swell up like a watermelon."

"You're very lucky," Keirran went on, and all traces of amusement had fled his voice. "Goblins poison the tips of their weapons. If you'd gotten cut at all…well, let's just say a watermelon knee is better than the alternative."

Anger and fear still buzzed through me, making me stupid, wanting to hit something, though there was nothing left to fight. I turned my rage on Keirran, instead.

"What the hell is wrong with you?" I snarled, stalking forward, wanting him farther away from Kenzie. He flinched, and I swung my rattan around the clearing, at the disintegrating piles of goblin. "You knew there were goblins here, you knew we would have to fight our way out, and you still brought us this way. You could've gotten us killed! You could've gotten *Kenzie* killed! Or was that your plan all along? Bring the stupid humans along as bait, so the goblins will be distracted? I should've known never to trust a faery."

"Ethan!" Kenzie scowled at me, but Keirran held up a hand.

"No, he's right," he murmured, and a flicker of surprise filtered through my anger. "I shouldn't have brought you this way. I thought I could deal with the goblins. If you had been seriously hurt, it would've been on my head. You have every reason to be angry." Turning to Kenzie, he bowed deeply, his gaze on the ground between them. "Forgive me, Mackenzie," he said in that clear, quiet voice. "I allowed pride to cloud my judgment, and you were injured because of it. I'm sorry. It won't happen again."

He sounded sincere, and I frowned as Kenzie quickly assured him it was all right. What kind of faery was he, anyway? The fey had no conscience, no real feelings of regret, no morals to get in the way of their decisions. Either Keirran was an exception or a very good actor.

Which reminded me…

"The chief said he smelled *three* humans," I told Keirran, who gave me a resigned look. "He didn't think you were fey. He thought you were human, too."

"Yeah." Keirran shrugged, offering a small grin. "I get that a lot."

Razor appeared on his shoulder with a buzzing laugh. "Stupid goblins," he crowed, bouncing up and down, making Keirran sigh. "Funny, stupid goblins think master is funny elf. Ha!" He buzzed once more and sat down, grinning like a psychotic piranha.

"You're a half-breed," I guessed, wondering how I hadn't

seen it earlier. He didn't look like any of the other Iron fey, but he couldn't be part of the Summer or Winter courts, either; normal fey couldn't enter the Iron Realm without harming themselves. (I was still trying to figure out how *Grimalkin* did it, but everything about that cat was a mystery.) But if Keirran was a half-breed, he didn't have the fey's deathly allergy to iron; his human blood would protect him from the ill effects of Meghan's court.

"I guess you could say that." Keirran sighed again and looked toward the trees, where most of the goblins had scattered. "More like three-quarters human, really. Can't blame them for thinking I was the real thing."

I stared at him. "Who are you?" I asked, but then the bushes snapped, and Keirran winced.

"I'll tell you later. Come on, let's get out of here. The goblins are coming back, probably with reinforcements."

I started to reach for Kenzie, but then I saw my hands, streaked with blood past my wrists, and let them drop. Keirran took her arm instead, helping her along, and she gave me an unreadable look as she limped past. I followed them up the stairs and ducked through the crumbling archway as furious cries echoed from the trees around us. The angry sounds faded as soon as I crossed the threshold, and everything went black.

CHAPTER FIFTEEN
GHOSTS OF THE FAIRGROUND

I emerged, squinting in the darkness, trying to see where I was. For a second, it didn't seem as if we'd left the Nevernever at all. Trees surrounded us, hissing in the wind, but I looked closer and saw they were regular, normal trees. A few yards away, three strands of barbed wire glinted in the moonlight, and beyond the wires, a scattering of fluffy white creatures peered at us curiously.

"Are those sheep?" Kenzie asked, sounding weary but delighted. Razor gave an excited buzz from Keirran's shoulder, leaped to the top of the first wire, and darted into the pasture. Sheep baaed in terror and fled, looking like clouds blowing across the field, and Keirran sighed.

"I keep telling him not to do that. They lose enough to the goblins as is."

"Where are we?" I asked, relieved to be back in the real world again, but not liking that I didn't know where we were. The wind here was cool, and the wooded hills beyond the pasture seemed to go on forever. Keirran watched Razor, buzzing happily from the back of a terrified sheep, and shook his head.

"Somewhere in rural Maryland."

"Maryland," I echoed in disbelief.

He grinned. "What, you think all trods lead to Louisiana?"

I took a breath to answer, but paused. *Wait. How does he know where I live?*

"Where to now?" Kenzie asked, grimacing as she leaned against a fencepost. "I don't think I'll be able to walk very fast with this knee. Someone might need to give me a piggyback ride later on."

"Don't worry." Keirran gestured over the rolling hills. "There's an abandoned fairground a couple miles from here. It's a hangout for the local fey, most of them exiled. The trod there will take us to where we need to go."

"And where is that?" I asked, but Keirran had moved up to the fence, peering over the wire at Razor, still tormenting the flock of sheep. "Razor!" he called over the bleating animals. "Come on, stop scaring the poor things. You're going to give them a heart attack."

The gremlin ignored him. I could just barely see him in the darkness, his electric-green eyes and glowing smile bouncing among the flock. I was about to suggest we just leave and let him catch up, when Kenzie stepped up to the fence, her expression puzzled.

"Where is he?" she asked, staring out over the field. "The sheep are going nuts, but I don't see Razor at all."

Oh, yeah. We were back in the real world now. Which meant Kenzie couldn't see the fey; they were invisible to humans unless they made a conscious effort to un-glamour themselves. I told her as much.

"Huh," she said in a neutral voice, then looked out over the pasture again, at the sheep racing through the grass like frantic clouds. A defiant expression crossed her face, and she took a breath.

"Razor!" she barked, making Keirran jump. "No! Bad gremlin! You stop that, right now!"

The gremlin, shockingly, looked up from where he was

bouncing on a rock, sheep scattering around him. He blinked and cocked his head, looking confused. Kenzie pointed to the ground in front of her.

"I want to see you. Come here, Razor. Now!"

And, he did. Blipping into sight at her feet, he gazed up expectantly, looking like a mutant Chihuahua awaiting commands. Keirran blinked in astonishment as she snapped her fingers and pointed at him, and Razor scurried up his arm to perch on his shoulder. She smiled, giving us both a smug look, and crossed her arms.

"Dog training classes," she explained.

The road stretched before us in the moonlight, a narrow strip of pavement that wove gently over and between the hills. Keirran led us on silently, Razor humming a raspy tune on his shoulder. No cars passed us; except for an owl and the flocks of sheep, snoozing in their pastures, we were alone.

"Wish I had my camera." Kenzie sighed as a black-faced ewe watched us from the side of the road, blinking sleepily. It snorted and trotted off, and Kenzie gazed after it, smiling. "Then again, maybe not. It might be weird, explaining how I could take pictures of the Maryland countryside when I never left Louisiana." She shivered, rubbing her arms as a cold breeze blew across the pasture, smelling of sheep and wet grass. I wished I had my jacket so I could offer it to her.

"What do you do?" Kenzie went on, her gaze still roaming the woods beyond the hills. "When you get home, I mean? We've been to Faeryland—we've seen things no one else has. What happens when you finally get home, knowing what you do, that no one else will ever understand?"

"You go back to what you were doing before," I replied. "You try to get on with your life and pretend it didn't happen. It'll be easier for you," I continued as she turned to me, frowning. "You have friends. Your life is fairly normal. You're not a freak who can see Them everywhere you go. Just try to forget about it. Forget the fey, forget the Nevernever, forget everything weird or strange or unnatural. Eventually, the nightmares will stop, and you might even convince yourself that everything you saw was a bad dream. That's the easiest way."

"Hey, tough guy, your bitterness is showing." Kenzie gave me an exasperated look. "I don't want to forget. Just burying my head in the sand isn't going to change anything. They'll still be out there, whether I believe in them or not. I can't pretend it never happened."

"But you won't ever see them," I said. "And that will either make you paranoid or drive you completely crazy."

"I'll still be able to talk to you, though, right?"

I sighed, not wanting to say it, but knowing I had to. "No. You won't."

"Why?"

"Because my life is too screwed up to drag you into it."

"Why don't you let me decide what's best for my life," Kenzie said softly, not quite able to mask her anger, the first I'd ever heard from her, "and who I want to be friends with?"

"What do you think is going to happen once we go home?" I asked, not meeting her stare. "You think I can be normal and hang out with you and your friends, just like that? You think your parents and your teachers will want you hanging around someone like me?"

"No," Kenzie said in that same low, quiet voice. "They won't. And you know what? I don't care. Because they haven't seen you like I have. They haven't seen the Nevernever, or the fey, or the Iron Queen, and they won't ever understand. *I* didn't understand." She paused, seeming to struggle with her next words. "The first time I saw you," she said, pushing her bangs from her eyes, "when we first talked, I thought you were this brooding, unfriendly, hostile, um…" She paused.

"Jerk," I finished for her.

"Well, yeah," Kenzie admitted slowly. "A pretty handsome jerk, I might add, but a huge, colossal megajerk nonetheless." She gave me a quick glance to see how I was taking this. I shrugged.

Not going to argue with that.

And then, a second later:

She thought I was handsome?

"At first, I just wanted to know what you were thinking." Kenzie pushed back her hair, the blue-and-black strands fluttering around her face. "It was more of a challenge, I guess, to get you to see me, to talk to me. You're the only one, in a very long time anyway, who talked to me like a real person, who treated me the same as everyone else. My friends, my family, even my teachers, they all tiptoe around me like I'm made of glass. They never say what they're really thinking if they feel it might upset me." She sighed, looking out over the fields. "No one is ever real with me anymore, and I'm sick and tired of it."

I held my breath, suddenly aware that I was very close to that dark thing Kenzie was hiding from me. *Tread softly, Ethan. Don't sound too eager or she might change her mind.* "Why is that?" I asked, trying to keep my voice light, like I didn't care. Wrong move.

"Um, because of my dad," Kenzie said quickly, and I swore under my breath, knowing I had screwed up. "He's this bigshot lawyer and everyone is terrified of him, so they pussyfoot around me, too. Whatever." She shrugged. "I don't want to talk about my dad. We were talking about you."

"The huge, colossal megajerk," I reminded her.

"Exactly. I don't know if you realize this, Ethan, but you're a good-looking guy. People are going to notice you, bad-boy reputation or not." I gave her a dubious look, and she nodded. "I'm serious. You didn't see the way Regan and the others were staring the first time you came into the classroom. Chelsea even dared me to go up and ask if you had a girlfriend." One corner of her mouth curled in a wry grin. "I'm sure you remember how *that* turned out."

I grimaced and looked away. *Yeah, I was a total jackass, wasn't I? Believe me, if I could take back everything I said, I would. But it wouldn't stop the fey.*

"But then, we came to the Nevernever," Kenzie went on, gazing a few yards up the road, where Keirran's bright form glided down the pavement. "And things started making a lot more sense. It must be hard, seeing all these things, knowing they're out there, and not being able to talk about it to anyone. It must be lonely."

Very lightly, she took my hand, sending electric tingles up my arm, and my breath caught. "But you have me now," she said in a near whisper. "You can talk to me…about Them. And I won't tease or make fun or call you crazy, and you don't have to worry about it frightening me. I *want* to know everything I can. I want to know about faeries and Mag Tuiredh and the Nevernever, and you're my only connection to them now." Her voice grew defiant. "So, if you think you can shut me out of your life, tough guy, and keep me in the dark, then you don't know me at all. I can be just as stubborn as you."

"Don't." I couldn't look at her, couldn't face the quiet sincerity in her voice. Fear stirred, the knowledge that she was only putting herself in danger the longer she stayed with me. "There is no connection, Kenzie," I said, pulling my hand from hers. "And I won't be telling you anything about the fey. Not now, not ever. Just forget that you ever saw them, and leave me alone."

Her stunned, hurt silence ate into me, and I sighed, stabbing my fingers through my hair. "You think I want to keep pushing people away?" I asked softly. "I don't enjoy being the freak, the one everyone avoids. I really, truly do not take pleasure in being a complete asshole." My voice dropped even lower. "Especially to people like you."

"Then why do it?"

"Because people who get close to me get hurt!" I snapped, finally whirling to face her. She blinked, and the memory of another girl swam through my head, red ponytail bobbing behind her, a spray of freckles across her nose. "Every time," I continued in a softer voice. "I can't stop it. I can't stop Them from following me. If it was just me that the fey picked on, I'd be okay with that. But someone else always pays for my Sight. Someone else always gets hurt instead of me." Tearing my gaze from hers, I looked out over the fields. "I'd rather be alone," I muttered, "than to have to watch that again."

"Again?"

"Hey," Keirran called from somewhere up ahead. "We're here."

Grateful for the interruption, I hurried to where the faery waited for us beneath the branches of a large pine by the side of the road. Striding through weeds, I followed Keirran's gaze to where the top of a Ferris wheel, yellow and spotted with rust, poked above the distant trees. Lights flickered through the branches.

"Come on," Keirran encouraged, sounding eager, and jogged forward. We followed, trailing him under branches, through knee-high grass and across an empty, weed-choked parking lot. Past a wooden fence covered in vines and ivy, the trees fell away, and we were staring at the remains of an abandoned fairground.

Though the park seemed empty, lanterns and torchlight

flickered erratically, lighting the way between empty booths, some still draped with the limp, moldy forms of stuffed animals. A popcorn cart lay overturned in the weeds a few yards away, the glass smashed, the innards picked clean by scavengers. We passed the bumper cars, sitting empty and silent on their tracks, and walked beneath a swing ride, the chains creaking softly in the wind. The carousel sat in the distance, peeling and rusted, dozens of once-colorful horses now flaking away with age and time.

Keirran skidded to a halt in front of a darkened funnel cake booth, his face grave. "Something is wrong," he muttered, turning slowly. "This place should be crawling with exiles. There's supposed to be a goblin market here year-round. Where is everyone?"

"Looks like your friend might not be here," I said, switching my sticks to both hands, just in case there was trouble. He didn't seem to hear me and abruptly broke into a sprint that took him between the midway aisles. Kenzie and I hurried after him.

"Annwyl!" he called, jogging up to a booth that at one point had featured a basketball game, as several nets dangled from the back wall. The booth was dark and empty, though flowers were scattered everywhere inside, dried stems and petals fluttering across the counter.

"Annwyl," Keirran said again, leaping easily over the wall, into the booth. "Are you here? Where are you?"

No one answered him. Breathing hard, the faery gazed around the empty stall for a moment, then turned and slammed his fist into the counter, making the whole structure shake. Razor squeaked, and Kenzie and I stared at him.

"Gone," he whispered, bowing his head, as the gremlin buzzed worriedly and patted his neck. "Where is she? Where is everyone? Are they all with *her*?"

"What's going on?" I leaned against the counter, brushing away drifts of petals and leaves. They had a rotten, sickly sweet smell, and I tried not to breathe in. "Who's with her? Who is Annwyl? Why—?"

I trailed off, my blood turning cold. Was it my imagination, or had I just seen a white shimmer float between the booths farther down the aisle? Carefully, I straightened, gripping my weapons, my skin starting to prickle with goose bumps. "Keirran, we have to get out of here now."

He looked up warily, reaching back for his weapon. And then, something slipped from the booths onto the dusty path, and we both froze.

At first, it looked like a giant cat. It had a sleek, muscular body, short fur and a long, thin tail that lashed its hindquarters. But when it turned its head, its face wasn't a cat's but an old, wrinkled woman's, her hair hanging limply around her neck, her eyes beady and cruel. She turned toward us, and I ducked behind the stall, pulling Kenzie down with me, as Keirran vanished behind the counter. I saw that the cat-thing's front paws were actually bony hands with long, crooked nails, but worst of all, her body flickered and shimmered in the air like heat waves. Like the creepy fey that had chased me and Kenzie into the Nevernever. Except this one seemed a bit more solid than the others. Not nearly so transparent.

I suddenly had a sinking suspicion of what had happened to the exiles.

Keirran squeezed through a crack in the cloth walls and crouched down beside us. "What is that?" he whispered, gripping his sword. "I've never seen anything like it before."

"I have." I peeked around the corner. The cat-thing was turning in slow circles, as if she knew something was there but couldn't see it. "Something similar took my friend and chased us—" I gestured to Kenzie and myself "—into the

Nevernever. I think they're the ones that have been kidnapping exiles and half-breeds."

Keirran's gaze darkened, and he suddenly looked extremely dangerous, eyes glowing with an icy light as he stood slowly. "Then perhaps we should make sure it doesn't hurt anyone else."

"You sure that's a good idea?"

"Ethan." Kenzie squeezed my arm, looking frightened but trying not to let it show. "I don't see it," she whispered. "I don't see anything."

"But the little boys can," hissed a voice behind us, and another cat-thing padded out of the darkness between the stalls.

I jumped to my feet, pulling Kenzie up with me. The cat-fey's wizened face creased in a smile, showing sharp feline teeth. "Little humans," she purred, as the other faery came around the corner, boxing us in. I shivered as the air around us grew cold. "You can see us and hear us. How encouraging."

"Who are you?" Keirran demanded, and raised his sword, pointing it at the nearest cat-thing. On his shoulder, Razor growled and buzzed at the faeries, baring his teeth. "What did you do to the exiles here?"

The cat-fey hissed and drew back at the sight of the iron weapon. "Not human," rasped the other behind us. "The bright one is not completely human. I can feel his glamour. He is strong." She growled, taking a step forward. "We should bring him to the lady."

I raised my sticks and eased back, closer to Keirran, trapping Kenzie between us. She glanced around wildly, trying to see the invisible threats, but it was obvious that she didn't even hear them.

The second cat-thing blinked slowly, running a tongue along her thin mouth. "Yes," she agreed, flexing her nails. "We will bring the half-breed to the lady, but it would be a shame to waste all that lovely glamour. Perhaps we will just take a little."

Her mouth opened, stretching impossibly wide, a gaping hole in her wrinkled face. I felt a ripple around us, a pulling sensation, as if the cat-fey was sucking the air into itself. I braced myself for something nasty, pressing close to Kenzie, but except for a faint sluggish feeling, nothing happened.

But Keirran staggered and fell to one knee, putting a hand against the booth to catch himself. As I stared, he seemed to fade a bit, his brightness getting dimmer, the color leeched from his hair and clothes. Razor screeched and flickered from sight, going in and out like a bad television station. The other faery cackled, and I glared at it, torn between helping Keirran and protecting the girl.

Suddenly, the cat-thing choked, convulsed and hurled itself back from Keirran. "Poison!" she screeched, gagging and heaving, as if she wanted to cough up a hairball. "Poison! Murder!" She spasmed again, curling in on herself as her body began to break apart, to dissolve like sugar in water. "Iron!" she wailed, clawing at the ground, at herself, her beady eyes wild. "He's an Iron abomination! Kill him, sister! Kill them all!"

She vanished then, blowing away in the breeze, as the other cat-thing screamed its fury and pounced.

I brought my rattan down, smashing it over the faery's skull, then sliding away to land a few solid blows on its shoulder. It screeched in pain and whirled on me, favoring its right leg. "So, you're real enough to hit, after all." I grinned. Snarling, it lunged, clawing at me, and I sidestepped again, angling out like Guro had taught me, whipping my rattan several times across the wizened face.

Shaking its head, the faery backed up, hissing furiously, one eye squeezed shut. Pale, silvery blood dripped from its mouth and jaw, writhing away as soon as it touched the ground. I twirled my sticks and stepped closer, forcing it back. Kenzie had retreated a few steps and was crouched next to Keirran; I could hear her asking if he was all right, and his quiet assurance that he was fine.

"Boy," the cat-faery hissed, her lips pulled back in a snarl of hate, "you will pay for this. You all will. When we return, there will be nothing that will save you from our wrath."

Turning, the cat-thing bounded into the darkness between the stalls and vanished from sight.

I breathed a sigh of relief and turned to Keirran, who was struggling upright, one hand still on the booth wall. Razor made angry, garbled noises on his shoulder, punctuated with the words "Bad kitty!"

"You okay?" I asked, and he nodded wearily. "What just happened there?"

"I don't know." He gave Kenzie a grateful smile and took a step forward, standing on his own. "When that thing turned on me, it felt like everything—my strength, my emotions, even my memory—was being sucked out. It was…awful." He shuddered, rubbing a forearm. "I feel like there are pieces of me missing now, and I'll never get them back."

I remembered the dead piskie, the way she'd looked right before she died, like all her color had been drained away. "It was draining your magic," I said, and Keirran nodded. "So, these things, whatever they are, they eat the glamour of regular fey, suck them dry until there's nothing left."

"Like vampires," Kenzie put in. "Vampire fey that hunt their own kind." She wrinkled her nose. "That's creepy. Why would they do that?"

I shook my head. "I have no idea."

"It got more than it bargained for, though," Keirran went on, gazing at the spot where the cat-faery had died. "Whatever they are, it looks like they're still deathly allergic to iron."

"So they're not Iron fey, at least."

"No." Keirran shivered and dropped his hands. "Though I have no idea *what* they are."

"Keirran!"

The shout echoed down the rows, making Keirran jerk his head up, hope flaring in his eyes. A moment later, a willowy girl in a green-and-brown dress turned a corner and sprinted toward us. Keirran smiled, and Razor gave a welcoming buzz, waving his arms.

I tensed. The girl was fey, I could see that easily. The tips of her ears peeked up through her golden-brown hair, which was braided with vines and flowers and hung several inches past her waist. She had that unnatural grace of all fey, that perfect beauty where it was tempting to stare at her and completely forget to eat, sleep, breathe or anything else.

Keirran stepped forward, forgetting Kenzie and me completely, his eyes only for the faery approaching us. The fey girl halted just shy of touching him, as if she'd intended to fling herself into his arms but thought better of it at the last moment.

"Annwyl." Keirran hesitated, as if he, too, wanted to pull her close, only to decide against it. His gaze never left the Summer faery, though, and she didn't seem to notice the two humans standing behind him.

There was a moment of awkward silence, broken only by Razor, chattering on Keirran's shoulder, before the faery girl shook her head.

"You shouldn't be here, Keirran," she said, her voice lilting and soft, like water over a rock bed. "It's going to get you in trouble. Why did you come?"

"I heard what was happening in the mortal realm," Keirran replied, stepping forward and reaching for her hand. "I heard the rumor that something is out here, killing off exiles and half-breeds." His other hand rose as if to brush her cheek. "I had to come see you, to make sure you were all right."

Annwyl hesitated. Longing showed on her face, but she stepped back before Keirran could touch her. His eyes closed, briefly, and he let his arm drop. "You shouldn't be here," the girl insisted. "It isn't safe, especially now. There are...creatures."

"We saw," Keirran replied, and Annwyl gave him a frightened look. His gaze hardened, ice-blue eyes glinting dangerously. "Those things," he went on. "Is *she* aware of them? Is that why the market has been disbanded?"

The fey girl nodded. "She knows you're here," she replied in her soft, rippling voice. "She's waiting for you. I'm supposed to bring you to her. But..."

Her gaze finally slid to mine, and the large, moss-green eyes widened. "You brought mortals here?" she asked, sounding confused. "Who...?"

"Ah. Yes, where are my manners?" Keirran glanced back, as well, as if just remembering us. "I'm sorry. Ethan, this is Annwyl, formerly of the Summer Court. Annwyl, may I introduce...Ethan Chase."

The faery gasped. "Chase? The queen's brother?"

"Yes," Keirran said, and nodded to Kenzie. "Also, Kenzie St. James. They're both friends of mine."

I glanced at Keirran, surprised by the casual way he threw out the word *friends*. We'd only just met and were virtually strangers, but Keirran acted as if he'd known us far longer. But that was crazy; I'd never seen him before tonight.

Solemnly, the Summer faery pulled back and dropped into a deep curtsy, directed at me, I realized. "Don't," I muttered, waving it off. "I'm not a prince. You don't have to do that with me."

Annwyl blinked large, moss-green eyes. "But...you are,"

she said in her rippling voice. "You're the queen's brother. Even if you're not one of us, we—"

"I said it's fine." Briefly, I wondered what would happen if all faeries knew who I was. Would they treat me with respect and leave me alone? Or would my life get even more chaotic and dangerous, as they saw me as a weak link that could be exploited? I had a feeling it would be the latter. "I'm not anyone special," I told the Summer girl, who still looked unconvinced. "Don't treat me any different than you would Keirran."

I couldn't be sure, but I was almost positive Keirran hid a small grin behind Annwyl's hair. The Summer girl blinked again, and seemed about to say something, when Kenzie spoke up.

"Um, Ethan? Sorry to be a normal human and all, but… who are we talking to?"

Keirran chuckled. "Oh, right." To Annwyl, he said, "I'm afraid Mackenzie can't see you right now. She's only human."

"What?" Annwyl glanced at Kenzie, and her eyes widened. "Oh, of course. Please excuse me." A shiver went through the air around her, and Kenzie jumped as the faery girl materialized in front of us. "Is this better?"

Kenzie sighed. "I'll never get used to that."

The Summer faery smiled, but then her eyes darkened and she drew back. "Come," she urged, glancing around the fairgrounds. "We can't stay out here. It's gotten dangerous." Her gaze swept the aisles like a wary deer's. "I'm supposed to bring you to the mistress. This way."

We followed Annwyl across the dead amusement park, through the silent fairway, past the Ferris wheel, creaking softly in the wind, until we came to the House of Mirrors in the shadow of a wooden roller coaster. Walking past weird, distorted reflections of ourselves—fat, short, tall with gorilla-like arms—we finally came to a narrow mirror in a shadowy corner, and Annwyl looked back at Keirran.

"It's a bit…crowded," she warned, her gaze flicking to me and Kenzie. "No one wants to be on this side of the Veil, not with those *things* out there." She shuddered, and I saw Keirran wince, too. "Fair warning," she continued, watching Keirran with undeniable affection. "The mistress is a little…cranky these days. She might not appreciate you showing up now, especially with two humans."

"I'll risk it," Keirran said softly, holding her gaze. Annwyl smiled at him, then put her hand to the mirror in front of us. It shimmered, growing even more distorted, and the fey girl stepped through the glass, vanishing from sight.

Keirran looked at us and smiled. "After you."

Taking Kenzie's hand, I stepped through the shifting glass, and the real world faded behind us once more.

We stepped through the doorway into a dark, underground room, a basement maybe, or even a dungeon. The Summer girl beckoned us forward, down the shadowy halls. Torches flickered in brackets as we followed Annwyl down the damp corridors, and gargoyles watched us from stone columns, sneering as we went by.

Fey also walked these halls: boggarts and bogies and a couple of goblins, fey that preferred the dank and damp and shadows, avoiding the light. They eyed us with hungry curiosity, and Kenzie eyed them back, able to See again now that we were back in Faery. They kept their distance, though, and we walked up a flight of long wooden steps, where a pair of crimson doors perched at the top. Annwyl pushed them open.

Noise and light flooded the stairway. The doors opened into an enormous, red-walled foyer, and the foyer was filled with fey.

Faeries stood or sat on the carpeted floors, talking in low murmurs. Goblins muttered amongst themselves, clumped in small groups, glancing around warily. Brownies, satyrs and piskies hovered through the room, looking lost. A couple redcaps stood in a corner, baring their fangs at whoever got too close. One of them noticed me and nudged his companion, jerking his chin in our direction. The other grinned, running a pale tongue over his teeth, and I glared stonily back, daring it to try something. The redcap sneered, made a rude gesture, and went back to threatening the crowd.

More fey clustered along the walls, some of them standing guard over tables and boxes of weird stuff. In one corner, a faery in a white cloak straightened a stand of feather masks, while near the fireplace, a crooked hag plucked a skewer of mice from the flames and set it, still smoking, next to a plate of frogs and what looked like a cooked cat. The stench of burning fur drifted to me across the room, and Kenzie made a tiny gagging noise.

But even with all the weird, unearthly and dangerous faeries in the room, there was only one that really mattered.

In the center of all the chaos, a cigarette wand in one hand and a peeved look on her face, was the most striking faery I'd ever seen. Copper-gold hair floated around her like a mane, and a gown hugged her slender body, the long slit up the side showing impossibly graceful legs. She was tall, regal and obviously annoyed, for she kept pursing her lips and blowing blue smoke into snarling wolves that ripped each other to pieces as they thrashed through the air. A black-bearded dwarf stood beneath her glare, a wooden box sitting beside him. The box had been draped with a dark cloth, and growling, hissing noises came from within as it shook back and forth.

"I don't care if the beast was already paid for, darling." The faery's high, clear voice rang out over the crowd. "You're not keeping that thing here." Her tone was hypnotic, exasperated as it was. "I will not have my human pets turned into stone because the Duchess of Thorns has an unnatural craving for cockatrice eggs."

"Please." The dwarf, held up his thick hands, pleading. "Leanansidhe, please, be reasonable."

I sucked in a breath, and my blood turned to ice.

Leanansidhe? Leanansidhe, the freaking Exile Queen? I leveled a piercing glare at Keirran, who offered a weak grin. Everyone in Faery knew who Leanansidhe was, myself included. Meghan had mentioned her name a few times, but beyond that, you couldn't meet an exiled fey who hadn't heard of the dangerous Dark Muse and wasn't terrified of her.

"Get it out of my house, Feddic." The Exile Queen pointed to the door we'd come through. "I don't care what you do with it, but I want it gone. Or would you like to be barred from my home permanently? Take your chances with the life-sucking monsters out in the real world?"

"No!" The dwarf shrank back, eyes wide. "I'll…I'll get rid of it, Leanansidhe," he stammered. "Right now."

"Be sure that you do, pet." Leanansidhe pursed her lips, sucking on her cigarette flute. She sighed, and the smoke image of a rooster went scurrying away over our heads. "If I find one more creature in this house turned to stone…" She trailed off, but the terrifying look in her eyes spoke louder than words.

The dwarf grabbed the hissing, cloth-covered box and hurried away, muttering under his breath. We stepped aside as he passed and continued down the stairs without glancing at us, then disappeared into the shadows.

Leanansidhe pinched the bridge of her nose, then straightened and looked right at us. "Well, well," she purred, smiling in a way I did not like at all, "Keirran, darling. Here you are again. To what do I owe the pleasure?" She gave me a cursory glance before turning back to Keirran. "And you brought a pair of humans with you, I see. More strays, darling?" She shook her head. "Your concern for hopeless waifs is very touching, but if you think you're going to dump them here, dove, I'm afraid I just don't have the room."

Keirran bowed. "Leanansidhe." He nodded, looking around at the crowd of fey. "Looks like you have a full house."

"Noticed that, did you, pet?" The Exile Queen sighed and puffed out a cougar. "Yes, I have been reduced to running the Goblin Market from my own living room, which makes it very difficult to concentrate on other things. Not to mention it's driving my human pets even more crazy than usual. They can barely strum a note or hold a tune with all the chaos around." She touched two elegant fingers to her temple, as if she had a headache. Keirran looked unimpressed.

The Exile Queen sniffed. "Sadly, I'm very busy at the moment, darling, so if you want to make yourself useful, why don't you be a good boy and take a message home? Tell the Iron Queen that something is going on in the real world, and she might want to know about it. If you're here just to make googly-eyes at Annwyl, my darling prince, I'm afraid I don't have time for you."

Prince? Wait. "Wait." I turned, very slowly, to stare at Keirran, ignoring the Exile Queen for the moment. Keirran grimaced and didn't look at me. "Care to say that again?" I asked, disbelief making my stomach knot. My mouth was suddenly dry. "You're a prince—of the Iron Realm? Then, you…you're Meghan's…" I couldn't even finish the thought.

From the corner of my eye, Leanansidhe straightened. "Ethan Chase." Her voice was low and dangerous, as if she'd just figured out who was standing in her living room.

I couldn't look at her now, though. My attention was riveted to Keirran.

He shot me a pained, embarrassed wince. "Yeah. I was going to tell you...sooner or later. There just wasn't a good time." He paused, his voice going very soft. "I'm sorry... Uncle."

Razor let out a high-pitched, buzzing laugh. "Uncle!" he howled, oblivious to the looks of horror and disgust he was getting from every faery in the room. "Uncle, uncle! Uncle Ethan!"

PART III

CHAPTER SIXTEEN
LEANANSIDHE'S PRICE

I felt numb. And slightly sick.

Keirran—this faery before me—was Ash and Meghan's *son*. How had I not figured it out before? Everything fit together: his human blood, his Iron glamour, even the familiar expressions on his face. They were familiar because I'd seen them before. On Meghan. I could see the resemblance now; his eyes, hair and facial features—they were all my sister's. But Ash's shadow hovered there as well, in his jaw, his stance, the way he moved.

For a second, I hated him.

Before either of us could say anything, the exiled fey in the room gasped and snarled, surging away from Keirran as if he had a disease. Murmurs of "the Iron prince," spread through the crowd, and the circle of fey seemed to hover between bowing down or fleeing the room. Leanansidhe gave us both an extremely exasperated glare, as if we were the cause of her headaches, and snapped her fingers at us.

"Annwyl, darling." The Exile Queen's tone made the fey girl cringe, and Keirran moved to stand protectively beside her. "Wait here, would you, dove? Try to keep the masses in check while I deal with this little bump. You three." She shifted that cold gaze to us, her tone brooking no argument. "Follow me, pets. And, Keirran, keep that wretched gremlin under control this time, or I'll be forced to do something drastic."

Kenzie, forgotten beside us all, shot me a worried glance, and I shrugged, trying to look unconcerned. We started to follow Leanansidhe, but Annwyl and Keirran lingered for a moment. Leanansidhe rolled her eyes. "Sometime today, pets." She sighed, as Annwyl finally turned away and Keirran looked dejected. "While I'm still in a reasonable enough mood not to turn anyone into a cello."

Turning in a swirl of blue smoke, the Exile Queen led us out of the room, down several long, red-carpeted hallways, and into a library. Huge shelves of books lined the walls, and a lively tune swam through the air, played by a human with a violin in the far corner.

"Out, Charles," Leanansidhe announced as she swept into the room, and the human quickly packed up his instrument and fled through another door.

The Exile Queen spun on us. "Well!" she exclaimed, gazing down at me, her hair writhing around her. "Ethan Chase. This *is* a surprise. The son and the brother of the Iron Queen, come to visit at the same time, what an occasion. How is your darling older sister, pet?" she asked me. "I assume you've been to see her recently?"

"Meghan's fine," I muttered, feeling self-conscious with Keirran standing there. Now that I knew we were…related… it felt weird, talking about Meghan in front of him.

Screw that. You want weird? Weird is having a nephew the same age as you. Weird is your sister having a kid, and not telling your family about him. Weird is being an uncle to a freaking half-faery! Forget weird, you are so beyond weird that it's not funny.

Leanansidhe *tsked* and looked at Keirran, and a slow smile crossed her lips. "And Keirran, you devious boy," she purred. "You didn't tell him, did you?" She laughed then, shaking her head. "Well, this is an unexpected family drama, isn't it? I wonder what the Iron Queen would say if she could be here now?"

"Wait a second." Kenzie's voice broke in, bewildered and incredulous. "Keirran is *your nephew?* He's the Iron Queen's son? But…you're the same age!" She gestured wildly. "How in the world does that work?"

"Ah, well." Keirran shrugged, looking embarrassed. "Remember the screwy time differences in Faery? That's part of it. Also, the fey mature at a faster rate than mortals—comes with living in a place as dangerous as the Nevernever, I guess. We grow up quickly until we hit a certain point, then we just… stop." He gave another sheepish grin. "Trust me, you're not the only ones to be shocked. It was a big surprise for Mom, too."

I glared at Keirran, forgetting Kenzie and Leanansidhe for the moment. "Why didn't you say anything?" I demanded.

Keirran sighed. "How?" he asked, lifting his hands away from his sides, before letting them drop. "When would it have come up? *Oh, by the way, I'm the prince of the Iron Realm, and your nephew. Surprise!*" He shrugged again, made a hopeless gesture. "It would've been weird. And…awkward. And I'm pretty sure you wouldn't have wanted anything to do with me if you knew."

"Why didn't Meghan say anything? That's kind of a big thing to keep from your family."

"I don't know, Ethan." Keirran shook his head. "She never talks about you, never speaks about her human life. I didn't even know I had another family until a few years ago." He paused, ran his fingers through his silver hair. "I was shocked when I heard that the queen had a brother living in the mortal world. But when I asked her about it, she told me that we had to live separate lives, that mingling the two families would only bring trouble to us both. I disagreed—I wanted to meet you, but she forbade me to come and see you at all."

He sounded sincere and genuinely sorry, that he hadn't been able to introduce himself. My anger with him dissolved a little, only to switch to another target. *Meghan,* I thought, furious. *How could you? How could you not tell us? What was the point?*

"When I heard you were at the palace," Keirran went on, his face earnest, as if he was willing me to believe him, "I couldn't believe it. I had to see for myself. But when Razor told me what you said—that something was killing off exiles and half-breeds—I knew I had to get to Annwyl, make sure she was safe. So I thought, *two birds with one stone, why not?*" He offered a shrug and a wry grin, before sobering once more. "I didn't tell you everything, and I'm sorry for that. But I had to make certain you would follow me out of the Iron Realm."

My head was still reeling. Meghan's son. My nephew. I could barely wrap my mind around it. I didn't know if I should be disgusted, horrified, ecstatic or completely weirded out. I *did* know that I was going to have to talk to Meghan about this, ask why she felt it was important to keep us in the dark. Screw this "living separate lives" crap. She had a kid! Half-faery or no, you did not keep that sort of thing from your family.

"Well," Leanansidhe interjected with a wave of her cigarette flute, "much as I'm enjoying this little drama, pets, I'm afraid we cannot sit around and argue the whole day. I have larger problems to attend to. I assume you boys did not see the abominations lurking around the fairgrounds?"

"We did, actually."

It wasn't Keirran who answered the Exile Queen. It was Kenzie. I grimaced and turned away from the Iron prince, vowing to deal with this later, when I had time to think it through. Right now, the Dark Muse had turned her attention on the girl who, up until this point, had been standing off to the side, watching the drama play out. Truthfully, I was happy for that; it was probably best that she avoid Leanansidhe's notice as much as she could. But, of course, Kenzie could never stay silent for long.

"We did see them," she repeated, and the Dark Muse blinked at her in surprise. "Well, *they* did," she continued, jerking her head at me and Keirran. "I couldn't see anything. But I do know something attacked us. They're the ones killing off your people, right?"

"And, who are you again, dove?"

"Oh, sorry," Kenzie went on, as Leanansidhe continued to stare as if she was seeing the girl for the first time. "I'm Mackenzie, Ethan's classmate. We sort of got pulled into the Nevernever together."

"How…tenacious," Leanansidhe mused after a moment. And I didn't know if she found Kenzie amusing or offensive. I hoped it was the former. "Well, if you must know, darling, yes, something out there is making exiles disappear. As you can see from the state of my living room, the exiled fey are practically tearing down my walls trying to get in. I haven't had this much trouble since the war with the Iron fey." She paused and leveled a piercing glare at Razor, humming on Keirran's shoulder. The gremlin seemed happily oblivious.

"Any idea what's causing it?" Kenzie asked, slipping into reporter mode like she had at the tournament. If she'd had a notebook, it would have been flipped open right now, pencil scribbling furiously. Leanansidhe sighed.

"Vague ideas, darling. Rumors of horrible monsters sucking the glamour out of their victims until they are lifeless husks. I've never seen the horrid things, of course, but there have been several disappearances from the fairgrounds, as well as all over the world."

"All over the world?" I broke in. "Is it really that wide-spread?"

Leanansidhe gave me an eerie stare. "You have no idea, darling," she said softly. "And neither do the courts. Your sister remains happily ignorant to the threat in the mortal realm, and Summer and Winter do not even care. But…let me show you something."

She strode to a table in the corner of the room, where a huge map of the world lay spread across the wood. Red dots marked the surface, some isolated, some clumped together. There were a fair number spread across North America, but also a bunch in England, Ireland and Great Britain. Scattered, perhaps. It wasn't as though a whole area was covered with red. No continent was unmarked, however. North America, Europe, Africa, Australia, Asia, South America. They all had their share of red dots.

"I've been tracking disappearances," Leanansidhe said into the stunned silence. "Exiles and half-breeds alike. As you can see, darlings, it's quite widespread. And each time I send someone out to investigate, they do not return. It's becoming—" Leanansidhe pursed her lips "—annoying."

I gazed at the map, my fingers hovering over a spot in the United States. Two bright red dots in the state of Louisiana, near my home town.

Todd.

Keirran scanned the table, his expression grave. "And the other courts do nothing?" he murmured. "Mab and Oberon and Titania don't know what's going on?"

"They've been informed, darling," Leanansidhe said, waving her cigarette flute in a dismissive manner. "However, the Summer and Winter courts do not think it important enough to intervene. What do they care about the lives of a few exiles and half-breeds? As long as the problem remains in the mortal realm, they are content to do nothing."

"Why didn't you tell Meghan?" I broke in. "She would've done something. She's trying to do something now."

Leanansidhe frowned at me. "That might be true, pet. But sadly, I have no way to get a message to the Iron Queen without my informants dropping dead from iron sickness. It is very difficult to contact the Iron Realm when no one is willing to set foot there. In fact, I was waiting for this one—" she waved her flute at Keirran "—to come sniffing around after Annwyl again, so that I could give him a message to bring back to Mag Tuiredh."

Keirran blushed slightly but didn't reply. Razor giggled on his shoulder.

I looked down at the map again, my thoughts whirling. So many gone. A part of me said not to care, that the fey were finally getting what they deserved after centuries of making humans disappear.

But there was more at stake now. Todd was still missing, and I'd promised to find him. Meghan would be getting involved soon. And now, there was Keirran.

I didn't want to think about Keirran right now.

"Then," I muttered, continuing to gaze at the map, "you're going to need someone who can investigate these things, someone who isn't a half-breed or an exile, who doesn't have any glamour they can suck dry." *Someone who's human.*

"Exactly, darling." Leanansidhe stared down with a chilling gleam in her eyes. I could feel it on the back of my neck without even seeing her. "So…are *you* volunteering, pet?"

I sighed.

"Yeah," I muttered and straightened to face her. "I am. I have a friend I've got to find, but this has become even bigger than that. I don't know what freaks are out there, and I don't like it. If these glamour-sucking things are so widespread, it's only a matter of time before all the exiles are gone, and then they might start on the Nevernever."

Where Meghan is.

"Excellent, darling, excellent." Leanansidhe beamed, looking pleased. "And what about you two?" she asked, gesturing to Kenzie and Keirran, on opposite ends of the table. "What will the son of the Iron Queen do, now that he's aware of the danger? You can always go home, you know, warn the kingdom. Though I can't imagine the Iron Queen will be pleased when she finds out what you've been doing."

"I'm going with Ethan," Keirran said softly. "I have to. Whatever these things are, I won't stand by while they kill off any more of our kind, exiled or not."

"Including Annwyl, is that right, pet?"

Keirran faced the Exile Queen directly, raising his chin. "Especially her."

"I'm going, too," Kenzie piped in, and frowned at me, as if guessing I was just about to suggest she go home. Which I *was,* but she didn't need to know.

"Kenzie, this isn't your fight anymore." I looked at Keirran, hoping he would back me on this. He just shrugged unhelpfully. "You don't have a stake in this," I continued, trying to be reasonable. "You have no family or siblings or—" I looked at Keirran "—girlfriends to worry about. You didn't even know Todd very well. We're closer to the mortal world than we've ever been now, and you can go home anytime. Why are you still here?"

"Because I want to be!" she snapped, like that was the end of it. We glared at each other, and she threw up her hands. "Jeez, Ethan, we've been over this already. Get it through your stubborn head, okay? Do you think, with everything I've seen, I can just go home and forget it all? I'm not here because of family or siblings or friends—I'm here because of you! And because I *want* to see this! I want to know what's out there."

"You can't even see them," I argued. "These things exist in the real world, remember? You don't have the Sight, so how are you going to help us when you won't even know where they are?"

She pursed her lips. "I'll…think of something."

"*I* may be able to help with that, darling," Leanansidhe broke in. We looked up, and the Exile Queen smiled at Kenzie, twiddling her cigarette holder. "You are a spunky little thing, aren't you, pet? I rather like you. With all the riffraff from the Goblin Market hanging out in my living room, I'm certain we'll be able to find something that will help you with your nonexistent Sight. However…" She raised one perfectly manicured nail. "A warning, my dove. This is not a simple request, nor does it come cheap. To grant a human the Sight is not something I take lightly. I will have something from you in return, if you agree."

"No!" My outburst made Kenzie start, though Leanansidhe blinked calmly, looking irritated and amused at the same time. "Kenzie, no," I said, taking a step toward her. "Never make a deal with the fey. The price is always too high."

Kenzie regarded me briefly, then turned back to the Exile Queen, her expression thoughtful. "What kind of price are we talking about?" she asked softly.

"Kenzie!"

"Ethan." Her voice was quiet but firm as she looked over her shoulder. "It's my decision."

"The hell it is! I'm not going to let you do this—"

"Ethan, darling," Leanansidhe ordered, and brought her finger and thumb together. "Shush."

And suddenly, I couldn't speak. I couldn't make a sound. My mouth opened, vocal chords straining to say something, but I had gone as mute as the paint on the wall. "This is my home," the Dark Muse continued, and the lights flickered on and off as she stared at me. "And here you will obey my rules. If you don't like it, pet, you're welcome to leave. But the girl and I have business to conduct now, so sit down and be a good boy, won't you? Don't make me turn you into a very whiny guitar."

I clenched my fists, wanting to hit something, wanting to grab Kenzie and get us both out of there. But even if I left, Leanansidhe wouldn't let Kenzie go, not without completing the bargain. Attacking someone as powerful as the Exile Queen was a very stupid idea, even for me. I wanted to protect Kenzie, but I couldn't do that if Leanansidhe turned me into a guitar. So I could only stand there, clenching and unclenching my fists, as Kenzie prepared to deal with the Exile Queen. Keirran watched me, his gaze apologetic, and I resisted the urge to hit him, too.

"Ethan." Kenzie looked back at me, horror crossing her face as she realized what had happened, then whirled on Leanansidhe. "Whatever you just did to him," she demanded, bristling, "stop it right now."

"Oh, pish, darling. He's just a little tongue-tied at the moment. Nothing he won't recover from. Eventually." The Exile Queen gave me a dismissive wave. "Now, my dove. I believe we have some business to conclude. You want to be able to see the Hidden World, and I want something from you, as well. The question is, what are you willing to pay?"

Kenzie stared at me a moment longer, then slowly turned back to the Dark Muse. "I take it we're not talking about money."

Leanansidhe laughed. "Oh, no, my pet. Nothing so crude as that." She strolled forward until Kenzie was just a foot away, gazing up at the Exile Queen looming over her. "You have something else that I'm interested in."

I started forward, but Keirran grabbed my arm.

"Ethan, don't," he whispered as I glared at him, wondering if I shouldn't lock his elbow out and force him to his knees. "She'll do something nasty if you try to interfere. I've seen it. Even if it's not on you, she could take it out on others. I can't let you hurt yourself…or Annwyl."

"I can feel the creative energy in you, pet," the Exile Queen mused, lightly stroking Kenzie's long black hair, and Keirran had to tighten his grip on my arm. "You are an artist, aren't you, darling? A smith of words, one might say."

"I'm a journalist," Kenzie replied cautiously.

"Exactly so, darling," said Leanansidhe, moving a few steps back. "You create music with words and sentences, not notes. Well, here is my bargain, my pet—I will offer you a little of my…shall we say 'divine inspiration,' for a very special piece I'm willing to commission."

"And…what do you want me to write about?"

"I want you to publish something about me, darling," Leanansidhe said, as if that were obvious. "That's not such a horrible price, is it, pet? Oh, but here is the real kicker—every word you put down on paper will practically sing from the page. It will touch everyone who reads it, in one form or another. The words will be yours, the thoughts will be yours. I will just add a little inspiration to make the work truly magnificent. Let me do this, and I will give you the ability to see the fey."

Kenzie, no! I wanted to shout. *If you let her do this, you'll be giving a piece of yourself to Leanansidhe. She'll take a bit of your life in exchange for the inspiration, that's how the Dark Muse works!*

Kenzie hesitated, considering. "One piece?" she said at last, as I turned desperately to Keirran, grabbing his collar. "That's all?"

Say something, I thought, beseeching the faery with my gaze. *Dammit, Keirran, you know what's going on. You can't let her agree without the full knowledge of what she's getting into. Say something!*

"Of course, darling," Leanansidhe said. "Just one tiny piece, written by you. With my help, of course.

"Please," I mouthed, and Keirran sighed.

"That's not all, Leanansidhe," he said, releasing my arm and stepping forward. "You're not telling her everything. She deserves to know the real price of your inspiration."

"Keirran, darling," Leanansidhe said, a definite note of irritation beneath the cheerful facade, "if I lose this deal because of you, I'm going to be very unhappy. And when I am unhappy, pet, *everyone* in my home is unhappy." She glowered at Keirran, and the lights on the walls flickered. "I did you a favor by taking the Summer girl in, darling. Remember that."

Keirran backed off, giving me a dark look, but it was enough. "What does he mean?" Kenzie asked as the Exile Queen huffed in frustration. "What's the 'real price'?"

"Nothing much, darling," Leanansidhe soothed, switching tones as she turned back to the girl. "Just…in the terms of the contract, you will agree to forfeit a tiny bit of your life to me, in exchange for the inspiration. Not much, mind you," she added, as Kenzie's mouth dropped open. "A month or two, give or take. Of course, this is your natural lifespan only—it does not count for fatal accidents, sickness, disease or other untimely demises. But that is my offer for the Sight, my pet. It really is one of my more generous offers. What say you?"

No, I thought at Kenzie. *Say no. That's the only thing you can say to an offer like that.*

"Sure," Kenzie said immediately, and I gaped at her. "Why not? A month of my life, in exchange for a lifetime of seeing the fey?" She shrugged. "That's not too bad, in the long run."

What? Stunned, I could only stare at the girl in horror. *Do you know what you just did? You gave away a month of your existence to a faery queen! You let her shorten your life for nothing.*

Leanansidhe blinked. "Well," she mused after a moment. "That was easy. How fortunate for me. Humans are usually extraordinarily attached to their lives, I've found. But, if that is your decision, then we have a deal, my pet. And I will get you the things you need to acquire the Sight." She smiled, terribly pleased with herself, and looked at me and Keirran. If she saw how I was staring at Kenzie, dumbstruck, she didn't comment. "I will fetch Annwyl to show you your rooms. Meet me here tomorrow, darlings, and we will discuss where you will go next. Until then, the mansion is yours."

My voice finally returned a few hours later.

I hadn't seen Annwyl or Keirran for a while, not since the Summer girl had brought us to Leanansidhe's guest rooms and quickly vanished, saying she had work to do. Keirran didn't wait very long before following her down the hall. Kenzie, I think, was avoiding me, for she disappeared into her room and didn't answer the door when I knocked a few minutes later.

So I prowled the mansion, which was huge, wandering its endless corridors, hoping some exiled fey would try to pick a fight with me. Nobody did, leaving me to brood without any distractions.

Keirran. Meghan's son…and my nephew, disturbing as that was. The whole situation was completely screwed up. I knew time flowed differently in Faery, but still. Keirran was *my* age, as were Meghan and Ash…

I shook my head, veering away from that train of thought. My family had just gotten a whole lot weirder. I wondered what Mom would say, if she knew about Keirran. She'd probably freak out.

Maybe that's why Meghan didn't tell us, I thought, glaring at a bogey crouched under a low shelf like a huge spider, daring it to do something. It took one look at me and vanished into the shadows. *Maybe she knew Mom wouldn't be able to handle it. Maybe she was scared of what I would think…but, no, that's not an excuse! She still should've told us. That's not something you can just hide away and hope no one finds out.*

Meghan had a reason for not telling us about Keirran, and for trying to keep him away from us, as well. What was it? As far as I could tell, Keirran had no prejudice against humans; he was polite, soft-spoken, respectful. *The complete opposite of me,* I thought, rolling my eyes. *Mom would absolutely love him.* But Meghan never wanted us to meet, which seemed really odd for her, as well. What could possibly be so horrible that you would have a child and keep it a secret from the rest of your family?

What wasn't she telling us about Keirran?

Voices drifted down the corridor from somewhere up ahead, the soft, garbled buzz of a conversation. I heard Annwyl's lyrical tone through an archway at the end of the hall, and Keirran's quiet voice echo it. Not wanting to disturb…whatever they were doing, I turned to leave, when Kenzie's name filtered through the conversation and caught my attention.

Wary now, I crept down the corridor until it ended at a large, circular room filled with vegetation. An enormous tree loomed up from the center, extending gnarled branches skyward, which was easy because the room had no ceiling. Bright sunlight slanted through the leaves, spotting the carpet of grass and wildflowers surrounding the trunk. Birds twittered overhead and butterflies danced through the flowers, adding to the dazzling array of color and light.

It wasn't real, of course. Leanansidhe's mansion, according to rumors, existed in a place called the Between, the veil that separated Faery from the mortal world. Supposedly, when using a trod, you passed very briefly through the Between, then into the other realm. How Leanansidhe managed to set up an entire mansion in the space between worlds was baffling, something you just shouldn't wonder about. No one knew what the outside of the mansion looked like, but I was pretty sure it didn't have sunlight and birdsong. This room was all faery glamour. A really good illusion—I could smell the wildflowers, hear the bees buzzing past my ear and feel the warmth of the sun—but an illusion nonetheless. I hadn't come here to smell the flowers, I was here to discover why two faeries were talking about Kenzie.

Keirran sat beneath the trunk, one knee drawn up to his chest, watching Annwyl as she moved gracefully through the flowers. Every so often, the Summer faery would pause, brushing her fingers over a petal or fern, and the plant would immediately straighten, unfurling new and brighter leaves. Butterflies danced around her, perching on her hair and clothes, as if she was an enormous blossom drifting through the field.

I eased closer, skirting the edges of the room, keeping a row of giant ferns between myself and the two fey. Peering through the fronds, feeling slightly ridiculous that I would stoop this low, I strained my ears in the direction of the tree.

"Leanansidhe wants the ceremony done tonight," Annwyl was saying, raising an arm to touch a low-hanging branch. It stirred, and several withered leaves grew full and green again. "I think it would be better if you performed the ritual, Keirran. She knows you, and the boy might object if I go anywhere near her."

"I know." Keirran exhaled, resting his chin on his knee. "I just hope Ethan doesn't hate me for my part in giving Kenzie the Sight. He's probably still reeling from that last load of bricks I dropped on his head."

"You mean that you're his nephew?" Annwyl asked mildly, and my gut twisted. I still wasn't used to the idea. "But, surely he understands how time works in both worlds. He had to realize that his sister would start her own family, even if she wasn't in the mortal realm, right?"

"How could he?" Keirran muttered. "She never told him. She never told *me*." He sighed again, and though I couldn't see his face very well, his tone was morose, almost angry. "She's hiding something, Annwyl. I think they all are. Oberon, Titania, Mab—they all know something. And no one will tell me what it is." His voice lowered, frustrated and confused. "Why don't they trust me?"

Annwyl turned, giving him a strange look. Snapping a twig from the nearest branch, she knelt in front of Keirran and held up the stick. "Here. Take this for a moment."

Looking bewildered, Keirran did.

"Do what I was doing just now," she ordered. "Make it grow."

His brow furrowed, but he shrugged and glanced down at the bare stick. It shivered, and tiny buds appeared along the length of the wood, before unfurling into leaves. A butterfly floated down from Annwyl's hair to perch on the end.

"Now, kill it," Annwyl said.

She received another puzzled look, but a second later frost crept over the leaves, turning them black, before the entire twig was coated in ice. The butterfly dropped away and spiraled toward the ground, lifeless in an instant. Annwyl flicked the branch with her fingers, and it snapped, one half of the stick spinning away into the flowers.

"Do you see what I'm getting at, Prince Keirran?"

He hung his head. "Yes."

"You're the Iron prince," Annwyl went on in a gentle voice. "But you're not simply an Iron faery. You have the glamour of all three courts and can use them seamlessly, without fail. No one else in Faery has that ability, not even the Iron Queen." She put a hand on his knee, and he looked down at it. "They fear you, Keirran. They're afraid of what you can become, what your existence might mean for them. It's the nature of the courts, sadly. They don't react well to change."

"Are you afraid of me?" Keirran asked, his voice nearly lost in the sighing leaves.

"No." Annwyl pulled her hand away and rose, gazing down at him. "Not when you were kind to me, and risked so much to bring me here. But I know the courts far better than you do, Keirran. I was just a humble servant to Titania, but you are the Iron prince." She took a step back, her voice mournful but resolved. "I know my place. I will not drag you into exile with me."

As Annwyl turned away, Keirran rose swiftly, not touching her but very close. "I'm not afraid of exile," he said quietly, and the Summer girl closed her eyes. "And I don't care what the courts say. My own parents defied those laws, and look where they are now." His hand rose, gently brushing her braid, causing several butterflies to flit skyward. "I would do the same for you, if you just gave me the chance—"

"No, Prince Keirran." Annwyl spun, her eyes glassy. "I won't do that, not to you. I wish things were different, but we can't... The courts would... I'm sorry."

She whirled and fled the room, leaving Keirran standing alone under the great tree. He scrubbed a hand over his eyes, then wandered back to lean against the trunk, staring out at nothing.

Feeling like an intruder who had just witnessed something he shouldn't have, I eased back into the corridor. My suspicions had been confirmed; Meghan *was* hiding something from us. I was definitely going to have to talk to her about that, demand why she thought it was so important to keep her family in the dark.

First, however, I had to find Kenzie, before this ritual was supposed to begin. She needed to know what having the Sight really meant, what the fey did to those who could See them. If she'd really understood the consequences, she never would have made that bargain.

Although, deep down, I knew that was a lie. Kenzie had known *exactly* what she was getting into and chose to do it anyway.

I finally found her in the library, hidden between towering shelves of books, leaning against the wall. She glanced up as I came into the aisle, the massive tome in her hands making her look even smaller. That strange, unfamiliar sensation twisted my stomach again, but I ignored it.

"Hey." She gave me a hesitant smile, as if she wasn't sure if I was mad at her or not. "Has your voice come back yet?"

"Yeah." It came out harsher than I'd wanted, but I plunged on. "I need to talk to you."

"I suppose you do." She sighed, pushing a strand of hair behind her ear. For a moment, she stared at the pages in front of her. "I guess…you want to know why I agreed to that bargain."

"Why?" I took a step forward, into the narrow space. "Why would you think your life was an acceptable trade for something that you have no business seeing in the first place?" Anger flickered again, but I couldn't tell if it was directed at Kenzie, Leanansidhe, Keirran or something else. "This isn't a game, Kenzie. You just shortened your life by trading it away to a faery. Don't think she won't collect. They always do."

"It's a month, Ethan. Two at the most. It won't matter in the long run."

"It's your life!" I stabbed my fingers through my hair, frustrated that she refused to see. "What would've been 'too much,' Kenzie? A year? Two? Would you have become her 'apprentice'? Giving away bits of your life for the inspiration she offers? That's what she does, you know. And every single person she helps dies an early death. Or becomes trapped in this crazy between-worlds house, entertaining her for eternity." I paused, fisting my hand against the shelf. "I can't watch that happen to you."

We both fell silent. Kenzie hesitated, picking at the pages of the book. "Look," she began, "I realize you know almost everything about the fey, but there are things you don't know about me. I don't like talking about it, because I don't want to be a burden on anyone, but…" She chewed her lip, her face tightening. "Let's just say I view things a little differently than most people. I want to learn everything I can, I want to *see* everything I can. That's why I want to become a reporter— to travel the world, to discover what's out there." Her voice wavered, and her eyes went distant. "I just don't want to miss anything."

I sighed. "Promise me you won't make any more deals," I said, taking another step toward her. "No matter what you see, no matter what they offer you, promise that you won't agree to it."

She watched me over the edge of the book, brown eyes solemn. "I can't make that promise," she said quietly.

"Why?"

"Why do you care?" she shot back, defiant. "You told me to leave you alone, to forget about you when we went back, because you're going to do the same. Those were your words, Ethan. You don't want me around and you don't care."

I huffed and closed the last few steps. Taking the book from her hands, I snapped it shut, replaced it on the shelf, and grabbed her shoulders, forcing her to look at me. She stiffened, raising her chin, glaring at me with wounded eyes.

"I care, all right?" I said in a low voice. "I know I come off as a bastard sometimes, and I'm sorry for that. But I do care about…what happens to you here. I don't want to see you get hurt because of Them. Because of me."

Kenzie met my gaze and stepped forward, so close that I could see my reflection in her dark eyes. "I want to see Them, Ethan," she said, firm and unshakable. "I'm not afraid."

"I know, that's what scares me." I released her, kicking myself for acting so roughly, yet reluctant to let her go. "You're going to have the Sight now," I said, feeling raw apprehension spread through my insides. "That means the fey will hound you relentlessly, wanting to bargain, or make a deal, or just make your life hell. You've seen it. You know what they're capable of."

"Yes," Kenzie agreed, and suddenly took my hand, sending a shiver up my arm. "But I've also spoken with a talking cat, fought a dragon, and watched the Iron Realm light up at night. I've seen a faery queen, climbed the towers of a huge castle, flown on a giant metal insect, and made a deal with a legend. How many people can say that? Can you blame me for not wanting to let it go?"

"And if it gets you killed?"

She shrugged and looked away. "No one lives forever."

I had no answer for that. There *was* no answer for that.

"Hey." Keirran appeared at the end of the aisle, and we jumped apart. His gremlin grinned manically from his shoulder, lighting the shelves with a blue-white glow. "What are you two doing?"

He gave me a half wary, half hopeful look, unsure of where we stood, if we were cool. I shrugged, not smiling, but not glaring at him, either. It was the best I could offer for now.

"Nothing," I said, and nodded to Kenzie. "Futilely trying to convince stubborn reporters not to go through with this."

She snorted. "Hi, Mr. Pot. Meet Mr. Kettle."

"Kenzie." Annwyl stepped forward. Her hair was loose, falling down her back in golden-brown waves, petals and leaves scattered throughout. Keirran watched her, his face blank, but he didn't say anything. A tiny glass vial gleamed from her fingertips as she held it up. "Leanansidhe told me to give this to you."

I clenched my fists to keep from dashing the vial to the floor. Kenzie reached out and plucked it from her hand, holding it up to the light. It sparkled dully, half-full with amber liquid, throwing tiny slivers of gold over the carpet.

"So," she mused after a moment, "is it 'down the hatch' right now and, *poof,* I'll be able to see the fey? Is that how this works?"

"Not yet," Annwyl said solemnly. "There is a ritual involved. To gain the Sight, you must stand in the middle of a faery ring at midnight, spill a few drops of your blood onto the ground, and then drink that. The Veil will lift, and you'll be able to see the Hidden World for the rest of your life."

"Doesn't sound too hard." Kenzie gave the vial a small shake, dislodging a few black specks that swirled around the glass. "What's in here, anyway?"

Keirran smiled. "Probably best you don't know," he warned. "In any case, Leanansidhe has a trod that will take us to a faery ring. There's a catch, though. When the full moon shines down on a faery ring, the local fey can't resist. We'll probably run into a few of them, dancing under the moonlight. You know, like they do."

"Well, then it's a good thing I'll have you two around to protect me." She glanced my way, a shadow of uncertainty crossing her face. "You'll be there, right?"

"Yeah." I gave her a resigned look. *I'd say what a stupid idea this is, but you won't listen to me. I only hope the cost will be worth it.*

"So," I muttered, looking at Keirran, "where is this faery ring?"

He grinned, reminding me suddenly of Meghan, and my stomach clenched. "Not far by trod, but probably farther than you've ever been," he said mysteriously. "This particular ring is several thousand years old, which is vital to the ritual tonight—the older the ring, the more power it holds. It's somewhere deep in the moors of Ireland."

Kenzie's head jerked up, her eyes brightening. "Ireland?"

"Yay!" Razor crowed, bouncing up and down on his shoulder. "Sheep!"

CHAPTER SEVENTEEN
THE FAERY RING

"Better hurry, darlings," Leanansidhe announced, walking into the dining room with a swooshing of fabric and smoke. "The witching hour is fast approaching, at least where you're headed. And it will be a full moon tonight, so you really don't want to miss your window." She glanced at me, wandering back to the corner of the room, and sighed. "Ethan, darling, why don't you sit down and eat? You're making my brownies very nervous with all that pacing."

Too bad for them, I thought, chewing a roll I'd snagged from the dining-room table in the middle of the room. The table was enormous and covered with enough food to feed an army, but I couldn't sit still. Keirran and Kenzie sat opposite each other, talking quietly and occasionally giving me worried looks as I paced around them, while Razor cavorted among the plates, scattering food and making small messes. Several redcaps, dressed in butler suits with pink bow ties, skulked back and forth, cleaning up and looking like they really wanted to bite the gremlin's head off. I kept a wary eye on them every time they approached Kenzie, tensing to jump in if they so much as looked at her. They reminded me of the motley that had chased me into the library and set it on fire, leading to my expulsion. If they made any threatening moves toward Kenzie, even a leer, they were going to get an expensive china plate to the back of the skull.

"Ethan," Leanansidhe warned, "you're wearing a hole through my carpet, darling. *Sit down*." She pointed to a chair with her cigarette holder, pursing her lips. "The minions aren't going to bite anyone's knees off, and I'd hate to have to turn you into a harp for the rest of the evening. Sit."

I pulled out a chair beside Kenzie and sat, still glaring at the biggest redcap, the guy with the fishhook through his nose. He sneered and bared his teeth, but then Razor knocked over a platter of fruit, and he hurried off with a curse. Leanansidhe threw up her hands.

"Keirran, dove. Your gremlin. *Please* keep it under control." The Exile Queen pinched the bridge of her nose and sighed heavily. "Worse than having Robin Goodfellow in my house," she murmured, as Kenzie clapped her hands, and Razor bounced happily into her lap. Leanansidhe shook her head. "Anyway, darlings, when you are finished here, I will have Annwyl show you the way to the trod. Meet her in the main hall, and she will take you out through the basement. If you have any questions about the ritual, I'm sure she can answer them for you." At the mention of Annwyl's name, Keirran glanced up, and Leanansidhe smiled at him. "I'm not a complete soulless harpy all the time, darling. Besides, you two remind me of another pair, and I just *adore* the irony." She snapped her fingers and handed her cigarette flute to the redcap who scurried up. "Now, I'm off to meet a jinn about another disappearance, so don't wait up for me, darlings. Oh, and, Kenzie, pet, when you finish the ritual, you might feel a bit odd for a moment."

"Odd?"

"Nothing to worry about, dove." The Exile Queen waved her hand. "Merely the completion of our bargain. I will see you three again soon, but not too soon, I hope." She looked directly at me when she said this, before turning away in a swirl of glitter and lights. "*Ciao,* darlings!"

And she was gone.

As soon as she left, Annwyl came into the room, not looking at any of us. "Leanansidhe has bid me to show you to the faery ring tonight," she said in her musical voice, gazing straight ahead. "We can leave whenever you are ready, but the ritual takes place at midnight, so we should depart soon—"

She paused as Keirran pushed back his chair and walked up to her. Taking her hand, the prince drew her to the table and pulled out the chair next to his, while Razor giggled and waved at her from Kenzie's lap.

"I really shouldn't be here," Annwyl said, perching gingerly on the seat. Her green eyes darted around the room, as if the Exile Queen was hiding somewhere, listening to her. "If Leanansidhe finds out—"

"She can take it up with me," Keirran broke in, sliding into his own chair. "Just because you have to be here doesn't mean Leanansidhe should treat you like a servant." He sighed, and for a second, his expression darkened. "I'm sorry. I know you miss Arcadia. I wish there was another place you could go."

"I'm fine, Keirran." Annwyl smiled at him, though her expression was wistful. "Avoiding Leanansidhe isn't much different than avoiding Queen Titania in one of her moods. I worry most for you. I don't want you to accede to Leanansidhe's every whim and favor because of me."

Keirran stared down at his plate. "If Leanansidhe asked me to fight a dragon," he said in his quiet, sincere voice, "if it meant keeping you safe, I would go into the depths of the Deep Wyld and fight Tiamat herself."

"How long have you two known each other?" Kenzie asked, as I gagged silently into a coffee mug. These two just needed to admit defeat and get on with it already.

Keirran spared her a quick glance and a smile. "I'm not sure," he admitted, shrugging. "It's hard to say exactly, especially in human years."

"We met at Elysium," Annwyl put in. "Midsummer's Eve. When Oberon was hosting. I was chosen to perform a dance for the rulers of the courts. And when it started, I noticed that the son of the Iron Queen couldn't stop staring at me the whole time."

"I remember that dance," Keirran said. "You were beautiful. But when I tried to talk to you, you ran away." He gave me and Kenzie a wry grin. "No one from Summer or Winter wants to talk to the Prince of the Iron Realm. I'd poison their blood or shoot toxic vapors from my nose or something. Annwyl even sicced a school of undine on me once when I was visiting Arcadia. I very nearly drowned."

Annwyl blushed. "But that didn't deter you, did it?"

"So, how did you end up here?" I asked. And Keirran's eyes narrowed.

"Summer Court politics," he said, frowning. "One of the minor nobles was jealous about Annwyl's proximity to Titania, that she was a personal favorite, so she started the rumor that Annwyl was more beautiful and graceful and gifted than even the Summer Queen, and that Oberon would be blind not to see her."

I winced. "That didn't go over well, I'm sure."

"Titania heard of it, of course." Annwyl sighed. "By then, the rumor had spread so far there was no telling who first mentioned such a thing. The Queen was furious, and even though I denied it, she still feared I would steal her husband's attention away."

"So she banished you," I muttered. "Yeah, that sounds like her."

"She banished you?" Kenzie repeated, sounding outraged,

"because someone said you were prettier? That's totally unfair! Can't any of the other rulers do something about it? You're the prince of the Iron Realm," she said, looking at Keirran. "Can't you get the Iron Queen to help?"

Keirran grimaced. "Ah, I'm not really supposed to be here," he said with a half embarrassed, half defiant smile. "If the other courts knew I was hanging around the Exile Queen, they wouldn't approve. They're afraid she'll put treasonous thoughts in my head, or use me to overthrow the other rulers. But…" And his eyes hardened, the shadow of his father creeping over him, making him look more fey than before. "I don't care what the courts dictate. Annwyl shouldn't suffer because Titania is a jealous shrew. So, I asked Leanansidhe to do me a favor, to let her stay here, with the rest of the exiles. It's not ideal, but it's better than being out in the real world."

"Why?" asked Kenzie.

"Because faeries banished to the real world, with no way to get home, eventually fade away into nothing," Annwyl said solemnly. "That's why exile is so terrifying. Cut off from the Nevernever, surrounded by iron and technology and humans that no longer believe in magic, we slowly lose ourselves, until we cease to exist at all."

"Except the Iron fey," I put in, glancing at Keirran. "So, you'd be in no danger."

"Well, that and I'm partly human," he replied, shrugging. "You're right—iron has no effect on me. But for a Summer fey…" He glanced at Annwyl, worry shining from his eyes. No explanation was needed.

The Summer girl sniffed. "I'm not as delicate as that, Prince Keirran," Annwyl said, giving him a wry smile. "You make me sound as fragile as a butterfly wing. I watched the druids perform their rites under the full moon long before your ancestors ever set foot on the land. I'm not going to blow away in the first strong wind that comes through the mortal world. Speaking of which," she went on, rising from the table, "we should get going. Midnight isn't far now, not where we're headed. I'll show you the way."

I followed Annwyl, Keirran and Kenzie back through Leanansidhe's huge basement—or dungeon, I guess—trailing a few steps behind to glare at the things skulking in the shadows. Annwyl had warned us that it might be cold once we emerged from the trod, and Kenzie wore a "borrowed" wool jacket that was two sizes too big for her. The Summer girl offered to find one for me, claiming Leanansidhe had tons of human clothes lying around that she'd never miss, but I didn't want to put myself into her or Leanansidhe's debt any more than I had to, so I refused. As usual, I carried my rattan sticks, in case we were jumped by anything nasty. They were starting to fray a little, though, and I found myself wishing more and more for the solid, steel blade in my room at home.

Was I ready for this? Or, more important, was *Kenzie* ready for this? I'd always considered my Sight a curse, something that I feared and hated and wished I didn't have. It had brought me nothing but trouble.

But to hear Kenzie talk about it, she considered the Sight a gift, something that she was willing to bargain for, something that was worth a tiny piece of her life. It staggered me; the fey were manipulative, untrustworthy and dangerous, that was something I'd always known. How could we see them so differently? And how was I going to protect her, once they realized she had the Sight, as well?

Wait. Why are you even thinking about that? What happened to your promise to not get involved? I felt a stab of annoyance with myself for bringing that up, but my thoughts continued ruthlessly. *You can't protect her. Once you find Todd and get home, she'll go back to her world, and you'll go back to yours. Everyone who hangs around you gets hurt, remember? The best protection you can give anyone is staying the hell away from them.*

Yeah, but it was different now. Kenzie was going to have the Sight. She'd be drawn even more heavily into my crazy, screwed-up world, and she was going to need someone to show her the ins and outs of Faery.

Don't kid yourself, Ethan. That's an excuse. You just want to see her. Admit it; you don't want to let her go.

So…what if I didn't?

"We're here," Annwyl said quietly, stopping at a large stone arch flanked by torch-holding gargoyles. "The ring isn't far. Past this doorway are woods, and then a stretch of moor, with the faery ring in the center of a small grove. It shouldn't be long now." She started forward, but Keirran caught her wrist.

"Annwyl, wait," he said, and she turned back. "Maybe you should stay here," he suggested, looking down at her hand. "We can find the ring on our own."

"Keirran…"

"If those things are anywhere nearby—"

"I'm sure you'll protect me. And I'm not entirely defenseless, either."

"But—"

"Keirran." Stepping close, Annwyl, placed a palm on his cheek. "I can't hide out at Leanansidhe's forever."

He sighed, covering the hand with his own. "I know. I just…worry." Releasing her, he gestured to the arch. "All right then, after you."

Annwyl ducked through the arch, disappearing into the black, Keirran close behind her. I looked at Kenzie, and she smiled back.

"Are you absolutely sure this is what you want?"

She nodded. "I'm sure."

"You know I'm probably going to hover around you for the rest of your life, now. I'll be that creepy stalker guy, always watching you through the fence or following you down the hallway, making sure you're all right."

"Oh?" She laughed. "Is that all it takes to get you to stick around? I should've done the whole bargain-your-life-away-to-the-faeries thing sooner."

I didn't see how she could joke about it, but I half smiled. "I'll be sure to wear a hockey mask, then. So you know it's me."

We went through the arch.

And emerged between two giant, rectangular-shaped rocks standing in the middle of an open field. As Annwyl had warned, the air on this side of the trod was icy. It swept across the rolling moors and sliced through my T-shirt, making my skin prickle. Above us, the sky was crystal clear, with a huge white moon blazing down directly overhead, turning everything black and silver. From where we stood, atop a small rise that sloped gently away into the moors, you could see for miles.

"Wow." Kenzie sighed. "Now I really, really wish I had my camera."

Annwyl pointed a graceful finger down the slope to a cluster of trees at the foot of a rocky hill. "The ring is there," she said quietly with a brief glance toward the sky. "And the moon is nearly right overhead. We must hurry. But remember," she warned, "when the full moon shines down on a faery ring, the fey will appear to dance. We will not be alone."

We started down the slope, picking our way over rocks and bramble, as the wind moaned softly around us and made me shiver with more than the cold. As we drew closer to the trees, I could hear faint strands of music on the wind, the whispers of many voices rising in song. My heart pounded, and I clenched my fists, ignoring the voices and the sudden urge to follow them, the pull that drew me steadily toward the dark clump of trees.

Movement flashed between the trunks, and the whispered song grew clearer, more insistent. I noticed Kenzie, tilting her head with a puzzled expression, as if she could just barely hear something on the wind.

Afraid that she might slip off without me, lured away by the intoxicating faery music, I reached for her hand, trapping it in mine. She blinked at me, startled, before giving me a smile and squeezing my palm. I kept a tight hold of her as we slipped through the forest, walking toward the music and lights, until the trees opened up and we stood at the edge of a clearing full of fey.

Music swirled around the clearing, dark and haunting and compelling. It took all my willpower not to walk toward the circle of unearthly dancers in the center of the glade. Summer sidhe, tall, gorgeous and elegant, swayed and danced in the moonlight, their movements hypnotic and graceful. Piskies and faery lights bobbed in the air, winking in and out like enormous fireflies.

"Ethan," Kenzie whispered, staring at the clearing. Her voice sounded dazed. "There is something here, right? I keep thinking I hear music, and…" Her fingers tightened around mine. "I really want to go stand in that ring over there."

I followed her gaze. Surrounding the dancers, seeming to glow in the darkness, a ring of enormous white toadstools stood in a perfect circle in the center of the glade. The ring was huge, nearly thirty feet across, the mushrooms forming a complete, unbroken circle. Strands of moonlight slanted in through the branches overhead, dappling the ground inside the circle, and even I could feel that this was a place of old, powerful magic.

"It's calling me," Kenzie whispered, as the circle of dancing fey suddenly stopped, their inhuman eyes trained on us. Smiling, they held out their hands, and the urge to join them returned, powerful and compelling. I clamped down on my will to stay where I was and squeezed Kenzie's hand in a death grip.

Keirran lifted his arm to let Razor scurry to an overhead branch. "I hope they don't mind us interrupting their dancing," he murmured. "Wait here. I'll explain what's going on."

I watched him walk confidently up to the observing sidhe, who waited for him with varying degrees of curiosity and alarm. They knew who he was, I realized. The son of the Iron Queen, the prince of the Iron Court, was probably someone you would remember, especially if his glamour was essentially fatal to you.

Keirran spoke quietly to the circle of dancers, who glanced up at us, smiled knowingly, and bowed.

Keirran stepped into the circle, turned and held out his hand. "All right, Kenzie," he called. "It's almost time. Are you ready?"

She gave me a brave smile, released my hand, and stepped forward. Crossing the line of mushrooms, not seeing the dancers that parted for her, she walked steadily toward Keirran, waiting in the center.

I started to follow, but Annwyl stopped me at the edge, putting out her arm.

"You cannot be there with her."

"The hell I can't," I shot back. "I'm not leaving her alone with them."

"Only the mortal who wishes the Sight is allowed in the ring," Annwyl continued calmly. "Otherwise the ritual will fail. Your girl must do this by herself." She smiled, giving me a soothing look. "She will be fine. As long as Keirran is there, nothing will harm her."

Worried, hating the barrier separating us now, I stood at

the edge of the toadstools and watched Kenzie walk up to the figure waiting in the center of the ring. It might've been the moonlight, the strangeness of the surroundings, or the unearthly dancers, but Keirran didn't look remotely human anymore. He looked like a bright, glowing faery, his silver hair reflecting the pale light streaming around him, his ice-blue eyes shining in the darkness. I clenched my fist around my rattan as Kenzie approached him, looking small and very mortal in comparison.

The faery prince smiled at her and suddenly drew a dagger, the deadly blade flashing in the shadows like a fang. I tensed, but he held it between them, point up, though the deadly cutting edge was still turned toward the girl.

"Blood must be spilled for the recipient to gain the Sight," Annwyl murmured as Keirran's lips moved, probably reciting the same thing to Kenzie. "For something to be given, something must be taken. A few drops are all that is needed."

Kenzie paused just a moment, then reached a hand out to the blade. Keirran kept the weapon perfectly still. I saw her brace herself, then quickly run her thumb along the sharp edge, wincing. Drops of blood fell from the blade and her hand, sparkling as they caught the light. A collective sigh went through the circle of fey around them as the crimson drops hit the earth, and I shivered.

"Now only one thing remains," Annwyl whispered, and there was a glint of amber as Kenzie pulled out the vial. "But be warned," she continued, speaking almost to herself, though I had the suspicion she was doing this for my benefit, letting me hear what was going on. "The Sight goes both ways. Not only will you be aware of the fey, they will be aware of you, as well. The Hidden Ones always know whose gazes can pierce the mist and the glamour, who can see through the Veil into the heart of Faery." Keirran stepped back a pace, raising his hand, as if calling her forward. "If you are prepared to embrace this world, to stand between them and be a part of neither, then complete your final task, and join us."

Kenzie looked back at me, blood slowly dripping from her cut fingers to spatter in the grass. I don't know if she expected me to leap in and try to stop her, or if she was just checking to see my reaction. Maybe she was asking, hoping, for my consent, my approval. I couldn't give her that; I'd be lying if I said I could, but I wasn't going to stop her. She had made up her mind for reasons of her own; all I could do now was watch over and try to keep her safe.

I managed a tiny nod, and that was all she needed. Tipping her head back, she put the vial to her lips, and the contents were gone in a heartbeat.

A breeze hissed through the clearing, rattling the branches and making the grass sway. I thought I heard tiny, whispering voices on the wind, a tangle of words spoken too fast to understand, but they were gone before I had the chance to listen. In the center of the ring, Kenzie stumbled, as if she was being battered by gale force winds, and fell to her knees.

I leaped across the toadstools, through the watching fey, who paid me no attention, and dropped beside her as she knelt in the grass. One hand clutched her heart, gasping. Her face was very pale, and I thought she was going to faint.

"Kenzie!" I caught her as she doubled over, gasping soundlessly. "Are you all right? What's happening?" I glared at Keirran, who hadn't moved from where he stood, and gestured sharply. "Keirran, what's going on? Get over here and help!"

"It's all right," Kenzie said, gripping my arm and slowly sitting up. She took a deep breath, and color returned to her cheeks and lips, easing my panic. "It's fine, Ethan. I'm fine. I just…couldn't catch my breath for a second. What happened?"

"Leanansidhe," Annwyl said, joining Keirran a few feet

away. Their gazes were solemn as they watched us, beautiful
and inhuman under the moon. "The Dark Muse has taken
her price."

Dread gripped my stomach with a cold hand. But Kenzie
wasn't looking at me, or any of us, anymore. Her mouth was
open in a small *O,* as she slowly stood up, staring at the ring
of fey surrounding us. "Have…have they been here the whole
time?" she whispered.

Keirran gave her a small, faintly sad smile. "Welcome to
our world."

One of the Summer sidhe came forward, tall and elegant in
a cloak of leaves, golden hair braided down his back. "Come,"
he said, holding out a long-fingered hand. "A mortal gaining the Sight is cause for celebration. One more to see us, one
more to remember. Tonight, we will dance for you. Prince
Keirran…." He turned and bowed his head to the silver haired
fey across from me. "With your permission…"

Keirran nodded solemnly. And the music rose up once
more, eerily compelling, haunting and beautiful. The fey
began to dance, swirling around us, flashes of color and graceful limbs. And suddenly, Kenzie was in that crowd, swept
from my side before I could stop it, eyes bright as she danced
among the fey.

I started forward, heart pounding, but Keirran held out his
arm. "It's all right," he said. I turned to glare at him, but his
face was calm. "Let her have this. Nothing will harm her tonight. I promise."

The promise thing threw me. If you were a faery and you
said the word *promise,* you were bound to carry it through,
no matter what. And if they couldn't keep that promise, they
would die, so it was a pretty serious thing. I didn't know if
Keirran's human side protected him from that particular rule,

or if he really meant it, but I forced myself to relax, watching Kenzie twirl and spin among the unearthly dancers.

Resentment bubbled. A part of me, a large part, actually, wanted to grab Kenzie and pull her back, away from the faeries and their world and the things that wanted to hurt her. I couldn't help it. The fey had tormented me all my life; nothing good had come out of knowing them, seeing them. My sister had ventured into their world, become their queen, and they'd taken her from me.

And now, Kenzie was a part of that world, too.

"Hey."

I turned. Kenzie had broken away from the circle and now stood behind me, the moonlight shining off her raven hair. She'd dropped her coat and looked like some kind of faery herself, graceful and slight, smiling at me. My breath caught as she extended a hand. "Come and dance," she urged.

I took a step back. "No thanks."

"Ethan."

"I don't want to dance with the faeries," I protested, still backing away. "It breaks my Things-Your-Classmates-Won't-Beat-You-Up-For rule."

Kenzie wasn't impressed. She rolled her eyes, grabbed my hand and tugged me forward even as I half resisted.

"You're not dancing with the faeries," she said, as I made one last attempt to stop, to hang on to my dignity. "You're dancing with me."

"Kenzie…"

"Tough guy," she answered, pulling me close. My heart stuttered, looking into her eyes. "Live a little. For me."

I sighed in defeat, let go of my resolve.

And danced with the fey.

It was easy, once you actually let yourself go. The faery music made it nearly impossible not to lose yourself, to close your eyes and let it consume you. I still kept a tiny hold on my willpower as I swayed with Kenzie, back and forth in the center of the ring, while beautifully inhuman Summer fey twirled around us.

Kenzie moved closer, leaning her head on my chest while her arms snaked around my waist. "You're actually really good at this," she murmured, while my heartbeat started thudding loudly in her ear. "Did they teach dancing in kali?"

I snorted. "Only the kind with sticks and knives," I muttered, trying to ignore the warmth spreading through my stomach, making it hard to think. "Though my old school did make us take a class in ballroom dancing. For our final grade, we had to wear formal attire and waltz around the gym in front of the whole school."

"Ouch." Kenzie giggled.

"That's not the worst of it. Half the class played sick that day, and I was one of the only guys to show up, so of course they made me dance with everyone. My mom still has the pictures." I looked down at the top of her head. "And if you tell anyone about that, I may have to kill you."

She giggled again, muffling her laughter in my shirt. I kept my hands on her slim hips, feeling her body sway against mine. As the eerie music swirled around us, I knew that if I remembered anything about this night, it would be this moment, right now. With Kenzie less than a breath away, the moonlight spilling down on her as she danced, graceful as any faery.

"Ethan?"

"Yeah?"

She paused, tracing the fabric along my ribs, not knowing how crazy it was making me. "How 'bout that interview now?"

I let out a long breath. "What do you want to know?"

"You said people around you get hurt, that I wasn't the only one the fey targeted because of you," she continued, and my stomach dropped. "Will you... Can you tell me what happened? Who was the other person?"

Groaning, I closed my eyes. "It's not something I like to talk about," I muttered. "It took years for the nightmares to finally stop. I haven't told anyone about it, ever..."

"It might help," Kenzie said quietly. "Getting it off your chest, I mean. But if you don't want to, I understand."

I held her, listening to the music, to the faeries spinning around us. I remembered that day; the horror and fear that people would find out, the crushing guilt because I knew I couldn't tell anyone. Would Kenzie hate me if I told her? Would she finally understand why I kept my distance? Maybe it *was* time...to tell someone. It would be a relief, perhaps. To voice the secret that had been hanging over me for years. To finally let it go.

All right, then. I'll...try.

"It was about six years ago," I began, swallowing the dryness in my throat. "We—my parents and I—had just moved into the city from our little backwater farm. My parents raised pigs, you know, before we came here. There's an interesting freebie for your interview. The tough guy's parents were pig farmers."

Kenzie was quiet, and I instantly regretted the cynical jab. "Anyway—" I sighed, squeezing her hand in apology "—I met this girl, Samantha. She lived on my block, and we went to the same school, so we became friends pretty quick. I was really shy back then—" Kenzie snorted, making me smile "—and Sam was pretty bossy, much like someone else whose name I won't mention." She pinched my ribs, and I grunted. "So, I usually ended up following her wherever she wanted to go."

"I'm having a hard time picturing that," Kenzie murmured with a faint smile. "I keep seeing this scowling little kid, stomping around and glaring at everyone."

"Believe what you want, I was actually pretty docile back then. The scowling and setting things on fire came later."

Kenzie shook her head, feathery black strands brushing my cheek. "So, what happened?" she asked softly.

I sobered. "Sam was horse crazy," I continued, seeing the red-haired girl in the back of my mind, wearing her cowboy hat. "Her room was full of horse posters and model ponies. She went to equestrian camp every summer, and the only thing she ever wanted for her birthday was an Appaloosa filly. We lived in the suburbs, so it was impossible for her to keep a horse in her backyard, but she was saving up for one just the same."

Kenzie's palm lingered on my chest, right over my heart, which was pounding against her fingers. "And then, one day," I continued, swallowing hard, "we were at the park, for her birthday, and this small black horse came wandering out of the trees. I knew what it was, of course. It had un-glamoured itself, so that Sam could see it, too, and didn't run away when she walked up to it."

"It was a faery?" Kenzie whispered.

"A phouka," I muttered darkly. "And it knew what it was doing, the way it kept staring at me. I was terrified. I wanted to leave, to go back and find the grown-ups, but Sam wouldn't listen to me. She kept rubbing its neck and feeding it bread crumbs, and the thing acted so friendly and tame that she was convinced it was just someone's pony that had gotten loose. Of course, that's what it wanted her to think."

"Phoukas," Kenzie muttered, her voice thoughtful. "I think I read about them. They disguise themselves as horses or ponies, to lure people onto their backs." She drew in a sharp breath. "Did Sam try to ride it?"

I closed my eyes. "I told her not to." My voice came out shaky at the end. "I begged her not to ride it, but she threatened she would make me sorry if I went and blabbed. And I didn't do anything. I watched her lead it to a picnic bench and swing up like she did with every horse in her summer camp. I knew what it was, and I didn't stop her." A familiar chill ran up my spine as I remembered, just before Sam hopped on, the phouka turned its head and gave me a grin that was more demonic than anything I'd ever seen. "As soon as she was on its back," I whispered, "it was gone. It took off through the trees, and I could hear her screaming the whole way."

Kenzie clenched her fingers in my shirt. "Did she—"

"They found her later in the woods," I interrupted. "Maybe a mile from where we had first seen the phouka. She was still alive but…" I stopped, took a careful breath to clear my throat. "But her back was broken. She was paralyzed from the waist down."

"Oh, Ethan."

"Her parents moved after that." My voice sounded flat in my ears, like a stranger's. "Sam didn't remember the black pony—that's another quirk about the fey. The memory fades, and people usually forget about them. No one blamed me, of course. It was a freak accident, only…I knew it wasn't. I knew if I had said more, argued more, I could have saved her. Sam would've been angry with me, but she would still be okay."

"It—"

"Don't say 'it's not your fault,'" I whispered harshly. There was a stinging sensation in my throat, and my eyes were suddenly blurry. Releasing her, I turned away, not wanting her to see me fall apart. "I knew what that thing was," I gritted out. "It was there because of me, not Sam. I could have physically stopped her from getting on, but I didn't, because I was afraid she wouldn't like me. All her dreams of riding her own horse, of competing in rodeos, she lost it all. Because I was too scared to do anything."

Kenzie was silent, though I could feel her watching me.

Around us, the faery dancers twirled in the moonlight, grace-ful and hypnotic, but I couldn't see their beauty anymore. All I could see was Sam, the way she laughed, the way she bounced from place to place, never still. She would never run again, or go hiking through the woods, or ride her beloved horses. Because of me.

"That's why I can't get let anyone get close," I rasped. "If Sam taught me anything, it's that I can't afford to have friends. I can't take that chance. I don't care if the fey come after me—I've dodged them all my life. But they're not satisfied with just hurting me. They'll go after anyone I care about. That's what they do. And I can't stop them. I can't protect anyone but my-self and my family, so it's better if people leave me alone. No one gets hurt that way."

"Except you."

"Yeah." I sighed, scrubbing a hand over my face. "Just me. I can handle that." A heaviness was spreading through me, gathering in my chest, that same feeling of helpless despair, the knowledge that I couldn't do anything, not really. That I could only watch as the people around me became targets, victims. "But, now…you're here. And…"

Her arms slipped around my waist from behind, making my heart jump. I drew in a sharp breath as she pressed her cheek to my back. "And you're scared I'm going to end up like Sam," she whispered.

"Kenzie, if something happened to you because of me—"

"Stop it." She gave me a little shake. "Ethan, you can't con-trol what they do," she said firmly. "Stop blaming yourself. Faeries will play their nasty tricks and games whether you can see them or not. The fey have always tormented humans, isn't that what you told me?"

"Yeah, but—"

"No buts." She shook me again, her voice firm. "You didn't

make that girl get on that phouka. You tried to warn her. Ethan, you were a little kid facing down a faery. You did nothing wrong."

"What about you?" My voice came out husky, ragged. "I pulled you into this mess. You wouldn't even be here if I hadn't—"

"I'm here because I want to be," Kenzie said in that soft, calm voice. "You said it yourself—I could've gone home anytime I wanted. But I stayed. And you're not going to cut me out of your life. Not now. Because no matter what you think, no matter how much you say you want to be alone, that it's better for everyone if you keep your distance, you can't go through this all by yourself." Her arms tightened around me, her voice dropping to a murmur. "I'm staying. I'm right here, and I'm not going anywhere."

I couldn't say anything for a few seconds, because I was pretty sure if I opened my mouth I would break down. Kenzie didn't say anything, either, and we just stood there for a little while, her arms wrapped around my waist, her slim body against mine. The fey danced and twirled their eerie patterns around us, but they were distant mirages, now. The only thing that was real was the girl behind me.

Slowly, I turned in her arms. She gazed up at me, her fingers still locked against the small of my back, holding me captive. I was suddenly positive that I didn't want to move, that I was content to stay like this, trapped in the middle of a faery ring, until the sun rose and the Fair Folk disappeared, taking their music and glamour with them. As long as she was here.

I slipped my hand into her hair, brushing a thumb over her cheek, and she closed her eyes. My heart was pounding, and a tiny voice inside was warning me not to do it, not to get close. If I did, They would only hurt her, make her a target, use her to get to me. But I couldn't fight this anymore, and I was tired of trying. Kenzie had been brave enough to stand with me against the fey and hadn't left my side once. Maybe it was time to stop living in fear...and just live.

Cupping her face with my other hand, I lowered my head...

And my nerves jangled a warning, that cold chill spreading over the back of my neck and down my spine. I tried not to listen, but years of vigilant paranoia, developing an almost unnatural sixth sense that told me I was being watched, could not be ignored so easily.

Growling a curse, I raised my head and scanned the clearing, trying to see past the unearthly dancers into the shadows of the trees. From the edge of the woods, high in the branches above the swirling fey, a pair of familiar golden eyes gleamed in the darkness, watching us.

I blinked, and the eyes vanished.

I swore again, cursing the rotten timing. Kenzie opened her eyes and raised her head, turning to glance at the now empty spot.

"Did you see something?"

I sighed. "Yeah." Reluctantly, I pulled back, determined to finish what we'd started—later. Kenzie looked disappointed but let me go. "Come on, then. Before he finds the others." Taking her hand, I strode out of the ring, parting ranks of fey as I did. Just inside the tree line, Keirran and Annwyl waited at the edge of the shadows, their backs to us.

"Keirran!" I called, breaking into a jog, Kenzie sprinting to keep up. Keirran didn't turn, and I tapped his shoulder as I stopped beside him. "Hey, we've got company—oh."

"So nice to see you, human," a voice purred from an overhead branch. Grimalkin sniffed, looking from me to Keirran, and smiled. "How amusing that you are both here. The queen is not at all happy with either of you."

CHAPTER EIGHTEEN

THE FEY OF CENTRAL PARK

Keirran visibly winced.

"What are you doing here, cat?" I demanded, and Grimalkin turned a slow, bored gaze on me. "If you're here to take us back to Meghan, you can forget it. We're not going anywhere."

He yawned, sitting up to scratch an ear. "As if I have nothing better to do than play nursemaid to a pair of wayward mortals," he sniffed. "No, the Iron Queen simply asked me to find you, to see if you were still alive. And to make sure that you did not wander into a dragon's lair or fall down a dark hole, as you humans are so prone to doing."

"So she sent you to babysit us." I crossed my arms. "We don't need your help. We're doing fine on our own."

"Oh?" Grimalkin curled his whiskers at me. "And where will you go after this, human? Back to Leanansidhe's? I have already been there, and she will tell you the same thing I am about to." He yawned again and stretched on the branch, arching his tail over his back, making us wait. Sitting back down, he raised a paw and gave it a few slow licks. I tapped my fingers impatiently on my arm. From the few stories Meghan had told me about the cait sith, I'd thought she might be exaggerating. Now I knew she was not.

"Leanansidhe has a lead she wishes you to follow up on,"

he finally announced, when I was just about ready to throw a rock at him. "There have been a great many disappearances around Central Park in New York. She thinks it would be prudent to search the area, see what you can turn up. If you are able to turn up anything."

"New York?" Kenzie furrowed her brow. "Why there? I thought New York would be a place the fey avoid, you know, because it's so crowded and, um…iron-y."

"It is indeed," the cat said, nodding. "However, Central Park has one of the highest populations of exiled fey in the world. Many half-breeds also come from that area. It is a small oasis in the middle of a vast population of humans. Also, there are more trods to and from Central Park than you would ever guess."

"So, how are we supposed to get to New York from Ireland?"

Grimalkin sighed. "One would think I would not have to explain how this works to mortals, again and again and again," he mused. "Worry not, human. Leanansidhe and I have already discussed it. I will lead you there, and then you can flounder aimlessly about to your heart's content."

Razor suddenly blipped onto Keirran's shoulder with a hiss, glaring at Grimalkin. "Bad kitty!" he screeched, making Keirran flinch and jerk his head to the side. "Evil, evil, sneaky kitty! Bite his tail off! Pull his toes out! Burn, burn!" He bounced furiously on Keirran's shoulder, and the prince put a hand over his head to stop him.

"What about the queen?" he asked over Razor's muffled hisses and occasional "bad kitties." "Doesn't she want you to return to the Iron Court?"

"The queen asked me to find you, and I did." Grimalkin scratched an ear, not the least bit concerned with the raging gremlin threatening to set him on fire. "Beyond that, I am afraid I cannot be expected to drag you back if you do not wish to go. Though…the prince consort did mention the phrase, *throw away the key,* at one point."

I couldn't be sure, but I thought I saw Keirran gulp. Razor gave a buzz that sounded almost worried.

"So, if we are done asking useless questions…" Grimalkin hopped to a lower branch, waving his tail and watching us with amusement. "And if you are all quite finished dancing under the moon, I will lead you to your destination. We will have to cut back through Leanansidhe's basement, but she has several trods to New York due to the amount of business she conducts there. And she is not exactly pleased with all the disappearances in her favorite city, so I suggest you hurry."

"Right now?"

"I do not see the point in repeating myself, human," Grimalkin said with a disdainful glance in my direction. "Follow along or not. It makes no difference to me."

I'd never been to New York City or Central Park, though I had seen images of them both online. As seen from above, the park was pretty amazing: an enormous, perfectly rectangular strip of nature surrounded by buildings, roads, skyscrapers and millions of people. It had woodlands, meadows, even a couple of huge lakes, smack-dab in the middle of one of the largest cities in the world. Pretty damn impressive.

It was no wonder that it was a haven for the fey.

It was early twilight when we went through yet another archway in Leanansidhe's dungeon and came out beneath a rough stone bridge surrounded by trees. At first, it was hard to believe we stood at the heart of a city of millions. Everything seemed quiet and peaceful, with the sun setting in the west and the birds still chirping in the branches. A few seconds later, however, it became clear that this wasn't the wilderness. The Irish moors had been completely silent; stand in one place long enough, and it felt as if you were the only person in the entire world. Here, though, the air held the quiet stillness of approaching night, you could still catch the faint sounds of horns and street traffic, filtering through the trees.

"Okay," I muttered, looking at Grimalkin, who strutted to a nearby log and hopped up on it. "We're here. Where to now?"

The cat sat down and licked dew off his paw. "That is up to you, human," he stated calmly. "I cannot look over your shoulder every step of the way. I brought you to your destination—what you do next is no concern of mine." He drew the paw over his ears and licked his whiskers before continuing. "According to Leanansidhe, there have been several disappearances in Central Park. So you are in the right place to start looking for...whatever it is that you are looking for."

"You do realize Central Park is over eight *hundred* acres. How are we supposed to find anything?"

"Certainly not by standing about and whining at me." Grimalkin yawned and stretched, curling his tail over his back. "I have business to attend to," he stated, hopping off the log. "So this is where we must part. If you find anything, return to this bridge—it will take you back to Leanansidhe's. Do try not to get lost, humans. It is becoming rather tedious hunting you down."

With a flick of his bushy tail, Grimalkin trotted away, leaped up an embankment, and vanished into the brush.

I looked at Kenzie and the others. "Any ideas? Other than wandering around a giant-ass park without a clue, that is."

Surprisingly, it was Annwyl that spoke. "I remember coming here a few times in the past," she said. "There are several places that are hot spots for the local fey. We could start there."

"Good enough." I nodded and gestured down the path. "Lead the way."

Yep, Central Park was enormous, a whole world unto itself, it seemed. We followed Annwyl down twisty forest paths, over wider cement roads lined with trees, across a huge flat lawn that still had people milling about, tossing footballs or lying together on blankets, watching the stars.

"Strange," Annwyl murmured as we crossed the gigantic field, passing a couple making out on a quilt. "There's always a few of us on the lawn at twilight—it's one of our favorite dancing spots. But this place feels completely empty." A breeze whispered across the lawn, and she shivered, hugging herself. Keirran put his hands on her shoulders. "I'm afraid of what we might find here."

"We haven't found anything yet, Annwyl," Keirran said, and she nodded.

"I know."

We continued past the lawn, walking by a large, open-air stage on the banks of a lake. A statue of two lovers embracing sat just outside the theater, together for all time. Again, Annwyl paused, gazing at the structure as if she expected to see someone there.

"Shakespeare in the park." She sighed, sounding wistful. "I watched *A Midsummer Night's Dream* here once. It was incredible—the Veil was the thinnest I'd ever seen at that point. So many humans were almost ready to believe in us." She shook her head, her face dark. "Something is very wrong. We haven't seen a single exile, half-blood or anyone. What has happened here?"

"We have to keep looking," Kenzie said. "There has to be someone who knows what's going on. Is there another place we could search?"

Annwyl nodded. "One more place," she murmured. "And if we don't find anyone there, then there's no one to be found. Follow me."

She took us down another path that turned into a rocky trail, winding its way through a serene landscape of flowers and plants. Rustic wooden railings and benches lined the path, and a few late-blooming flowers still poked up from the vegetation. *Quaint* was the word that came to mind as we trailed Annwyl through the lush gardens. Quaint and picturesque, though I didn't voice my opinion out loud. Keirran and Annwyl were faeries, and Kenzie was a girl, so it was okay for them to notice such things. As a card-carrying member of the guy club, I wasn't going to comment on the floral arrangements.

"Where are we?" I asked instead. "What is this place?"

Annwyl stopped at the base of a tree, fenced in by wooden railings and in full bloom despite the cool weather. "This," she said, gazing up at the branches, "is Shakespeare's Garden. The most famous human of our world. We come to this place to pay tribute to the great Bard, the mortal who opened people's minds again to magic. Who made humans remember us once more." She reached out to the tree and gently touched a withered leaf with her finger. The branch shuddered, and the leaf uncurled, green and alive again. "The fact that it's empty now, that no one is here, is terrifying."

I craned my neck to look up at the tree. It was empty, except for a lone black bird near the top branches, preening its feathers. Annwyl was right; it was strange that we hadn't run into any fey, especially in a place like this. Central Park had everything they could ask for: art and imagination, huge swaths of nature, a never-ending source of glamour from all the humans who passed through. This place should be teeming with faeries.

"Aren't there other places we could check?" Kenzie asked. "Other...faery hangouts?"

"Yes," Annwyl said, but she didn't sound confident. "There are other places. Sheep Meadow—"

"Sheep!" Razor buzzed.

"—Tavern on the Green and Strawberry Fields. But if we didn't run into anyone by now, I doubt we're going to have much luck."

"Well, we can't give up," Kenzie insisted. "It's a big park. There have to be other places we can—"

A cry shattered the silence then, causing us all to jerk up. It was faint, echoing over the trees, but a few seconds later it came again, desperate and terrified.

Keirran drew his sword. "Come on!"

We charged back down the path, following the echo of the scream, hoping we were going in the right direction. As we left Shakespeare's Garden, the path split before us, and I paused a second, panting and looking around. I could just see the top of the theater off to the left, but directly ahead of us…

"Is that…a castle?" I asked, staring at the stone towers rising over the trees.

"Belvedere Castle," Annwyl said, coming up behind me. "Not really a castle, either. More of an observatory and sight-seeing spot."

"Is that why it's so small?"

"Look!" Kenzie gasped, grabbing my arm and pointing to the towers.

Ghostly figures, white and pale in the moonlight, swarmed the top of the stone castle, crawling over its walls like ants. Another scream rang out, and a small, dark figure appeared in the midst of the swarm, scrambling for the top of the tower.

"Hurry!" Keirran ordered and took off, the rest of us close behind.

Reaching the base of the castle steps, I whirled, stopping Kenzie from following me up. "Stay here," I told her, as she took a breath to protest. "Kenzie, you can't go charging up there! There're too many of them, and you don't have anything to fight with."

"Screw that," Kenzie retorted, and grabbed a rattan stick from my hand. "I do now!"

"Ethan," Keirran called before I could argue. The faery prince stood a few steps up, glaring at the top of the staircase. "They're coming!"

Ghostly fey swarmed over the walls and hurled themselves down the steps toward us. They were small faeries, gnome- or goblin-sized, but their hands were huge, twice as big as mine. As they drew closer, I saw that they had no mouths, just two giant, bulging eyes and a pair of slits for a nose. They dropped from the walls, crawling down like lizards or spiders, and flowed silently down the steps toward us.

At the head of our group, Keirran raised his hand, eyes half-closed in concentration. For a second, the air around him turned cold, and then he swept his arm down toward the approaching fey. Ice shards flew before him in a vicious arc, ripping into the swarm like an explosion of shrapnel. Wide-eyed, several of them jerked, twisted into fog and disappeared.

Damn. Where have I seen that *before?*

Brandishing his weapon, Keirran charged up the steps with me close behind him. The evil, mouthless gnomes scuttled toward us, eyes hard and furious, raising their hands as they lunged. One of them clawed at my arm as I jerked back. Its palm opened up—or rather, a gaping, tooth-lined mouth opened up on its palm, hissing and chomping as it snatched for me.

"Aagh!" I yelped, kicking the gnome away. "That is not cool! Keirran!"

"I saw." Keirran's sword flashed, and an arm went hurtling away, mouth shrieking. The ghostly fey pressed in, raising their horrible hands. Surrounded by tiny, gnashing teeth, Keirran stood his ground, cutting at any faery that got too close. "Are the others all right?" he panted without looking back.

I spared a split-second glance at Kenzie and Annwyl. Keirran and I were blocking the lower half of the steps, so the gnomes were focused on us, but Kenzie stood in front of Annwyl, her rattan stick raised to defend the Summer girl if needed.

I almost missed the gnome that ducked through Keirran's guard and leaped at me, both hands aiming for my throat. I stumbled back, raising my stick, but a vine suddenly whipped over the stair rail and coiled around the faery in midair, hurling it away. I looked back and saw Annwyl, one hand outstretched, the plants around her writhing angrily. I nodded my thanks and lunged forward to join Keirran.

Gradually, we fought our way up the steps until we reached the open courtyard at the base of the towers. The ugly gnomes fell back, swiping at us with their toothy hands as we pressed forward. One managed to latch onto my belt; I felt the razor-sharp teeth slice through the leather as easily as paper before I smashed the hilt of my weapon into its head with a curse. We fought our way across the deck, battling gnomes that swarmed us from all directions, until we stood in the shadow of the miniature castle itself. Kenzie and Annwyl hung back near the top of the steps, Annwyl using Summer magic to choke and entangle her opponents, while Kenzie whapped them with her stick once they were trapped.

But more kept coming, scaling the walls, rushing us with arms raised. A cry behind us made me look back. Several gnomes stood in a loose circle around Kenzie and Annwyl. They weren't attacking, but the faery's hands were stretched toward the Summer girl, the horrible mouths opened wide. Annwyl had fallen to her hands and knees, her slender form fraying around the edges as if she was made of mist and the wind was blowing her away. Kenzie rushed forward and swung at one gnome, striking it in the shoulder. It turned with a hiss and grabbed the stick in both hands. There was a splintering crack, and the rattan shredded, breaking apart, as the faery's teeth made short work of the wood.

"Annwyl!" Keirran turned back, rushing forward to defend the Summer girl and Kenzie, and in that moment of distraction a wrinkled, gnarled hand landed on my arm. Jagged teeth sank into my wrist, and I cried out, shaking my arm to dislodge it, but the thing clung to me like a leech, biting and chewing. Gritting my teeth, I slammed my arm into the wall several times, ignoring the burst of agony with every hit, and the gnome finally dropped away.

The gnomes pressed forward, sensing blood. My wrist and forearm were soaked red and felt as if I'd just stuck my arm into a meat grinder. As I staggered back, half-blind with pain, a big raven swooped down and landed on the wall across from me. And, maybe it was the delirium from the pain and loss of blood, but I was almost sure it winked.

There was a burst of cold from Keirran's direction, and the bird took off. Several shrieks of pain showed the Iron prince was taking revenge for the Summer faery, but that didn't really help me, backed against a wall, dripping blood all over the flagstones. I braced myself as the swarm tensed to attack.

"You really do meet the strangest people in New York," called a new voice somewhere overhead.

I looked up. A lean figure stood atop one of the towers, arms crossed, gazing down with a smirk. He shook his head, dislodging several feathers from his crimson hair, giving me a split-second glance of his pointed ears.

"For example," he continued, still grinning widely, "you look *exactly* like the brother of a good friend of mine. I mean, what are the odds? Of course, he's supposed to be safely home in Louisiana, so I have no idea what he's doing in New York City. Oh, well."

The gnomes whirled, hissing and confused, looking from me to the intruder and back again. Sensing he was the bigger threat, they started edging toward the tower, raising their hands to snarl at him.

"Huh, that's kinda disturbing. I bet none of you have pets, do you?"

A dagger came flying through the air from his direction, striking a gnome as it rushed forward, turning it into mist. A second later, the stranger landed next to me, still grinning, pulling a second dagger from his belt. "Hey there, Ethan Chase," he said, looking as smug and irreverent as I remembered. "Fancy meeting you here."

The pack lifted their arms again, mouths opening, and I felt that strange, sluggish pull. The faery beside me snorted. "I don't think so," he scoffed, and lunged into their midst.

Pushing myself off the wall, I started to follow, but he really didn't need much help. Even with the gnomes sucking away at his glamour, he danced and whirled among them with no problem, his dagger cutting a misty path through their ranks. "Oy, human, go help your friends!" he called, dodging as a piranha-gnome leaped at him. "I can finish up here!"

I nodded and ran to the foot of the stairs where Keirran had drawn back, placing himself between the gnomes, Annwyl and Kenzie, his eyes flashing as he dared anything to come close. Annwyl slumped against the ground, and Kenzie stood protectively beside her, still holding one half of the broken rattan. A few gnomes surrounded them, arms outstretched and glaring at Keirran; one was doubled over a few feet away as if sick.

Leaping from the stairs, I dropped behind one of the faeries with a yell, bringing my stick crashing down on its skull.

It dropped like a stone, fading into nothing, and I quickly stepped to the side, kicking another in the head, flinging it away.

Hissing, the rest of the pack scattered. Screeching and jabbering through their nasty hand-mouths, they scuttled into the bushes and up the walls, leaving us alone at the foot of the stairs.

Panting, I looked toward the others. "Everyone okay?"

Keirran wasn't listening. As soon as the gnomes had gone, he sheathed his weapon and immediately turned to Annwyl, dropping down beside her. I heard them talking in low murmurs, Keirran's worried voice asking if she was all right, the Summer girl insisting she was fine. I sighed and turned to Kenzie; they would probably be unreachable for a while.

Kenzie approached sheepishly, one half of the broken rattan in her hand. "Sorry," she said, holding up the ruined weapon with a helpless gesture. "It...uh...died a noble death. I can only hope it gave that thing a wicked tongue splinter."

I took the broken stick from her hand, tossed it into the bushes, and drew her into a brief, one-armed hug.

"Better the stick than you," I muttered, feeling her heart speed up, her arms circling my waist to cling to me. "Are you all right?"

She nodded. "They were doing something to Annwyl when Keirran came leaping in. He killed several, but they backed off and started doing that creepy thing with their hands, and Annwyl..." She shivered, looking back at the Summer faery in concern. "It was a good thing you came and chased them off. Annwyl wasn't looking so good...and you're bleeding again!"

"Yeah." I gritted my teeth as she stepped away and gently took my arm. "One of them mistook my arm for the stick. Ow!" I flinched as she drew back the torn sleeve, revealing a mess of blood and sliced skin. "You can thank Keirran for this," I muttered as Kenzie gave me a horrified, apologetic look. "He went swooping in to rescue his girlfriend and left me alone with a half dozen piranha fey."

And speaking of swooping…

"Hey," came a familiar, slightly annoyed voice from the top of the stairs, "not to rain on your little reunion or anything, but did you forget something back there? Like, oh, I don't know…me?"

I heard a gasp from Annwyl as the redheaded faery came sauntering down the steps, lips pulled into a smirk.

"Remember me?" he said, hopping down the last step to face us, still grinning. Kenzie eyed him curiously, but he looked past her to Keirran and Annwyl. "Oh, hey, and the princeling is here, too! Small world! And what, may I ask, are you doing way out here with the queen's brother?"

"What are *you* doing here?" I growled, as Keirran and Annwyl finally joined us. Keirran had on a wide, relieved smile, and the other faery grinned back at him; obviously they knew each other. Annwyl, on the other hand, looked faintly star-struck. I guess you couldn't blame her, considering who this was.

"Me?" The faery laced his hands behind his skull. "I was supposed to meet a certain obnoxious furball near Shakespeare's Garden, but then I heard a racket so I decided to investigate." He shook his head, giving me a bemused look. "Jeez, you're just as much trouble as your sister, you know that? It must run in the family."

"Um, excuse me," Kenzie put in, and we stared at her. "Sorry," she continued, looking around at each of us, "but do you all know each other? And if you do, would you mind letting me in on the secret?"

The Great Prankster grinned at me. "You wanna tell her? Or should I?"

I ignored him. "Kenzie," I sighed, "this is Robin Goodfellow, a friend of my sister's." Her eyes went wide, and I nodded. "You might know him better as—"

"Puck," she finished for me in a whisper. She was staring at him now, awe and amazement written across her face. "Puck, like from *A Midsummer Night's Dream?* Love potions and Nick Bottom and donkey heads? That Puck?"

"The one and only." Puck grinned. Pulling a green hankie from his pocket, he wadded it up and tossed it in my direction. I caught it with my good hand. "Here. Looks like those things chewed on you pretty good. Wrap that up, and then someone can tell me what the heck is going on here."

"That's what we were trying to figure out," Keirran explained, as Kenzie took the handkerchief and started wrapping my mangled wrist. The slashes weren't deep, but they were extremely painful. Damn piranha-faery. I clenched my teeth and endured, as Keirran went on. "Leanansidhe sent us here to see what was happening with the exiles and half-breeds. We were trying to find them when you showed up."

Razor abruptly winked into sight on Keirran's shoulder. Seeing Puck, the gremlin gave a trill that wasn't quite welcoming, making Puck wrinkle his nose. "Oh, hey, Buzzsaw. Still hanging around, are you?" He sighed. "So, let me get this straight. Scary Dark Muse has got you tromping all over Central Park on some sort of crazy secret mission, and she didn't tell *me* about it? Well, I'm kinda hurt." Crossing his arms, he gave Keirran and me a scrutinizing look, and his green eyes narrowed sharply. "How did you two get involved in this, anyway?"

Something in his voice made the hairs rise along my arm. Me and Keirran. Not Kenzie or Annwyl; he wasn't even looking at them. Puck knew something. Just like Meghan. It was as if he'd confirmed that Keirran and I were never supposed to meet, that seeing us together was definitely a bad thing.

I couldn't think about that now, though. Puck was certainly not going to tell me anything. "My friend Todd was kidnapped," I said, and he arched an eyebrow at me. "He's a half-breed, and was taken by the same type of creatures that suck out the glamour of normal fey."

"I *thought* that's what they were doing. Ugh." Puck gave an exaggerated shiver and brushed at his arms. "Nasty creepy things. I'm feeling very violated right now." He shook himself, then frowned at me. "So, you just decided to go look for him? Just like that? Without telling anyone about it? Wow, you *are* just like your sister."

"We had to do something, Puck," Keirran broke in. "Exiles and half-breeds all over the world are disappearing. And these…glamour-eaters…are making them disappear. Summer and Winter weren't offering any help. I could go to Oberon, but he won't listen to me."

Kenzie finished wrapping my arm, tying it off as gently as she could. I nodded my thanks and turned to the Summer faery. "But he'll listen to you," I told Puck. "Someone has to tell the courts about this."

"And you think *I* should be messenger boy?" Puck crossed his arms. "What do I look like, a carrier pigeon? What about you? What are you four planning?" He looked at all of us, Keirran especially, and smiled. "Whatever it is, I think I should stick around for it."

"What about Grimalkin?"

"Furball?" Puck snorted. "He probably set this whole thing up. If he wants to see me, he'll find me. Besides, this sounds much more exciting."

"We've got this."

"Really? Your arm begs to differ, kid. What would Meghan

say if she knew you were out here? *Both* of you?" he added, glancing at Keirran.

"We'll be fine," I insisted. "I don't need Meghan's help. I survived without her for years. She never bothered to keep tabs on me until now."

Puck narrowed his eyes to glowing slits, looking rather dangerous now, and I quickly switched tactics. "And we're just going back to Leanansidhe, to let her know what we found. There's nothing here, anyway."

"But the courts have to know what's going on," Keirran added. "You felt what those things were doing. How long before they kill all the exiles in the real world and start eyeing the Nevernever?"

"You have to go to them," I said. "You have to let them know what's going on. If you tell Oberon—"

"He might not listen to me, either." Puck sighed, scratching the back of his neck. "But...I see your point. Fine, then." He blew out a noisy breath. "Looks like the next stop on my list is Arcadia." That grin crept up again, eager and malicious. "I guess it's about time I went home. Titania is going to be *so* happy to see me."

At the mention of Titania, Annwyl shivered and wrapped her arms around herself. The longing on the Summer girl's face was plain; it was obvious that she wanted to go home, back to the Summer Court. Keirran didn't touch her but leaned in and whispered something in her ear, and she smiled at him gratefully.

They didn't see the way Puck stared at them, his eyes hooded and troubled, a shadow darkening his face. They didn't see the way his gaze narrowed, his mouth set into a grim line. It caused a chill to skitter up my back, but before I could say anything, the Summer Prankster yawned noisily and stretched, raising long limbs over his head, and the scary look on his face vanished.

"Well," he mused, dusting off his hands, "I guess I'm off to the Summer Court, then. You sure you four don't need any help? I feel a little left out of the action."

"We'll be fine, Puck," Keirran said. "If you see my parents, tell them I'm sorry, but I had to go."

Puck winced. "Yeah, that's going to go over so well for me," he muttered. "I can already hear what ice-boy is going to say about this." Shaking his head, he backed up, leaves and dust starting to swirl around him. "You two remind me of a certain pair." He grinned, looking from me to Keirran. "Maybe that's why I like you so much. So be careful, okay? If you get into trouble, I'll probably get blamed for it."

The whirlwind of dust and leaves whipped into a frenzy, and Puck twisted into himself, growing smaller and darker, until a huge black raven rose from the cyclone and flapped away over the trees.

"Wow," murmured Kenzie, uncharacteristically quiet until now. "I actually met Robin Goodfellow."

"Yeah," I said, cradling my arm. My wrist hurt like hell, and the mention of my sister was making me moody. "He's a lot less insufferable in the plays."

For some reason, Razor found that hilarious and cackled with laughter, bouncing up and down on Keirran's back. The prince sighed. "He won't go back to Arcadia," he said grimly, staring at the spot where the raven had disappeared. "Not immediately. He'll go to Mag Tuiredh, or he'll at least try to get a message there. He's going back to tell my parents where we are."

"Great," I muttered. "So we don't have a lot of time, whatever we do."

Keirran shook his head. "What now?" he asked. "Should

we go back to Leanansidhe and tell her the park is basically a dead zone?"

"My vote is yes," I said. I shifted my arm to a more comfortable position, gritting my teeth as pain stabbed through my wrist. "If we run into any more of those things, I'm not going to be able to fight very well."

"Back to the bridge, then?"

"Wait," Kenzie said suddenly. She was staring back toward the castle, her gaze turned toward one of the towers, dark and hazy in the moonlight. "I thought I saw something move."

I turned, following her gaze, just as a head poked up from one of the observation platforms, looking around wildly. Its eyes glowed orange in the shadows.

CHAPTER NINETEEN

PASSING DOWN THE SWORDS

"Todd!" I called, rushing forward.

The dark figure jerked its head toward me, eyes going wide. I leaped up the steps, taking them two at a time, the others close behind. "Hey!" I barked, as the shadowy figure scrambled over the edge of the wall, landing on the deck with a grunt. "Todd, wait!"

I put on a burst of speed, but the figure raced across the courtyard, leaped over the edge and plummeted into the pond at the bottom with a splash.

"Annwyl," Keirran said as we reached the spot the half-breed went over. He was swimming for the edge of the pond, drawing rapidly away. "Can you stop him?"

The Summer girl nodded. Waiting until the half-breed reached the shore, she immediately flung out a hand, and coils of vegetation erupted from the ground, snaking around him. There was a yelp of fear and dismay and the sound of wild thrashing as Annwyl continued to wrap him in vines.

"Got him," Keirran muttered, and leaped onto the wall. He crouched there for a split second, balanced gracefully on the edge, then dropped the long way down to the ground, landing on a sliver of solid ground below us as lightly as a cat. Sheathing his sword, he started across the pond.

I scowled at the back of his head, as I, being a mere mortal, had to retrace my steps back down the stairs and around the pond. Kenzie followed. By the time we reached the place the half-breed was trapped, Keirran stood a few feet from the writhing lump of vegetation, hands outstretched as he tried to quiet him.

"Easy, there." Keirran's quiet, soothing voice drifted over the rocks. "Calm down. I'm not going to hurt you."

The half-breed responded by howling and swiping at him with a claw-tipped hand. Keirran dodged easily. I saw his eyes half close in concentration and felt a slow pulse of magic extend out from where he stood, turning the air thick, making me feel sluggish and sleepy. The half-breed's wild struggles slowed, then stilled, until a loud snore came from the vegetation lump.

Keirran looked up almost guiltily as I joined him, staring at the tangle of vines, weeds, flowers and half-breed. "He was going to hurt himself," he murmured, stepping back as I knelt beside the unconscious form. "I figured this was the easiest way to calm him down."

"No complaints here," I muttered, using my uninjured hand to peel back the tangle of vines. A face emerged within the vegetation, an older, bearded face, with short tusks curling up from his jaw.

I slumped. "It's not Todd," I said, standing back up. Disappointment flickered, which surprised me. What had I been expecting? Todd's last known location was Louisiana. There was no reason he would show up in New York.

Kenzie leaned over my shoulder. "Not Todd," she agreed, blinking at the thick, bearded face, the blunt yellow teeth poking from his jaw. "What is he, then?"

"Half-troll," Keirran supplied. "Homeless, by the looks of it. He probably made part of Central Park his territory."

I stared at the half-troll, annoyed that he wasn't Todd, and frowned. "So, what do we do with him?"

"Hold on," Kenzie said, stepping around me. Kneeling down, she pushed aside weeds and vines, grunting in concentration, until she emerged with a small square item in her hand.

"Wallet," she said, waving it at us, before flipping it open and squinting at it. "Shoot, it's too dark to see anything. Anyone have a minilight?"

Keirran gestured. A small globe of heatless fire appeared overhead, making her jump. "Oh, well, that's handy," she said with a wry grin. "I bet you're fun on camping trips."

The prince smiled faintly. "I can also open cans and make your drinks cold."

"What does the license say?" I asked, trying not to sound impatient. "Who is this guy?"

Kenzie peered at the card. "Thomas Bend," she read, holding the driver's license underneath the pulsing faery light. "He's from…Ohio."

We all stared at him. "Then what the heck is he doing here?" I muttered.

"Oh, you're back, darlings," Leanansidhe said, sounding faintly resigned. "And *what,* may I ask, is *that?*"

"We found him in the park," I said, as Thomas the half-troll stumbled in behind us, shedding mud and leaves and gaping at his surroundings. After he'd woken up, he'd seemed to calm down, remaining passive and quiet when we spoke to him. He'd followed us here without complaint. "He's not from New York. We thought he might be one of yours."

"Not mine, darlings." Leanansidhe wrinkled her nose as the troll blinked at her, orange eyes huge and round. "And why did you feel the need to bring the creature here, pets? You could have asked him yourself and spared my poor carpets."

"Lady," whispered the half-troll, cringing back from the Exile Queen. "Lady. Big Dark. Lady."

"That's all he'll say," Kenzie said, looking worriedly back at the troll. "We tried talking to him. He doesn't remember anything. I don't even think he knows who he is."

"He was being chased through Central Park by our ghostly friends," Keirran added, sounding grim and protective. He hadn't let Annwyl out of his sight the entire way back to Leanansidhe's, and now stood between her and Leanansidhe, watching both the Exile Queen and the half-troll. Razor peeked down from the back of his neck, muttering nonsense. "We fought them off with Goodfellow's help, but we didn't see anyone else there."

"Goodfellow?" The Exile Queen pulled a face. "Ah, so that's what Grimalkin was talking about, devious creature. Where is our darling Puck now?"

"He went back to the Seelie Court to warn Oberon."

"Well, that is something, at least." Leanansidhe regarded the half-breed with cool disinterest. "And what of the park locals, darlings?" she asked without looking up. "Did they mention anything about ladies and dark places?"

"There weren't any others," I told her, and she did look at me then, raising her eyebrows in surprise. "He's the only one we could find."

"The park is a dead zone," Annwyl said. I could see she was shivering. "They're all gone. No one is left. Just those horrible glamour-eaters. I think…I think they killed them all."

Glamour-eaters. The term was catching on, though that was a good name for them. They couldn't hurt me or Kenzie that way, because we had no magic. And Keirran was the son of the Iron Queen; his glamour was poison to them. But everyone else, including Annwyl, the exiles and the rest of Summer and Winter, were at risk.

I suddenly wondered what they could do to half-breeds. Maybe they couldn't make them disappear like the regular fey; maybe a half-breed's human side prevented them from ceasing to exist. But what would draining their magic do to them? I looked at Thomas, standing forlornly in the center of the room, eyes empty of reason, and felt my skin crawl.

Leanansidhe must've been thinking the same thing. "This," she said, her voice cold and scary, "is unacceptable. Darlings…" She turned to us. "You need to go back, pets. Right now. Go back to the park and find what is doing this. I will not stand by while my exiles and half-breeds are killed right out in the open."

"Go back?" I frowned at her. "Why? There's nothing there. The park is completely dead of fey."

"Ethan darling." The Exile Queen regarded me with scary blue eyes. "You are not thinking, dove. The half-breed you found—" she glanced at Thomas, now sitting in a dazed lump on the carpet "—is not from New York. He was obviously taken and brought to Central Park. The park is empty, but so many half-breeds cannot simply vanish into thin air. And the normal fey are gone. Where did they all go, pet? They certainly didn't come to me, and as far as I know, no one has seen them in the mortal world."

I didn't know what she was getting at, but Kenzie spoke up, as if she'd just figured it out. "Something is there," she guessed. "Something is in the park."

Leanansidhe smiled at her. "I knew I liked you for a reason, darling."

"The glamour-eaters might have a lair in Central Park," Keirran added, nodding grimly. "That's why there are no fey there anymore. But where could they be? You'd think such a large population of exiles and half-breeds would notice a group of strange faeries wandering around."

"I don't know, darlings," Leanansidhe said, pulling her cigarette flute out of thin air. "But I think this is something you should find out. Sooner, rather than later."

"Why don't you come with us?" Keirran asked. "You haven't been banished from the mortal realm, Leanansidhe. You could see what's going on yourself."

Leanansidhe looked at him as if he'd just said the sky was green. "Me, darling? I would, but I'm afraid the Goblin Market rabble would make quite the mess while I'm gone. Sadly, I cannot go traipsing across the country whenever I please, pet—I have obligations here that make that impossible." She glanced at me and wrinkled her nose. "Ethan, darling, you're dripping blood all over my clean carpets. Someone should take care of that."

She snapped her fingers, and a pair of gnomes padded up, beckoning to me. I tensed, reminded of the piranha-palmed creatures, but I also knew many gnomes were healers among the fey. I let myself be taken to another room and, while the gnomes fussed over my arm, considered our next course of action.

Return to the park, Leanansidhe had said. Return to the place where a bunch of creepy, transparent, glamour-sucking faeries waited for us, maybe a whole nest of them. Kenzie was right; something was there, lurking in that park, unseen and unknown to fey and human alike. *The lady,* Thomas had mumbled. The lady and the big dark. What the heck did he mean by that?

The door creaked open, and Kenzie came into the room, dodging the gnome who padded out with a bloody rag. "Leanansidhe is keeping Thomas here for now," she said, perching on the stool beside mine. "She wants to see if he'll regain any of his memory, see if he can remember what happened to him. How's your arm?"

I held it up, drawing an annoyed reprimand from the gnome. They'd put some sort of smelly salve over the wound and wrapped it tightly with bandages so it no longer hurt; it was just numb. "I'll live."

"Yes, you will," muttered the gnome with a warning glower at me. "Though you're lucky it didn't get your hand—you might've lost a few fingers. Don't pick at the bandages, Mr. Chase." Gathering the supplies, it gave me a last glare and padded off with its partner, letting the door swing shut behind them.

Kenzie reached over and gently wrapped her hand around mine. I stared at our entwined fingers, dark thoughts bouncing around in my head. This was getting dangerous. No, forget that, this was already dangerous, more than ever. People were dying, vanishing from existence. A deadly new breed of fey was on the rise, killing their victims by draining their glamour, their very essence. Half-breeds were disappearing, right off the streets, from their homes and schools. And there was something else. Something dark and sinister, hidden somewhere in that park, waiting.

The big dark. The lady.

I felt lost, overwhelmed. As if I was a tiny speck of driftwood, bobbing in a huge ocean, waiting for something to swallow me whole. I wasn't ready for this. I didn't want to get pulled into this faery madness. What did they want from me? I wasn't my sister, half-fey and powerful, with the infamous Robin Goodfellow and the son of Mab at my side. I was only human, one human against a whole race of savage, dangerous faeries. And, as usual, I was going to put even more people in harm's way.

Kenzie ran her fingers over my skin, sending tingles up my arm. "I don't suppose there's any way I could convince you to stay behind," I murmured, already knowing the answer.

"Nope," said Kenzie with forced cheerfulness. I looked up, and she gave me a fierce smile. "Don't even think about it, Ethan. You'll need someone to watch your back. Make sure you don't get chomped by any more nasty faeries with sharp teeth. I didn't gain the Sight just to sit back and do nothing."

I sighed. "I know. But I don't have anything to protect you with anymore. Or *me*, for that matter." Gingerly, I clenched my fist, wincing at the needles of pain that shot up my arm. "If we're going to go look for this nest, I don't want a stick. It's not enough. I want my knife or something sharp between me and those faeries. I can't hold back with them any longer."

Cold dread suddenly gripped me. This wasn't a perverse game; me playing keep-away with a redcap motley in the library, or trying to avoid getting beaten up by Kingston's thugs. These fey, whatever they were, were savage and twisted killers. There would be no reasoning with them, no pleas for favors or bargains. It was kill or be torn to shreds myself.

I think I shivered, for Kenzie inched closer and leaned into me, resting her head on my shoulder. "We need a plan," she said calmly. "A strategy of some sort. I don't like the idea of rushing back with no clue of where to go. If we knew where this lair was…" She paused, as I closed my eyes and soaked in her warmth. "I wish I had a computer," she said. "Then I could at least research Central Park, try to figure out what this 'big dark' is. I don't suppose Leanansidhe has any laptops lying around?"

"Not a chance," I muttered. "And my phone is dead. I checked back in the real world."

"Me, too." She sighed and tapped her finger against my knee in thought. "Could we…maybe…go home?" she asked in a hesitant voice. "Not to stay," she added quickly. "I could check some things online, and you could grab your weapons or whatever it is you'll need. Our folks wouldn't have to know."

She snorted, and a bitter edge crept into her voice. "My dad might not even realize I've been gone."

I thought about it. "I don't know," I admitted at last. "I don't like the idea of going home and having those things follow me. Or waiting for me. And I don't want to drag your family into it, either."

"We're going to have to do something, Ethan." Kenzie's voice was soft, and her fingers very gently brushed the bandage on my wrist. "We're in way over our heads—we need all the help we can get."

"Yeah." Frustration rose up, and I resisted the urge to lash out, to snarl at something. Right now, the only someone around was Kenzie, and I wasn't going to take out my fear and anger on her. I wished there was someone I could go to, some grown-up who would understand. I'd never wanted to be the one everyone looked to for direction. Keirran wasn't here; this was my call. How had it all come to rest on me?

Wait. Maybe there *was* someone I could ask. I remembered his face in the locker room, the way he'd looked around as if he knew something was there. I remembered his words. *If you need help, Ethan, all you have to do is ask. If you're in trouble, you can come to me. For anything, no matter how small or crazy it might seem. Remember that.*

Guro. Guro might be the only one who would understand. He believed in the invisible things, the creatures you couldn't see with the naked eye. That's what he'd been trying to tell me in the locker room. His grandfather was a *Mang-Huhula,* a spiritual leader. Spirits to faeries wasn't that big of a leap, right?

Of course, I might be reading too much into it. He might think that I'd finally gone off the deep end and call the people in the white coats.

"What are you brooding over?" Kenzie murmured, her breath soft on my cheek.

I squeezed her hand and stood, pulling her up with me. "I think," I began, hoping the others would be okay with a detour, "that I'm going to have to ask Leanansidhe for one last favor."

She wasn't entirely happy with the idea of us running off to Louisiana again. "How will I know you won't just decide to go home, darlings?" the Dark Muse said, giving me a piercing stare. "You might see your old neighborhood, get homesick, return to your families, and leave me high and dry. That wouldn't work out for me, pets."

"I'm not running away," I said, crossing my arms. "I'm not going to lead those things right to my home. Besides, they might already be hanging around my neighborhood, looking for me. I'm coming back. I swear, I'm not backing out until this is finished, one way or another."

Leanansidhe raised a slender eyebrow, and I realized I'd just invoked one of the sacred vows of Faery. Damn. Well, I was in it for the long haul, now. Not that I couldn't have broken my promise if I wanted to; I was human and not bound by their complex word games, but making an oath like that, in front of a faery queen no less, meant I'd better carry it out or unpleasant things might happen. The fey took such vows seriously.

"Very well, darling." Leanansidhe sighed. "I still do not see the point of this ridiculous side quest, but do what you must. Since Grimalkin is no longer around, I will have to find someone else to take you home. When did you want to leave?"

"As soon as Keirran joins us."

"I'm here," came a quiet voice from the hallway, and the Iron prince came into the room. He looked tired, more solemn than usual, with shadows crouched under his eyes that hadn't been there before. Annwyl was not with him.

"Where are we going?" he asked, looking from me to Kenzie and back again. "Back to the park already?"

"Not yet." I held up my single rattan stick. "If we're going
to be walking into this lady's lair or nest or whatever, I'm
going to need a better weapon. I think I can convince my
kali master to lend me one of his. He has a whole collection
of knives and short swords."

*And I want to talk to Guro one more time, let him know what's
going on, that I didn't just drop out. I owe him that much, at least.
And maybe he can tell my folks I'm all right. For now, anyway.*

Keirran nodded. "Fair enough," he said.

"Where's Annwyl?" asked Kenzie. "Is she okay?"

"She's fine. The fight—the glamour-eaters—it took more
out of her than we first realized. She's sleeping right now.
Razor is with her—he'll come to me when she wakes up."

"Do you want to wait for her?" Kenzie asked. "We don't
mind, if you wanted to let her sleep a bit."

"No." Keirran shook his head. "I'm ready. Let's go."

I watched him, the way he looked back nervously, as if he
was afraid Annwyl could come through the door at any moment. "She doesn't know we're leaving," I guessed, narrowing my eyes. "You're taking off without her."

Keirran raked a guilty hand through his bangs. "You saw
what they did to her," he said grimly. "Out of all of us, she's
the one in the most danger. I can't take that risk again. She'll
be safer here."

Kenzie shook her head. "So you're just leaving her behind?
She's going to be *pissed*." Putting her hands on her hips, she
glared at him, and he wouldn't meet her eyes. "I know I'd
kick your ass if you pulled that stunt with me. Honestly, why
do boys always think they know what's best for us? Why can't
they just *talk?*"

"I've often wondered the same, darling," Leanansidhe

sighed. "It's one of the mysteries of the universe, trust me. But I need an answer, pets, so I know whether or not to call a guide. Are you three going to wait for the Summer girl, or are you going on without her?"

I looked at Keirran, questioning. He hesitated, looking back toward the door, eyes haunted. I saw the indecision on his face, before he shook his head and turned away. "No," he said, ignoring Kenzie's annoyed huff. "I want her to be safe. I'd rather have her angry at me than lose her to those monsters. Let's go."

It took most of the night. Leanansidhe's piskie guide knew of only one trod to my hometown; Guro's house was still clear across town where we came out, and we had to call a taxi to take us the rest of the way. During the half-hour cab ride, Kenzie dozed off against my shoulder, drawing a knowing smile from both Keirran and the driver. I didn't mind the journey, though I did find myself thinking that I wished Grimalkin was here—he would have found us a quicker, easier way to Guro's house—before I caught myself.

Whoa, when did you start relaying on the fey, Ethan? That can't happen, not now, not ever.

Careful not to disturb Kenzie, I crossed my arms and stared out the window, watching the streetlamps flash by. And I tried to convince myself that I still wanted nothing to do with Faery. As soon as this business with the glamour-eaters was done, so was I.

Somehow, I knew it wasn't going to be that simple.

The taxi finally pulled up to Guro's house in the early hours of the morning. I paid the driver with the last of my cash, then gazed up the driveway to the neat brick house sitting up top.

Hope Guro is an early riser.

I knocked on the front door, and immediately a dog started

barking from within, making me wince. Several seconds later, the door opened, and Guro's face stared at me through the screen. A big yellow lab peered out from behind his legs, wagging its tail.

"Ethan?"

"Hey, Guro." I gave an embarrassed smile. "Sorry it's so early. Hope I didn't wake you up."

Before I could even ask to come in, the screen door swung open and Guro beckoned us inside. "Come in," he said in a firm voice that set my heart racing. "Quickly, before anyone sees you."

We crowded through the door. The interior of his home looked pretty normal, though I don't know what I was expecting. Mats on the floor and knives on the walls, maybe? We followed him through the kitchen into the living room, where an older, scruffy-looking dog gave us a bored look from the sofa and didn't bother to get up.

"Sit, please." Guro turned to me, gesturing to the couch, and we all carefully perched on the edge. Kenzie sat next to the old dog and immediately started scratching his neck. Guro watched her a moment, then his dark gaze shifted back to me.

"Have you been home yet?"

"I…" Startled by his question, I shook my head. "No, Guro. How did you—"

"The news, Ethan. You've been on the news."

I jerked. Kenzie looked up at him with a small gasp.

Guro nodded grimly. "You, the girl and another boy," he went on, as a sick feeling settled in my stomach. "All vanished within a day of each other. The police have been searching for days. I don't know you—" he nodded at Keirran "—but I can only assume you're a part in this, whatever it is."

Keirran bowed his head respectfully. "I'm just a friend,"

he said. "I'm only here to help Ethan and Kenzie. Pay no attention to me."

Guro looked at him strangely. His eyes darkened, and for a second, I almost thought he could see through the glamour, through the Veil and Keirran's human disguise, to the faery beneath.

"Who was that at the door, dear?" A woman came into the room, dark-haired and dark-eyed, blinking at us in shock. A little girl of maybe six stared at us from her arms. "These…" She gasped, one hand going to her mouth. "Aren't these the children that were on TV? Shouldn't we call the police?"

I gave Guro a pleading, desperate look, and he sighed.

"Maria." He smiled and walked over to his wife. "I'm sorry. Would you be able to entertain our guests for a moment? I need to speak to my student alone." She looked at him sharply, and he took her hand. "I'll explain everything later."

The woman glanced from Guro to us and back again, before she nodded stiffly. "Of course," she said in a rigidly cheerful voice, as if she was trying to accept the whole bizarre situation. I felt bad for her; it wasn't every day three strange kids landed on your doorstep, two of whom were wanted by the police. But she smiled and held out a hand. "We can sit in the kitchen until your friend is done here."

Kenzie and Keirran looked at me. I nodded, and they rose, following the woman into the hall. I heard her asking if they wanted something to eat, if they'd had breakfast yet. Both dogs hopped up and trailed Kenzie as she left the room, and I was alone with my master.

Guro approached and sat on the chair across from me. He didn't ask questions. He didn't demand to know where I'd been, what I was doing. He just waited.

I took a deep breath. "I'm in trouble, Guro."

"That I figured," Guro said in a quiet, non-accusing voice. "What's happened? Start from the beginning."

"I'm...not even sure I can explain it." I ran my hands through my hair, trying to gather my thoughts. Why had I come here? Did I think Guro would believe me if I started talking about invisible faeries? "Do you remember what you said in the locker room that night? About not trusting what your eyes tell you?" I paused to see his reaction, but I didn't get much; he just nodded for me to go on. "Well...something was after me. Something that no one else can see. Invisible things."

"What type of invisible things?"

I hesitated, reluctant to use the word *faery,* knowing how crazy I already sounded. "Some people call them the Fair Folk. The Gentry. The Good Neighbors." No reaction from Guro, and I felt my heart sink. "I know it sounds insane, but I've always been able to see them, since I was a little kid. And *They* know I can see them, too. They've been after me all this time, and I don't think I can run from them any longer."

Guro was silent a moment. Then he said, very softly: "Does this have anything to do with what happened at the tournament?"

I looked up, a tiny spring of hope flaring in my chest. Guro didn't smile. "You were being chased, weren't you?" he asked solemnly. "I saw you. You and the girl both. I saw you run out the back door, and I saw something strike you just as you went outside."

"How—"

"Your blood was on the door frame." Guro's voice was grave, and I heard the worry behind it. "That, if anything, told me what I saw was real. I followed you out, but by the time I reached the back lot, you were both gone."

I held my breath.

"My grandfather, the *Mang-Huhula* who trained me, he

would often tell me stories of spirits, creatures invisible to the naked eye. He said there is a whole unknown world that exists around us, side by side, and no one knows it is there. Except for a few. A very rare few, who can see what no one else can. And the spirits of this world can be helpful or harmful, friendly or wicked, but above all, those who see the invisible world are constantly trapped by it. They will always walk between two lives, and they will have to find a way to balance them both."

"Do they ever succeed?" I asked bitterly.

"Sometimes." Guro's voice didn't change. "But they often have help. If they can accept it."

I chewed my lip, trying to put my thoughts into words. "I don't know what to do, Guro," I said at last. "I've been trying to stay away from all this—I didn't want to get involved. But they're threatening my friends and family now. I'm going to have to fight them, or they'll never leave me alone. I'm just… I'm scared of what they'll do to my family if I don't do something."

Guro didn't say anything for a moment. Then he stood and left the room for several minutes, while I sat on the couch and wondered if he was calling the police. If my story was still too crazy for him to accept, despite his apparent belief in "the invisible world." I was wondering if I should get Kenzie and Keirran and just leave, when he reappeared holding a flat wooden box. Setting it reverently on the coffee table between us, he looked at me with a serious expression.

"Remember when I told you I do not teach kali for violence?" he asked. I nodded.

"What *do* I teach it for?"

"Self-defense," I recited. Guro nodded at me to go on. "To…pass on the culture. To make sure the skills don't fade away." Guro still waited. My answers were correct, but I still wasn't saying what he wanted.

"And?"

I racked my brain for a few seconds, before I had it. "To protect your family," I said quietly. "To defend the ones you care about."

Guro smiled. Bending forward, he flipped the latches on the case and pulled back the top.

I drew in a slow breath. The swords lay there on the green felt, nestled in their leather sheaths. The same blades I had used in the tournament.

Guro's gaze flickered to me. "These are yours," he explained. "I had them made a few years after you joined the class. I had a feeling you might need them someday." He smiled at my astonishment. "They have no history, not yet. That will be up to you. And someday, hopefully, you can pass them down to your son."

I unstrapped the swords and picked them up in a daze. I could feel the balance, the lethal sharpness of the edges, and I gripped the hilts tightly. Rising, I gave them a practice twirl, hearing the faint hum of the blades cutting through the air. They were still perfectly balanced, fitting into my hands like they'd been waiting for me all along. I couldn't help but smile, seeing my reflection in the polished surface of the weapons.

Okay, *now* I was ready to face whatever those glamour-sucking bastards could throw at me.

"One more thing." Guro reached into the box and pulled out a small metal disk hanging from a leather thong. A triangle was etched into the center of the disk, and between the lines was a strange symbol I didn't recognize.

"For protection," Guro said, holding it up. "This kept my grandfather safe, and his father before him. It will protect you now, as well."

Guro draped the charm around my neck. It was surprisingly heavy, the metal clinking against my iron cross as I tucked it into my shirt. "Thank you," I murmured.

"Whatever you have to face, Ethan, you don't have to do it alone."

Embarrassed now, I looked down. Guro seemed to pick up on my unease, for he turned away, toward the hall. "Come. Let's see what your friends have gotten themselves into."

Keirran was in the kitchen, sitting at the counter with his elbows resting on the granite surface, a mug of something hot near his elbow. The little girl sat next to him, scrawling on a sheet of paper with a crayon, and the half-faery—the prince of the Iron Realm—seemed wholly intrigued by it.

"A…lamia?" he asked as I came up behind him, peering over his shoulder. A squat, four-legged thing with two heads stood amid a plethora of crayon drawings, looking distinctly unrecognizable.

The kid frowned at him. "A pony, silly."

"Oh, of course. Silly me. What else can you draw?"

"Hey," I muttered, as the little girl huffed and started scribbling again. "Where's Kenzie?"

"In the office," Keirran replied, glancing up at me. "She asked if she could use the computer for a little while. I think she's researching the park. You should go check on her."

I smirked. "You gonna be okay out here?"

"There!" announced the girl, straightening triumphantly. "What's that?"

Keirran smiled and waved me off. I left the kitchen, nodding politely to Guro's wife as I wandered down the hall, hearing Keirran's hopeless guesses of dragons and manticores fade behind me.

I found Kenzie in a small office, sitting at a desk in the

corner, the two dogs curled around her chair. The younger lab raised his blocky head and thumped his tail, but Kenzie and the older dog didn't move. Her eyes were glued to the computer screen, one hand on the mouse as it glided over the desk. Releasing it, she typed something quickly, slender fingers flying over the keys, before hitting Enter. The current screen vanished and another took its place. The lab sat up and put his big head on her knee, looking up at her hopefully. Her gaze didn't stray from the computer screen, but she paused to scratch his ears. He groaned and panted against her leg.

I eased into the room. Reaching into my shirt, I withdrew Guro's amulet, pulling it over my head. Stepping up behind Kenzie, I draped it gently around her neck. She jerked, startled.

"Ethan? Jeez, I didn't hear you come in. Make some noise next time." She glanced at the strange charm hanging in front of her. "What's this?"

"A protection amulet. Guro gave it to me, but I want you to have it."

"Are you sure?"

"Yeah." I felt the weight of the swords at my waist. "I already have what I need." Looking past her to the computer screen, I leaned forward, bracing myself on the desk and chair. "What are you looking up?"

She turned back to the screen. "Well, I wanted to see if there was a place in Central Park that might be the nest or something. Thomas said something about a 'big dark,' so I wondered if maybe he meant the underground or something like that. I did some digging—" she scrolled the mouse over a link and clicked "—and I found something very interesting. Look at this."

I peered at the screen. "There's a cave? In Central Park?"

"Somewhere in the section called the Ramble." Kenzie scrolled down the site. "Not many people know about it, and it was sealed off a long time ago, but yeah…there's a cave in Central Park."

Suddenly, both dogs raised their heads and growled, long and low. Kenzie and I tensed, but neither of them were looking at us. At once, they bolted out of the room, barking madly, claws scrabbling over the floor. In the kitchen, the little girl screamed.

We rushed into the room. Keirran was on his feet, standing in front of the girl, while Guro's wife shouted something over the racket of the barking dogs. Both animals were in front of the refrigerator, going nuts. The younger lab was bouncing off the door as it barked and howled, trying to reach something on top.

A pair of electric green eyes glared down from the top of the freezer, and a spindly black form hissed at the two dogs below.

"No! Bad dogs! Bad! Go away!" it buzzed, and Keirran rushed forward.

"Razor! What are you doing here?"

"Master!" the gremlin howled, waving his long arms hopelessly. "Master help!"

I cringed. This was the last thing I'd wanted—to pull Guro and his family into this craziness. We had to get out of here before it went any further.

Grabbing Keirran's arm, I yanked him toward the door. "We're leaving," I snapped as he turned on me in surprise. "Right now! Tell your gremlin to follow us. Guro," I said as my instructor appeared in the door, frowning at the racket, "I have to go. Thank you for everything, but we can't stay here any longer."

"Ethan!" Guro called as I pushed Keirran toward the exit. I looked back warily, hoping he wouldn't insist that we stay. "Go home soon, do you hear me?" Guro said in a firm voice.

"I won't alert the authorities, not yet. But at least let your parents know that you're all right."

"I will," I promised and hurried outside with the others.

We rushed across the street, ducked between two houses, and came out in an abandoned lot choked with weeds. A huge oak tree, its hanging branches draped in moss, loomed out of the fog, and we stopped beneath the ragged curtains.

"Where's Razor?" Kenzie asked, just as the gremlin scurried up and leaped onto Keirran, jabbering frantically. The Iron prince winced as Razor scrabbled all over him, buzzing and yanking at his shirt.

"Ouch! Razor!" Keirran pried the gremlin away and held him at arm's length. "What's going on? I thought I told you to stay with Annwyl."

"Razor did!" the gremlin cried, pulling at his ears. "Razor stayed! Pretty elf girl didn't! Pretty elf girl left, wanted to find Master!"

"Annwyl?" Abruptly, Keirran let him go. Razor blipped out of sight and appeared in the nearby tree, still chattering but making no sense now. "She left? Where—?" The gremlin buzzed frantically, flailing his arms, and Keirran frowned. "Razor, slow down. I can't understand you. Where is she now?"

"She is with the lady, little boy."

We spun. A section of mist seemed to break off from the rest, gliding toward us, becoming substantial. The cat-thing with the old woman's face slid out of the fog, wrinkled lips pulled into an evil smile. Behind her, two more faeries appeared, the thin, bug-eyed things that had chased Kenzie and me into the Nevernever. The screech of weapons being drawn shivered across the misty air.

The cat-thing hissed, baring yellow teeth. "Strike me down, and the Summer girl will die," she warned. "The Iron monster speaks the truth. We watched as she entered the real world again, looking for you. We watched, and when she was away from the Between, we took her. She is with the lady now. And if I perish, the Summer faery will become a snack for the rest of my kin. It's up to you."

Keirran went pale and lowered his weapon. The faery smiled. "That's right, boy. Remember me? I watched you, after you killed my sister with your foul poison glamour. I saw you and your precious Summer girl lead the humans to the Exile Queen." She curled a withered lip. "Pah! Exile Queen. She is no more a true queen than that bloated slug Titania, sitting on her throne, feeding on her ill-gotten fame. Our lady will destroy these silly notions of Summer and Winter courts."

"I don't care about Titania," Keirran said, stepping forward. "Where's Annwyl? What have you done with her?"

The cat-faery smiled again. "For now, she is safe. When we took her, our lady gave specific orders that she was not to be harmed. How long she remains that way depends on you."

I saw Keirran's shoulders rise as he took a deep, steadying breath. "What do you want from us?" he asked.

"From the mortals? Nothing." The cat-thing barely glanced and me and Kenzie, giving a disdainful sniff. "They are human. The boy may have the Sight, but our lady is not interested in humans. They are of no use to her. She wants you, bright one. She sensed your strange glamour while you were in the park, the magic of Summer, Winter and Iron. She has never felt anything like it before." The faery bared her yellow fangs in a menacing smile. "Come with us to meet the lady, and the Summer girl will live. Otherwise, we will feed on her glamour, suck out her essence, and drain her memories until there is nothing left."

Keirran's arms shook as he clenched his fists. "Do you

promise?" he said firmly. "Do you promise not to harm her, if I come with you to see this lady?"

"Keirran!" I snapped, stepping toward him. "Don't! What are you doing?"

He turned on me, a bright, desperate look in his eyes.

"I have to," he whispered. "I have to do this, Ethan. You'd do the same if it was Kenzie."

Dammit, I would, too. And Keirran would do anything for Annwyl—he'd proven that already. But I couldn't let him march happily off to his destruction. Even if he was part fey, he was still family.

"You're going to get yourself killed," I argued. "We don't even know if they really took her. They could be lying to get you to come with them."

"Lying?" The cat-thing growled, sounding indignant and outraged. "We are fey. Mankind has forgotten us, the courts have abandoned us, but we are still as much a part of Faery as Summer and Winter. We do not lie. And your Summer girl will not survive the night if you do not come back with us, now. *That* is a promise. So, what will it be, boy?"

"All right," Keirran said, spinning back. "Yes. You have a deal. I'll come with you, if you swear not to harm my friends when we leave. Promise me that, at least."

The cat-faery sniffed. "As you wish."

"Keirran—"

He didn't look at me. "It's up to you, now," he whispered, and sheathed his blade. "Find us. Save everyone."

Razor buzzed frantically and leaped from the tree, landing on Keirran's shoulder. "No!" he howled, tugging on his collar, as if he could drag him away. "No leave, Master! No!"

"Razor, stay with Kenzie," Keirran murmured, and the gremlin shook his head, huge ears flapping, garbling nonsense. Keirran's voice hardened. "Go," he ordered, and Razor cringed back from the steely tone. "Now!"

With a soft wail, the gremlin vanished. Reappearing on Kenzie's shoulder, he buried his face in her hair and howled. Keirran ignored him. Straightening his shoulders, he walked steadily toward the trio of glamour-eaters, until he was just a few feet away. I noticed that the two thin faeries drifted a space away from him as he approached, as if afraid they would accidentally catch his deadly Iron glamour. "Let's go," I heard him say. "I'm sure the lady is waiting."

Do something, I urged myself. *Don't just stand there and watch him leave.* I thought of rushing the glamour-eaters and slicing them all to nothingness, but if Annwyl died because of it, Keirran would never forgive me. Clenching my fists, I could only watch as the fey drew back, one of the thin faeries turning to slash the very mist behind them. It parted like a curtain, revealing darkness beyond the hole. Darkness, and nothing else.

"Do not follow us, humans," the cat-faery hissed, and padded through the hole in the fog, tail twitching behind her. The thin fey jerked their claws at Keirran, and he stepped through the hole without looking back, fading into the darkness. The two fey pointed at us silently, threateningly, then swiftly vanished after him. The mist drew forward again, the tear in realities closed, and we were alone in the fog.

CHAPTER TWENTY

THE FORGOTTEN

Great. Now what?

I heard Kenzie trying to calm Razor down as I stared at the spot from which the glamour-eaters and the Iron prince had vanished a moment before. How were they able to create a trod right here? As I understood it, only the rulers of Faery—Oberon, Mab, Titania—or someone of equal power could create the paths into and out of the Nevernever. Even the fey couldn't just slip back and forth between worlds wherever they liked; they had to find a trod.

Unless someone of extreme power created that trod for them, knowing we'd be here.

Unless whatever lurked in Central Park could rival Oberon or Mab.

That was a scary thought.

Kenzie finally managed to get Razor to stop wailing. He sat on her shoulder, ears drooping, looking miserable. She sighed and turned to me. "Where to now? How do we get to Central Park from here?"

"I don't know," I said, fighting down my frustration. "We have to find a trod, but I don't know where any would be located. I never kept track of the paths into Faery. And even if we find one, humans can't open it by themselves."

Razor suddenly sniffed, raising his head. "Razor knows," he chirped, blinking huge green eyes. "Razor find trod, open trod. Trod to scary Muse lady. Razor knows."

"Where?" Kenzie asked, pulling the gremlin off her shoulder, holding him in both hands. "Razor, where?" He buzzed and squirmed in her grip.

"Park," he said, and she frowned. He pointed back at me. "Park near funny boy's house. Leads to scary lady's home."

"What?" I glared at him. "Why is there a trod to Leanansidhe's so close to my house? Was she sending her minions to spy on me, too?"

He yanked on his ears. "Master asked!" he wailed, flashing his teeth. "Master asked scary lady to make trod."

I stared at him, my anger fading. Keirran. Keirran had had Leanansidhe create a trod close to where I lived. Why?

Maybe he was curious. Maybe he wanted to see the other side of his family, the human side. Maybe he was hoping to meet us one day, but was afraid to reveal himself. I'd never seen him hanging around, but maybe he had been there, hidden and silent, watching us. Abruptly, I wondered if it had been lonely in the Iron Court, if he ever felt out of place, a half-human prince surrounded by fey.

Another thought came to me, the memory of a gremlin peering in my bedroom window. Could it have been Razor all along? Had Keirran been sending his pet to spy on me, since he couldn't come himself?

I'd have to ask him about that, if we rescued him from the lady. *When* we rescued him. I wouldn't let myself think that we might not.

"I know that park," I told Kenzie, as Razor scrambled to her shoulder again. "Let's go."

Another cab ride—Kenzie paid for it this time, since I was out of cash—and we were soon standing in a familiar neighborhood at the edge of the little park where I'd spoken to the dryad. It seemed like such a long time ago now. The sun had burned away the last of the mist, and people were beginning to stir inside their homes. I gazed toward the end of the street. Just a few blocks away stood my house, where Mom would be getting ready for work and Dad would still be asleep. So close. Were they thinking of me now? Did they worry?

"Ethan." Kenzie touched my elbow. "You okay?"

"Yeah," I muttered, turning away from the direction of my house. I couldn't think of home, not yet. "Sorry, I'm fine. Tell your gremlin to show us the trod."

Razor buzzed indignantly but hopped off Kenzie's shoulder and scampered to the old playground slide. Leaping to the railing, he jabbered and pointed frantically to the space beneath the steps. "Trod here!" he squeaked, looking at Kenzie for approval. "Trod to scary lady's house here! Razor did good?"

As Kenzie assured him that he did fine, I shook my head, still amazed that a trod to the infamous Exile Queen had been this close. But we couldn't waste any time. Todd, Annwyl and now Keirran were out there, with the lady, and every second was costly.

Taking Kenzie's hand, we ducked beneath the slide and into the Between once more.

The trod didn't dump us into Leanansidhe's basement this time. Rather, as we left the cold whiteness between worlds, we appeared in a closet that led to an empty bedroom. I felt a moment of dizziness as we stepped through the frame, and wondered if all this frequent trod jumping was hazardous to our health.

The room we entered was simple: a rumpled bed, a night-stand, a desk in the corner. All in shades of white or gray. The only thing of color in the room was a vase of wildflowers on the corner of the desk, Annwyl's handiwork, probably. Razor buzzed sadly as we came in, and his ears wilted.

"Master's room," he sniffled. Kenzie reached up and patted his head.

Voices and music drifted down the hallway as I opened the door. Not singing; just soft notes played at random, barely muffling a conversation. As we ventured down the corridor, the voices and notes grew stronger, until we came to a pair of double doors leading to a red-carpeted music room. An enormous piano sat in the center of the room, surrounded by various instruments on the walls and floor, many vibrating softly. A harp sat in a corner, the strings humming, though there was no one to play it. A lute plinked a quiet tune on the far wall, and a tambourine answered it, jingling softly. For a moment, it made me think that the instruments were talking to each other, as if they were sentient and alive, which was more than a little disturbing.

Then Leanansidhe glanced up from a sofa, and Grimalkin turned to stare at us with big golden eyes.

"Ethan, darling, there you are!" The Exile Queen rose in a fluttering of fabric and blue smoke, beckoning us into the room with her cigarette flute. "You've arrived just in time, pet. Grimalkin and I were just talking about you." She blinked as Kenzie and I stepped through the door, then looked down the empty hallway. "Um, where is the prince, darlings?"

"They have him," I said, and Leanansidhe's lips thinned dangerously. "They met us outside Guro's house and wanted Keirran to come back with them to see the lady."

"And you didn't *stop* him, pet?"

"I couldn't. The glamour-eaters kidnapped Annwyl and threatened to kill her if Keirran didn't do what they said."

"I see." Leanansidhe sighed, and a smoke hound went loping away over our heads. "I knew taking in that girl was a mistake. Well, this puts a rather large damper on our plans, doesn't it, darling? How do you intend to fix this little mess? I suggest you get started soon, before the Iron Queen hears that her darling son has gone missing. That wouldn't bode well for either of us, would it, dove?"

"I'll find him," I said, clenching my fist around a sword hilt. "We know where they are now."

"Oh?" The Exile Queen raised an eyebrow. "Do share, darling."

"The glamour-eaters said something about the Between." I watched as Leanansidhe's other eyebrow arched in surprise. "Maybe you aren't the only one who knows how to build a lair in the space between Faery and the mortal realm. If you can do it, others should be able to as well, right?"

"Technically, yes, darling." Leanansidhe's voice was stiff; obviously she didn't like the idea that she wasn't the only one to think of it. "But the Between is a very thin plane of existence, a curtain overlapping both realms you might say. For anything to survive here, it must have an anchor in the real world. Otherwise, a person could wander the Between forever."

"There's a cave in Central Park," Kenzie broke in, stepping up beside me. "It's a small cave, and it's been sealed off for years, but I bet that isn't a problem for faeries, right? If it exists in the real world, it could be an entrance to the Between."

"Well done, pet. That could very well be your entrance." The Exile Queen gave Kenzie an approving smile. "Of course, space isn't a problem here, as you might have noticed. That 'small cave' in the real world could be a huge cavern in the Between, or a tunnel system that runs for miles."

A huge hidden world, right under Central Park. Talk about eerie. "That's where we're going, then," I said. "Keirran, Annwyl and Todd must be down there somewhere." I turned to the girl. "Kenzie, let's go. The longer we stand around here, the harder it will be to find them."

On the piano bench, Grimalkin yawned and sat up. "Before you go rushing off into the unknown," he mused, regarding us lazily, "perhaps you would like to know what you are up against."

"I know what we're up against, cat."

"Oh? The intelligent strategist always learns as much as he can about his opposition." Grimalkin sniffed and examined a paw, giving it a lick. "But of course, if you wish to go charging off without a plan, send my regards to the Iron prince when you are inevitably discovered."

"Grimalkin and I have been discussing where these glamour-eaters could have come from," Leanansidhe said as I glared at the cat. He scratched behind an ear and ignored me. "They are not Iron fey, for they still have our deathly allergies to iron and technology. So it stands to reason that, at one point, they were just like us. Yet I have not been able to recognize a one of them, have you, darling?"

"No," I said. "I've never seen them before."

"Precisely." Grimalkin stood, and leaped from the bench to the sofa, regarding us coolly. He blinked once, then sat down, curling his tail around his feet as he got comfortable. After a moment, he spoke, his voice low and solemn.

"Do you know what happens to fey whom no one remembers anymore, human?"

Fey whom no one remembers anymore? I shook my head. "No. Should I?"

"They disappear," Grimalkin continued, ignoring my question. "One would say, they 'fade' from existence, much as the exiles do when banished to the mortal realm. Not just individual fey, however. Entire races can disappear and vanish into oblivion, because no one tells their stories, no one remembers their names, or what they looked like. There are rumors of a place, in the darkest reaches of the Nevernever, where these fey go to die, gradually slipping from existence, until they are simply not there anymore. Faded. Unremembered. Forgotten."

A chill slithered up my back. *"We are forgotten,"* the creepy faery had hissed to me, so long ago it seemed. *"No one remembers our names, that we ever existed."*

"Okay, great. We know what they are," I said. "That doesn't really explain why they're sucking the glamour from normal fey and half-breeds."

Grimalkin yawned.

"Of course it does, human," he stated, as if it were obvious. "Because they have none of their own. Glamour—the dreams and imagination of mortals—is what keeps us alive. Even half-breeds have a bit of magic inside them. But these creatures have been forgotten for so long, the only way for them to exist in the real world is to steal it from others. But it is only temporary. To truly exist, to live without fear, they need to be remembered again. Otherwise they are in danger of fading away once more."

"But…" Kenzie frowned, while Razor mumbled a half-hearted "bad kitty" from her shoulder, "how can they be remembered, when no one knows what they are?"

"That," Grimalkin said, as I tried to wrap my brain around all of this, "is a very good question."

"It doesn't matter." I shook myself and turned to Leanansidhe, who raised an eyebrow and puffed her cigarette flute. "I'm going back for Keirran, Todd and the others, no matter what these things are. We need the trod to Central Park right now." Her eyes narrowed at my demanding tone, but I didn't back down. "We have to hurry. Keirran might not have a lot of time."

Grimalkin slid from the sofa, sauntering past us with his tail in the air. "This way, humans," he mused, ignoring Razor, who hissed and spat at him from Kenzie's shoulder. "I will take you to Central Park. Again."

"Are you coming with us this time?" Kenzie asked, and the cat snorted.

"I am not a tour guide, human," he said, peering over his shoulder. "I shall be returning to the Nevernever shortly, and the trod you wish to use happens to be on my way. I will not be tromping about Central Park with a legion of creatures bent on sucking away glamour. You will have to do your floundering without me."

"Yeah, that just breaks my heart," I returned.

Grimalkin pretended not to hear. With a flick of his tail, he turned and trotted out of the room with his head held high. Leanansidhe gave me an amused look.

"Bit of advice, darling," she said as we started to leave. "Unless you want to find yourselves in a dragon's lair or on the wrong end of a witch's bargain, it's never a good idea to annoy the cat."

"Right," I muttered. "I'll try to remember that when we're not fighting for our lives."

"Bad kitty," Razor agreed, as we hurried to catch up with Grimalkin.

CHAPTER TWENTY-ONE

THE BIG DARK

One more time, we stepped through the trod into Central Park, feeling the familiar tingle as we passed through the barrier. It was night now, and the streetlamps glimmered along the paths, though it wasn't very dark. The lights from the surrounding city lit up the sky, glowing with an artificial haze and making it impossible to see the stars.

I looked at Kenzie. "Where to now?"

"Um." She looked around, narrowing her eyes. "The Ramble is south of Belvedere Castle, where we found Thomas, so...this way, I think."

We started off, passing familiar trails and landmarks, though everything looked strange at night. We passed Belvedere Castle and continued walking, until the land around us grew heavily wooded, with only small, winding trails taking us through the trees.

"Where is this cave?" I asked, keeping my eyes trained on the forest, looking for ghostly shimmers of things moving through the darkness.

"I couldn't find any pictures, but I did find an article that said it's near a small inlet on the west side of the lake," was the answer. "Really, it's just a very small cave. More of a grotto, actually."

"Best lead we've got right now," I replied. "And you heard what Leanansidhe said. If these Forgotten things have a lair in the Between, size doesn't matter. They just need an entrance in from the real world."

Kenzie was silent a few minutes, before murmuring, "Do you think Keirran is okay?"

Man, I hope so. What would Meghan do if something happened to him? *What would* Ash *do?* That was a scary thought. "I'm sure he'll be fine," I told Kenzie, willing myself to believe it. "They can't drain his glamour without poisoning themselves, and they wouldn't have gone through all the trouble of kidnapping Annwyl if they wanted him dead."

"Maybe they want him as a hostage," Kenzie went on, her brow furrowed thoughtfully. "To get the Iron Queen to do what they want. Or to do nothing when they finally make their move."

Dammit, I hadn't thought of that. "We'll find him," I growled, clenching my fists. "All of them." I wasn't going to allow any more people to be dragged into this mess. I was not going to have my entire family manipulated by these things. If I had to look under every rock and bush in the entire park, I wasn't leaving without Keirran, Annwyl or Todd. This was going to end tonight.

The paths through the Ramble woods became even more twisted. The trees grew closer together, shutting out the light, until we were walking through shadow and near darkness. It was very quiet in this section of the park, the sounds of the city muffled by the trees, until you could almost imagine you were lost in this huge, sprawling forest hundreds of miles from everything.

"Ethan?" Kenzie murmured after a few minutes of silent walking.

"Yeah?"

"Don't you ever get scared?"

I glanced at her to see if she was serious. "Are you kidding?" I asked, as her solemn brown eyes met mine. "You don't think I'm scared right now? That marching into a nest of blood-thirsty faeries isn't freaking me out just a little?"

She snorted, giving me a wry look. "You could've fooled me, tough guy."

All right, I'd give her that. I'd done the whole "prickly bas-tard" thing for so long, I didn't know what was real anymore. "Truthfully?" I sighed, looking ahead into the trees. "I've been scared nearly my whole life. But one of the first rules I learned was that you never show it. Otherwise, They'll just torment you more." With a bitter chuckle, I dropped my head. "Sorry, you're probably sick of hearing me whine about the fey."

Kenzie didn't answer, but a moment later her hand slipped into mine. I curled my fingers around hers, squeezing gently, as we ventured farther into the tangled darkness of the Ram-ble.

Razor suddenly let out a hiss on Kenzie's shoulder. "Bad faeries coming," he buzzed, flattening his huge ears. Kenzie and I exchanged a worried glance, and my pulse started rac-ing under my skin. This was it. The lair was close.

"How many?" Kenzie whispered, and Razor hissed again. "Many. Coming quickly!"

I tugged her off the path. "Hide!"

We ducked behind a tree just as a horde of Forgotten sidled out of the woods, making no sound as they floated over a hill. They were pointed, thin faeries, the ones that had threatened me and Kenzie, the ones that had given me the scar on my shoulder. They flowed around the trees like wraiths and con-tinued on into the park, perhaps on the hunt for their nor-mal kin.

Kenzie and I huddled close to the tree trunk as the Forgotten drifted past us like ghosts, unseeing. I hugged her close, and her heart pounded against my chest, but none of the faeries looked our way. Maybe they didn't really notice us, maybe two humans in the park at night wasn't cause for attention. They were out hunting exiles and half-breeds, after all. We were just another human couple, for all they knew. I kept my head down and my body pressed close to Kenzie, like we were making out, as the faeries drifted by without a second glance.

Then Razor hissed at a Forgotten that passed uncomfortably close.

The thing stopped. Turned. I felt its cold eyes settle on me.

"Ethan Chase," it whispered. "I see you there."

Damn. Well, here we go.

I leaped away from Kenzie and drew my swords as the Forgotten gave a piercing shriek and lunged, slashing at me with long, needlelike talons.

I met the blow with an upward strike, and the razor edge of my weapon cut through the fragile limb as if was a twig, shearing it off. The Forgotten howled as its arm dissolved into mist and lurched back, flailing wildly with the other. I dodged the frantic blows, stepped close, and ripped my blade through the spindly body, cutting it in half. The faery split apart, fraying into strands of fog and disappeared.

Oh, yeah. Definitely better than wooden sticks.

A wailing sound jerked me to attention. The horde of Forgotten were coming back, black insect eyes blazing with fury, slit mouths open in alarm. Howling in their eerie voices, they glided through the trees, talons raised to tear me to shreds. I gripped my swords and whirled to face them.

"Kenzie, stay back!" I called, as the first faery reached me, ripping its claws at my face. I smacked its arm away with one sword and slashed down with the other, cutting through the spindly neck. Two more came right through the dissolving faery, grabbing at me, and I dodged aside, letting them pass while whipping the sword at the back of their heads. Turning, I lashed out with the second blade, catching another rushing me from behind. Then the rest of the horde closed in and everything melted into chaos—screaming, slashing claws, whirling blades—until I was aware of nothing except my next opponent and the blades in my hands. Claws scored me, tearing through clothes, raking my skin, but I barely registered the pain. I didn't know how many Forgotten I destroyed; I just reacted, and the air grew hazy with mist.

"Enough!"

The new voice rasped through the ranks of Forgotten, and the faeries drew back, staring at me with blackest hate. I stood there, panting, blood trickling down my arms from countless shallow cuts. The old woman with the cat's body stood a few yards away, flanked by more spindly Forgotten, observing the carnage with cold, slitted eyes.

"You again?" she spat at me, baring jagged yellow fangs. "You are not supposed to be here, Ethan Chase. We told you to stay out of our affairs. How did you find this place?"

I pointed my sword at her. "I'm here for my friends. Keirran, Annwyl and Todd. Let them go, right now."

She hissed a laugh. "You are in no position to give orders, boy. You are just one human—there are far more of us than you think. No, the lady will decide what to do with you. With the son and brother of the Iron Queen, the courts will not dare strike against us."

My hands were shaking, but I gripped the handle of my swords and stepped closer, causing several Forgotten to skitter back. "I'm not leaving without my friends. If I have to carve a path through each and every one of you to the lady herself, I'm taking them out of here." Twirling my blades, I gave the cat-faery an evil smirk. "I wonder how resistant your lady is to iron weapons."

But the ancient Forgotten simply smiled. "I would worry more about your own friends, boy."

A scream jerked my attention around. There was a short scuffle, and two Forgotten dragged Kenzie out from behind a tree. She snarled and kicked at them, but the spindly fey hissed and sank their claws into her arms, drawing blood. Gasping, she flinched, and one of them grabbed her hair, wrenching her head back.

I started forward, but the cat-lady bounded between us with a growl. "Not another step, little human!" she warned as I raised my weapons. "Or we will slit her open from ear to ear." One of the spindly fey raised a thin, pointed finger to Kenzie's throat, and I froze.

Razor suddenly landed on the cat-faery's head, hissing and baring his teeth. "Bad kitty!" he screeched, and the Forgotten howled. "Bad kitty! Not hurt pretty girl!"

He beat the faery's head with his fists, and the cat-thing roared. Reaching up, she yanked the gremlin from her neck and slammed him to the ground, crushing his small body between her bony fingers. Razor cried out, a shrill, painful wail, and the Forgotten's hand started to smoke.

With a screech, the cat-faery flung the gremlin away like he was on fire, shaking her fingers as if burned. "Wretched, wretched Iron fey!" she gasped, as I stared at the place Razor had fallen. I could see his tiny body, crumbled beneath a bush, eyes glowing weakly.

Before they flickered out.

No! I turned on the cat-faery, but she hissed an order, and the two Forgotten holding Kenzie forced her to her knees with a gasp. "I will give you one chance to surrender, human," the cat-thing growled, as the rest of the horde closed in, surrounding us. "Throw away your horrid iron weapons now, or this girl's blood will be on your hands. The lady will decide what to do with you both."

I slumped, desperation and failure making my arms heavy. *Dammit, I couldn't save anyone. Keirran, Todd, even Razor. I'm sorry, everyone.*

The cat-faery waited a moment longer, watching me with hateful eyes, before turning to the Forgotten holding Kenzie. "Kill her," she ordered, and my heart lurched. "Slit her throat."

"No! You win, okay?" Shifting my blades to both hands, I hurled them away, into the trees. They glinted for a brief second, catching the moonlight, before they fell into shadow and were lost from view.

"A wise move," the cat-thing purred, and nodded to the faeries holding the girl. They dragged her upright and shoved her forward, as the rest of the Forgotten closed in. She stumbled, and I caught her before she could fall. Her heart was racing, and I held her tight, feeling her tremble against me.

"You all right?" I whispered.

"Yeah," she replied, as the Forgotten made a tight circle around us, hemming us in. "I'm fine. But if they touch me again, I'm going to snap one of their stupid pointed legs off and stab them with it."

Jokes again. Kenzie being brave because she was terrified. As if I couldn't see the too-bright gleam in her eyes, the way she looked back at the place where Razor had fallen, crumpled and motionless. *I'm sorry,* I wanted to tell her. *This is my fault. I never should have brought you here.*

The circle of Forgotten began to drift forward, poking us with bony talons, forcing us to move. I looked back once, at the shadows that held the limp body of the gremlin, before being herded into the trees.

★ ★ ★

The Forgotten escorted us through the woods, down a winding path that looked much like every other trail in the Ramble, and deeper into the forest. We didn't walk far. The narrow cement path led us through a dense gully of boulders and shrubs, until we came to a strange stone arch nestled between two high outcroppings. The wall was made of rough stone blocks and was a good twenty or more feet high. The narrow arch set in the middle was only five or six feet across, barely wide enough for two people to pass through side-by-side.

It was also guarded by another Forgotten, a tall, skeletal creature that looked like a cross between a human and a vulture. It squatted atop the wall, bristling with black feathers, and its head was a giant bird skull with blazing green eye sockets. Long talons were clasped to its chest, like a huge bird of prey's, and even hunched over it was nearly ten feet tall. Kenzie shrank back with a gasp, and the cat-thing sneered at her.

"Don't worry, girl," she said as we approached the arch without the giant bird creature noticing us. "He doesn't bother humans. Only fey. He can see the location of a single faery miles away. Now that the park is virtually empty, we're going to have to hunt farther afield again. The lady is growing stronger, but she still requires glamour. We must accede to her wishes."

"You don't think the courts will catch on to what's happening?" I demanded, glaring at the Forgotten who poked me in the back when I stopped to stare at the huge creature. "You don't think they might notice the disappearance of so many fey?"

The cat-faery laughed. "They haven't so far," she cackled as we continued down the path, toward the arch and its monstrous guardian. "The Summer and Winter courts don't care about the exiles on this side of the Veil. And a few scraggly half-breeds are certainly below their notice. As long as we don't bother the fey in the Nevernever, they have no idea what is happening in the real world. The only unknown factor is the new Iron Court and its half-human queen." She smiled at me, showing yellow teeth. "But now, we have the bright one. And *you*."

We'd come to the opening in the wall, directly below the huge bird-creature perched overhead. Beyond the arch, I could see the path winding away, continuing between several large boulders and out of sight. But as the first of the Forgotten went through the arch, the air around them shimmered, and they disappeared.

I stopped, causing a couple of Forgotten to hiss impatiently and prod me in the back, but I didn't move. "Where does this go?" I asked, though I sort of knew the answer.

The cat-faery gestured, and the Forgotten crowded close, making sure we couldn't back away. "Your Dark Muse isn't the only one who can move through the Between, little boy. Our lady knew about the spaces between the Nevernever and the real world long before Leanansidhe ever thought to take over the courts. The cave here in the park is only the anchor—it exists in the same place, but we have fashioned it to our liking. This isn't the only entrance, either. We have dozens of tunnels running throughout the park, so we can appear anywhere, at any time. The silly faeries that lived here didn't even know what was going on until it was too late. But enough talking. The lady is waiting. Move."

She gestured, and the fey behind us dug a long talon into my ribs. I grunted in pain and went through the arch with Kenzie behind me.

As the blackness cleared and my eyes adjusted to the darkness, I looked around in astonishment. We were in a huge cavern, the ceiling spiraling up until I could just make out a tiny hazy circle directly overhead. That was the real world, way up there, beyond our reach. Down here, it looked like an enormous ant or termite nest, with tunnels snaking off in every direction, ledges running along walls, and bridges spanning the gulfs between. The walls and floor of the cave were spotted with thousands of glowing crystals, and they cast a pale, eerie luminance over the hundreds of Forgotten that roamed the cavern. Except for the thin faeries and the dwarves with killer hands, I didn't recognize any of these fey.

The Forgotten escorted us across the chamber, down a long, winding tunnel with fossils and bones poking out of the walls. More passageways and corridors wound off in every direction, bleached skeletons staring at us from the stone: lizards, birds, giant insects. I saw the fossil of what looked like a winged snake, coiled around a huge column, and wondered how much of the cave was real and how much was in the Between.

We walked through a long, narrow tunnel, under the rib cage of some giant beast, and entered another cavern. Here, the floor was dotted with large holes, and above us, the ceiling glittered with thousands of tiny crystals, looking like the night sky. A burly fey with an extra arm growing right out of his chest stood guard at the entrance, and eyed us critically as we approached.

"Eh? We're bringing humans down here now?" He peered at me with beady black eyes and curled a lip. "This one has the Sight, but no more glamour than the rocks on the ground. And the rest of the lot are all used up. What do we need 'em for?"

"That is not your concern," snapped the cat-faery, lashing her tail against her flanks. "You are not here to ask questions or attempt to be intelligent. Just make sure they do not escape."

The burly fey snorted. Turning away, it used its extra hand

to snatch a long wooden ladder leaning against the wall, then dropped it down into a pit.

"Get down there, mortal." A jab to the ribs prodded me forward. I walked to the edge and peered down. The ladder dropped away into black, and the sides of the hole were steep and smooth. I stared hard into the darkness, but I couldn't see the bottom.

Afraid that if I stood there much longer I'd get forcibly shoved into the black pit, I started down the ladder. My footsteps echoed dully against the wood, and with every step, the darkness grew thicker, until I could barely see the rungs in front of me.

I hope there's not something nasty down here, I thought, then immediately wished I hadn't.

My shoes finally hit a sandy floor, and I backed carefully away from the ladder, as Kenzie was coming down, as well. As soon as she hit the bottom, the ladder zipped up the wall and vanished through the opening, leaving us in near blackness.

I gazed around, waiting for my eyes to adjust. We stood in the center of a large chamber, the walls made of smooth, seamless stone. No handholds, no cracks or ledges, just flat, even rock. Above us, I could barely make out the hazy gray circles that were the holes in the floor above. The ground was covered in pale sand, with bits of garbage scattered here and there; the wrapper of a granola bar or a chewed apple core. Something had been down here recently, by the looks of it.

And then, a shuffle in the corner of the room made my heart skip a beat. My earlier thoughts were correct. Something *was* still down here with us. *Lots* of things. And they were getting closer.

CHAPTER TWENTY-TWO
KENZIE'S CONFESSION

Grabbing Kenzie, I pulled her behind me, backing away as several bodies shuffled forward into the beam of hazy light.

Humans. All of them. Young and old, male and female. The youngest was probably no more than thirteen, and the oldest had a gray beard down to his chest. There were about two dozen of them, all ragged and filthy-looking, like they hadn't bathed or eaten in a while.

Staring at them, my nerves prickled. There was something about this group that was just...wrong. Sure, they were ragged and filthy and had probably been captives of the Forgotten for a while now, but no one came forward to greet us or demand who we were. Their faces were blank, their features slack, and they gazed back with no emotion in their eyes, no spark of anger or fear or anything. It was like staring into a herd of curious, passive sheep.

Still, there were a lot of them, and I tensed, ready to fight if they attacked us. But the humans, after a somewhat disappointed glance, like they were expecting us to be food, turned away and shuffled back into the darkness.

I took a step forward. "Hey, wait!" I called, the echo bouncing around the pit. The humans didn't respond, and I raised my voice. "Just a second! Hold up!"

A few of them turned, regarding me without expression, but at least it was something. "I'm looking for a friend of mine," I went on, gazing past their ragged forms, trying to peer into the shadows. "His name is Todd Wyndham. Is there anyone by that name down here? He's about my age, blond hair, short."

The humans stared mutely, and I sighed, frustration and hopelessness threatening to smother me. End of the road, it seemed. We were stuck here, trapped by the Forgotten and surrounded by crazy humans, with no hope of rescuing Keirran or Annwyl. And Todd was still nowhere to be found.

There was a shuffle then, somewhere in the darkness, and a moment later a human pushed his way to the front of the crowd. He was about my age, small and thin, with scruffy blond hair and...

A jolt of shock zipped up my spine.

It was Todd. But he was *human*. The furry ears were gone, as were the claws and canines and piercing orange eyes. It was still Todd Wynham, there was no question about that; he still wore the same clothes as when I saw him last, though they were filthy and ragged now. But the change was so drastic it took me a few seconds to accept that this was the same person. I could only stare in disbelief. Except for the grime and the strange, empty look on his face, Todd seemed completely mortal, with no trace of the faery blood that ran through him a week ago.

"Todd?" Kenzie eased forward, holding out her hand. Todd watched her with blank hazel eyes and didn't move. "It is you! You're all right! Oh, thank goodness. They didn't hurt you, did they?"

I clenched my fists. She didn't know. She couldn't realize what had happened. Kenzie had only seen Todd as a human before; she didn't know anything was wrong.

But I knew. And a slow flame of rage began to smolder inside. *Well, you wanted to know what happened to half-breeds when their glamour was drained away, Ethan. There's your answer. All these humans were half-fey once, before the Forgotten took their magic.*

Todd blinked slowly. "Who are you?" he asked in a mono-tone, and I shivered. Even his voice sounded wrong. Flat and hollow, like everything he was had been stripped away, leaving no emotion behind. I remembered the eager, defiant half-breed from before; comparing him to this hopeless stranger made me sick.

"You know me," Kenzie said, walking toward him. "Kenzie. Mackenzie, from school. Ethan is here, too. We've been looking everywhere for you."

"I don't know you," Todd stated in that same empty, chilling voice. "I don't remember *him,* or school or anything. I don't remember anything but this hole. But…" He looked away, into the darkness, his brow furrowing. "But…it feels like I should remember something. Something important. I think…I think I lost something." An agonized expression crossed his face, just for a moment, before it smoothed out again. "Or, maybe not," he continued with a shrug. "I can't remember. It must not have been very important."

I was shaking with fury, and took a deep breath to calm myself. *Bastards,* I thought, filled with a sudden, fiery hatred. *Killing faeries is one thing. But this?* I looked at Todd, at the slack face, the hollow eyes, and resisted the urge to punch the wall. *This is worse than killing. You stripped away everything that made him who he was, took something that he can't ever get back and left him…like this. To keep yourselves alive. I won't let you get away with that.*

"What about your parents?" Kenzie continued, still trying to cajole an answer out of the once half-faery. "Don't you remember them? Or any of your teachers?"

"No," was the flat reply, and Todd backed away, his eyes

clouding over, into the darkness. "I don't know you," he whispered. "Go away."

"Todd—" Kenzie tried again, but the human turned away from her, huddling down against the wall, burying his face in his knees.

"Leave me alone."

She tried coaxing him to talk again, asking him questions about home, school, how he came to be there, telling him about our own adventures. But she was met with a wall of silence. Todd didn't even look up from his knees. He seemed determined to pretend we didn't exist, and after a few minutes of watching this and getting nothing, I walked away, needing to move before I started shaking him. Kenzie's stubbornly cheerful voice followed me as I stalked into the shadows, and I left her to it; if anyone could persuade him to talk, she could.

Weaving through hunched forms of indifferent humans, I wandered the perimeter, halfheartedly searching for anything we might've missed. Anything that might allow us to escape. Nothing. Just steep, smooth walls and sand. We were well and truly stuck down here.

Putting my back against the wall, I slid to the floor, feeling cold sand through my jeans. I wondered what my parents were doing right now. I wondered how long the Forgotten would keep us down here. Weeks? Months? If they finally let us go, would we return to the mortal realm to find we'd been missing for twenty years, and everyone had given us up for dead?

Or, would they simply kill us and leave our bones to rot in this hole, gnawed on by a bunch of former half-breeds?

Kenzie joined me, looking tired and pale. Purple marks streaked her arms from where the Forgotten had grabbed her, and her eyes were dull with exhaustion. Anger flared, but it was damped by the feeling of hopelessness that clung to everything in this place. She gave me a brave smile as she came up, but I could see her mask crumbling, falling to pieces around her.

"Anything?" I asked, and she shook her head.

"No. I'll try again in a little while, when he's had a chance to think about it. I think poking him further will just make him retreat more." She slid down next to me, gazing out into the darkness. I felt the heat of her small body against mine, and an almost painful urge to reach out for her, to draw her close. But my own fear held me back. I had failed. Again. Not only Kenzie, but Todd, Keirran, Annwyl, everyone. I wished I had been stronger. That I could've kept everyone around me safe.

But most of all, I wished Kenzie didn't have to be here. That I'd never shown her my world. I'd give anything to get her out of this.

"How long do you think they'll keep us here?" Kenzie whispered after a few beats of silence.

"I don't know," I murmured, feeling the weight in my chest get bigger. Kenzie rubbed her arms, running her fingers over the bruises on her skin, making my stomach churn.

"We…we're gonna make it home, right?"

"Yeah." I half turned, forcing a smile. "Yeah, don't worry, we'll get out of here, and you'll be home before you know it. Your sister will be waiting for you, and your Dad will probably yell that you've been gone so long, but they'll both be relieved that you're back. And you can call my house and keep me updated on everything that happens at school, because my parents will probably ground me until I'm forty."

It was a kind lie, and we both knew it, but I couldn't tell her the truth. That I didn't know if we would make it home, that no one knew where we were, that right above our heads waited a legion of savage, desperate fey and their mysterious lady. Keirran was gone, Annwyl was missing, and the person we'd come to find was a hollow shell of himself. I'd hit rock bottom and had dragged her down with me, but I couldn't tell her that all hope was gone. Even though I had none of it myself.

So I lied. I told her we would make it home, and Kenzie returned the small smile, as if she really believed it. But then she shivered, and the mask crumpled. Bringing both knees to her chest, she wrapped her arms around them and closed her eyes.

"I'm scared," she admitted in a whisper. And I couldn't hold myself back any longer.

Reaching out, I pulled her into my lap and wrapped her in my arms. She clung to me, fists clenched in my shirt, and I folded her against my chest, feeling our hearts race together.

"I'm sorry," I whispered into her hair. "I wanted to protect you from all of this."

"I know," she whispered back. "And I know you're thinking this is your fault somehow, but it isn't." Her hand slipped up to my face, pressing softly against my cheek, and I closed my eyes. "Ethan, you're a sweet, infuriating, incredible guy, and I think I…might be falling for you. But there are things in my life you just can't protect me from."

My breath caught. I felt my heartbeat stutter, then pick up, a little faster than before. Kenzie hunched her shoulders, burying her face in my shirt, suddenly embarrassed. I wanted to tell her she had nothing to be afraid of; that I couldn't stay away from her if I tried, that she had somehow gotten past all my bullshit—the walls, the anger, the constant fear, guilt and self-loathing—and despite everything I'd done to drive her away and make her hate me, I couldn't imagine my life without her.

I wished I knew how to tell her as much. Instead, I held her and smoothed her hair, listening to our breaths mingle together. She was quiet for a long time, one hand around my neck, the other tracing patterns in my shirt.

"Ethan," she murmured, still not looking at me. "If—when—we get home, what will happen, to *us?*"

"I don't know," I said honestly. "I guess…that will mostly depend on you."

"Me?"

I nodded. "You've seen my life. You've seen how screwed up it is. How dangerous it can be. I wouldn't force that on anyone, but…" I trailed off, closing my eyes, pressing my forehead to hers. "But I can't stay away from you anymore. I'm not even going to try. If you want me around, I'll be there."

"For how long?" Her words were the faintest whisper. If we hadn't been so close, I wouldn't have caught them. Hurt, I stared at her, and she peered up at me, her eyes going wide at the look on my face.

"Oh, no! I'm sorry, Ethan. That wasn't for you. I just…" She sighed, hanging her head again, clenching a fist in my shirt. "All right," she whispered. "Enough of this, Kenzie. Before this goes any further." She nodded to herself and looked up, facing me fully. "I guess it's time you knew."

I waited, holding my breath. *Whatever secrets you have,* I wanted to say, *whatever you've been hiding, it doesn't matter. Not to me.* My whole life was one big lie, and I had more secrets than one person should have in a lifetime. Nothing she said could scare or shock me away from her.

But there was still that tiny sense of unease, that dark, ominous thing Kenzie had been keeping from me since we'd met. I knew some secrets weren't meant to be shared, that knowing them could change your perspective of a person forever. I suspected this might be one of those times. So I waited, as the silence stretched between us, as Kenzie gathered her thoughts. Finally, she pushed her hair back, still not looking at me, and took a deep breath.

"Remember…when you asked why I would trade a piece

of my life away to Leanansidhe?" she began in a halting voice. "When I made that bargain to get the Sight. Do you remember what I said?"

I nodded, though she still wasn't looking at me. "That no one lives forever."

Kenzie shivered. "My mom died three years ago," she said, folding her arms protectively to her chest. "It was a car accident—there was nothing anyone could do. But I remember when I was little, she would always talk about traveling the world. She said when I got older, we would go see the pyramids together, or the Great Wall or the Eiffel Tower. She used to show me travel magazines and brochures, and we would plan out our trip. Sometimes by boat, or train or even by hot air balloon. And I believed her. Every summer, I asked if *this* was the year we would go." She sniffed, and a bitter note crept into her voice. "It never was, but dad swore that when he wasn't so busy, when work slowed down a bit, we would all take that trip together.

"But then she died," Kenzie went on softly, and swiped a hand across her eyes. "She died, and she never got the chance to see Egypt, or Paris or any of the places she wanted to see. And I always thought it was so sad, that it was such a waste. All those dreams, all those plans we had, she would never get to do any of them."

"I'm sorry, Kenzie."

She paused, taking a breath to compose herself, her voice growing stronger when she spoke again. "Afterward, I thought maybe Dad and I could…take that trip together, in her honor, you know? He was so devastated when he found out. I thought that if we could go someplace, just the two of us, he'd remember all the good times. And I wanted to remind him that he still had me, even though Mom was gone."

I remembered the way Kenzie had spoken about her father before, the anger and bitterness she'd shown, and my gut twisted. Somehow, I knew that hadn't happened.

"But, my dad…" Kenzie shook her head, her eyes dark. "When Mom died, he sort of…forgot about me. He never talked to me if he could help it, and just…threw himself into his job. He started working more and more at the office, just so he didn't have to come home. At first, I thought it was because he missed Mom so much, but that wasn't it. It was me. He didn't want to see me." At my furious look, she shrugged. "Maybe I reminded him too much of Mom. Or maybe he was just distancing himself, in case he lost me, too. I would try talking to him—I really missed her sometimes—but he'd just give me a wad of cash and then lock himself in his office to drink." Her eyes glimmered. "I didn't want money. I wanted someone to talk to me, to listen to me. I wanted him to be a dad."

Anger burned. And guilt. I thought of my family, of how we had lost Meghan all those years ago, and how my parents clung to me even more tightly, for fear of that same thing. I couldn't imagine them ignoring me, forgetting I existed, in case they woke up one day and found me gone. They were paranoid and overprotective, but that was infinitely better than the alternative. What was wrong with Kenzie's father? How could he ignore his only daughter, especially after she'd just lost her mom?

"That's insane," I muttered. "I'm sorry, Kenzie. Your dad sounds like a complete tool. You shouldn't have had to go through that alone." She didn't say anything, and I rubbed her arms, trying to get her to look at me, keeping my voice gentle. "So, you do all these crazy things because you don't want to end up like your mom?"

"No." Kenzie hunched her shoulders, looking off into the distance, and her eyes glimmered. "Well, that's part of it, but…" She paused again and went on, even softer than before. "When Dad remarried, things got a little better. I had a stepsister, Alexandria, so at least I wasn't stuck in a big empty house all day, alone. But Dad still worked all the time, and the nights he *was* home, he was so busy with his new wife and Alex, he didn't pay much attention to me." She shrugged, as if she'd gotten over it and didn't need any sympathy, but I still seethed at her father.

"Then, about a year ago," Kenzie went on, "I started getting sick. Nausea, sudden dizzy spells, things like that. Dad didn't notice, of course. No one really did…until I passed out in the middle of class one afternoon. In history. I remember, because I begged the school nurse not to call my dad. I knew he'd be angry if he had to come pick me up in the middle of the workday." Kenzie snorted, her eyes and voice bitter as she stared at the ground. "I collapsed just picking up my books, and the freaking *school nurse* had to tell him to take me to a doctor. And he was still pissed about it. Like I got sick on purpose, like he thinks all the tests and treatments and doctor appointments are just a way of getting attention."

Something cold settled in my stomach, as many small things clicked into place. The bruises. The protectiveness of her friends at school. Her fearlessness and burning desire to see all that she could. The dark thing hovered between us now, turning my blood to ice as I finally figured it out. "You're sick now, aren't you?" I whispered. "The serious kind."

"Yeah." She looked down, fiddling with my shirt, and took a shaky breath. "Ethan I…I have leukemia." The words trailed off into a whisper at the end, and she paused, but when she continued her voice was calm and matter-of-fact. "The doctors won't tell me much, but I did some research, and the survival rate for the type I have, with treatment and chemo and everything, is about forty percent. And that's if I even make it through the first five years."

It felt as if someone had punched a hole in my stomach, grabbed my insides and pulled them out again. I stared at Kenzie in horror, unable to catch my breath. Leukemia. Cancer. Kenzie was…

"So, now you know the real reason I wanted the Sight. Why I wanted to see the fey." She finally looked at me, one corner of her lip turned up in a bitter smile. "That month I traded to Leanansidhe? That's nothing. I probably won't live to see thirty."

I wanted to do something, anything. I wanted to jump up and punch the walls, scream out my frustration and the unfairness of it all. Why her? Why did it have to be Kenzie, who was brave and kind and stubborn and absolutely perfect? It wasn't right. "You should've gone back," I finally choked out. "You shouldn't be here with me, not when you could be…" I couldn't even get the word past my lips. The sudden thought that this dark pit could be the last place she would ever see nearly made me sick. "Kenzie, you should be with your family," I moaned in despair. "Why did you stay with me? You should've gone home."

Kenzie's eyes gleamed. "To what?" she snapped, making a sharp gesture. "Back to my dad, who can't even look at me? Back to that empty house, where everyone tiptoes around and whispers things they don't think I can hear? To the doctors who won't tell me anything, who treat me like I have no idea what's going on? Haven't you been listening, Ethan? What do I have to go back to?"

"You would be safe—"

"Safe," she scoffed. "I don't have time to be safe. I want to *live*. I want to travel the world. See things no one else has. Go bungee jumping and skydiving and all those crazy things. If

I'm living on borrowed time, I want to make the most of it. And you showed me this whole other world, with dragons and magic and queens and talking cats. How could I pass that up?"

I couldn't answer, mostly because my own throat felt suspiciously tight. Kenzie reached out with both arms and laced her hands behind my head, gazing up at me. Her eyes were tender as she leaned in. "Ethan, this sickness, this thing inside me…I've made my peace with it. Whatever happens, I can't stop it. But there are things I want to do before I die, a whole list that I know I probably won't get to, but I'm sure as hell going to try. 'Seeing the fey' wasn't on the list, but 'go someplace no one has ever seen before' was. So is 'have my first kiss.'" She ducked her head, as if she was blushing. "Of course, there's never been a boy that I've wanted to kiss me," she whispered, biting her lip, "until I met you."

I was still reeling from her last words, so that admittance sent another jolt through my stomach, turning it inside out. That this strange, stubborn, defiantly cheerful girl—this girl who fought lindwurms and bargained with faery queens and faced her own mortality every single day, who followed me into Faery and didn't leave my side, even when she was offered a way home—this brave, selfless, incredible girl wanted me to kiss her.

Damn. I was in deep, wasn't I?

Yeah, and I don't care.

Kenzie was still staring at the ground, and I realized I hadn't answered her, still recovering from being blindsided by my own emotions. "But I understand if you don't want to," she went on in a forced, cheerful voice, dropping her arms. "It's not fair to you, to get involved with someone like me. It was stupid of me to say anything." She spoke quickly, trying to convince herself, and I shook myself out of my trance. "I don't know how long I'll have, and who wants to go through that?

It'll just end up breaking both our hearts. So, if you don't want to start anything, that's fine, I understand. I just—"

I kissed her, stopping any more arguments. She made a tiny noise of surprise before she relaxed into me with a sigh. Her arms laced around my neck; mine slid into her hair and down to the small of her back, holding us together. No more illusions, no more hiding from myself. I needed this girl; I needed her laughter and fearlessness, the way she kept pushing me, refusing to be intimidated. I'd kept people at arm's length for so long, scared of what the fey would do to them if I got close, but I couldn't do that anymore. Not to her.

It seemed a long time before we finally pulled back. The shuffle of the former half-breeds echoed around us, the pit was still dark and cold and unscalable, but I was no longer content just to sit here and accept our fate. Everything was different. I had something to fight for, a real reason to get home.

Kenzie didn't say anything immediately after. She blinked and looked a little dazed as I drew back. I couldn't help but smirk.

"Oh, wow," I teased quietly. "Did I actually render Mackenzie St. James speechless?"

She snorted. "Hardly, but you're welcome to try again."

Smiling, I pulled her to me for another kiss. She shifted so that her knees were straddling my waist and buried her hands in my hair, holding my head still. I wrapped my arms around the small of her back and let the feel of her lips take me away.

This time, Kenzie was the one who pulled back, all traces of amusement gone as she stared at me, my reflection peering back from her eyes. "Promise you won't disappear when we get home, tough guy," she whispered, and, though her tone was light, her gaze was solemn. "I like this Ethan. I don't want him to turn into the one I met at the tournament once we're safe."

"I can't promise that you won't ever see him again," I told

her. "The fey will still hang around me, no matter what I do. But I'm not going anywhere." Reaching up, I brushed the hair from her eyes, smiling ruefully. "I'm still not sure how this will work when we get home, but I want to be with you. And if you want me to be your boyfriend and go to parties and hang out with your meathead friends…I'll try. I'm not the best at being normal, but I'll give it a shot."

"Really?" She smiled, and her eyes glimmered. "You… you're not just saying that because you feel sorry for me, are you? I don't want to guilt you into doing anything, just because I'm sick."

No, Mackenzie. I fell for you long before then, I just didn't know it. "I'll prove it to you, then," I told her, running my hands up her back, drawing her closer. "Once we get out of here, I'll show you nothing has changed." *And everything's changed.* "Deal?"

She nodded, and a tear finally spilled over, running down her cheek. I brushed it away with my thumb. "Deal," she whispered, as I reached up to kiss her once more. "But, um… Ethan?"

"Yeah?"

"I think something is watching us."

CHAPTER TWENTY-THREE

THE ESCAPE

Warily, I looked up, just as something bright fell from the ceiling, flashing briefly as it struck the ground a few yards away.

Puzzled, I released Kenzie and stood, squinting as I walked up to it. When I could see it clearly in the darkness, my heart stood still.

My swords. Or one of them, anyway. Standing up point first in the sand. Incredulous, I picked it up, wondering how it got here.

There was a familiar buzz on the wall overhead. Heart leaping, I looked up to see a pair of smug, glowing green eyes. Razor grinned down at me, his teeth a blue-white crescent in the darkness. One spindly arm still clutched my second blade.

"Found you!" he buzzed.

Kenzie gasped, and the gremlin cackled, tossing the sword down. It soared through the air in a graceful arc and landed hilt up at my feet. Scuttling along the wall, the gremlin launched himself at Kenzie, landing in her arms with a gleeful cry. "Found you!" he exclaimed again, as she quickly shushed him. He beamed but dropped his voice to a staticky whisper. "Found you! Razor help! See, see? Razor brought swords silly boy dropped."

"Razor, are you all right?" Kenzie asked, holding him at

arm's length to look at him closely. One of his ears was torn, hanging limply at an angle, but other than that, he seemed okay. "That Forgotten threw you pretty hard," she mused, touching the wounded ear. "Are you hurt?"

"Bad kitty!" growled Razor, shaking his head as if he was shooing off a fly. "Evil, sneaky, nasty kitty! Boy should cut its nose off, yes. Tie rock to tail and throw kitty in lake. Watch kitty sink, ha!"

"Seems like he's fine," I said, sheathing my second blade. Relief and hope spread through me. Now that I was armed again, the future looked a lot less bleak. We might actually make it out of here. "Razor, did you happen to see Keirran anywhere? Or Annwyl?"

Before he could answer, a shuffle of movement up top silenced us, and we pressed back into the wall, staring up at the lip. A moment later, the old woman's voice floated down into the hole.

"Ethan Chase. The lady will see you now."

Kenzie shivered and pressed close, gripping my hand, as the gleam of the cat-faery's eyes appeared over the mouth of the pit. "Did you hear me, humans?" she called, sounding impatient. "When we lower the rungs, only the Chase boy is to come up. He will be escorted to the lady. Anyone who follows will be tossed back into the hole, without a ladder. So don't try anything."

Her wrinkled face split into an evil grin, and she disappeared. I turned to Kenzie.

"When I get up there," I whispered, "can you and Razor give me a distraction?" I glanced at Razor, hiding in her long black hair, then back to the girl. "I only need a few seconds. Think you can do that?"

She looked pale but determined. "Sure," she whispered. "No problem. Distractions are our specialty, right, Razor?"

The gremlin peeked out from the curtain of her hair and gave a quiet buzz. I brushed a strand from her eyes, trying to sound calm. "Wait until I'm almost at the very top," I told her, untucking my shirt, pulling the hem over the sword hilts. "Then, do whatever you have to do. Nothing dangerous, just make sure they're not looking at me when I come up. Also, here." I pulled out a sword, sheath and all, and handed it to her. "In case this doesn't go as planned. This will give you a fighting chance."

"Ethan."

I took her hand, fighting the urge to pull her close. "We're getting out of here, right now."

With a scraping sound, the ladder dropped into the pit. I squeezed Kenzie's arm and stepped forward, walking across the sand to the opposite wall. I saw Todd huddled in the corner, his head buried in his knees, not even looking at the ladder, and clenched my fists. *Dammit, what they did to you was unforgivable. Even if I can't fix that, I'll get you home, I swear. I'll get all of us home.*

My footsteps clunked loudly against the rungs as I started up, echoing my pounding heart.

Six steps from the top, I could see the hulking, three-armed Forgotten, yawning as it stared off into the distance.

Four steps from the top, I could see the old cat-faery and a pair of insect fey, one holding a coil of rope in its long talons. Another two guarded the entrance, floating a few inches above the ground.

Two steps from the top, Razor abruptly dropped onto the three-armed faery's head.

"BAD KITTY!" he screeched at the top of his lungs, making everything in the room jump in shock. The three-armed Forgotten gave a bellow and slapped at the thing on his head, but Razor leaped off just in time, and the huge fey smacked its own skull with enough force to knock it back a step.

I drew my sword and leaped out of the pit, blade flashing. I cut through one spindly body, dodged the second as it slashed at me, and sliced through its neck. Both dissolved into mist, and I went for the old cat-faery, intending to cut that evil grin from her withered face. She hissed and leaped away, landing behind the two guards at the mouth of the tunnel.

"Stop him!" she spat, and the Forgotten closed in on me, including the huge three-armed faery, a club clutched in his third hand. I dodged the first swing, parried the vicious claw swipes, and was forced back. "You cannot escape, Ethan Chase!" the cat-fey called triumphantly, as I fought to avoid being surrounded. The club swished over my head and smashed into the wall, showering me with rock. "Give up, and we will take you to the lady. Your death might be a painless one if you surrender no—aaaaaagh!"

Her warning melted into a yowl of pain as Razor dropped behind her, grabbed her skinny tail, and chomped down hard. The cat-faery spun, clawing at him, and I lost them both as the three fey crowded in. Battling Forgotten, I saw Kenzie pull herself out of the pit, sword in hand. Her eyes gleamed as she stepped up behind the hulking faery and swung a vicious blow at the back of its knees. Bellowing in pain, the Forgotten stumbled, lurched backward, and toppled over. Kenzie dodged aside as the big faery dropped into the pit with a howl.

Slicing through the last two guards, I lunged to where the cat-thing was twisting and clawing the air behind her, trying to reach the gremlin doggedly clinging to her tail. She looked up as I came in, made one last attempt to flee, but my sword flashed down across her neck and she erupted into mist.

Panting, I lowered my sword, stumbling back as Razor blinked, grinning as what had been the cat-faery rippled over the ground and evaporated. "Bad kitty," he buzzed, sounding smug as he looked up at me. "No more bad kitty. Ha!"

I smiled, turning to Kenzie, but then my heart seized up and I started to shout a warning.

The hulking Forgotten she had dropped into the pit had somehow clawed its way out again, looming behind her with its club raised. At the look on my face, she realized what was happening and started to turn, throwing up her arms, but the club swept down and I knew I would get there far too late.

And then…I don't know what happened. A dark, featureless shadow sprang up, seemingly out of nowhere, between Kenzie and the huge Forgotten. A sword flashed, and the blow that probably would've crushed her skull hit her shoulder instead. The impact was still enough to knock her aside, and she crumpled against the wall, gasping in pain, as the shadow vanished as suddenly as it appeared.

Rage blinded me. Rushing forward, I leaped at the Forgotten with a scream, cutting at it viciously. It bellowed and swiped its club at my head, but I met the blow with my sword, severing the arm from its chest. Howling in pain, the faery resorted to pounding at me with its huge fists. I dodged back, snatching the fallen sword from the ground, and stepped up to meet the raging Forgotten. Ducking wild swings, I lunged past its guard and sank both blades into its chest with a snarl.

The Forgotten melted into fog, still bellowing curses. Without a second glance, I rushed through its dissolving form to the body on the far side of the wall. Kenzie was struggling upright, grimacing, one hand cradling her arm. Razor hopped up and down nearby, buzzing with alarm.

"Kenzie!" Reaching her, I took her arm and very gently felt along the limb, checking for lumps or broken bones. Miraculously everything seemed intact, despite the massive green bruise already starting to creep down her shoulder. *Badge of courage,* Guro would've called it. He would've been proud.

"Nothing's broken," I muttered in relief, and looked up at her. "Are you all right?"

She winced. "Well, considering today I have been stabbed, poked, pummeled and threatened with having my throat cut open, I guess I can't complain." Her brow furrowed, and she glanced around the cave. "Also, I thought there was... Did you see...?"

I nodded, remembering the shadow that had appeared, deflected the killing blow, and vanished just as suddenly. It had happened so fast; if Kenzie hadn't mentioned it, too, I might've thought I was seeing things.

"Oh, good. I thought I was having some weird near-death hallucination or something." Kenzie looked at the place the huge Forgotten had died and shuddered. "Any idea what just happened there?"

"No clue," I muttered. "But it probably saved your life. That's all I care about."

"Maybe for you," Kenzie said, wrinkling her nose. "But if I'm going to have some sort of shadowy guardian angel hanging around me, I kind of want to know why. In case I'm in the shower or something."

"Kenzie?" A faint, familiar voice drifted from the darkness before I could answer. We both jumped and gazed around wildly. "Ethan? Are you up there?"

"Annwyl?" Kenzie looked around, as Razor hopped to her shoulder. "Where are you?"

"Here," came the weak reply, as if muffled through the walls. I peered along the edge of the cave and saw a wooden door at the far corner of the room, nearly hidden in shadow. A thick wooden beam barred it shut. Hurrying over, we pushed the heavy beam out of the way and pulled on the door. It opened reluctantly, creaking in protest, and we stepped through.

Kenzie gasped. The room beyond was full of cages—bronze

or copper by the looks of them—hanging from the ceiling by thick chains. They groaned as they swung back and forth, narrow, cylindrical cells that barely gave enough room to turn around. All of them were empty, save one.

Annwyl huddled down in one of the cages, her knees drawn to her chest and her arms wrapped around them. In the darkness of the room, lit only by a single flickering torch on the far wall, she looked pale and sick and miserable as she raised her head, her eyes going wide.

"Ethan," she whispered in a trembling voice. "Kenzie. You're here. How…how did you find me?"

"We'll tell you later," Kenzie said, looking furious as she gripped the bars separating them. Razor buzzed furiously and leaped to the top of the cage, rattling the frame. "Right now, we're getting out of here. Where are the keys?"

Annwyl nodded to a post where a ring of bronze keys hung from a wooden peg. After unlocking the cage, we helped Annwyl climb down. The Summer girl stumbled weakly as she left the cage, leaning on me for support. The Forgotten had probably drained most of her glamour; she felt as thin and brittle as a bundle of twigs.

"Are there others?" I asked as she took several deep breaths, as if breathing clean air once again. Annwyl shuddered violently and shook her head.

"No," she whispered. "Just me." She turned and nodded to the empty cages, swinging from their chains. "When I was first brought here, there were a few other captives. Exiled fey like me. A satyr and a couple wood nymphs. One goblin. But…but then they were taken away by the guards. And they never came back. I was sure it was just a matter of time… before I was brought to her, as well."

"The lady," I muttered darkly. Annwyl shivered again.

"She…she *eats* them," she whispered, closing her eyes. "She drains their glamour, sucks it into herself, just like her followers, until there's nothing left. That's why so many exiles are gone. She needs a constant supply of magic to get strong again, at least that's what her followers told me. So they go out every night, capture exiles and half-breeds, and drag them back here for her."

"Where's Keirran?" I asked, holding her at arm's length. "Have you seen him?"

She shook her head frantically. "He's…with *her*," she said, on the verge of tears. "I'm so worried…what if she's done something to him?" She covered her face with one hand. "What will I do if he's gone?"

"Master!" Perched on Kenzie's shoulder again, Razor echoed her misery, pulling on his ears. "Master gone!"

I sighed, trying to think over the gremlin's wailing. "All right," I muttered, and turned to Kenzie. "We have to get Todd and the others out of here. Do you remember the way they brought us in?"

She winced, trying to shush the tiny Iron fey. "Barely. But the cave is crawling with Forgotten. We'd have to fight our way out."

Annwyl straightened then, taking a deep breath. "Wait," she said, seeming to compose herself, her voice growing stronger. "There is another way. I can sense where the trods are in this place, and one empties under a bridge in the mortal world. It isn't far from here."

"Can you lead everyone there? Open it?"

"Yes." Annwyl nodded, and her eyes glittered. "But I'm not leaving without Keirran."

"I know. Come on." I led her out of the room, back to the chamber that held the giant pit. Dragging the ladder from the wall, I dropped it down into the hole.

"All right," I mumbled, peering into the darkness. Mutters

and shuffling footsteps drifted out of the pit, and I winced. "Wait here," I told Kenzie and Annwyl. "I'll be right back, hopefully with a bunch of crazy people."

"Wait," Kenzie said, stopping me. "I should go," she said, and held up a hand as I protested. "Ethan, if something comes into this room, I won't be able to stop it. You're the one with the mad sword skills. Besides, you're not the most comforting presence to lead a bunch of scared, crazy people to safety. If they start crying, you can't just crack your knuckles and threaten them to get them to move."

I frowned. "I wouldn't use my fists. A sword is much more threatening."

She rolled her eyes and handed me the gremlin, who scurried to my shoulder. "Just stand guard. I'll start sending them up."

A few minutes later, a crowd of ragged, dazed-looking humans clustered together in the tunnel, muttering and whispering to themselves. Todd was among them. He gazed around the cavern with a blank expression that made my skin crawl. I hoped that when we got him out of here he would go back to normal. No one looked at Annwyl or Razor, or seemed to notice them. They stood like sheep, passive and dull-witted, waiting for something to happen. Annwyl gazed at them all and shivered.

"How awful," she whispered, rubbing her arms. "They feel so…empty."

"Empty," Razor buzzed. "Empty, empty, empty."

"Is this everyone?" I asked Kenzie as she crawled back up the ladder. She nodded as Razor bounced back to her. "All right, everyone stay together. This is going to be interesting."

Drawing my weapons, I walked to the edge of the tunnel, where it split in two directions, and peered out. No Forgotten, not yet.

"Ethan." Kenzie and Annwyl joined me at the edge, the group following silently. Annwyl gripped my arm. "I'm not leaving. Not without him."

"I know. Don't worry." I shook off her fingers, then turned and handed a sword to Kenzie. "Get them out of here," I told her. "Take Annwyl, get to the exit, and don't look back. If anything tries to stop you, do whatever you can not to get caught again."

"What about you?"

I sighed, glancing down the tunnel. "I'm going back for Keirran."

She blinked. "Alone? You don't even know where he is."

"Yes, I do." Raking a hand through my hair, I faced the darkness, determined not to be afraid. "He'll be with the lady. Wherever *she* is, I'll find him, too."

"Master?" Razor perked up, eyes flaring with hope. "Razor come? Find Master?"

"No, you stay, Razor. Protect Kenzie."

The gremlin buzzed sadly but nodded.

Dark murmurs echoed behind us. The group of former half-breeds were shifting fretfully, muttering "the lady," over and over again, like a chant. It made my stomach turn with nerves.

"Here, then." Kenzie handed back the sword. "Take it. I won't need it this time."

"But—"

"Ethan, trust me, if something finds us, we won't be fighting—we'll be running. If you're going back, you're going to need it more than me."

"I'll come with you," Annwyl said.

"No." My voice came out sharp. "Kenzie needs you to open the trod when you get there. It won't work for humans. Besides, if something happens to you, if you get caught or threatened in any way, Keirran won't try to escape. He'll only come with me if he knows you're safe."

"I want to help. I won't abandon him—"

"Dammit, if you love him, the best thing you can do is leave!" I snapped, whirling on her. She blinked and drew back. "Keirran is here because of you! That's what got us into this mess in the first place." I glared at her, and the faery dropped her gaze. Sighing, I lowered my voice. "Annwyl, you have to trust me. I won't come back without him, I promise."

She struggled a moment longer, then nodded. "I'll hold you to that promise, human," she murmured at last.

Kenzie suddenly took my arm. "I will, too," she whispered as I looked into her eyes. She smiled faintly, trying to hide her fear, and squeezed my hand. "So you'd better come back, tough guy. You have a promise to keep, remember?"

The urge to kiss her then was almost overpowering. Gently, I cupped her cheek, trying to convey my promise, what I felt, without words. Kenzie put her hand over mine and closed her eyes. "Be careful," she whispered. I nodded.

"You, too."

Opening her eyes, she released me and stepped back. "We'll be at Belvedere Castle," she stated, her eyes suspiciously bright. "So meet us there when you find Keirran. We'll be waiting for you both."

Todd spoke up then, his voice echoing flatly over the rest. "If you're looking for the lady, she'll be on the very last floor," he stated. "That's where the screams used to come from."

A chill went through me. Giving Kenzie and the others one last look, I turned, gripping my weapons and disappeared into the tunnel.

CHAPTER TWENTY-FOUR

THE LADY

I made my way through the darkness of the Forgotten hive, keeping to the shadows, pressed flat against rocks or behind boulders. In a real cave, with no artificial light, it would be impossible to see your hand in front of your face. Here, in the Between, the cave glowed with luminescent crystals and mushrooms, scattered on the walls and along the ceiling. Colorful moss and ferns grew around a clear green pool in the center of the main cavern, where a small waterfall trickled in from the darkness above.

Forgotten drifted through the tunnels, pale and shimmery against the gloom, though there weren't as many as I'd first feared. Maybe most of them were out hunting exiles, since they had to feed on the glamour of the regular fey to live. Some were just transparent shadows, while others seemed much more solid, even gaining some color back. I noticed the less "real" the faery was, the more it tended to wander around in a daze, as if it couldn't remember what it was doing. I nearly ran right into a snakelike creature with multiple arms coming out of a tunnel, and dove behind a stalactite to avoid it, making a lot of noise as I did. The faery stared at my hiding spot for a few seconds, blinking, then appeared to lose interest and slithered off down another corridor. Breathing a sigh of relief, I continued.

Hugging the walls, I slowly made my way through the caverns and tunnels, searching for Keirran and the lady. I hoped Kenzie and Annwyl had gotten the others out, and I hoped they were safe. I couldn't worry about them now. If this lady was as powerful as I feared—the queen of the Forgotten, I suspected—then I had more than enough to worry about for myself.

Past another glittering pool, a stone archway rose out of the wall and floor, blue torches burning on either side. It looked pretty official, like the entrance to a queen's chamber, perhaps.

Gripping my weapons, I took a deep breath and walked beneath the arch.

The tunnel past the doorway was winding but short, and soon a faint glow hovered at the end. I crept forward, staying to the shadows, and peeked into the throne room of the Lady.

The cavern through the arch wasn't huge, though it glittered with thousands of blue, green and yellow crystals, some tiny, some as big as me, jutting out of the walls and floor. Several massive stone columns, twined with the skeletons of dragons and other monsters, lined the way to a crystal throne near the back of the room.

Sitting on that throne, flanked by motionless knights in bone armor, was a woman.

My breath caught. The Lady of the Forgotten wasn't monstrous, or cruel-looking or some terrible, crazy queen wailing insanities.

She was beautiful.

For a few seconds, I couldn't stop staring, couldn't even tear my eyes away. Like the rest of the Forgotten, the Lady was pale, but a bit of color tinged her cheeks and full lips, and her eyes were a striking crystal blue, though they shifted colors in the dim light—from blue to green to amber and back again. Her long hair was colorless, writhing away to mist at the ends, as if she still wasn't quite solid. She wore billowing robes with a high collar, and the face within was young, perfect and achingly sad.

For one crazy moment, my brain shut off, and I wondered if we had this all wrong. Maybe the Lady was a prisoner of the Forgotten, as well, maybe she had nothing to do with the disappearances and killings and horrible fate of the half-breeds.

But then I saw the wings, or rather, the shattered bones of what had been wings, rising from her shoulders to frame the chair. Like the other Forgotten. Her eyes shifted from green to pure black, and I saw her reach a slender white hand out to a figure standing at the foot of the throne.

"Keirran," I whispered. The Iron prince looked none the worse for wear, unbound and free, as he took the offered hand and stepped closer to the Lady. She ran long fingers through his silver hair, and he didn't move, standing there with his head bowed. I saw her lips move, and he might've said something back, but their voices were too soft to hear.

Anger flared, and I clenched my fists around my swords. Keirran was still armed; I could see the sword across his back, but he wouldn't do anything that would endanger Annwyl. How strong was the Lady? If I burst in now, could we fight our way out? I counted four guards surrounding the throne, eyes glowing green beneath their bony helmets. They looked pretty tough, but we might be able to take them down together. If I could only get his attention…

A second later, however, it didn't matter.

The Lady suddenly stopped talking to Keirran. Raising her head, she looked right at me, still hidden in the shadows. I saw her eyebrows lift in surprise, and then she smiled.

"Hello, Ethan Chase." Her voice was clear and soft, and her smile was heartbreaking "Welcome to my kingdom."

Dammit. I burst from my hiding spot, as Keirran whirled around, eyes widening in shock. "Ethan," he exclaimed as I walked forward, my blades held at my side. The guards started forward, but the Lady raised a hand, and they stopped. "What are you doing here?"

"What do you think I'm doing here?" I snapped. "I'm here to get you out. You can relax—Annwyl is safe." I met the Lady's gaze. "So are Todd and all the other half-breeds you kidnapped. And you won't hurt anyone else, I swear."

I wasn't expecting an answer. I expected Keirran to spin around, draw his sword, and all hell to break loose as we beat a hasty retreat for the exit. But Keirran didn't move, and the next words spoken weren't his. "What do you mean, Ethan Chase?" The Lady's voice surprised me, genuinely confused and shocked, trying to understand. "Tell me, how have I hurt your friends?"

"You're kidding, right?" I halted a few yards from the foot of the throne, glaring up at her. Keirran, rigid beside her, looked on warily. I wondered when he was going to step down, in case we had to fight our way out. Those bony knights at each corner of the throne looked pretty tough.

"Let me give you a rundown, then," I told the Forgotten queen, who cocked her head at me. "You kidnapped my friend Todd from his home and dragged him here. You kidnapped Annwyl to force Keirran to come to you. You've killed who knows how many exiles, and, oh, yeah…you turned all those half-breeds mortal by sucking out their glamour. How's that for harm, then?"

"The half-breeds were not to be harmed," the Lady said in a calm, reasonable voice. "We do not kill if there is no need. Eventually, they would have been returned to their homes. As for losing their 'fey-ness,' now that they are mortal, the Hidden World will never bother them again. They can live happier, safer lives now that they are normal. Wouldn't you agree that is the better option, Ethan Chase? You, who have been tormented by the fey all your life? Surely you understand."

"I... That's...that's not an excuse."

"Isn't it?" The Lady gave me a gentle smile. "They are happier now, or they will be, once they go home. No more nightmares about the fey. No more fear of what the 'pure-bloods' might do to them." She tilted her head again, sympathetic. "Don't *you* wish you could be normal?"

"What about the exiles?" I shot back, determined not to give her the upper hand in this bizarre debate. *Dammit, I shouldn't even have to argue about this. Keirran, what the hell are you doing?* "There's no question of what you did to them," I continued. "You can't tell me that they're happier being dead."

"No." The Lady closed her eyes briefly. "Sadly, I cannot. There is no excuse for it, and it breaks my heart, what we must do to our former brethren to survive."

A tiny motion from Keirran, just the slightest tightening of his jaw. *Well, at least that's something. I still don't know what you think you're doing, Prince. Unless she's got a debt or a glamour on you.* Somehow, I doubted it. The Iron prince looked fine when I first came in. He was still acting of his own free will.

"But," the Lady continued, "our survival is at stake here. I do what I must to ensure my people do not fade away again. If there was another way to live, to exist, I would gladly take it. As such, we feed only on exiles, those who have been banished to the mortal realm. That they will fade away eventually is small comfort to what we must do, but we must take our comfort where we can."

I finally looked at Keirran. "And you. You're okay with all this?"

Keirran bowed his head and didn't meet my gaze. The Lady reached out and touched the back of his neck.

"Keirran understands our plight," she whispered as I stared at him, disbelieving. "He knows I must protect my people from nonexistence. Mankind has been cruel and has forgotten us, as have the courts of Faery. We have just returned to the world again. How can we go back to nothing?"

I shook my head, incredulous. "I hate to break it to you, but I promised someone I wouldn't leave without the Iron prince, there." I stabbed a sword at Keirran, who raised his head and finally looked at me. I glared back. "And I'm going to keep my promise, even if I have to break both his legs and carry him out myself."

"Then, I am sorry, Ethan Chase." The Lady sat back, watching me sadly. "I wish we could have come to an agreement. But I cannot allow you to return to the Iron Queen with our location. Please understand—I do this only to protect my people."

The Lady lifted her hand, and the bone knights suddenly lunged forward, drawing their swords as they did. Their weapons were pure white and jagged on one end, like a giant razor tooth. I met the first warrior bearing down on me, knocking aside his sword and instantly whipping my second blade at his head. It happened in the space of a blink, but the faery dodged back, the sword missing him by inches.

Damn, they're fast. Another cut at me from the side, and I barely twisted away, feeling the jagged edge of the sword catch my shirt. Parrying yet another swing, I immediately had to dodge as the others closed in, not giving me any time to counter. They backed me toward a corner, desperately fending off blindingly quick stabs and thrusts. Too many. There were too many of them, and they were *good*. "Keirran!" I yelled, ducking behind a column. "A little help?"

The knights slowly followed me around the pillar, and through the short lull, I saw the Iron prince still standing beside the throne, watching. His face was blank; no emotion showed on his face or in his eyes as the knights closed on me again. Fear gripped my heart with icy talons. Even after everything, I still believed he would back me up when I needed it. "Keirran!" I yelled again, ducking as the knight's sword smashed into the column, spraying me with grit. "Dammit, what are you doing? Annwyl is safe—help me!"

He didn't move, though a tortured expression briefly crossed his face. Stunned and abruptly furious, I whirled, stepped inside a knight's guard as it cut at me, and lunged deep. My blade finally pierced the armored chest, lancing between the rib slits and sinking deep. The warrior convulsed, staggered away, and turned into mist.

But my reckless move had left my back open, and I wasn't able to dodge fast enough as another sword swept down, glancing off my leg. For just a second, it didn't hurt. But as I backed away, blood blossomed over my jeans, and then the pain hit in a crippling flood. I stumbled, gritting my teeth. The remaining three knights followed relentlessly, swords raised. All the while, Keirran stood beside the throne, not moving, as the Lady's remote blue eyes followed me over his head.

I can't believe he's going to stand there and watch me die. Panting, I desperately fended off another assault from all three knights, but a blade got through and hit my arm, causing me to drop one of my swords. I lashed out and scored a hit along the knight's jaw, and it reeled away in pain, but then another swung viciously at my head, and I knew I wouldn't be able to completely avoid this one.

I raised my sword, and the knight's blade smashed into it and my arm, knocking me to the side. My hurt leg crumpled beneath me, and I fell, the blade ripped from my hands, skidding across the floor. Dazed, I looked up to see the knights looming over me, sword raised for the killing blow.

That's it, then. I'm sorry, Kenzie. I wanted to be with you, but at least you're safe now. That's all that matters.

The blade flashed down. I closed my eyes.

The screech of weapons rang directly overhead, making my hair stand up. For a second, I held my breath, wondering when the pain would hit, wondering if I was already dead. When nothing happened, I opened my eyes.

Keirran knelt in front of me, arm raised, blocking the knight's sword with his own. The look on his face was one of grim determination. Standing, he threw off the knight and glared at the others, who eased back a step but didn't lower their weapons. Without looking in my direction but still keeping himself between me and the knights, he turned back to the throne.

"This isn't the way, my lady," he called. Cursing him mentally, I struggled to sit up, fighting the pain clawing at my arms, legs, shoulders, everywhere really. Keirran gave me a brief glance, as if making sure I was all right, still alive, and faced the Forgotten Queen again. "I sympathize with your plight, I do. But I can't allow you to harm my family. Killing the brother of the Iron Queen would only hurt your cause, and bring the wrath of all the courts down upon you and your followers. Please, let him go. Let us both go."

The Lady regarded him blankly, then raised her hand again. Instantly, the bone knights backed off, sheathing their weapons and returning to her side. Keirran still didn't look at me as he sheathed his own blade and gave a slight bow. "We'll be taking our leave, now," he stated, and though his voice was polite, it wasn't a question or a request. "I will think on what you said, but I ask that you do not try to stop us."

The Lady didn't reply, and Keirran finally bent down, putting my arm around his shoulders. I was half tempted to shove him off, but I didn't know if my leg would hold. Besides, the room seemed to be spinning.

"Nice of you to finally step in," I growled, as he lifted us both to our feet. Pain flared, and I grit my teeth, glaring at him. "Was that a change of heart at the end, or were you just waiting for the last dramatic moment?"

"I'm sorry," Keirran murmured, steadying us as I stumbled. "I was hoping…it wouldn't come to this." He sighed and gave me an earnest look. "Annwyl. Is she all right? Is she safe?"

"I already told you she was." My leg throbbed, making my temper flare. "No thanks to you! What the hell is wrong with you, Keirran? I thought you cared for Annwyl, or don't you care that they left her in a *cage,* all alone, while you were out here having tea with the Lady or whatever the hell you were doing?"

Keirran paled. "Annwyl," he whispered, closing his eyes. "I'm sorry. Forgive me, I didn't know…." Opening his eyes, he gave me a pleading look. "They wouldn't let me see her. I didn't know where she was. They told me she would be killed if I didn't cooperate."

"Well, you were certainly doing that," I shot back, and pushed him toward one of my fallen weapons. "Don't leave my swords. I want them in case your wonderful Lady decides to double-cross us."

"She wouldn't do that," Keirran said, dragging me over and kneeling to pick up my blade. "She's more honorable than you think. You just have to understand what's happened to her, what she's trying to accomplish—"

I snatched the weapon from him and glared. "Whose side are you on, anyway?"

That tortured look crossed his face again. "Ethan, please…"

"Never mind," I muttered, wincing as my leg started to throb. "Let's just get out of here, while I can still walk out."

We started across the floor again, but hadn't gone very far when the Lady's voice rang out again. "Prince Keirran," she called. "Wait, please. One more thing."

Keirran paused, but he didn't look back.

"The killings can stop," the Lady went on in a quiet but earnest voice. "No more exiles will be sacrificed to keep us alive, and no more half-breeds will be taken. I can order my people to do this, if that is what you want."

"Yes," Keirran said immediately, still not looking back. "It is."

"However," the Lady went on, "if I do this, you must come and speak with me again. One day soon I will call for you, and you must come to me, of your own free will. Not as a prisoner, but as a guest. An equal. Will you give me that much, at least?"

"Keirran," I muttered as he paused, "don't listen to her. She just wants you under her thumb again because you're the son of the Iron Queen. You *know* faery bargains never turn out right."

He didn't answer, staring straight ahead, at nothing.

"Iron Prince?" The Lady's voice was low, soothing. "What is your answer?"

"Keirran…" I warned.

His eyes hardened. "Agreed," he called back. "You have my word."

I wanted to punch him.

"Dammit, what is wrong with you?" I seethed as we left the queen's chamber. "Have you forgotten what she's done? Did you happen to see all the half-breeds she's kidnapped? Did you see what they did to them, drained all their magic so they're

just shells of what they were? Have you forgotten all the exiles they've killed, just to keep themselves alive?" He didn't
answer, and I narrowed my eyes. "Annwyl could've been one
of them, or are you so enamored with your new lady friend
that you forgot about her, too?"

The last was a low blow, but I wanted to make him angry,
get him to argue with me. Or at least to confirm that he hadn't
forgotten the atrocities committed here or what we'd come
to do. But his blue eyes only got colder, though his voice remained calm.

"I wouldn't expect a human to understand."

"Then explain it to me," I said through gritted teeth,
though hearing him say that sent a chill up my spine.

"I don't agree with her methods," Keirran said as two pi-
ranha-palm gnomes stepped aside for us, bowing to Keirran. "But she's only trying to achieve what every good ruler
wants—the survival of her people. You don't know how horrible it is for exiles, for all of them, to face nothingness. Losing
pieces of yourself every day, until you cease to exist."

"And the harm she's caused so that her people can survive?"

"That was wrong," Keirran agreed, furrowing his brow.
"Others shouldn't have had to die. But the Forgotten are only
trying to live and not fade away, just like the exiles. Just like
everyone in Faery." He sighed and turned down a side tunnel filled with crystals and bone fragments. But the farther we
walked, the more the gems and skeletons faded away, until the
ground was just normal rock under our feet. Ahead, I could see
the end of the tunnel and a small paved path that cut through
the trees. The shadows of the cavern fell away. "There has to
be a way for them to survive without hurting anyone else,"
Keirran muttered at last. I looked at him and frowned.

"And if there isn't?"

"Then we're all going to have to choose a side."

★ ★ ★

We left the cave of the Forgotten and stepped into the real world from beneath a stone bridge, emerging in Central Park again. I didn't know how long we had been in the Between, but the sky overhead blazed with stars, though the air held a stillness that said it was close to dawn. Keirran dragged me to a green bench on the side of the trail, and I collapsed on top of it with a groan.

The prince hovered anxiously on the edge of the path. "How's the leg?" he asked, sounding faintly guilty. *Not guilty enough,* I thought sourly. I prodded the gash and winced.

"Hurts like hell," I muttered, "but at least the bleeding's slowed down." Removing my belt, I wrapped it several times around my leg to make a rough bandage, clenching my jaw as I cinched it tight. The gash on my arm was still oozing sluggishly, but I'd have to take care of it later.

"Where to now?" Keirran asked.

"Belvedere Castle," I replied, desperately hoping Kenzie and the others were already there, waiting for us. "We agreed to meet there, when this was all over."

Keirran looked around the dense woods and sighed. "Any idea what direction it might be?"

"Not really," I gritted out and glared at him. "You're the one with faery blood. Aren't you supposed to have some innate sense of direction?"

"I'm not a compass," Keirran said mildly, still gazing around the forest. Finally, he shrugged. "Well, I guess we'll pick a trail and hope for the best. Can you walk?"

Despite my anger, I felt a tiny twinge of relief. He was starting to sound like his old self again. Maybe all that madness down in the Lady's throne room was because he'd been glamoured, after all.

"I'll be fine," I muttered, struggling to my feet. "But I'm

going to have to tell Kenzie that you're really not at all help-ful on camping trips."

He chuckled, and it sounded relieved, too. "Be sure to break it to her gently," he said, and took my weight again.

Fifteen minutes later, we still had no idea where we were going. We were wandering up a twisty, narrow path, hoping it would take us someplace familiar, when Keirran suddenly stopped. A troubled look crossed his face, and I glanced around warily, wondering if I should pull my swords. Of course, it was going to be really awkward fighting while hopping around on one leg or leaning against Keirran. I had hoped our fight-ing was done for the night.

"What is it?" I asked. Keirran sighed.

"They're here."

"What? Who?"

"Master!"

A familiar wail rent the night, and Keirran grimaced, brac-ing himself, as Razor hurled himself at his chest. Scrabbling to his shoulders, the gremlin gibbered and bounced with joy. "Master, master! Master safe!"

"Hey, Razor." Keirran smiled, wincing helplessly as the gremlin continued to bounce on him. "Yeah, I'm happy to see you, too. Is the court far behind?"

I frowned at him. "Court?"

They emerged from the trees all around us, dozens of sidhe knights in gleaming armor, the symbol of a great iron tree on their breastplates. They slid out of the woods, amazingly si-lent for an army in plate mail, until they formed a glittering half circle around us. Leading them all was a pair of familiar faces: a dark faery dressed all in black with silver eyes, and a grinning redhead.

Keirran stiffened beside me.

"Well, well," Puck announced, smirking as he and Ash approached side-by-side. "Look who it is. See, ice-boy, I told you they'd be here."

Ash's glittering stare was leveled at Keirran, who quickly bowed his head but, to his credit, didn't cringe or back away. Which took guts, I had to admit, facing down that icy glare.

"Are you two all right?" From Ash's tone, I couldn't tell if he was relieved, secretly amused or completely furious. His gaze swept over me, quietly assessing, and his eyes narrowed. "Ethan, you're badly wounded. What happened?"

"I'm fine." A weak claim, I knew, as my shirt and half my pant leg were covered in blood. Beside me, Keirran was rigid, motionless. Razor gave a worried buzz from his neck. *What's the matter?* I thought. *Afraid I'm going to tell Daddy that you nearly let me be skewered to death?* "I got into a fight with a few guards." I shrugged, then grimaced as the motion tore the dried wound on my shoulder. "Turns out, fighting multiple opponents in armor isn't a very smart idea."

"You think?" Puck came forward, shooing Keirran away and pointing me to a nearby rock. "Sit down. Jeez, kid, do I look like a nurse? Why are you always bleeding whenever I see you? You're worse than ice-boy."

Ash ignored that comment as Puck briskly started tying bandages around my various cuts and gashes, being not particularly gentle. "Where are they?" the dark faery demanded.

I clenched my teeth as Puck yanked a strip of cloth around my arm. "There's a trod under a bridge that will take you to their lair," I said, pointing back down the path. "I'd be careful, though. There's a lot of them running around."

"Don't hurt them," Keirran burst out, and everyone, even Razor, glanced at him in surprise. "They're not dangerous," he pleaded, as I gave him an are-you-crazy look. He ignored me. "They're just…misguided."

Puck snorted, looking up from my shoulder. "Sorry, but are

we talking about the same creepy little faeries that tried to kill us atop the castle that night? Evil gnomes, toothy hands, tried to suck out everyone's glamour—this ringing any bells?" He stood, wiping off his hands, and I pushed myself to my feet, gingerly putting weight on my leg. It was just numb now, making me wonder what Puck had done to it. Magic, glamour or something else? Whatever it was, I wasn't complaining.

"The killings will stop," Keirran insisted. "The queen promised me they would stop."

"They have a queen?" Ash's voice had gone soft and lethal, and even Puck looked concerned. Keirran drew in a sharp breath, realizing his mistake.

"Huh, another queen," Puck mused, an evil grin crossing his face. "Maybe we should drop in and introduce ourselves, ice-boy. Do the whole, hey, we were just in the neighborhood, and we were just wondering if you had any plans to take over the Nevernever. Have a fruit basket."

"Father, please." Keirran met Ash's gaze. "Let them go. They're only trying to survive."

The dark faery stared Keirran down a few moments, then shook his head. "We didn't come here to start a war," he said, and Keirran relaxed. "We came here for you and Ethan. The courts will have to decide what to do with the emergence of another queen. Right now, let's get you both out of here. And, Keirran—" he glared at his son, who flinched under that icy gaze "—this isn't over. The queen will be waiting for you when we get home. I hope you have a good explanation."

Meghan, I thought as Keirran and Puck took my weight again, and we started hobbling down the path. Questions swirled, all centered on her and Keirran. I needed to talk to my sister, not just to ask about my nephew and the "other" side of my family, but to let her know that I understood. I knew why she left us so long ago. Or at least, I was beginning to.

I couldn't speak to her now, but I would, soon. Keirran was my way back to Faery, back to my sister, because now that we'd met, I was pretty sure not even the Iron Queen herself could keep him away.

"Ah." Puck sighed, shaking his head as we headed into the forest. "This brings back memories." He glanced over his shoulder and grinned. "Don't they remind you of a pair, ice-boy, from way back when?"

Ash snorted. "Don't remind me."

EPILOGUE

Belvedere Castle looked eerie and strange under the moon-light, with armored knights standing guard along the top and the banner of the Iron Queen flapping in the wind. It was as if we'd stepped through time into King Arthur's court or something. But the small group of humans clustered on the balcony sort of ruined that image, though it was obvious they couldn't see the unearthly knights milling around them. Occasionally one would break away from the group and walk toward the steps, though when they reached the edge they would turn and wander back, a dazed look on their face. So, a glamour barrier had been placed over the castle, preventing them from going anywhere. Probably a good idea; the former half-breeds didn't even know who they were and wouldn't survive for long, out there on their own. Still, it was faery magic, repressing the will of normal humans, keeping them trapped, and it made my skin crawl.

"What will happen to the half-breeds now that they're human?" I asked as we approached the first flight of stairs, knights bowing to us on either side.

Ash shook his head. "I don't know." Gazing up at the top of the steps, he narrowed his eyes. "Some of them are probably Leanansidhe's, so she might take them back, see if they regain their memories. Beyond that…" He shrugged. "Some of them may have been reported missing. We'll let the human authorities know they're here. Their own will have to take care of them now."

"One of them is a friend of ours," I said. "He's been missing for days. We need to take him back to Louisiana with us."

Ash nodded. "I'll make sure he gets home."

Keirran stopped at the foot of the stairs, his breath catching. I gritted my teeth as the abrupt halt jolted my leg, then followed his gaze up to where Annwyl stood at the top of the steps, waiting for him.

I sighed and pulled my arm from his shoulders. "Go on," I said, rolling my eyes, and he instantly leaped up the steps, taking them three at a time, until he reached the top. Uncaring of Ash, Puck or any of the surrounding knights, he pulled the Summer girl into his arms and kissed her deeply, while Razor jabbered with delight, beaming his manic smile at them both.

Puck shot a look at Ash, his green eyes solemn. "I told you, ice-boy. That kid of yours is trouble. And that's coming from *me*."

Ash scrubbed a hand over his face. "Leanansidhe," he muttered, and shook his head. "So that's where he's been disappearing to." He sighed, and his silver gaze narrowed. "The three of us are going to have to have a talk."

Where's Kenzie? I thought, gazing up the stairs. If Annwyl and the former half-breeds were safe, she had to be here, too. But I didn't see her near the top of the steps with Keirran and Annwyl, or in the cluster of humans wandering around the balcony. I felt a tiny prick of hurt, that she wasn't here to greet me and tried to ignore it. She must have her reasons.

Though you'd think me standing here bleeding all over the place would warrant some type of reaction.

"Sire." Glitch suddenly appeared from the trees, leading another squad of knights behind him. The lightning in his hair glowed purple as he bowed. "We found a second entrance to the strange faeries' lair," he said solemnly, and Ash nodded. "However, the cave was empty when we investigated. There was evidence of other trods, leading in from various points in the park, but nothing remained of the inhabitants themselves. They cleared out very recently."

I looked at Ash, frowning. "You had a second squad, coming from another direction," I guessed. He ignored me, giving Glitch a brief nod.

"Good work. Though if they've fled, there is nothing to do but wait for them to reemerge. Return to Mag Tuiredh and inform the queen. Tell her I will return shortly with Keirran."

"Yes, sire." Glitch bowed, took his knights, and vanished into the darkness.

"Guess that's our cue, as well," Puck said, stepping away from me. "Back to Arcadia, then?"

"Not yet." Ash turned to gaze into the forest, his eyes solemn. "I want to do one more sweep, one last search around the cave, just in case we missed anything." He glanced over his shoulder, smirking. "Care to join me, Goodfellow?"

"Oh, ice-boy. A moonlight stroll with you? Do you even have to ask?"

"Ethan," Ash said, as Puck gave me a friendly arm punch and sauntered into the trees, "we'll return in a few minutes. Tell Keirran that if he even *thinks* about moving from this spot, I will freeze his legs to the floor of his room." His eyes flashed silver, and I didn't doubt his threat. "Also..." He sighed, glancing over my shoulder. "Let him know that the Summer girl probably shouldn't be here when we get back. She's been through enough."

Surprised, I nodded. *Huh. Guess you're not a complete heartless bastard, after all,* I thought grudgingly, as the dark faery turned and melted into the woods with Puck. *I didn't think you'd be the type to look the other way.* Catching myself, I snorted. *I still don't like you, though. You can still drop dead anytime.*

"They won't find anything," Keirran stated, a few steps away, and I turned. The Iron prince stood behind Annwyl with his arms around her waist, gazing over her shoulder. His eyes were dark as he stared into the forest. "The Lady will have taken her followers and fled to another part of the Between. Maybe she'll never reemerge. Maybe we'll never see them again."

"I hope so." Annwyl sighed, and Razor hissed in agreement. But Keirran continued to stare into the trees, as if he hoped the Lady would step out of the shadows and call to him.

And, one day, she will.

"Where's Kenzie?" I asked, clutching the railing as I limped up the stairs, pushing dark thoughts out of my head for now. Keirran and Annwyl hurried down to help, but I waved away their offered hands. "I didn't see her with any of the humans," I continued, marching doggedly forward, up the stairs. "Is she okay?"

"She's talking to one of the half-breeds," Annwyl said. "Todd? The smaller human. I think he was starting to remember her, at least a little bit. He was crying when I saw them last."

I nodded and hurried toward the top, pushing myself to go faster, though my leg was beginning to throb again. As I persisted up the steps, I heard Annwyl's and Keirran's voices drift up behind me.

"I think I should go, too," Annwyl said. "While I still can, if Leanansidhe even takes me back." Her voice grew softer, frightened. "I don't know what will happen to us, Keirran. Everyone saw…"

"I don't care." Keirran's voice was stubbornly calm. "Let

them exile me if they want. I'm not backing down now. I'll beg Leanansidhe to take you back, if that's what it takes." A dark, determined note crept into his words. "I won't watch you fade away into nothing," he swore in a low voice. "There has to be a way. I'll *find* a way."

Leaving them embracing in the middle of the stairs, I reached the balcony where the group of humans still milled aimlessly about, looking as if they were sleepwalking. Pushing my way through the crowd, I spotted a pair of figures sitting by the wall, one hunched over with his head buried in his knees, the other crouched beside him, a slender hand on his shoulder.

Kenzie looked up, and her eyes widened when she saw me. Bending close to Todd, she whispered something in his ear, and he nodded without raising his head.

Standing, she walked across the balcony, dodged the humans that shuffled in front of her, and then we were face-to-face.

"Oh, Ethan." The whisper was half relief, half horror. Her eyes flickered to my face, the blood streaking my arm, splattered across my shirt and jeans. She looked as if she wanted to hug me close but was afraid of hurting me. I gave her a tired smile. "Are you all right?"

"Yeah." I took one step toward her, so that only a breath separated us. "I'm fine enough to do this." And I pulled her into my arms.

Her arms came around me instantly, hugging me back. Closing my eyes, I held her tight, feeling her slim body pressed against mine. She clung to me fiercely, as if daring something to take me away, and I relaxed into her, feeling nothing but relief. I was alive, Todd was safe, and everyone I cared for was all right. That was enough for now.

She finally pulled back, gazing up at me, tracing a shallow

cut on my cheek. "Hi, tough guy," she whispered. "Looks like you made it."

I smiled. Taking her hand, I led her over to the railing, where the wall dropped away and we could see the pond, the forest and most of the park stretched out before us.

I jerked my head toward the lump huddled in the opposite corner. "How is he?"

"Todd?" She sighed, shaking her head. "He still doesn't remember me. Or our school. Or any of his friends. But he said he does remember a woman, very vaguely. His mom, I hope. He started crying after that, so I couldn't get much more out of him." She leaned against the railing, resting her arms on the ledge. "I hope he can get back to normal."

"Me, too," I said, though I seriously doubted it. How could you be normal again when a huge piece of you had been stripped away? Was there even a cure, a remedy, something that could restore a creature's glamour, once it had been lost?

I suddenly realized the irony: here I was, wishing I could give someone back their magic, to return them to the world of Faery, when a few days ago I didn't want anything to do with the fey.

When did I change so much?

Kenzie sighed again, gazing out over the pond. The moonlight gleamed off her hair, outlining her slender body, casting a hazy light around her. And I knew. I knew exactly when I had changed.

It started the day I met you.

"It sure has been a crazy week," she murmured, resting her chin on the back of her hands. "Getting kidnapped, being chased around the Nevernever, faeries and Forgotten and talking cats. Things will seem very dull when we go home." She groaned, hiding her face in her arms. "God, we are going to be in *sooooooo* much trouble when we get back."

I stepped behind her, putting my hands on her waist. "Yeah," I agreed, making her groan again. "So let's not think about that right now." There would be plenty of time to worry about the trouble we were in, the Forgotten, the Lady, Kenzie's disease and Keirran's promise. Right now, I didn't want to think about them. The only thing on my mind was a promise of my own.

I wrapped my arms around Kenzie's waist and brought my lips close to her ear. "Remember what I promised you?" I murmured. "Down in the cave?"

She froze for a second, then turned slowly, her eyes wide and luminous in the moonlight. Smiling, I drew her close, slipping one arm around her waist, the other sliding up to her neck. I lowered my head as her eyes fluttered shut. And on that balcony under the stars, in front of everyone who might be watching, I kissed her.

And for the first time, I wasn't afraid.

★ ★ ★ ★ ★

ACKNOWLEDGMENTS

First and foremost, a huge shout out to my Guro, Ron. Thanks for answering all my crazy kali questions, for all the "badges of courage" I picked up in sparring, and for making Hit-People-With-Sticks class the best night of the week. I could not have written this book without you.

To Natashya Wilson, T. S. Ferguson, and all the awesome MIRA Ink people, you guys rock. Tashya, you especially deserve a standing ovation. I don't know how you juggle so much and still manage to make it look easy.

To my agent, Laurie McLean. This has been one crazy ride, and I'm so grateful to be taking it with you. Let's keep shooting for the stars.

And of course, to my husband, sparring partner, first editor, and best friend, Nick. To many more years of writing, laughs and giving each other "badges of courage" in kali. You keep me young (and deadly).

QUESTIONS FOR DISCUSSION

1. Ethan almost gets into a fight on his first day of school. What did you think about his response to Brian Kingston's bullying of Todd? What would you have done? What do you think is an effective way of responding to a bully?

2. When we first meet Todd, he seems to be the victim of bullies. Later we learn that perhaps the situation is not as simple as Ethan first believes. Todd even lets Ethan take the fall for his retaliation against Kingston. Why do you think Ethan still decides to look for Todd and help him? Did you agree with Ethan's actions, or would you have done something else?

3. Ethan is angry with his sister, Meghan, for what he sees as her desertion of their family. What do you think of the way he handles his feelings? What do you think Meghan would say if she knew how he felt? If someone left you and stayed away to protect you, how would that make you feel? What kinds of things do you do to protect people you care about?

4. Kenzie gives Leanansidhe a month of her life in exchange for gaining the Sight. What do you think of her decision? Are there any circumstances under which you would knowingly give up a month of your life?

5. Guro Javier believes Ethan when Ethan comes to him for help. What, if any, circumstances in your life require you to believe in something you can't see? What do you think would happen if Ethan did open up to kids at school?

6. Julie Kagawa's Iron Fey world began with the addition of the Iron faeries, who live with metal and technology that is poisonous to traditional faeries. Now she has added another type of faery to this world, the Forgotten. What do you think can make someone live on after death? What does immortality mean to you?

7. The Forgotten must steal the glamour of other faeries to survive. How do you feel about their circumstances? What would you do if you knew your life depended on stealing someone else's?

Turn the page for an exclusive excerpt from book 2
of Julie Kagawa's dark and riveting
BLOOD OF EDEN *series*
THE ETERNITY CURE

In a future world, vampires rule and humans are blood cattle.
New vampire Allison Sekemoto is on a quest to find and save her
creator, Kanin, from the sadistic vampire Sarren. Blood calls to
blood—but Allie's path has never been as simple as it seems....

A "big white house" and a pointed finger was all I had to go on, but I found what the human was talking about easily enough. Almost due north from the tower, past a crumbling street lined with rusty cars and across another swampy lawn, a bristling fence rose out of the ground to scar the horizon. Twelve feet tall, made of black iron bars topped with coils of barbed wire, it was a familiar sight. I'd seen many walls in my travels across the country; concrete and wood, steel and stone. They were everywhere, surrounding every settlement, from tiny farms to entire cities. They all had one purpose: to keep rabids from slaughtering the population.

And there were a lot of rabids shambling about the perimeter, a pale, dead swarm. They prowled the walls, always searching, always hungry, looking for a way in. As I stopped in the shadow of a tree to watch, I noticed something weird. The rabids didn't rush the fence, clawing and biting, like they had the tower. They skulked around the edge, always a couple feet away, never touching the iron bars.

Looming above the gates, a squat white building crouched in the weeds. The entrance to the place was circular, lined with columns, and I could make out flickering lights through the windows.

Kanin, I thought. *Sarren. Where are you? I can feel you in there, somewhere.*

The breeze shifted, and the stench of the rabids hit me full force, making my nose wrinkle. They probably weren't going to let me saunter up and knock on the Prince's door, and I really didn't want another fight so soon after my last two. I was Hungry, and any more blood loss would drive me closer to the monster. Besides, there were a lot of rabids this time, a whole huge swarm, not just a few. Taking on this many would venture very close to suicide. Even I could be dragged under and torn apart by sheer numbers.

Frowning, I pondered my plan of attack. I needed to get inside, past the rabids, without being seen. The fence was only twelve feet tall; maybe I could vault over it?

One of the rabids snarled and shoved another that had jostled it, sending it stumbling toward the fence. Hissing, the other rabid put out a hand to catch itself and landed square on the iron bars.

There was a blinding flash and an explosion of sparks, and the rabid shrieked, convulsing on the metal. Its body jerked in spasms, sending the other rabids skittering back. Finally, the smoke pouring off its blackened skin erupted into flame and consumed the monster from the inside.

Okay, definitely not touching the fence.

I growled in frustration. Dawn wasn't far, and soon I would have to fall back to find shelter from the sun. Which meant abandoning any plans to get past the gate until tomorrow night. I was so close! I was right here, mere yards from my target, and the only thing keeping me from my goal was a rabid horde and a length of electrified metal.

Wait. Dawn was approaching. Which meant that the rabids would have to sleep soon. They couldn't face the light any better than a vampire; they would have to burrow into the ground to escape the burning rays of the sun.

Under normal circumstances, I would, as well.

But these weren't normal circumstances. And I wasn't your average vampire. Kanin had taught me better than that.

To keep up the appearance of being human, I'd trained myself to stay awake when the sun rose. Even though it was very, very difficult and something that went against my vampire instincts, I could remain awake and active if I had to. For a little while, at least. But the rabids were slaves to instinct and wouldn't even try to resist. They would vanish into the earth, and with the threat of rabids gone, the power that ran through the fence would probably be shut off. There'd be no need to keep it running in the daytime, especially with fuel or whatever powered the fence in short supply. If I could stay awake long enough, I'd have a clear shot to the house and whoever was inside it. I just had to deal with the sun.

It might not be smart, continuing my quest in the daylight. I would be slow, my reactions muted. But if Sarren was in that house, he would be slowed, as well. He might even be asleep, not expecting Kanin's vengeful daughter to come looking for him here. I could get the jump on him, if I could stay awake myself.

I scanned the grounds, marking where the shadows were thickest, where the trees grew close together. Smartly, the area surrounding the fence was clear of brush and trees, with no places a rabid could climb or hide from the sun. Indirect sunlight wouldn't harm us, but it could still cause a great deal of pain.

Finally, as the sky lightened and the sun grew close to breaking the horizon, the horde began to disappear. Breaking away from the fence, they skulked away to bury themselves in the soft mud, their pale bodies vanishing beneath water and earth until there wasn't a rabid to be seen.

I stayed up, leaning against the trunk of a thick oak, fighting the urge to follow the vicious creatures beneath the earth, to sleep and hide from the sun. It was madly difficult to stay awake. My thoughts grew sluggish, my body heavy and tired. I waited until the sun had risen nearly above the trees, to allow time for the fence to be shut down. It would be hilariously tragic if I avoided the rabids and the sun only to be fried to a crisp on a damn electric fence because I was too impatient. But my training to remain aboveground paid off. About twenty or so minutes after the horde disappeared, the faint hum coming from the metal barrier finally clicked off.

Now came the most dangerous part.

Pulling up my coat, I drew it over my head and tugged the sleeves down so they covered my hands. Direct sunlight on my skin would cause it to blacken, rupture and eventually burst into flame, but I could buy myself some time if it was covered.

Still, I was not looking forward to this.

All my vampire instincts were screaming at me to stop when I stepped out from under the branches, feeling even the weak rays of dawn beating down on me. Keeping my head down, I hurried across the grounds, moving from tree to tree and darting into shade whenever I could. The stretch closest to the fence was the most dangerous, with no trees, no cover, nothing but short grass and the sun heating the back of my coat. I clenched my teeth, hunched my shoulders and kept moving.

I scooped up a branch as I approached the black iron barrier, hurling it in front of me. It arced through the air and struck the bars with a faint clatter before dropping to the ground. No sparks, no flash of light, no smoke rising from the wood. I didn't know much about electric fences, but I took that as a good sign as I drew close enough to touch the bars.

Let's hope that fence is really off.

I leaped toward the top, feeling a brief stab of fear as my fingers curled around the bars. Thankfully, they remained cold and dead beneath my hands, and I scrambled over the fence in half a second, landing on the other side in a crouch.

In the brief moment it took me to leap over the iron barrier, my coat had slipped off my head, exposing it to the sun. My relief at being inside the fence without cooking myself was short-lived as a blinding flare of pain seared my face and hands. I gasped, frantically tugging my coat up while scrambling under the nearest tree. Crouching down, I examined my hands and winced. They were red and painful from just a few seconds of being hit by the sun.

I've got to get inside.

Keeping close to the ground, I hurried across the tangled, snowy lawn, feeling horribly exposed as I drew closer to the building. If someone pushed aside those heavy curtains that covered the huge windows, they would most definitely spot me. But the windows and grounds remained dark and empty as I reached the oval wall and darted beneath an archway, relieved to be out of the light.

Okay. Now what?

The faint tug, that subtle hint of knowing, was stronger than ever as I crept up the stairs and peeked through a curtained window. The strange, circular room beyond was dark and surprisingly intact. A table stood in the center, and several chairs sat around it, all thankfully deserted. Beyond that room was an empty hallway, and even more rooms beyond that.

I stifled a groan. Judging from the size of this place, finding one comatose vampire in such a huge house was going to be a challenge. But I couldn't give up. Kanin was in there somewhere. And so was Sarren.

The glass on the windows was shockingly unbroken, but

the window itself was unlocked. I slid through the frame and dropped silently onto the hardwood floor, glancing warily about. Humans lived here, I realized; a lot of them. I could smell them on the air, the lingering scent of warm bodies and blood. If Sarren was here, he'd likely painted the walls with it.

But I didn't run into any humans, alive or dead, as I made my way through the gigantic house, and that worried me. Especially since it was obvious this place was well taken care of. Nothing appeared broken. The walls and floor were clean and uncluttered, the furniture, though old, remarkably intact. The vampire Prince who lived here either had a lot of servants to keep the place up and running, or he was unbelievably dedicated to cleaning.

I kept expecting to run into someone, a human at the least and Sarren or the Prince at the worst. I continued to scan the shadows and the dozens of empty rooms, wary and alert, searching for movement. But the house remained dark and lifeless as I crept up a long flight of steps, down an equally long corridor and stopped outside a thick wooden door at the end.

This…this is it.

I could feel it, the pull that I'd followed over half the country to this spot, the sudden knowing that what I searched for was so close. Kanin was here. He was just on the other side. Or…I stopped myself from grasping the handle…would it be Sarren that I'd face, grinning manically as I opened the door? Would he be asleep, lying helpless on a bed? Or was he expecting me, as I'd begun to imagine from the silent, empty house? Something was wrong. Getting here had been way too easy. Whoever was on the other side of that door knew I was coming.

Carefully, I grasped my sword and eased it out, being sure the metal didn't scrape against the sheath. If Sarren was expecting me, I'd be ready, too. If Kanin was in there, I wasn't leaving until I got him out safe.

Grasping the door handle, I wrenched it to the side and flung the door open.

A figure stood at the back, waiting for me as I'd feared. He wore a black leather duster, and his thick dark hair tumbled to his broad shoulders. Leaning against the wall with his arms crossed, he didn't even raise an eyebrow as the door banged open. A pale, handsome face met mine over the room, lips curled into an evil smile. But it was the wrong face. I'd gotten everything wrong. I'd followed the wrong pull—and this vampire was supposed to be dead.

"Hello, sister," Jackal greeted, his gold eyes shining in the dim light. "It's about time you showed up."

A chat with
Julie Kagawa

What inspired you to write The Iron Fey series?

I've always loved faery tales, the old, creepy faery tales, where the fey were primal and wicked and dangerous. But when I first began writing a faery story, I got to thinking: what are the fey afraid of? In myth, the answer is iron, so what if there was a type of faery that was immune to iron, that had evolved with progress and technology? How would that affect the more traditional fey? And then I remembered we already have "creatures" lurking in machines: gremlins and bugs and worms and such, and from that thought the Iron Fey were born.

Who is your favourite character in the series?

I would have to say Ash, because I have a thing for dark, brooding bad boys who can wield pointy objects. But Grimalkin runs a very, very close second.

What is your favourite aspect of the faery world?

All the strange, beautiful, and fascinating creatures you can meet in Faery. Be it a dragon or a kelpie or a talking cat, it's never boring.

Is there one element from The Iron Fey universe that you would like to exist in the real world?

Trods, or faery paths between worlds, would be nice. It would make travel so much quicker.

Did you always want to be a writer?

Not always. I wanted to be a veterinarian for years and years, until high school, when I realised you actually had to be somewhat good at math and science to be a vet. And since numbers hate me, I figured making up stories and writing them down would be much easier. (Though I can tell you now, it's *not*.)

Of the books you've written, which is your favourite?

The Iron King, the first book of The Iron Fey series, will always have a special place in my heart because it was the first to get published. But so far, I think *The Iron Queen* is my favourite book I've written.

Do you have a writing routine?

I'm one of those extremely lucky authors who gets to stay home and write, so I start in the morning and try for at least a thousand to twelve hundred words a day.

Favourite author of all time?

Oh goodness. There are too many; I can't pick just one. I will say Neil Gaiman is one of my favourite authors, because his books are so inspiring. (And he has a sexy voice.)

Which book do you wish you could have written?

Harry Potter. And not just because of Rowling's success; because I love the world and want to live there.

HAMILTON COLLEGE LIBRARY